'[
',
r

']
a

'(
s

"
t
k

,
b

,
f
g

'Robert Crais is a major crime-writing talent, exciting
and thought-provoking' *Sunday Express*

'Crais tells a compelling tale that glints with wit, intel-
ligence and expertise' *Literary Review*

527 523 42 4

Robert Crais is the author of eighteen novels, including the international bestsellers *The Forgotten Man*, *The Last Detective*, *Demolition Angel* and the Edgar-nominated *L.A. Requiem*. He has two additional Edgar nominations as well as Anthony and Macavity awards for his series of Elvis Cole and Joe Pike crime novels. Crais has also written for acclaimed television shows such as *L.A. Law* and *Hill Street Blues*. *Hostage* has been made into a major motion picture featuring Bruce Willis. He lives in Los Angeles. Visit his website at www.robertcrais.com

By Robert Crais

The Monkey's Raincoat
Stalking the Angel
Lullaby Town
Free Fall
Voodoo River
Sunset Express
Indigo Slam
L.A. Requiem
Demolition Angel
Hostage
The Last Detective
The Forgotten Man
The Two Minute Rule
The Watchman
Chasing Darkness
The First Rule
The Sentry
Taken

the two minute rule

ROBERT CRAIS

An Orion paperback

First published in Great Britain in 2006
by Orion
This paperback edition published in 2006
by Orion Books Ltd,
an imprint of The Orion Publishing Group Ltd,
Carmelite House, 50 Victoria Embankment
London EC4Y 0DZ

An Hachette UK company

3 5 7 9 10 8 6 4 2

Reissued 2012

A CIP catalogue record for this book
is available from the British Library.

ISBN 978-1-4091-3825-9

Printed and bound in Great Britain by
CPI Group (UK) Ltd, Croydon, CR0 4YY

The Orion Publishing Group's policy is to use papers
that are natural, renewable and recyclable products and
made from wood grown in sustainable forests. The logging
and manufacturing processes are expected to conform to
the environmental regulations of the country of origin.

www.orionbooks.co.uk

Dedicated to the memory of

Detective Terry Melancon, Jr.
Baton Rouge Police Department
August 10, 2005

Hero.

"Thank you, Mr. Policeman."

ACKNOWLEDGMENTS

MANY PEOPLE helped with the research and writing of this novel and must be thanked.

In the FBI's Los Angeles Field Office, Supervisory Special Agent John H. McEachern (boss of the L.A. Field Office's legendary Bank Squad) and Special Agent Laura Eimiller (FBI Press and Public Relations) were generous with their time and patient with my questions. Errors and purposeful alterations in description and procedure are my responsibility.

Assistant United States Attorney Garth Hire of the Los Angeles AUSA office was similarly helpful in the matters of federal sentencing guidelines and federal incarceration, and by pointing the way toward additional research in these areas. Again, the inconsistencies between actual fact and what is depicted in this novel are my responsibility.

Former Special Agent Gerald Petievich of the United States Secret Service provided facts and history about the Hollywood Sign and Mount Lee, as well as additional insights into criminal behavior.

Christina Ruano counseled me regarding all things

Latin—from East L.A. locations to gang lore and language, as well as providing engineering information about the Los Angeles River channel and downtown bridges.

Finally, special thanks and appreciation must be extended to my editor, Marysue Rucci, who worked with insight and diligence to help me realize the innate integrity of Max Holman.

PROLOGUE

MARCHENKO AND PARSONS circled the bank for sixteen minutes, huffing Krylon Royal Blue Metallic to regulate the crystal as they worked up their nut. Marchenko believed Royal Blue Metallic gave them an edge in the bank, made them fierce and wild-eyed, Royal Blue being a warrior's color; Parsons just enjoyed the spacey out-of-body buzz, like being separated from the world by an invisible membrane.

Marchenko suddenly slapped the dash, his wide Ukrainian face purple and furious, and Parsons knew they were on.

Marchenko screamed, "Let's get this bitch DONE!"

Parsons jerked the charging bolt on his M4 rifle as Marchenko swerved their stolen Corolla into the parking lot. Parsons was careful not to place his finger on the trigger. It was important not to fire the weapon until Marchenko gave the word, Marchenko being the leader of their little operation, which was fine by Parsons. Marchenko had made them both millionaires.

They turned into the parking lot at seven minutes

after three that afternoon, and parked near the door. They pulled on black knit ski masks as they had twelve times before, rapped their gloved fists together in a flash of *esprit de corps,* now both shouting in unison like they meant it—

"Get this bitch *DONE!*"

They pushed out of the car, the two of them looking like black bears. Marchenko and Parsons were both decked out in matching black fatigues, boots, gloves, and masks; they wore load-bearing gear over armored vests they had bought on eBay, with so many extra magazines for their rifles bristling from their vests that their already bloated bodies looked swollen. Parsons carried a large nylon bag for the money.

Broad daylight, as obvious as two flies in a bowl of milk, Marchenko and Parsons sauntered into the bank like two WWF wrestlers casually entering the ring.

Parsons never once thought the police might show up or that they would be caught. The first couple of times they took over a bank he had worried, but this was their thirteenth armed bank robbery, and robbing banks had turned out to be the easiest money either of them had ever made: these banking people, they flat out just *gave* you the money, and security guards were a thing of the past; banks didn't employ rent-a-cops anymore because the liability costs were too high—all you had to do was step through the doors and take what you wanted.

As they entered the bank, a woman in a business suit was on her way out. She blinked at them in their black commando gear and guns, and she tried to reverse course, but Marchenko grabbed her face, kicked her legs out from under her, and pushed her down to the floor. Then he raised his rifle and shouted as loud as he could.

"This is a robbery, you muthuhfuckuhs! We *OWN* this fuckin' bank!"

That being Parsons' cue, he raked the ceiling with two horrific bursts from his rifle that knocked loose ceiling tiles and shattered three rows of lights. Shrapnel, debris, and ricochets spattered the walls and pinged off desks. Spent casings streamed from his rifle, tinkling like silverware at a furious feast. The noise of his automatic weapon's fire was so loud in the enclosed space that Parsons never heard the tellers scream.

Their thirteenth bank robbery had officially begun. The clock was running.

•••

Lynn Phelps, the third woman waiting in line for a teller, startled at the sound of the gunfire like everyone else, then dropped to the floor. She grabbed the legs of the woman standing behind her, pulled her down, then carefully checked the time. Her Seiko digital showed three-oh-nine, exactly. Nine minutes after three. Time would be critical.

Mrs. Phelps, sixty-two years old, was overweight, dowdy, and a retired sheriff's deputy from Riverside, California. She had moved to Culver City with her new husband, a retired Los Angeles police officer named Steven Earl Phelps, and had been a customer at this branch for only eight days. She was unarmed, but would not have reached for her weapon if she had been carrying it. Lynn Phelps knew the two A-holes robbing

3

her bank were not professionals by the way they wasted time waving their guns and cursing rather than getting down to the business of stealing money. Professionals would have immediately grabbed the managers and had the tellers dump their drawers. Professionals knew that speed was life. These A-holes were clearly amateurs. Worse, they were amateurs who were armed to the teeth. Professionals wanted to get out alive; amateurs would kill you.

Lynn Phelps checked the time again. Three-ten. One minute had passed, and these two idiots were still waving their guns. Amateurs.

•••

Marchenko shoved a Latino man into a counter laden with deposit slips. The man was short and dark, with baggy work clothes streaked with white paint and dust. His hands were dusty and white, too. Parsons thought the guy had probably been installing drywall before he came to the bank. The poor bastard probably didn't speak English, either, but they didn't have time for language lessons.

Marchenko screamed, "Get your fucking ass DOWN!"

With that, Marchenko butt-stroked the guy with his rifle. The man's head split and he slumped onto the counter, but he didn't go down, so Marchenko hit him again, knocking him to the floor. Marchenko spun away, his voice furious and his eyes bulging out of the ski mask.

"Everybody stay on the floor. Anyone gives us any shit you better kiss your ass good-bye. C'mere, you fat cow!"

Parsons' job was easy. He kept an eye on everyone, and kept an eye on the door. If new people walked in, he grabbed them and shoved them down. If a cop walked in, he would ace the fucker. That's the way it worked. And he shook down the tellers while Marchenko went for the key.

Banks kept their cash in two places, the teller drawers and the cash locker in the vault. The manager had the key to the cash locker.

While Marchenko got the customers on the floor, Parsons whipped out his nylon bag and confronted the tellers. It was an easy mid-afternoon scene: four tellers, all young Asian and Middle Eastern women, and an older broad at a desk behind the tellers who was probably the manager. Another banker who was probably a loan officer or assistant manager sat at one of the two desks on the public side of the tellers.

Parsons made his voice fierce like Marchenko and waved his gun. His gun scared the shit out of these chicks.

"Stand away from the counter! *Step back, goddamnit!* Stand up! Don't get down, fuckin' bitch! *Stand UP!*"

One of the tellers, already crying, had dropped to her knees, the dumb bitch. Parsons leaned across the counter, jabbing his gun at her.

"Get up, you stupid bitch!"

Behind him, Marchenko had pulled the desk jockey to his feet, screaming for the manager.

"Which one of you has the key? Goddamnit, who's the manager? I gotta fuckin' cap your ass, I will!"

The woman at the desk behind the tellers stepped forward, identifying herself as the manager. She raised

5

both hands to show her palms, walking slowly forward.

"You can have the money. We're not going to resist you."

Marchenko shoved the one he had down, then stalked around the pass-through behind the tellers. While he took care of his end, Parsons ordered the tellers to step forward to their stations and warned them not to trip the alarms under their counters. He told them to dump their drawers on their desks and leave out the fuckin' dye packs. He held his rifle in his right hand and the bag in his left. He ordered them to put their cash into the bag. Their hands shook as they did it. Each and every one of them trembled. Their fear gave Parsons an erection.

He had a problem with the stupid bitch on the floor. She wouldn't get up. She didn't seem able to control her legs or even to hear his commands. He wanted to jump over the counter and beat the bitch silly until the next teller offered to empty her drawer.

Parsons said, "Do it. Come over here and give me the money."

While the helpful teller bagged the cash, a man with short grey hair and weathered skin entered the bank. Parsons saw him only because he noticed one of the tellers looking at the man. When Parsons glanced over, the man was already turning to leave.

The rifle jerked up with a life of its own and three rounds ripped out with a short sharp *brrp*. The tellers screamed as the man windmilled and fell. Parsons didn't give it another thought. He glanced at the people on the floor to make sure no one was trying to get up, then turned back to the tellers.

"Give me the goddamned money."

6

The last teller had put her money into his bag when Marchenko returned from the vault. His bag bulged large. The real money was always in the vault.

Parsons said, "We cool?"

Marchenko smiled behind his mask.

"We're golden."

Parsons zipped his bag closed. If a dye pack exploded the money would be ruined, but the nylon bag would protect him from the color. Sometimes the dye packs were on timers and sometimes they were on proximity fuses that were triggered when you left the bank. If a dye pack went off, the cops would be looking for anyone wearing indelible colored ink.

With the money, they stood together, looking back at the bank and the people on the floor.

Marchenko, as always, shouted his signature farewell.

"Don't get up, don't look up. If you look up, I'm gonna be the last fuckin' thing you see."

When he turned for the door, Parsons followed, not even glancing at the man he had killed, anxious to get out and get home and count their money. When they reached the door, Parsons turned for a last glance to make sure everyone was still on the floor, and, like always, they were—

—because robbing banks was so goddamned easy.

Then he followed Marchenko into the light.

●●●

Lynn Phelps checked her watch as the two robbers stepped out the door. It was three-eighteen; nine minutes since the two bozos with their black costumes

7

and big guns had entered the bank. Professional bank robbers knew they had less than two minutes to make their robbery and get away. Two minutes was the minimum amount of time it took for a bank employee to trigger a silent alarm, for that alarm to register at the security firms that banks hired to monitor such things, and for the police to respond once they were notified a robbery was in progress. Every second past two minutes increased the odds that a bank robber would be caught. A professional would leave a bank when the clock struck two whether he had the money or not. Lynn Phelps knew these guys were amateurs, dicking around in the bank for nine minutes. Sooner or later they would get bagged.

Lynn Phelps stayed on the floor and waited. The time clicked over. Ten minutes. She grunted.

Lynn Phelps did not know for certain what was waiting outside, but she had a good idea.

•••

Parsons backed out of the bank, making sure the people they had just robbed didn't rush up behind them. Backing out, he bumped into Marchenko, who had stopped only a few feet from the door when the amplified voice echoed across the parking lot.

"Police! Do not move. Stand absolutely still."

Parsons absorbed the scene in a heartbeat: Two nondescript sedans were parked across the parking lot, and a black-and-white police car was blocking the drive. A beat-up Econoline van was on the street behind the black-and-white. Hard-looking men in plainclothes were set up behind the vehicles, aiming pistols, shotguns, and rifles. Two uniformed officers were at either end of their radio car.

Parsons said, "Wow."

He did not feel afraid or any great surprise, though his heart was pounding. Marchenko raised his rifle without hesitation and opened fire. The movement of Marchenko's gun was like the okay sign. Parsons opened up, too. Their modified M4s operated flawlessly, hosing out streams of bullets. Parsons felt light punches in his stomach, chest, and left thigh, but barely noticed them. He dumped his magazine, jammed in another, and recharged. He swung toward the black-and-white, rattled off a stream, then swung back toward the nondescript sedans as Marchenko fell. Marchenko didn't stagger or spin or any of that; he dropped like a puppet with cut strings.

Parsons wasn't sure where to go or what to do except keep shooting. He stepped over Marchenko's body, then saw that one of the men behind the sedans had a rifle very much like his own. Parsons lined up, but not quite in time. Bullets snapped through his vest and staggered him. The world was suddenly grey and hazy, and his head buzzed with a feeling far different than the Royal Blue Metallic. Parsons didn't know it, but his right lung had been destroyed and his aorta had burst. He sat down hard on his ass but did not feel the impact. He slumped backwards, but did not feel his head strike the concrete. He realized that all of it had gone terribly wrong, but he still did not believe he was dying.

Shapes and shadows floated above him, but he did not know what they were and did not care. Parsons thought about the money as his abdominal cavity filled with blood and his blood pressure dropped. His last thoughts were of the money, the cash, all those perfect green bills they had stolen and stashed, each dollar a wish and a fantasy, millions of unfulfilled wishes that were beyond his reach and moving farther away. Parsons had always known that robbing banks was wrong, but he had enjoyed it. Marchenko had made them rich. And they had been rich.

Parsons saw their money.

It was waiting for them.

Then Parsons went into cardiac arrest, his breathing stopped, and only then did his dreams of the money vanish on the hot bright street in Los Angeles.

Long past their two minutes, Parsons and Marchenko had run out of time.

Part One
86 DAYS LATER

I

"YOU'RE NOT TOO OLD. Forty-six isn't old, these days. You got a world of time to make a life for yourself."

Holman didn't answer. He was trying to decide how best to pack. Everything he owned was spread out on the bed, all neatly folded: four white T-shirts, three Hanes briefs, four pairs of white socks, two short-sleeved shirts (one beige, one plaid), one pair of khaki pants, plus the clothes he had been wearing when he was arrested for bank robbery ten years, three months, and four days ago.

"Max, you listening?"

"I gotta get this stuff packed. Lemme ask you something—you think I should keep my old stuff, from before? I don't know as I'll ever get into those pants."

Wally Figg, who ran the Community Correctional Center, which was kind of a halfway house for federal prisoners, stepped forward to eye the pants. He picked them up and held them next to Holman. The cream-colored slacks still bore scuff marks from when the police had wrestled Holman to the floor in the First

United California Bank ten years plus three months ago. Wally admired the material.

"That's a nice cut, man. What is it, Italian?"

"Armani."

Wally nodded, impressed.

"I'd keep'm, I was you. Be a shame to lose something this nice."

"I got four inches more in the waist now than back then."

In the day, Holman had lived large. He stole cars, hijacked trucks, and robbed banks. Fat with fast cash, he hoovered up crystal meth for breakfast and Maker's Mark for lunch, so jittery from dope and hung over from booze he rarely bothered to eat. He had gained weight in prison.

Wally refolded the pants.

"Was me, I'd keep'm. You'll get yourself in shape again. Give yourself something to shoot for, gettin' back in these pants."

Holman tossed them to Wally. Wally was smaller.

"Better to leave the past behind."

Wally admired the slacks, then looked sadly at Holman.

"You know I can't. We can't accept anything from the residents. I'll pass'm along to one of the other guys, you want. Or give'm to Goodwill."

"Whatever."

"You got a preference, who I should give'm to?"

"No, whoever."

"Okay. Sure."

Holman went back to staring at his clothes. His suitcase was an Albertsons grocery bag. Technically, Max Holman was still incarcerated, but in another hour he would be a free man. You finish a federal stretch, they don't just cross off the last X and cut you loose; being released from federal custody happened in stages. They started you off with six months in an Intensive Confinement Center where you got field trips into the outside world, behavioral counseling, additional drug counseling if you needed it, that kind of thing, after which you graduated to a Community Correctional Center where they let you live and work in a community with real live civilians. In the final stages of his release program, Holman had spent the past three months at the CCC in Venice, California, a beach community sandwiched between Santa Monica and Marina del Rey, preparing himself for his release. As of today, Holman would be released from full-time federal custody into what was known as supervised release—he would be a free man for the first time in ten years.

Wally said, "Well, okay, I'm gonna go get the papers together. I'm proud of you, Max. This is a big day. I'm really happy for you."

Holman layered his clothes in the bag. With the help of his Bureau of Prisons release supervisor, Gail Manelli, he had secured a room in a resident motel and a job; the room would cost sixty dollars a week, the job would pay a hundred seventy-two fifty after taxes. A big day.

Wally clapped him on the back.

"I'll be in the office whenever you're ready to go. Hey, you know what I did, kind of a going-away present?"

Holman glanced at him.

"What?"

15

Wally slipped a business card from his pocket and gave it to Holman. The card showed a picture of an antique timepiece. *Salvadore Jimenez, repairs, fine watches bought and sold, Culver City, California.* Wally explained as Holman read the card.

"My wife's cousin has this little place. He fixes watches. I figured maybe you havin' a job and all, you'd want to get your old man's watch fixed. You want to see Sally, you lemme know, I'll make sure he gives you a price."

Holman slipped the card into his pocket. He wore a cheap Timex with an expandable band that hadn't worked in twenty years. In the day, Holman had worn an eighteen-thousand-dollar Patek Philippe he stole from a car fence named Oscar Reyes. Reyes had tried to short him on a stolen Carrera, so Holman had choked the sonofabitch until he passed out. But that was then. Now, Holman wore the Timex even though its hands were frozen. The Timex had belonged to his father.

"Thanks, Wally, thanks a lot. I was going to do that."

"A watch that don't keep time ain't much good to you."

"I have something in mind for it, so this will help."

"You let me know. I'll make sure he gives you a price."

"Sure. Thanks. Let me get packed up here, okay?"

Wally left as Holman returned to his packing. He had the clothes, three hundred twelve dollars that he had earned during his incarceration, and his father's watch. He did not have a car or a driver's license or friends or family to pick him up upon his release. Wally was going to give him a ride to his motel. After that, Holman would be on his own with the Los Angeles public transportation system and a watch that didn't work.

Holman went to his bureau for the picture of his son. Richie's picture was the first thing he had put in the room here at the CCC, and it would be the last thing he packed when he left. It showed his son at the age of eight, a gap-toothed kid with a buzz cut, dark skin, and serious eyes; his child's body already thickening with Holman's neck and shoulders. The last time Holman actually saw the boy was his son's twelfth birthday, Holman flush with cash from flipping two stolen Corvettes in San Diego, showing up blind drunk a day too late, the boy's mother, Donna, taking the two thousand he offered too little too late by way of the child support he never paid and on which he was always behind. Donna had sent him the old picture during his second year of incarceration, a guilty spasm because she wouldn't bring the boy to visit Holman in prison, wouldn't let the boy speak to Holman on the phone, and wouldn't pass on Holman's letters, such as they were, however few and far between, keeping the boy out of Holman's life. Holman no longer blamed her for that. She had done all right by the boy with no help from him. His son had made something of himself, and Holman was goddamned proud of that.

Holman placed the picture flat into the bag, then covered it with the remaining clothes to keep it safe. He glanced around the room. It didn't look so very different than it had an hour ago before he started.

He said, "Well, I guess that's it."

He told himself to leave, but didn't. He sat on the side of the bed instead. It was a big day, but the weight of it left him feeling heavy. He was going to get settled in his new room, check in with his release supervisor, then try to find Donna. It had been two years since her last note, not that she had ever written all that much anyway, but the five letters he had written to her since had all been returned, no longer at this address. Holman figured she had gotten married, and the new guy probably didn't want her convicted-felon boyfriend messing in their life. Holman didn't blame her for that, either. They had never married, but they did have the boy together and that had to be worth something even if she hated him. Holman wanted to apologize and let her know he had changed. If she had a new life, he wanted to wish her well with it, then get on with his. Eight or nine years ago when he thought about this day he saw himself running out the goddamned door, but now he just sat on the bed. Holman was still sitting when Wally came back.

"Max?"

Wally stood in the door like he was scared to come in. His face was pale and he kept wetting his lips.

Holman said, "What's wrong? Wally, you having a heart attack, what?"

Wally closed the door. He glanced at a little notepad like something was on it he didn't have right. He was visibly shaken.

"Wally, what?"

"You have a son, right? Richie?"

"Yeah, that's right."

"What's his full name?"

"Richard Dale Holman."

Holman stood. He didn't like the way Wally was fidgeting and licking his lips.

"You know I have a boy. You've seen his picture."

"He's a kid."

"He'd be twenty-three now. He's twenty-three. Why you want to know about this?"

"Max, listen, is he a police officer? Here in L.A.?"

"That's right."

Wally came over and touched Holman's arm with fingers as light as a breath.

"It's bad, Max. I have some bad news now and I want you to get ready for it."

Wally searched Holman's eyes as if he wanted a sign, so Holman nodded.

"Okay, Wally. What?"

"He was killed last night. I'm sorry, man. I'm really, really sorry."

Holman heard the words; he saw the pain in Wally's eyes and felt the concern in Wally's touch, but Wally and the room and the world left Holman behind like one car pulling away from another on a flat desert highway, Holman hitting the brakes, Wally hitting the gas, Holman watching the world race away.

Then he caught up and fought down an empty, terrible ache.

"What happened?"

"I don't know, Max. There was a call from the Bureau of Prisons when I went for your papers. They didn't have much to say. They wasn't even sure it was you or if you were still here."

Holman sat down again and this time Wally sat beside him. Holman had wanted to look up his son after he spoke with Donna. That last time he saw the boy, just two months before Holman was pinched in the bank gig, the boy had told him to fuck off, running

19

alongside the car as Holman drove away, eyes wet and bulging, screaming that Holman was a loser, screaming fuck off, you loser. Holman still dreamed about it. Now here they were and Holman was left with the empty sense that everything he had been moving to for the past ten years had come to a drifting stop like a ship that had lost its way.

Wally said, "You want to cry, it's okay."

Holman didn't cry. He wanted to know who did it.

●●●

Dear Max,

I am writing because I want you to know that Richard has made something of himself despite your bad blood. Richard has joined the police department. This past Sunday he graduated at the police academy by Dodger stadium and it was really something. The mayor spoke and helicopters flew so low. Richard is now a police officer. He is strong and good and not like you. I am so proud of him. He looked so handsome. I think this is his way of proving there is no truth to that old saying "like father like son."

Donna

●●●

This was the last letter Holman received, back when he was still at Lompoc. Holman remembered getting to the part where she wrote there was no truth about being like father like son, and what he felt when he read those words wasn't embarrassment or shame; he felt relief. He remembered thinking, *thank God, thank God.*

He wrote back, but the letters were returned. He wrote to his son care of the Los Angeles Police Department, just a short note to congratulate the boy, but never received an answer. He didn't know if Richie received the letter or not. He didn't want to force himself on the boy. He had not written again.

2

"WHAT SHOULD I DO?"

"What do you mean?"

"I don't know what to do about this. Is there someone I'm supposed to see? Something I'm supposed to do?"

Holman had served a total of nine months juvenile time before he was seventeen years old. His first adult time came when he was eighteen—six months for grand theft auto. This was followed by sixteen months of state time for burglary, then three years for a stacked count of robbery and breaking and entering. Altogether, Holman had spent one-third of his adult life in state and federal facilities. He was used to people telling him what to do and where to do it. Wally seemed to read his confusion.

"You go on with what you were doing, I guess. He was a policeman. Jesus, you never said he was a policeman. That's intense."

"What about the arrangements?"

"I don't know. I guess the police do that."

Holman tried to imagine what responsible people

did at times like this, but he had no experience. His mother had died when he was young and his father had died when Holman was serving the first burglary stretch. He had nothing to do with burying them.

"They sure it's the same Richie Holman?"

"You want to see one of the counselors? We could get someone in here."

"I don't need a counselor, Wally. I want to know what happened. You tell me my boy was killed, I want to know things. You can't just tell a man his boy was killed and let it go with that. Jesus Christ."

Wally made a patting gesture with his hands, trying to keep Holman calm, but Holman didn't feel upset. He didn't know what else to do or what to say or have anyone to say it to except Wally.

Holman said, "Jesus, Donna must be devastated. I'd better talk to her."

"Okay. Can I help with that?"

"I don't know. The police gotta know how to reach her. If they called me they would've called her."

"Let me see what I can find out. I told Gail I'd get back to her after I saw you. She was the one got the call from the police."

Gail Manelli was a businesslike young woman with no sense of humor, but Holman liked her.

"Okay, Wally," Holman said. "Sure."

Wally spoke with Gail, who told them Holman could obtain additional information from Richie's commander at the Devonshire Station up in Chatsworth, where Richie worked. Twenty minutes later Wally drove Holman north out of Venice on the 405 and into the San Fernando Valley. The trip took almost thirty minutes. They parked outside a clean, flat building that looked more like a modern suburban library than a police station. The air tasted like pencil lead. Holman had resided at the CCC for twelve weeks, but had not been outside of Venice, which always had great air because it was on the water. Living on a short leash like that, cons in transition called it being on the farm. Cons in transition were called transitionary inmates. There were names for everything when you were in the system.

Wally got out of the car like he was stepping into soup.

"Jesus, it's hotter'n hell up here."

Holman didn't say anything. He liked the heat, enjoying the way it warmed his skin.

They identified themselves at the reception desk and asked for Captain Levy. Levy, Gail said, had been Richie's commanding officer. Holman had been arrested by the Los Angeles Police Department on a dozen occasions, but had never seen the Devonshire Station before. The institutional lighting and austere government decor left him with the sense that he had been here before and would be again. Police stations, courts, and penal institutions had been a part of Holman's life since he was fourteen years old. They felt normal. His counselors in prison had drummed it home that career criminals like Holman had difficulty going straight because crime and the penalties of crime were a normal part of their lives— the criminal lost his fear of the penalties of his actions. Holman knew this to be true. Here he was surrounded by people with guns and badges, and he didn't feel a thing. He was disappointed. He thought he might feel afraid or at least apprehensive, but he might as well have been standing in a Ralphs market.

A uniformed officer about Holman's age came out, and the desk officer waved them over. He had short silvery hair and stars on his shoulders, so Holman took him for Levy. He looked at Wally.

"Mr. Holman?"

"No, I'm Walter Figg, with the CCC."

"I'm Holman."

"Chip Levy. I was Richard's commander. If you'll come with me I'll tell you what I can."

Levy was a short, compact guy who looked like an aging gymnast. He shook Holman's hand, and it was then Holman noticed he was wearing a black armband. So were the two officers seated behind the desk and another officer who was push-pinning flyers into a bulletin board: *Summer Sports Camp!! Sign up your kids!!*

"I just want to know what happened. I need to find out about the arrangements, I guess."

"Here, step around through the gate. We'll have some privacy."

Wally waited in the reception area. Holman went through the metal detector, then followed Levy along a hall and into an interview room. Another uniformed officer was already waiting inside, this one wearing sergeant's stripes. He stood when they entered.

Levy said, "This is Dale Clark. Dale, this is Richard's father."

Clark took Holman's hand in a firm grip, and held on longer than Holman found comfortable. Unlike Levy, Clark seemed to study him.

"I was Richard's shift supervisor. He was an outstanding young man. The best."

Holman muttered a thanks, but didn't know what to say past that; it occurred to him that these men had known and worked with his son, while he knew absolutely nothing about the boy. Realizing this left him feeling uncertain how to act, and he wished Wally was with him.

Levy asked him to take a seat at a small table. Every police officer who ever questioned Holman had hidden behind a veneer of distance, as if whatever Holman said was of no importance. Holman had long ago realized their eyes appeared distant because they were thinking; they were trying to figure out how to play him in order to get at the truth. Levy looked no different.

"Can we get you some coffee?"

"No, I'm good."

"Water or a soft drink?"

"No, uh-uh."

Levy settled across from him and folded his hands together on the table. Clark took a seat to the side on Holman's left. Where Levy tipped forward to rest his forearms on the table, Clark leaned back with his arms crossed.

Levy said, "All right. Before we proceed I need to see some identification."

Right away, Holman felt they were jacking him up. The Bureau of Prisons had told them he was coming, and here they were asking for his ID.

"Didn't Ms. Manelli talk to you?"

"It's just a formality. When something like this happens, we have people walking in off the street claiming to be related. They're usually trying to float some kind of insurance scam."

Holman felt himself redden even as he reached for his papers.

"I'm not looking for anything."

26

Levy said, "It's just a formality. Please."

Holman showed them his release document and his government-issued identity card. Realizing that many inmates had no form of identification upon release, the government provided a picture ID similar to a driver's license. Levy glanced at the card, then returned it.

"Okay, fine. I'm sorry you had to find out the way you did—through the Bureau of Prisons—but we didn't know about you."

"What does that mean?"

"You weren't listed in the officer's personnel file. Where it says 'father,' Richard had written 'unknown.'"

Holman felt himself redden even more deeply, but stared back at Clark. Clark was pissing him off. It was guys like Clark who had been busting his balls for most of his life.

"If you didn't know I existed, how did you find me?"

"Richard's wife."

Holman took it in. Richie was married, and neither Richie nor Donna had told him. Levy and Clark must have been able to read him because Levy cleared his throat.

"How long have you been incarcerated?"

"Ten years. I'm at the end of it now. I start supervised release today."

Clark said, "What were you in for?"

"Banks."

"Uh-huh, so you've had no recent contact with your son?"

Holman cursed himself for glancing away.

"I was hoping to get back in touch now that I'm out."

Clark made a thoughtful nod.

27

"You could've called him from the correction center, couldn't you? They give you guys plenty of freedom."

"I didn't want to call while I was still in custody. If he wanted to get together I didn't want to have to ask permission. I wanted him to see me free with the prison behind me."

Now it was Levy who seemed embarrassed, so Holman pushed ahead with his questions.

"Can you tell me how Richie's mother is doing? I want to make sure she's okay."

Levy glanced at Clark, who took his cue to answer.

"We notified Richard's wife. Our first responsibility was her, you understand, her being his spouse? If she notified his mother or anyone else she didn't tell us, but that was up to her. It was Mrs. Holman—Richard's wife—who told us about you. She wasn't sure where you were housed, so we contacted the Bureau of Prisons."

Levy took over.

"We'll bring you up to date with what we know. It isn't much. Robbery-Homicide is handling the case out of Parker Center. All we know at this point is that Richard was one of four officers murdered early this morning. We believe the killings were some sort of ambush, but we don't know that at this time."

Clark said, "Approximately one-fifty. A little before two is when it happened."

Levy continued on as if he didn't mind Clark's intrusion.

"Two of the officers were on duty, and two were off—Richard was not on duty. They were gathered together in—"

Holman interrupted.

"So they weren't killed in a shoot-out or anything like that?"

"If you're asking whether or not they were in a gun battle we don't know, but the reports I have don't indicate that to be the case. They were gathered together in an informal setting. I don't know how graphic I should be—"

"I don't need graphic. I just want to know what happened."

"The four officers were taking a break together—that's what I meant by informal. They were out of their cars, their weapons were holstered, and none of them radioed that a crime was in progress or a situation was developing. We believe the weapon or weapons used were shotguns."

"Jesus."

"Understand, this happened only a few hours ago. The task force has just been formed, and detectives are working right now to figure out what happened. We'll keep you informed on the developments, but right now we just don't know. The investigation is developing."

Holman shifted, and his chair made a tiny squeal.

"Do you know who did it? You have a suspect?"

"Not at this time."

"So someone just shot him, like when he was looking the other way? In the back? I'm just trying to, I don't know, picture it, I guess."

"We don't know any more, Mr. Holman. I know you have questions. Believe me, we have questions, too. We're still trying to sort it out."

Holman felt as if he didn't know any more than when he arrived. The harder he tried to think, the more he saw the boy running alongside his car, calling him a loser.

"Did he suffer?"

Levy hesitated.

"I drove down to the crime scene this morning when I got the call. Richard was one of my guys. Not the other three, but Richard was one of us here at Devonshire so I had to go see. I don't know, Mr. Holman—I want to tell you he didn't. I want to think he didn't even see it coming, but I don't know."

Holman watched Levy and appreciated the man's honesty. He felt a coldness in his chest, but he had felt that coldness before.

"I should know about the burial. Is there anything I need to do?"

Clark said, "The department will take care of that with his widow. Right now, no date has been set. We don't yet know when they'll be released from the coroner."

"All right, sure, I understand. Could I have her number? I'd like to talk to her."

Clark shifted backwards, and Levy once more laced his fingers on the table.

"I can't give you her number. If you give us your information, we'll pass it on to her and tell her you'd like to speak with her. That way, if she wants to contact you, it's her choice."

"I just want to talk to her."

"I can't give you her number."

Clark said, "It's a privacy issue. Our first obligation is to the officer's family."

"I'm his father."

"Not according to his personnel file."

30

There it was. Holman wanted to say more, but he told himself to take it easy, just like when he was inside and another con tried to front him. You had to get along.

Holman looked at the floor.

"Okay. I understand."

"If she wants to call, she will. You see how it is."

"Sure."

Holman couldn't remember the number at the motel where he would be living. Levy walked him out to the reception area where Wally gave them the number, and Levy promised to call when they knew something more. Holman thanked him for his time. Getting along.

When Levy was heading back inside, Holman stopped him.

"Captain?"

"Yes, sir?"

"Was my son a good officer?"

Levy nodded.

"Yes, sir. Yes, he was. He was a fine young man."

Holman watched Levy walk away.

Wally said, "What did they say?"

Holman turned away without answering and walked out to the car. He watched police officers entering and leaving the building as he waited for Wally to catch up. He looked up at the heavy blue sky and at the nearby mountains to the north. He tried to feel like a free man, but he felt like he was still up in Lompoc. Holman decided that was okay. He had spent much of his life in prison. He knew how to get along in prison just fine.

HOLMAN'S NEW HOME was a three-story building one block off Washington Boulevard in Culver City, sandwiched between the Smooth Running Transmission Repair Service and a convenience store protected by iron bars. The Pacific Gardens Motel Apartments had been one of six housing suggestions on a list Gail Manelli provided when it was time for Holman to find a place to live. It was clean, cheap, and located on a no-transfer bus route Holman could use to get to his job.

Wally pulled up outside the front entrance and turned off his car. They had stopped by the CCC so Holman could sign his papers and pick up his things. Holman was now officially on supervised release. He was free.

Wally said, "This isn't any way to start, man, not your first day back with news like this. Listen to me—if you want a few more days at the house you can stay. We can talk this out. You can see one of the counselors."

Holman opened the door but didn't get out. He

knew Wally was worried about him.

"I'll get settled, then I'll call Gail. I still want to get to the DMV today. I want to get a car as soon as I can."

"It's a blow, man, this news. Here you are back in the world, and already you have this to deal with. Don't let it beat you, man. Don't yield to the dark side."

"No one's going to yield."

Wally searched Holman's eyes for some kind of reassurance, so Holman tried to look reassuring. Wally didn't seem to buy it.

"You're going to have dark times, Max—black moments like you're trapped in a box with the air running out. You'll pass a hundred liquor stores and bars, and they're going to prey on your mind. If you feel weak, you call me."

"I'm okay, Wally. You don't have to worry."

"Just remember you have people pulling for you. Not everyone would've went down the way you went down, and that shows you got a strong natural character. You're a good man, Max."

"I gotta go, Wally. There's a lot to do."

Wally put out his hand.

"I'm a call away, twenty-four seven."

"Thanks, bro."

Holman took his bag of clothes from the back seat, climbed out of the car, and waved as Wally drove away. Holman had arranged for one of the eight studio apartments at the Pacific Gardens. Five of the six other tenants were civilians, and one, like Holman, was on supervised release. Holman wondered if the civilians got a break on rent for living with criminals. Holman figured they were probably Section Eight Housing recipients and lucky to have a roof over their heads.

Something wet hit Holman's neck and he glanced up. The Pacific Gardens didn't have central air. Window units hung over the sidewalk, dripping water. More water hit Holman on the face, and this time he stepped to the side.

The manager was an elderly black man named Perry Wilkes, who waved when he saw Holman enter. Even though the Pacific Gardens called itself a motel, it didn't have a front desk like a real motel. Perry owned the building and lived in the only ground-floor apartment. He manned a desk that filled a cramped corner of the entry so he could keep an eye on the people who came and left.

Perry glanced at Holman's bag.

"Hey. That all your stuff?"

"Yeah, this is it."

"Okay then, you're officially a resident. You get two keys. These are real metal keys, so if you lose one you're gonna lose your key deposit."

Holman had already filled out the rental agreement and paid his rent two weeks in advance along with a one-hundred-dollar cleaning fee and a six-dollar key deposit. When Holman first looked at the place, Perry had lectured him on noise, late-night doings, smoking pot or cigars in the rooms, and making sure his rent was paid on time, which meant exactly two weeks in advance on the dot. Everything was set so all Holman had to do was show up and move in, which is the way Gail Manelli and the Bureau of Prisons liked it.

Perry took a set of keys from his center drawer and handed them to Holman.

"This is for two-oh-six, right at the top in front here.

I got one other empty right now up on the third floor in back, but you look at two-oh-six first—it's the nicest. If you want to see the other I'll let you take your pick."

"This is one of the rooms looking at the street?"

"That's right. In front here right at the top. Set you up with a nice little view."

"Those air conditioners drip water on people walking past."

"I've heard that before and I didn't give a shit then, either."

Holman went up to see his room. It was a simple studio with dingy yellow walls, a shopworn double bed, and two stuffed chairs covered in a threadbare floral print. Holman had a private bath and what Perry called a kitchenette, which was a single-burner hot plate sitting on top of a half-size refrigerator. Holman put his bag of clothes at the foot of the bed, then opened the refrigerator. It was empty, but gleamed with cleanliness and a fresh bright light. The bathroom was clean, too, and smelled of Pine-Sol. Holman cupped his hand under the tap and drank, then looked at himself in the mirror. He had worked up a couple of mushy bags under his eyes and crow's-feet at the corners. His short hair was dusty with grey. He couldn't remember ever looking at himself up at Lompoc. He didn't look like a kid anymore and probably never had. He felt like a mummy rising from the dead.

Holman rinsed his face in the cool water, but realized too late that he had no towels and nothing with which to dry himself, so he wiped away the water with his hands and left the bathroom wet.

He sat on the edge of his bed and dug through his

wallet for phone numbers, then called Gail Manelli.

"It's Holman. I'm in the room."

"Max. I am so sorry to hear about your son. How are you doing?"

"I'm dealing. It's not like we were close."

"He was still your son."

A silence developed because Holman didn't know what to say. Finally he said something because he knew she wanted him to.

"I just have to keep my eye on the ball."

"That's right. You've come a long way and now is no time to backslide. Have you spoken to Tony yet?"

Tony was Holman's new boss, Tony Gilbert, at the Harding Sign Company. Holman had been a part-time employee for the past eight weeks, training for a full-time position that he would begin tomorrow.

"No, not yet. I just got up to the room. Wally took me up to Chatsworth."

"I know. I just spoke with him. Were the officers able to tell you anything?"

"They didn't know anything."

"I've been listening to the news stories. It's just terrible, Max. I'm so sorry."

Holman glanced around his new room, but saw he had no television or radio.

"I'll have to check it out."

"Were the police helpful? Did they treat you all right?"

"They were fine."

"All right, now listen—if you need a day or two off because of this, I can arrange it."

"I'd rather jump on the job. I think getting busy would be good."

"If you change your mind, just let me know."

"Listen, I want to get to the DMV. It's getting late and I'm not sure of the bus route. I gotta get the license so I can start driving again."

"All right, Max. Now you know you can call me anytime. You have my office and my pager."

"Listen, I really want to get to the DMV."

"I'm sorry you had to start with this terrible news."

"Thanks, Gail. Me, too."

When Gail finally hung up Holman picked up his bag of clothes. He removed the top layer of shirts, then fished out the picture of his son. He stared at Richie's face. Holman, not wanting to pock the boy's head with pinholes, had fashioned a frame out of maple scraps in the Lompoc woodworking shop and fixed the picture to a piece of cardboard with carpenter's glue. They wouldn't let inmates have glass in prison. You had glass, you could make a weapon. Broken glass, you could kill yourself or someone else. Holman set the picture on the little table between the two ugly chairs, then went downstairs to find Perry at his desk.

Perry was tipped back in his chair, almost like he was waiting for Holman to turn the corner from the stairs. He was.

Perry said, "You have to lock the deadbolt when you leave. I could hear you didn't lock the deadbolt. This isn't the CCC. You don't lock your room, someone might steal your stuff."

Holman hadn't even thought to lock his door.

"That's a good tip. After so many years, you forget."

"I know."

"Listen, I need some towels up there."

"I didn't leave any?"

"No."

"You look in the closet? Up on the shelf?"

Holman resisted his instinct to ask why towels would be in the closet and not in the bathroom.

"No, I didn't think to look in there. I'll check it out. I'd like a television, too. Can you help me with that?"

"We don't have cable."

"Just a TV."

"Might have one if I can find it. Cost you an extra eight dollars a month, plus another sixty security deposit."

Holman didn't have much of a nest egg. He could manage the extra eight a month, but the security deposit would bite pretty deep into his available cash. He figured he would need that cash for other things.

"That sounds steep, the security deposit."

Perry shrugged.

"You throw a bottle through it, what do I have? Look, I know it's a lot of money. Go to one of these discount places. You can pick up a brand-new set for eighty bucks. They make'm in Korea with slave labor and damn near give'm away. It'll be more up front, but you won't have to pay the eight a month and you'll have a better picture, too. These old sets I have are kind of fuzzy."

Holman didn't have time to waste shopping for a Korean television.

He said, "You'll give back the sixty when I give back the set?"

"Sure."

"Okay, hook me up. I'll give it back to you when I get one of my own."

"That's what you want, you got it."

Holman went next door to the convenience store for a *Times*. He bought a carton of chocolate milk to go with the paper and read the newspaper's story about the murders while standing on the sidewalk.

Sergeant Mike Fowler, a twenty-six-year veteran, had been the senior officer at the scene. He was survived by a wife and four children. Officers Patrick Mellon and Charles Wallace Ash had eight and six years on the job, respectively. Mellon was survived by a wife and two small children; Ash was unmarried. Holman studied their pictures. Fowler had a thin face and papery skin. Mellon was a dark man with a wide brow and heavy features who looked like he enjoyed kicking ass. Ash was his opposite with chipmunk cheeks, wispy hair so blond it was almost white, and nervous eyes. The last of the officers pictured was Richie. Holman had never seen an adult picture of his son. The boy had Holman's lean face and thin mouth. Holman realized his son had the same hardened expression he had seen on jailbirds who had lived ragged lives that left them burned at the edges. Holman suddenly felt angry and responsible. He folded the page to hide his son's face, then continued reading.

The article described the crime scene much as Levy described it, but contained little information beyond that. Holman was disappointed. He could tell the reporters had rushed to file their story before press time.

The officers had been parked in the L.A. River channel beneath the Fourth Street Bridge and had apparently been ambushed. Levy told Holman that all four officers had holstered weapons, but the paper reported that Officer Mellon's weapon had been drawn, though

39

not fired. A police spokesman confirmed that the senior officer present—Fowler—had radioed to announce he was taking a coffee break, but was not heard from again. Holman made a soft whistle—four trained police officers had been hammered so quickly that they hadn't been able to return fire or even take cover to call for assistance. The article contained no information about the number of shots fired or how many times the officers were hit, but Holman guessed at least two shooters were involved. It would be difficult for one man to take out four officers so quickly they didn't have time to react.

Holman was wondering why the officers were under the bridge when he read that a police spokesman denied that an open six-pack of beer had been found on one of the police cars. Holman concluded that the officers had been down there drinking, but wondered why they had chosen the riverbed for their party. Back in the day, Holman had ridden motorcycles down in the river, hanging out with dope addicts and scumbags. The concrete channel was off limits to the public, so he had climbed the fence or broken through gates with bolt-cutters. Holman thought the police might have had a passkey, but he wondered why they had gone to so much trouble just for a quiet place to drink.

Holman finished the article, then tore out Richie's picture. His wallet was the same wallet that had been in his possession when he was arrested for the bank jobs. They returned it when Holman was transferred to the CCC, but by then everything in it was out of date. Holman had thrown away all the old stuff to make room for new. He put Richie's picture into the wallet and walked back upstairs to his room.

Holman sat by his phone again, thinking, then finally dialed information.

"City and state, please?"

"Ah, Los Angeles. That's in California."

"Listing?"

"Donna Banik, B-A-N-I-K."

"Sorry, sir. I don't show anyone by that name."

If Donna had married and taken another name, he didn't know. If she had moved to another city, he didn't know that, either.

"Let me try someone else. How about Richard Holman?"

"Sorry, sir."

Holman thought what else he might try.

"When you say Los Angeles, is that just in the three-ten and two-one-three area codes?"

"Yes, sir. And the three-two-three."

Holman had never even heard of the 323. He wondered how many other area codes had been added while he was away.

"Okay, how about up in Chatsworth? What is that, eight-one-eight?"

"Sorry, I show no listing in Chatsworth by that name, or anywhere else in those area codes."

"Okay, thanks."

Holman put down the phone, feeling irritated and anxious. He went back into his bathroom and washed his face again, then walked over to his window where he stood in front of the air conditioner. He wondered if the water from its drain was falling on anyone. He took out his wallet again. His remaining savings were tucked in the billfold. He was supposed to open savings and checking accounts to demonstrate his return to the normal world, but Gail had told him anytime in the next couple of weeks would be fine. He fished through the bills and found the corner of the envelope he had torn from Donna's last letter. It was the address where he had written her only to have his letters returned. He studied it, then slipped it back between the bills.

When he left his room this time, he remembered to lock the deadbolt.

Perry nodded at him when he reached the bottom of the stairs.

"There you go. I heard you shoot the lock this time."

"Perry, listen, I need to get over to the DMV and I'm running way late. You got a car I could borrow?"

Perry's smile faded to a frown.

"You don't even have a license."

"I know, but I'm running late, man. You know what those lines are like. It's almost noon."

"Have you gone stupid already? What would you do if you got stopped? What you think Gail's gonna say?"

"I won't get stopped and I won't say you loaned me a car."

"I don't loan shit to anyone."

Holman watched Perry frowning, and knew he was considering it.

"I just need something for a few hours. Just to get over to the DMV. Once I start my job tomorrow it'll be hard to get away. You know that."

"That's true."

"Maybe I could work something out with one of the other tenants."

"So you're in a jam and you want a favor?"

"I just need the wheels."

"I did you a favor like this, it couldn't get back to Gail."

"Come on, man, look at me."

Holman spread his hands. Look at me.

Perry tipped forward in his chair, and opened the center drawer.

"Yeah, I got an old beater I'll let you use, a Mercury. It ain't pretty, but it'll run. Cost is twenty, and you gotta bring it back full."

"Jesus, that's steep. Twenty bucks for a couple of hours?"

"Twenty. And if you get fancy and don't bring it back, I'll say you stole it."

Holman passed over the twenty. He had been officially on supervised release for only four hours. It was his first violation.

4

PERRY'S MERCURY looked like a turd on
wheels. It blew smoke from bad rings and had a nasty
case of engine knock, so Holman spent most of the
drive worried that some enterprising cop might tag
him for a smog violation.

Donna's address led to a pink stucco garden apartment in Jefferson Park, south of the Santa Monica Freeway and dead center in the flat plain of the city. It was
an ugly two-story building with a parched skin
bleached by an unrelenting sun. Holman felt depressed
when he saw the blistered eaves and spotty shrubs. He
had imagined Donna would live in a nicer place; not
Brentwood or Santa Monica nice, but at least something hopeful and comforting. Donna had complained
of being short of cash from time to time, but she had
held steady employment as a private nurse for elderly
clients. Holman wondered if Richie had helped his
mother move to a better area when he got on with the
cops. He figured the man that Richie had become
would have done that even if it crimped his own
lifestyle.

The apartment building was laid out like a long U with the open end facing the street and a shrub-lined sidewalk winding its way between twin rows of apartments. Donna had lived in apartment number 108.

The building had no security gate. Any passerby was free to walk up along the sidewalk, yet Holman couldn't bring himself to enter the courtyard. He stood on the sidewalk with a nervous fire flickering in his stomach, telling himself he was just going to knock and ask the new tenants if they knew Donna's current address. Entering the courtyard wasn't illegal and knocking on a door wasn't a violation of his release, but it was difficult to stop feeling like a criminal.

Holman finally worked up the nut and found his way to 108. He knocked on the doorjamb, immediately discouraged when no one answered. He was knocking again, a little more forcefully, when the door opened and a thin, balding man peered out. He held tight to the door, ready to push it closed, and spoke in an abrupt, clipped manner.

"You caught me working, man. What's up?"

Holman slipped his hands into his pockets to make himself less threatening.

"I'm trying to find an old friend. Her name is Donna Banik. She used to live here."

The man relaxed and opened the door wider. He stood like a stork with his right foot propped on his left knee, wearing baggy shorts and a faded wife-beater. He was barefoot.

"Sorry, dude. Can't help you."

"She lived here about two years ago, Donna Banik, dark hair, about this tall."

"I've been here, what, four or five months? I don't know who had it before me, let alone two years ago."

Holman glanced at the surrounding apartments, thinking maybe one of the neighbors.

"You know if any of these other people were here back then?"

The pale man followed Holman's glance, then frowned as if the notion of knowing his neighbors was disturbing.

"No, man, sorry, they come and go."

"Okay. Sorry to bother you."

"No problem."

Holman turned away, then had a thought, but the man had already closed the door. Holman knocked again and the man opened right away.

Holman said, "Sorry, dude. Does the manager live here in the building?"

"Yeah, right there in number one hundred. The first apartment as you come in, on the north side."

"What's his name?"

"Her. She's a woman. Mrs. Bartello."

"Okay. Thanks."

Holman went back along the sidewalk to number one hundred, and this time he knocked without hesitation.

Mrs. Bartello was a sturdy woman who wore her grey hair pulled back tight and a shapeless house dress. She opened her door wide and stared out through the screen. Holman introduced himself and explained he was trying to find the former tenant of apartment 108, Donna Banik.

"Donna and I, we were married once, but that was a long time ago. I've been away and we lost track."

46

Holman figured saying they were married would be easier than explaining he was the asshole who knocked Donna up, then left her to raise their son on her own.

Mrs. Bartello's expression softened as if she recognized him, and she opened the screen.

"Oh my gosh, you must be Richard's father, *that* Mr. Holman?"

"Yes, that's right."

Holman wondered if maybe she had seen the news about Richie's death, but then he understood that she hadn't and didn't know that Richie was dead.

"Richard is such a wonderful boy. He would visit her all the time. He looks so handsome in his uniform."

"Yes, ma'am, thanks. Can you tell me where Donna is living now?"

Her eyes softened even more.

"You don't know?"

"I haven't seen Richie or Donna for a long time."

Mrs. Bartello opened the screen wider, her eyes bunching with sorrow.

"I'm sorry. You don't know. I'm sorry. Donna passed away."

Holman felt himself slow as if he had been drugged; as if his heart and breath and the blood in his veins were winding down like a phonograph record when you pulled the plug. First Richie, now Donna. He didn't say anything, and Mrs. Bartello's sorrowful eyes grew knowing.

She wedged the screen open with her ample shoulders to cross her arms.

"You didn't know. Oh, I'm sorry, you didn't know. I'm sorry, Mr. Holman."

Holman felt the slowness coalesce into a kind of distant calm.

"What happened?"

"It was those cars. They drive so fast on the free-ways, that's why I hate to go anywhere."

"She was in an auto accident?"

"She was on her way home one night. You know she worked as a nurse, didn't you?"

"Yes."

"She was on her way home. That was almost two years ago now. The way it was explained to me some-one lost control of their car, and then more cars lost control, and one of them was Donna. I'm so sorry to tell you. I felt so badly for her and poor Richard."

Holman wanted to leave. He wanted to get away from Donna's old apartment, the place she had been driving back to when she was killed.

He said, "I need to find Richie. You know where I can find him?"

"It's so sweet you call him Richie. When I met him he was Richard. Donna always called him Richard. He's a policeman, you know."

"You have his phone number?"

"Well, no, I just saw him when he came to visit, you know. I don't think I ever had his number."

"So you don't know where he lives?"

"Oh, no."

"Maybe you have Richie's address on her rental application."

"I'm sorry. I threw those old papers out after—well, once I had new tenants there was no reason to keep all that."

Holman suddenly wanted to tell her that Richie was

dead, too; he thought it would be the kind thing to do, her saying such kind things about both Donna and Richie, but he didn't have the strength. He felt depleted, like he had already given all of himself and didn't have any more to give.

Holman was about to thank her for all of it when another thought occurred to him.

"Where was she buried?"

"That was over in Baldwin Hills. The Baldwin Haven Cemetery. That was the last time I saw Richard, you know. He didn't wear his uniform. I thought he might because he was so proud and all, but he wore a nice dark suit."

"Did many people attend?"

Mrs. Bartello made a sad shrug.

"No. No, not so many."

Holman walked back to Perry's beater in a dull funk, then drove west directly into the sun, trapped in lurching rush hour traffic. It took almost forty minutes to cover the few miles back to Culver City. Holman left Perry's car in its spot behind the motel, then entered through the front door. Perry was still at his desk, the little radio tinny with the Dodgers play-by-play. Perry turned down the volume as Holman handed him the keys.

"How was your first day of freedom?"

"It was shit."

Perry leaned back and turned up his radio.

"Then it can only get better."

"Anyone call for me?"

"I don't know. You got a message machine?"

"I gave some people your number."

"Give them your own number, not mine. Do I look

49

like a message service?"

"A police captain named Levy and a young woman. Either of them call?"

"Nope. Not that I answered and I been here all day."

"You set up my TV?"

"I been here all day. I'll bring it tomorrow."

"You got a phone book or you gotta bring it tomorrow?"

Perry lifted a phone book from behind his desk.

Holman took the phone book upstairs and looked up the Baldwin Haven Cemetery. He copied the address, then lay on the bed in his clothes, thinking about Donna. After a while he held up his father's watch. The hands were frozen just the way they had been frozen since his father died. He pulled the knob and spun the hands. He watched them race around the dial, but he knew he was kidding himself. The hands were frozen. Time moved only for other people. Holman was trapped by his past.

5

HOLMAN ROSE EARLY the next morning and went down to the convenience store before Perry was at his desk. He bought a pint of chocolate milk, a six-pack of miniature powdered donuts, and a *Times*, and brought them back to his room to eat while he read the paper. The investigation into the murders was still front-page news, though today it was below the fold. The chief of police had announced that unnamed witnesses had come forward and detectives were narrowing a field of suspects. No specifics were presented except for an announcement that the city was offering a fifty-thousand-dollar reward for the arrest and conviction of the shooter. Holman suspected the cops had nothing, but were floating bullshit witnesses to bait real witnesses into making a move on the reward.

Holman ate the donuts and wished he had a television to see the morning news coverage. A lot could have happened since the paper went to bed.

Holman finished his chocolate milk, showered, then dressed for work in his one set of fresh clothes. He needed to catch the 7:10 bus to arrive at his job by eight. One bus, no changes, one long ride to his job and back again that night. Holman just had to do it every day, a single ride at a time, and he could turn his life around.

When he was ready to leave he called the Chatsworth police station, identified himself, and asked for Captain Levy. He didn't know if Levy would be at work so early and expected to leave a message, but Levy came on the line.

"Captain, it's Max Holman."

"Yes, sir. I don't have anything new to report."

"Okay, well, I have another number I'd like you to have. I don't have an answering machine yet, so if something comes up during the day you can reach me at work."

Holman read off the work number.

"One other thing. Did you have a chance to talk with Richie's wife?"

"I spoke with her, Mr. Holman."

"I'd appreciate it if you gave her this number, too. If she tries to call me here at the motel I'm not sure I'll get the message."

Levy answered slowly.

"I'll give her your work number."

"And please tell her again that I'd like to speak with her as soon as possible."

Holman wondered why Levy hesitated, and was about to ask if there was a problem when Levy interrupted.

"Mr. Holman, I'll pass along this message, but I'm going to be direct with you about this situation, and you won't like what I'm about to say."

Levy plowed on as if it was going to be just as difficult for him to say it as for Holman to hear it.

"I was Richard's commanding officer. I want to
respect his wishes and the wishes of his widow, but
I'm also a father—it wouldn't be right to leave you
waiting for something that isn't going to happen.
Richard wanted nothing to do with you. His wife, well,
her world has been turned upside down. I wouldn't
hold my breath waiting for her to call. Do you understand what I'm telling you?"

"I don't understand. You told me she's the one who
told you about me. That's why you called the Bureau
of Prisons."

"She thought you should know, but that doesn't
change how Richard felt. I don't like being in this position, but there it is. Whatever was between you and
your son is none of my business, but I am going to
respect his wishes and that means I'm going to respect
whatever his widow wants to do. I'm not a family
counselor in this matter. Are we clear on that?"

Holman stared at his hand. It lay in his lap like a
crab on its back, flexing to right itself.

"I stopped expecting anything a long time ago."

"Just so you understand. I'll pass along this new
number, but I'm not going to push her. As far as you go,
I am here to answer your questions about the investigation if I can and I'll call to update you when we have
something to report."

"What about the funeral?"

Levy didn't answer. Holman hung up without saying
more, then went downstairs and was waiting in the
lobby when Perry showed up.

Holman said, "I need that car again."

"You got another twenty?"

Holman held up the bill like a middle finger and Perry scooped it away.

"Bring it back full. I'm telling you. I didn't check last night or this morning, but I want that ride full."

"I need the TV."

"You look like something's wrong. If you're mad you didn't have the TV last night I'm sorry, but it's in storage. I'll get it this morning."

"I'm not mad about the TV."

"Then why the face?"

"Just give me the fucking keys."

Holman picked up Perry's Mercury and headed south to the City of Industry. Taking the bus would have been smarter, but Holman had a lot of ground to cover. He never exceeded the speed limit and was wary of other drivers.

Holman arrived at work ten minutes early and parked on the far side of the building because he didn't want his boss, Tony Gilbert, to see him driving. Gilbert was familiar with inmate hires, and knew Holman would not yet have his license.

Holman worked for the Harding Sign Company in a plant that printed art for Harding billboards. The art was printed on huge wallpaper-like sheets that were cut and rolled so they could be transported all over California, Nevada, and Arizona. When they reached their assigned billboards, special crews hung the rolls in huge strips and pasted them in place. During the past two months, Holman had trained part-time as a trimmer in the printing plant, which meant his job was to load five-, six-, and eight-foot-wide rolls of fabric into the printer, make sure the fabric fed square, then make sure the automatic trimmers at the end of the process made a clean cut. A moron could do it. Holman had learned the job in about two minutes, but he was lucky to have the gig and knew it.

He clocked in, then looked up Gilbert so his boss would know he had shown up on time. Gilbert was going over the day's schedule with the printer operators, who were responsible for color-coordinating and correcting the art that would be reproduced that day. Gilbert was a short thick man with a bald crown who swaggered when he walked.

Gilbert said, "So, you're officially a free man. Congratulations."

Holman thanked him, but let their conversation die. He didn't bother alerting the office receptionist or anyone else that Richie's wife might call. After his conversation with Levy, he figured her call wouldn't come.

Throughout the morning Holman was congratulated on making his release and welcomed as a full-time hire even though he had already been working there for two months. Holman kept an eye on the clock as he worked, anxious for the free hour he would have at lunch.

Holman took a piss break at ten minutes after eleven. While he was standing at the urinal another inmate hire named Marc Lee Pitchess took the next stall. Holman didn't like Pitchess and had avoided him during his two-month training period.

Pitchess said, "Ten years is a long time. Welcome back."

"You've been seeing me five days a week for the past two months. I haven't been anywhere."

"They still gonna test you?"

"Get away from me."

"I'm just saying. I can get you a kit, you keep a little sample with you ready to go, you'll be all set when they spring it on you, piss in a cup."

Holman finished and stepped back from the urinal. He turned to face Pitchess, but Pitchess was staring ahead at the wall.

"Stay the fuck away from me with that shit."

"You feel the need, I can hook you up, your basic pharmaceuticals, sleep aids, blow, X, oxy, whatever."

Pitchess shook off and zipped, but still didn't move. He stared at the wall. Someone had drawn a picture of a cock with a little word balloon. The cock was saying *smoke this, bitch*.

Pitchess said, "Just tryin' to help a brother."

Pitchess was still smiling when Holman walked out and looked up Gilbert.

Tony said, "How's it going, your first day?"

"Doin' fine. Listen, I want to ask you, I need to get to the DMV to take the test and after work is too late. Could you cut me an extra hour at lunch?"

"Don't they open on Saturday morning?"

"You have to make an appointment and they're booked three weeks. I'd really like to get this done, Tony."

Holman could tell that Gilbert didn't appreciate being asked, but he finally went along.

"Okay, but if there's some kind of problem, you call. Don't take advantage. This isn't getting off to a good start, you asking for time on your first day."

"Thanks, Tony."

"Two o'clock. I want you back by two o'clock. That should be plenty of time."

"Sure, Tony. Thanks."

Gilbert hadn't mentioned Richie and Holman didn't bring it up. Gail hadn't called, which suited Holman. He didn't want to have to explain about Richie, and have Richie lead into Donna and the whole fucking mess he had made of his life.

When Gilbert finally turned away and steamed off across the floor, Holman walked back to the office and punched out even though it wasn't yet noon.

6

HOLMAN BOUGHT a small bunch of red roses from a Latin cat at the bottom of the freeway off-ramp. Here was this dude, probably illegal, with a cowboy hat and a big plastic bucket filled with bundles of flowers, hoping to score with people on their way to the graveyard. The dude asked eight—*ocho*—but Holman paid ten, guilty he hadn't thought to bring flowers before seeing the cat with his bucket, even more guilty because Donna was gone and Richie hadn't thought enough of him to let him know.

Baldwin Haven Cemetery covered the wide face of a rolling hillside just off the 405 in Baldwin Hills. Holman turned through the gates and pulled up alongside the main office, hoping no one had seen the crappy condition of his car. Perry's old Mercury was such a shitpile that anyone who saw him pull up would think he was here to hustle work trimming weeds. Holman brought the flowers inside with him, thinking he would make a better impression.

The cemetery office was a large room divided by a counter. Two desks and some file cabinets sat on one side of the counter; landscape plans were laid out on a large table on the other side. An older woman with grey hair glanced up from one of the desks when he entered.

Holman said, "I need to find someone's grave."

She stood and came to the counter.

"Yes, sir. Could I have the party's name?"

"Donna Banik."

"Banner?"

"B-A-N-I-K. She was buried here about two years ago."

The woman went to a shelf and took down what looked to Holman like a heavy frayed ledger. Her lips moved as she flipped the pages, mumbling the name, Banik.

She found the entry, wrote something on a note slip, then came out from behind the counter and led Holman to the landscape plans.

"Here, I can show you how to find the site."

Holman followed her as she circled the landscape map. She checked the coordinates written on the slip, then pointed out a tiny rectangle in a uniform rank and file of tiny rectangles, each labeled by number.

"She's here, on the south face. We're here in the office, so what you'll do is turn right out of the parking lot and follow the road to this fork, then veer left. She's right in front of the mausoleum here. Just count the rows, third row from the street, the sixth marker from the end. You shouldn't have any trouble, but if you do, just come back and I'll show you."

Holman stared at the tiny blue rectangle with its indecipherable number.

"She's my wife."

"Oh, I'm sorry."

"Well, she wasn't my wife, but like that, a long time ago. We hadn't seen each other in a long time. I didn't even know she had passed until yesterday."

"Well, if you need any help just let me know."

Holman watched the woman return to her place behind the counter, clearly uninterested in who Donna was to him. Holman felt a flash of anger, but he had never been one to share his feelings. During the ten years he spent at Lompoc he had rarely mentioned Donna or Richie. What was he going to do, swap family stories with shitbird convicts and predatory criminals like Pitchess? Real people talked about their families with other real people, but Holman didn't know real people and had abandoned his family, and now lost them. He had suddenly needed to tell someone about Donna, but the best he could do was an uninterested stranger. Recognizing the need left him feeling lonely and pathetic.

Holman climbed back into the Mercury and followed the directions to Donna's grave. He found a small bronze plaque set into the earth bearing Donna's name and the years of her birth and death. On the plaque was a simple legend: *Beloved Mother*.

Holman laid the roses on the grass. He had rehearsed what he wanted to tell her when he got out a thousand times, but now she was dead and it was too late. Holman didn't believe in an afterlife. He didn't believe she was up in Heaven, watching him. He told her anyway, staring down at the roses and the plaque.

"I was a rotten prick. I was all those things you ever called me and worse. You had no idea how rotten I really was. I used to thank God you didn't know, but now I'm ashamed. If you had known you would've given up on me, and you might've married some decent guy and had something. I wish you had known. Not for me, but for you. So you wouldn't have wasted your life."

Beloved Mother.

Holman returned to his car and drove back to the office. The woman was showing the map of the grounds to a middle-aged couple when Holman walked in, so he waited by the door. The cold air in the little office felt good after standing in the sun. After a few minutes, the woman left the couple talking over available sites and came over.

"Did you find it okay?"

"Yeah, thanks, you made it real easy. Listen, I want to ask you something. Do you remember who made the arrangements?"

"For her burial?"

"I don't know if it was her sister or a husband or what, but I'd like to share in the cost. We were together a long time, then I was away, and, well, it's not right that I didn't share the expenses."

"It's been paid for. It was paid for at the time of the service."

"I figured that, but I still want to offer to pay. Part of it, at least."

"You want to know who paid for the burial?"

"Yes, ma'am. If you can give me a phone number or an address or something. I'd like to offer to help out on the costs."

The woman glanced at her other customers but they were still talking over the various sites. She went back around the counter to her desk and searched through the trash can until she found the slip with the plot numbers.

"That was Banik, right?"

"Yes, ma'am."

"I'll have to look it up for you. I have to find the records. Can you leave a phone number?"

Holman wrote Perry's number on her note-pad.

She said, "This is very generous. I'm sure her family will be glad to hear from you."

"Yes, ma'am. I hope so."

Holman went out to his car and drove back toward the City of Industry. With the time and the traffic he figured he would get back to work before two o'clock, but then he turned on the radio and all of that changed. The station had broken into their regular programming with news that a suspect had been named in the murders of the four officers, and a warrant had been issued for his arrest.

Holman turned up the volume and forgot about work. He immediately began looking for a phone.

7

HOLMAN DROVE until he spotted a tiny sports bar with its front door wedged open. He jockeyed the beater into a red zone, then hesitated in the door, taking the measure of the place until he saw a television. Holman hadn't been in a bar since the week before he was arrested, but this was no different: A young bartender with sharp sideburns worked a half-dozen alkies sipping their lunch. The television was showing ESPN but no one was looking at it. Holman went to the bar.

"You mind if we get the news?"

The bartender glanced over like the toughest thing he would do that day was pour Holman a drink.

"Whatever you want. Can I get you something?"

Holman glanced at the two women next to him. They were watching him.

"Club soda, I guess. How about that news?"

The bartender added a squeeze of lime to the ice, brimmed the glass, then set it on the bar before changing the channel to a couple of heads talking about the Middle East.

Holman said, "How about the local news?"

"I don't know if you're gonna get news right now. It's nothing but soap operas."

The nearest of the two women said, "Try five or nine."

The bartender found a local station and there it was, several high-ranking LAPD suits holding a press conference.

The bartender said, "What happened? This about those cops who were killed?"

"Yeah, they know who did it. Let's listen."

The second woman said, "What happened?"

Holman said, "Can we listen?"

The first woman said, "I saw that this morning. There isn't anything new."

Holman said, "Can we listen to what they're saying, please?"

The woman made a snorting sound and rolled her eyes like where did Holman get off. The bartender turned up the sound, but now an assistant chief named Donnelly was recounting the crime and stating information Holman already knew. Pictures of the murdered officers flashed on the screen as Donnelly identified them, Richie being the last. It was the same picture Holman had seen in the papers, but now the picture left Holman feeling creepy. It was as if Richie was staring down at him from the screen.

A man at the far end of the bar said, "I hope they catch the bastard did this."

The first woman said, "Can't we get something else? I'm tired of all this killing."

Holman said, "Listen."

She turned to her friend as if they were having a private conversation, only loud.

"Nothing but the bad news and they wonder why no one watches."

Holman said, "Shut the fuck up and listen."

The picture cut back to Donnelly, who looked determined as another picture appeared on the screen to his right.

Donnelly said, "We have issued a warrant for the arrest of this man, Warren Alberto Juarez, for the murder of these officers."

The woman swiveled toward Holman.

"You can't talk to me like that. How dare you use the F word when you're talking to me?"

Holman strained to hear past her as Donnelly continued.

"Mr. Juarez is a resident of Cypress Park. He has an extensive criminal history including assault, robbery, possession of a concealed weapon, and known gang associations—"

The woman said, "Don't pretend you can't hear me!"

Holman concentrated on what Donnelly was saying, but he still missed some of it.

"—contact us at the number appearing on your screen. Do NOT—I repeat—do NOT try to apprehend this man yourself."

Holman stared hard at the face on the screen. Warren Alberto Juarez looked like a gangbanger, with a thick mustache and hair slicked tight like a skullcap. He was making his eyes sleepy to look tough for the booking photo. The sleepy look was popular with black and Latino criminals, but Holman wasn't impressed. Back in the day when he pulled state time at Men's Colony and Pleasant Valley, he had kicked the shit out of plenty of sleepy assholes just to stay alive.

The woman said, "I'm talking to you, goddamnit. How dare you say such a thing, using that word with me!"

Holman nodded at the bartender.

"How much for the soda?"

"I said I'm talking to you."

"Two."

"You got a pay phone?"

"Look at me when I'm talking to you."

"Back by the bathrooms."

Holman put two dollars on the bar, then followed the bartender's finger back toward the pay phone as the woman called him an asshole. When Holman reached the phone he dug out his list for Levy's number up at the Devonshire Station. He had to wait while Levy got off another call, then Levy came on.

Holman said, "I heard on the news."

"Then you know what I know. Parker Center called less than an hour ago."

"Do they have him yet?"

"Mr. Holman, they just issued the warrant. They'll notify me as soon as an arrest is made."

Holman was so jacked up that he shook as if he had been on meth for a week. He didn't want to put off Levy, so he took a couple of deep breaths and forced himself to relax.

"All right, I understand that. Do they know why it happened?"

"The word I have so far is it was a personal vendetta

between Juarez and Sergeant Fowler. Fowler arrested Juarez's younger brother last year, and apparently the brother was killed in prison."

"How was Richie involved with Juarez?"

"He wasn't."

Holman waited for more. He waited for Levy to tell him the reason that would stitch the four murders together but Levy was silent.

"Waitaminute—wait—this asshole killed all four of these people just to get Fowler?"

"Mr. Holman, listen, I know what you're looking for here—you want this to make sense. I would like this to make sense, too, but sometimes they don't. Richard had nothing to do with the Juarez arrest. So far as I know neither did Mellon or Ash. I can't say that definitively, but that's the impression I have from speaking with their captains. Maybe we'll know more later and this will make sense."

"They know who was with him?"

"It's my understanding that he acted alone."

Holman felt his voice shake again and fought hard to stop it.

"This doesn't make sense. How did he know they were down under that bridge? Did he follow them? Was he laying in wait, *one guy,* and he shotguns four men just to get one of them? This doesn't make sense."

"I know it doesn't. I'm sorry."

"They're sure it was Juarez?"

"They are positive. They matched fingerprints found on shell casings at the scene with Mr. Juarez. My understanding is they also have witnesses who heard Juarez make numerous threats and placed him at the

67

scene earlier that night. They attempted to arrest Juarez at his home earlier today, but he had already fled. Listen, I have other calls—"

"Are they close to an arrest?"

"I don't know. Now I really do—"

"One more thing, Captain, please. On the news, they said he was a gangbanger."

"That's my understanding, yes."

"You know his gang affiliation?"

"I don't—no, sir. I really do have to go now."

Holman thanked him, then went back to the bartender for change of a dollar. The woman with the loud mouth gave him a nasty glance, but this time she didn't say anything. Holman took his change back to the phone and called Gail Manelli.

"Hey, it's Holman. You got a second?"

"Of course, Max. I was just about to call you."

Holman figured she wanted to tell him that the police had named a suspect, but he plowed on.

"Remember you said if I needed a few days you'd square it with Gilbert?"

"Do you need some time off?"

"Yes. There's a lot to deal with, Gail. More than I thought."

"Have you spoken with the police today?"

"I just got off the phone with Captain Levy. Can you square a few days with Gilbert? That guy has been good to me with the job—"

"I'll call him right now, Max—I'm sure he'll understand. Now listen, would you like to see a counselor?"

"I'm doing fine, Gail. I don't need a counselor."

"This isn't a time to lose sight of everything you've learned, Max. Use the coping tools you have. Don't try to be an iron man and think you have to weather this alone."

Holman wanted to ask her if she would like to share the guilt and shame he felt. He was tired of everyone treating him as if they were scared shitless he would explode, but he reminded himself Gail was doing her job.

"I just need the time, is all. If I change my mind about the counselor I'll let you know."

"I just want you to understand I'm here."

"I know. Listen—I have to go. Thanks for squaring up the job for me. Tell Tony I'll call him in a few days."

"I will, Max. You take care of yourself. I know you're hurting, but the most important thing you can do right now is take care of yourself. Your son would want that."

"Thanks, Gail. I'll see you."

Holman put down the phone. Gail had her ideas about what was important, but Holman had his. The criminal world was a world he knew. And knew how to use.

8

CRIMINALS DID not have friends. They had associates, suppliers, fences, whores, sugar daddies, enablers, dealers, collaborators, co-conspirators, victims, and bosses, any of whom they might rat out and none of whom could be trusted. Most everyone Holman met on the yard during his ten years at Lompoc had not been arrested and convicted because Dick Tracy or Sherlock Holmes made their case; they had been fingered by someone they knew and trusted. Police work only went so far; Holman wanted to find someone who would rat out Warren Juarez.

That afternoon, Gary "L'Chee" Moreno said, "You gotta be the dumbest gringo ever shit between two feet."

"Tell me you love me, bro."

"Here's what I'm tellin' you, Holman: Why didn't you run? I been waiting ten years to ask that, dumbfuckinAnglo."

"Didn't have to wait ten years, Chee. You coulda come seen me in Lompoc."

"That's why they caught you, thinkin' like that,

dumbfuckinHolman! Me, I would'a jetted outta that bank straight to Zacatecas like a chili pepper was up my ass. C'mere. Give a brother some love."

Chee came around the counter there at his body shop in East L.A. He wrapped Holman in a tight hug, it being ten years since they had seen each other—since the day Chee had waited outside the bank for Holman as the police and FBI arrived; whereupon—by mutual agreement—Chee had driven away.

Holman first met Chee when they were serving stints at the California Youth Authority, both fourteen years old; Holman for a string of shoplifting and burglary arrests, Chee on his second auto theft conviction. Chee, small but fearless, was being pounded by three bloods on the main yard when Holman, large for his size even then with the thick neck and shoulders, whaled in and beat the bloods down. Chee couldn't do enough for him after that, and neither could Chee's family. Chee was a fifth-generation White Fence homeboy, nephew to the infamous Chihuahua Brothers from Pacoima, two miniature Guatemalans who macheted their way to the top of the L.A. stolen car market in the seventies. In the day, Holman had fed Porsches and 'vettes to Chee when he was sober enough to steal them, which wasn't so very often toward the end, and Chee had even driven on a few of the bank jobs; done it, Holman knew, only for the in-your-face outlaw rush of living crazy with his good buddy Holman.

Now, Chee stepped back, and Holman saw that his eyes were serious. Holman really did mean something to him; meant something deep for all those past times.

"Goddamn, it's good to see you, bro. Goddamn. You

crazy or what? It's a violation for you even to be standing here."

"I'm federal release, homes. It's not like a state parole. They don't say who I can roll with."

Chee looked doubtful.

"No shit?"

"Up."

Chee was clearly mystified and impressed at the vagaries of the federal system.

"C'mon back here, we'll get away from this noise."

Chee led Holman behind the counter into a small office. These same offices had once been the center of a chop shop Chee managed for his uncles, breaking down stolen cars into their component parts. Now, older, wiser, and with his uncles long dead, Chee ran a mostly legitimate body shop employing his sons and nephews. Holman made a show of looking around the body shop office.

"Looks different."

"*Is* different, homes. My daughter works here three days a week. She don't wanna see titty pictures on the walls. You want a beer?"

"I'm sober."

"No shit? Well, good, man, that's real good. God-damned, we're gettin' old."

Chee laughed as he dropped into his chair. When Chee laughed, his leathery skin accordioned with acne craters and tattoos from his gang days. He was still White Fence, a certified veterano, but out of the street life. Chee's weathered face grew sad, staring at nothing until he finally looked at Holman.

"You need some money? I'll front you, homes. You don't even have to pay me back. I mean it."

"I want a homeboy named Warren Alberto Juarez."

Chee swiveled in his chair to pull a thick phone book from the clutter. He flipped a few pages, circled a name, then pushed the book across his desk.

"Here you go. Knock yourself out."

Holman glanced at the page. Warren A. Juarez. An address in Cypress Park. A phone number. When Holman looked up, Chee was staring like Holman was stupid.

"Homes, that why you came down here, cash in on the reward? You think he's hidin' in a closet down here? *Ese, please.*"

"You know where he went?"

"Why you think I'd know something like that?"

"You're Little Chee. You always knew things."

"Those days are gone, bro. I am Mister Moreno. Look around. I ain't in the life anymore. I pay taxes. I got hemorrhoids."

"You're still White Fence."

"To the death and beyond, and I'll tell you this—if I knew where the homeboy was I'd nail that fifty myself—he ain't White Fence. He's Frogtown, homes, from up by the river, and right now he ain't nothing to me 'cept a pain in the ass. Half my boys called in sick today, wantin' that money. My work schedule's in the shitter."

Chee showed his palms, like enough already with Warren Juarez, and went on with his rant.

"Forget that reward bullshit, Holman. I tol' you, I'll give you money, you want it."

"I'm not looking for a loan."

"Then what?"

"One of the officers he killed was my son. Richie

grew up to be a policeman, you imagine? My little boy."

Chee's eyes went round like saucers. He had met the boy a few times, the first when Richie was three. Holman had convinced Donna to let him take the boy to the Santa Monica pier for the Ferris wheel. Holman and Chee had hooked up, but Holman had left Richie with Chee's girlfriend so he and Chee could steal a Corvette they saw in the parking lot. Real Father of the Year stuff.

"*Ese. Ese,* I'm sorry."

"That's his mother, Chee. I used to pray for that. Don't let him be a fuckup like me; let him be like his mother."

"God answered."

"The police say Juarez killed him. They say Juarez killed all four of them just to get the one named Fowler, some bullshit about Juarez's brother."

"I don't know anything about that, man. Whatever, that's Frogtown, *ese.*"

"Whatever, I want to find him. I want to find out who helped him, and find them, too."

Chee shifted in his chair, making it creak. He rubbed a rough hand over his face, muttering and thinking. Latin gangs derived their names from their neighborhoods: Happy Valley Gang, Hazard Street, Geraghty Lomas. Frogtown drew its name from the old days of the Los Angeles River, where neighborhood homies fell asleep to croaking bullfrogs before the city lined the river with concrete and the frogs died. Juarez being a member of the Frogtown gang wasn't lost on Holman. The officers had been murdered at the river.

Chee slowly fixed his eyes on Holman.

"You gonna kill him? That what you wanna do?"

Holman wasn't sure what he would do. He wasn't sure what he was doing sitting with Chee. The entire Los Angeles Police Department was looking for Warren Juarez.

"Holman?"

"He was my boy. Someone kills your boy you can't just sit."

"You're not a killer, Holman. Tough motherfucker, yeah, but a man would do murder? I never seen that in you, homes, and, believe me, I seen plenty of cold-hearted killers, homies stab a child then go eat a prime rib dinner, but that wasn't you. You gonna kill this boy, then ride the murder bus back to prison, thinking you done the right thing?"

"What would you do?"

"Kill the muthuhfuckuh straight up, homes. Cut off the boy's head, hang it from my rearview so everyone see, and ride straight down Whittier Boulevard. You gonna do something like that? Could you?"

"No."

"Then let the police do their business. They lost four of their own. They're gonna take lives findin' this boy."

Holman knew Chee was right, but tried to put his need into words.

"The officers, they have to fill out this next-of-kin form at the police. Where they have a place for the father, Richie wrote 'unknown.' He was so ashamed of me he didn't even claim me—he put down that his father was unknown. I can't have that, Chee. I'm his father. This is the way I have to answer."

Chee settled back again, quietly thoughtful as Holman went on.

"I can't leave this to someone else. Right now, they're saying Juarez did this thing by himself. C'mon, Chee, how'd some homeboy get good enough to take out four armed officers all by himself, so fast they didn't shoot back?"

"A lot of homies are coming back from Iraq, bro. If the boy tooled up overseas, he might know exactly how to do what he did."

"Then I want to know that. I need to understand how this happened and find the bastards who did it. I'm not racing the cops. I just want this bastard found."

"Well, you're gonna have a lot of help. Over there outside his house in Cypress Park, it looks like a cop convention. My wife and daughter drove by there at lunchtime just to see, a couple of goddamned looky-loos! His wife's gone into hiding herself. The address I gave you, that place is empty right now."

"Where'd his wife go?"

"How can I know something like that, Holman? That boy ain't White Fence. If he was and he killed your son, I would shoot him myself, *ese*. But he's in with that Frogtown crew."

"Little Chee?"

Witnesses at two of the bank jobs had seen Holman get into cars driven by another man. After Holman's arrest, the FBI had pressured him to name his accomplice. They had asked, but Holman had held fast.

Holman said, "After my arrest—how much sleep did you lose, worrying I was going to rat you out?"

"Not one night. Not a single night, homes."

"Because why?"

"Because I knew you were solid. You were my brother."

"Has that fact changed or is it the same?"

"The same. We're the same."

"Help me, Little Chee. Where can I find the girl?"

Holman knew Chee didn't like it, but Chee did not hesitate. He picked up his phone.

"Get yourself some coffee, homes. I gotta make some calls."

An hour later, Holman walked out, but Chee didn't walk with him. Ten years later, some things were the same, but others were different.

9

HOLMAN DECIDED to drive past Juarez's house first to see the cop convention. Even though Chee had warned him that the police commanded the scene, Holman was surprised. Three news vans and an LAPD black-and-white were parked in front of a tiny bungalow. Transmission dishes swayed over the vans like spindly palms, with the uniformed officers and newspeople chatting together on the sidewalk. One look, and Holman knew Juarez would never return even if the officers were gone. A small crowd of neighborhood civilians gawked from across the street, and the line of cars edging past the house made Holman feel like he was passing a traffic fatality on the 405. No wonder Juarez's wife had split.

Holman kept driving.

Chee had learned that Maria Juarez had relocated to her cousin's house in Silver Lake, south of Sunset in an area rich with Central Americans. Holman figured the police knew her location, too, and had probably even helped her move to protect her from the media; if she had gone into hiding on her own they would have declared her a fugitive and issued a warrant.

The address Chee provided led to a small clapboard box crouched behind a row of spotty cypress trees on a steep hill lined with broken sidewalks. Holman thought the house looked like it was hiding. He parked at the curb two blocks uphill, then tried to figure out what to do. The door was closed and the shades were drawn, but it was that way for most of the houses. Holman wondered if Juarez was in the house. It was possible. Holman knew dozens of guys who were bagged in their own garages because they didn't have anyplace else to go. Criminals always returned to their girlfriends, their wives, their mothers, their house, their trailer, their car—they ran to whatever or whoever made them feel safe. Holman probably would have been caught at home, too, only he hadn't had a home.

It occurred to Holman the police knew this and might be watching the house. He twisted around to examine the neighboring cars and houses, but saw nothing suspicious. He got out of his car and went to the front door. He didn't see any reason to get dramatic unless no one answered. If no one answered, he would walk around the side of the place and break in through the back. He knocked.

Holman didn't expect someone to answer so quickly, but a young woman threw open the door right away. She couldn't have been more than twenty or twenty-one, even younger than Richie. She was butt-ugly, with a flat nose, big teeth, and black hair greased flat into squiggly sideburns.

She said, "Is he all right?"

She thought he was a cop.

Holman said, "Maria Juarez?"

79

"Tell me he is all right. Did you find him? Tell me he is not dead."

She had just told Holman everything he needed to know. Juarez wasn't here. The police had been here earlier, and she had been cooperative with them. Holman gave her an easy smile.

"I need to ask a few questions. May I come in?"

She moved back out of the door and Holman went in. A TV was showing Telemundo, but other than that the place was quiet. He listened to see if anyone was in the back of the house, but heard nothing. He could see through the dining room and the kitchen to a back door which was closed. The house smelled of chorizo and cilantro. A central hall opened off the living room and probably led to a bathroom and a couple of bedrooms. Holman wondered if anyone was in the bedrooms.

Holman said, "Is anyone else here?"

Her eyes flickered, and Holman knew he had made his first mistake. The question left her suspicious.

"My aunt. She is in the bed."

He took her arm, bringing her toward the hall.

"Let's take a look."

"Who are you? Are you the police?"

Holman knew a lot of these homegirls would kill you as quick as any veterano and some would kill you faster, so he gripped her arm tight.

"I just want to see if Warren is here."

"He is not here. You know he isn't here. Who are you? You are not one of the detectives."

Holman brought her back along the hall, glancing in the bathroom first, then the front bedroom. An old lady wrapped in shawls and blankets was sitting up in bed, as withered and tiny as a raisin. She said something in Spanish that Holman didn't understand. He gave her an apologetic smile, then pulled Maria out to the second bedroom, closing the old lady's door behind them.

Maria said, "Don't go in there."

"Warren isn't in here, is he?"

"My baby. She is sleeping."

Holman held Juarez's wife in front of him and cracked open the door. The room was dim. He made out a small figure napping in an adult's bed, a little girl who was maybe three or four. Holman stood listening again, knowing that Juarez might be hiding under the bed or in the closet, but not wanting to wake the little girl. He heard the buzz of a child's gentle snore. Something in the child's innocent pose made Holman think of Richie at that age. Holman tried to remember if he had ever seen Richie asleep, but couldn't. The memories didn't come because they didn't exist. He was never around long enough to see his baby sleeping.

Holman closed the door and brought Maria into the living room.

She said, "You weren't here with the policemen—I want to know who you are."

"My name is Holman. You know that name?"

"Get out of this house. I don't know where he is. I already tol' them. Who are you? You don't show me your badge."

Holman forced her down onto the couch. He leaned over her, nose to nose, and pointed at his face.

"Look at this face. Did you see this face on the news?"

She was crying. She didn't understand what he was

saying, and she was scared. Holman realized this but was unable to stop himself. His voice never rose above a whisper. Just like when he was robbing the banks.

"My name is Holman. One of the officers, his name was Holman, too. Your fucking husband murdered my son. Do you understand that?"

"No!"

"Where is he?"

"I don't know."

"Did he go to Mexico? I heard he went under the fence."

"He did not do this. I showed them. He was with us."

"Where is he?"

"I don't know."

"Tell me who's hiding him."

"I don't know. I told them. I showed them. He was with us."

Holman hadn't thought through his actions and now he felt trapped. The prison counselors had harped on that—criminals were people who were unable or unwilling to anticipate the consequences of their actions. No impulse control, they called it. Holman suddenly grabbed her throat. His hand encircled her from ear to ear as if acting with a will of its own. He grabbed her with no sense of what he was doing or why—

—but then she made a choking gurgle and Holman saw himself in the moment. He released her and stepped back, his face burning with shame.

The little girl said, "Mommy?"

She stood in the hall outside the old lady's room, so small she looked like a miniature person. Holman wanted to run, sick with himself and humiliated that the child might have seen him.

Maria said, "It's okay, my love. Go back to bed. I'll be in with you soon. Go on, now."

The little girl returned to her room.

Richie, turning away as Donna cursed him for being a loser.

Holman said, "I'm sorry. Are you all right?"

Maria stared at him, soundless. She touched her throat where he had gripped her. She touched a curl gelled to her cheek.

Holman said, "Listen, I'm sorry. I'm upset. He killed my son."

She gathered herself and shook her head.

"It was her birthday, the day before yesterday. He was with us for her birthday. He wasn't killing no policemen."

"Her birthday? The little girl?"

"I can prove it. I showed them the tape. Warren was with us."

Holman shook his head, fighting away the depressing memories of loss as he tried to understand what she was saying.

"I don't know what you're telling me. You had a party for the little girl? You had guests?"

Holman wouldn't believe any witness she could produce and neither would the cops, but she waved toward the television.

"Warren brought us one of these video cameras. It's at my house. We took videos of her blowing out the candles and playing with us, the day before yesterday."

"That doesn't prove anything."

"You don't understand. That show was on, that one

with the comedian? Warren put her on his back so she could ride him like a donkey and he was going around the living room in front of the TV. You could see the show when Warren was here. That *proves* he was with us."

Holman had no idea what show she was talking about.

"Those officers were murdered at one-thirty in the morning."

"Yes! The show starts at one. It was on the TV when Warren was giving her rides. You can see on the tape."

"You were having a party for your kid in the middle of the night? C'mon."

"He has the warrants, you know? He has to be careful when he comes by. My father, he saw the tape I took. He told me the show proved Warren was home with us."

She seemed to believe what she was saying, and it would be easy enough to check. If her videotape showed a television show on the tube, all you had to do was call the TV station and ask what time the show had aired.

"Okay. Lemme see it. Show me."

"The police took it. They said it was evidence."

Holman worked through what she was telling him. The police took the tape, but clearly hadn't believed it cleared Warren of the crime—they had issued the warrant. Still, Holman thought she was being sincere, so he figured she was probably telling the truth about not knowing her husband's whereabouts.

The little girl said, "Mama."

The little girl was back in the hall.

Holman said, "How old are you?"

The little girl stared at the floor.

Maria said, "Answer him, Alicia. Where are your manners?"

The little girl held up a hand, showing three fingers.

Maria said, "I'm sorry your son was killed, but it was not Warren. I know what is in your heart now. If you kill him, that will be in your heart, too."

Holman pulled his eyes from the little girl.

"I'm sorry about what I did."

He went out the front door. The sun was blinding after being in the dim house. He walked back to Perry's car, feeling like a boat without a rudder, trapped in a current. He had no place to go and no idea what to do. He thought he should probably just go back to work and start earning money. He couldn't think of anything else to do.

Holman was still trying to decide when he reached Perry's car. He put the key in the lock, then was suddenly hit from behind so hard that he lost his breath. He smashed into the side of the car as his feet were kicked from beneath him, and they rode him down hard onto the street, proning him out with the grace of true professionals.

When Holman looked up, a red-haired guy in sunglasses and plainclothes held up a badge.

"Los Angeles Police Department. You're under arrest."

Holman closed his eyes as their handcuffs shut on his wrists.

IO

IT WAS FOUR plainclothes officers who hooked him up, but only two of them brought him to Parker Center, the red-haired officer whose name was Vukovich and a Latino officer named Fuentes. Holman had been arrested by the Los Angeles Police Department on twelve separate occasions, and in every case except his last (when he was arrested by an FBI agent named Katherine Pollard) he had been processed through one of LAPD's nineteen divisional police stations. He had been in the Men's Central Jail twice and the Federal Men's Detention Center three times, but he had never been to Parker Center. When they brought him to Parker, Holman knew he was in deep shit.

Parker was the Los Angeles Police Department's main office: A white-and-glass building that housed the Chief of Police, the Internal Affairs Group, various civilian administrators and administration agencies, and LAPD's elite Robbery-Homicide Division, which was a command division overseeing Homicide Special, Robbery Special, and Rape Special. Each of the nineteen divisions had homicide, robbery, and sex crimes detectives, but those detectives worked only in their respective divisions; Robbery-Homicide detectives worked on cases that spanned the city.

Vukovich and Fuentes walked Holman into an interview room on the third floor and questioned him for more than an hour, after which another set of detectives took over. Holman knew the drill. The cops always asked the same questions over and over, looking to see if your answers changed. If your answers changed they knew you were lying, so Holman told them the truth about everything except Chee. When the red-haired guy, Vukovich, asked how he knew Maria Juarez was with her cousins, Holman told them he heard it in a bar, some Frogtown paco bragging he screwed Maria in junior high, him and sixty-two other guys, the girl was such a slut, the paco spouting the cops Warren killed had probably been bagging the little slut, too. Covering for Chee was something he had done before and now it was the only lie Holman told. One lie, it was easy to remember even though telling it frightened him.

Eight-forty that night, Holman was still in the room, having been questioned on and off for more than six hours without being offered an attorney or being booked. Eight forty-one, the door opened again and Vukovich entered with someone new.

The new man studied Holman for a moment, then put out his hand. Holman thought he looked familiar.

"Mr. Holman, I'm John Random. I'm sorry about your son."

Random was the first of the detectives to offer his hand. He wore a long-sleeved white shirt and tie without a jacket. A gold detective's shield was clipped to his belt. Random took a seat opposite Holman as Vukovich leaned against the wall.

Holman said, "Am I being charged with anything?"

"Has Detective Vukovich explained why we pulled you in?"

"No."

Holman suddenly realized why Random was familiar. Random had been part of the press conference that Holman had seen in the bar. He hadn't known Random's name, but he recognized him.

Random said, "When the officers ran your vehicle they found thirty-two unpaid parking violations and another nine outstanding traffic violations."

Holman said, "Jesus."

Vukovich smiled.

"Yeah, and you didn't match the DMV description we got of the vehicle's owner, you not being a seventy-four-year-old black male. We thought you had a hot car, bud."

Random said, "We spoke with Mr. Wilkes. You're in the clear so far as the car, even though you've been driving it without a license. So forget the car and let's get back to Ms. Juarez. Why did you go see her?"

The same question he had been asked three dozen times. Holman gave them the same answer.

"I was looking for her husband."

"What do you know about her husband?"

"I saw you on TV. You're looking for him."

"But why were *you* looking for him?"

"He killed my son."

"How'd you find your way to Ms. Juarez?"

"Their address was in the phone book. I went to

their house but the place was crawling with people. I started hitting the bars in their neighborhood and found some people who knew them, and pretty soon I ended up in Silver Lake and met this guy said he knew her. He told me she was staying with her cousins, and I guess he was telling the truth—that's where I found her."

Random nodded.

"He knew her address?"

"Information operator gave me the address. The guy I met, he just told me who she was staying with. It wasn't any big deal. Most folks don't have unlisted numbers."

Random smiled, still staring at him.

"Which bar was this?"

Holman met Random's eye, then casually glanced at Vukovich.

"I don't know the name of the place, but it's on Sunset a couple of blocks west of Silver Lake Boulevard. On the north side. I'm pretty sure it had a Mexican name."

Holman had driven past earlier. Sunset was lined with Mexican places.

"Uh-huh, so you could take us there?"

"Oh, yeah, absolutely. I told Detective Vukovich three or four hours ago I could take you there."

"And this man you spoke with, if you saw him again, could you point him out?"

Holman met Random's stare again, but relaxed, not making a point of it.

"Absolutely. Without a doubt. If he's still there after all this time."

Vukovich, smiling again, said, "Hey, you busting my balls or what?"

Random ignored Vukovich's comment.

"So tell me, Mr. Holman, and I am very serious in asking you this question—did Maria Juarez tell you anything that would help us find her husband?"

Holman suddenly found himself liking Random. He liked the man's intensity and his desire to find Warren Juarez.

"No, sir."

"She didn't know where he was hiding?"

"She said she didn't."

"Did she tell you why he killed the officers? Or any details of the crime?"

"She said he didn't do it. She told me he was with her when the murders were committed. They have a little girl. She said it was the little girl's birthday and they made a video that proved Warren was with them at the time of the murders. She said she gave it to you guys. That's it."

Random said, "She admitted no knowledge of her husband's whereabouts?"

"She just kept saying he didn't do it. I don't know what else to tell you."

"What were you planning to do when you left her?"

"Same thing I was doing before. Talk to people to see if I could pick up something else. But then I met Mr. Vukovich."

Vukovich laughed and changed his position against the wall.

Holman said, "Mind if I ask a question?"

Random shrugged.

"You can ask. Not saying I'll answer, but let's see."

"They really have a tape?"

"She gave us a tape, but it doesn't show what she

claims that it shows. There are questions about when that tape was made."

Vukovich said, "They didn't have to make their video at one A.M. on Tuesday morning. We had our analyst look at it. She believes they recorded the talk show, then played it back on their VCR to use it as an alibi. You watch her video, you aren't seeing the talk show when it originally aired; you're seeing a recording of a recording. We believe they made their tape the morning after the murders."

Holman frowned. He understood how such a tape could be produced, but he had also seen the fear in Maria's eyes when he grabbed her throat. He had been eye to eye with terrified people when he was stealing cars and robbing banks, and he had left her with the sense she was telling the truth.

"Waitaminute. You're saying she conspired with her husband?"

Random seemed about to answer, then thought better of it. He checked his watch, then stood as if lifting a great load.

"Let's leave it at what I've said. This is an ongoing investigation."

"Okay, but one more thing. Richie's commander told me this was a personal beef between Juarez and one of the other officers, Fowler. Is that what it was?"

Random nodded at Vukovich, letting Vukovich answer.

"That's right. It started a little over a year ago. Fowler and his trainee stopped a kid for a traffic violation. That was Jaime Juarez, Warren's younger brother. Juarez grew belligerent. Fowler knew he was high, pulled him out of the car, and found a few crack rocks in his pants. Juarez, of course, claimed Fowler planted the stuff, but he still got hit for three years in the State. Second month in, a fight broke out between black and Latino prisoners, and Jaime was killed. Warren blamed Fowler. Went all over the Eastside saying he was going to do Fowler for killing the kid. He didn't keep it a secret. We have a witness list two pages long of people who heard him making the threats."

Holman took it in. He could absolutely see Juarez killing the man he blamed for his brother's death, but that wasn't what bothered him.

"Have you named any other suspects?"

"There are no other suspects. Juarez acted alone."

"That doesn't make sense, Juarez doing this by himself. How did he know they were down there? How'd he find them? How does one street dick take four armed police officers and none of them even get off a shot?"

Holman's voice grew loud and he regretted it. Random seemed irritated. He pursed his lips, then checked his watch again as if someone or something was waiting for him. He made some kind of decision, then looked back at Holman.

"He approached them from the east using the bridge supports for cover. That's how he got close. He was right at thirty feet away when he started shooting. He used a Benelli combat shotgun firing twelve-gauge buckshot. You know what buckshot is, Mr. Holman?"

Holman nodded. He felt sick.

"Two of the officers were shot in the back, indicating they never knew it was coming. The third officer was likely seated on the hood of his car. He jumped off, turned, and took his shot head-on. The fourth officer did manage to draw his sidearm, but he was dead before he could return fire. Don't ask me which was your son, Mr. Holman. I won't tell you."

Holman felt cold. His breaths were short. Random checked his watch again.

"We know there was one shooter and only one because all the shell casings came from the same gun. It was Juarez. This video is just a half-assed attempt he made to cover his ass. As for you, we're going to cut you free. That wasn't a unanimous decision, but you're free to go. We'll arrange for a ride back to your car."

Holman stood, but he still had questions and for the first time in his life he wasn't in a hurry to leave a police station.

"Where are you in finding the sonofabitch? You guys have a line on him or what?"

Random glanced at Vukovich. Vukovich's face was empty. Random looked back at Holman.

"We already have him. At six-twenty this evening Warren Alberto Juarez was found dead of a self-inflicted gunshot wound."

Vukovich touched the underside of his chin.

"Same shotgun he used to murder your son. Straight up through here, took the top of his head off. Still had the gun in his hand."

Random extended his hand once more. Holman felt numb with the news, but took the hand automatically.

"I'm sorry, Mr. Holman. I'm truly sorry that four officers were lost like this. It's a goddamned shame."

Holman didn't respond. Here they were, keeping him here all evening, and Juarez was dead.

Holman said, "Then why in hell did you ask me if his wife knew where he was and what I would do?"

"To see if she lied to me. You know how it works."

Holman felt himself growing angry but fought it down. Random opened the door.

"Let's make sure we're clear on this—don't go back to Ms. Juarez. Her husband might be dead, but she is still the subject of an active investigation."

"You think she was involved in the killings?"

"She helped him try to get away with it. Whether or not she knew before the fact is still to be determined. Don't get involved in this again. We're giving you a break because you lost your son, but that consideration ends now. If we bring you back to this room, Holman, I'll charge you and see that you're prosecuted. Do we understand each other?"

Holman nodded.

"Rest easy, Mr. Holman. We got the bastard."

Random left without waiting for an answer. Vukovich peeled himself from the wall and gently slapped Holman on the back, like two guys who had been through the mill together.

"C'mon, bud. I'll take you back to your car."

Holman followed Vukovich out.

11

HOLMAN THOUGHT about Maria Juarez as they drove past her house on the way to his car. He looked for the remaining surveillance team but couldn't find them.

Vukovich said, "Random means it about hassling that woman, Holman. Stay away from her."

"You say they faked that tape I guess they faked it, but she seemed sincere to me."

"Thank you for your expert opinion. Now tell me something—when you were waiting in line to rob those banks, did you look innocent or guilty?"

Holman let it go.

Vukovich said, "One point me, zero Holman."

They stopped alongside the beater and Holman opened the door.

"Thanks for the ride."

"Maybe I should take you home instead of letting you drive. You don't even have a license."

"First thing I hear when I get my release is that Richie was killed. I had more on my mind than the DMV."

"Get it done. I'm not just being an asshole. You get stopped, you're just going to end up in trouble."

"Tomorrow. First thing."

Holman stood in the street as he watched Vukovich drive away. He looked at Maria Juarez's house. The windows were lit and very likely the cousins were home. Holman wondered what they were talking about. He wondered whether the police had informed her that her husband was dead. Holman told himself he didn't care, but knowing the little house was probably filled with pain bothered him. He climbed into his car and drove home.

Holman made it back to the motel without being stopped and left Perry's car in the alley. Perry was up and waiting when Holman entered the lobby, leaning back behind his desk with his arms folded, his legs crossed, and his face pinched. He was pulled so tight he reminded Holman of a spider waiting to launch itself on the first bug that walked by.

Perry said, "You fucked me up good. You know how much I hadda pay in back fines?"

Holman wasn't in the best of moods, either. He walked over and put himself right at the edge of Perry's desk.

"Fuck you and your fines. You should've told me I was driving around in a wanted vehicle. You rented me a piece of shit that could've put me back in prison."

"Fuck you, too! I didn't know about those tickets! Guys like you get'm driving around and don't even tell me. Now I'm fucking stuck with the bill—two thousand four hundred eighteen dollars!"

"You should've told them to keep it. It's a piece of shit."

"They were gonna boot it and hit me for the tow and the impound. I hadda go all the way downtown in rush hour to fork over that dough."

Holman knew Perry was dying to hit him up for a reimbursement, but he also knew Perry was worried about the repercussions. If it got back to Gail Manelli she would know that Perry was illegally and knowingly renting his vehicle to unlicensed drivers. Then he would lose out on the tenants she fed him through the Bureau of Prisons.

Holman said, "Tough shit. I was downtown, too, thanks to your fucking car. Did you bring my television today?"

"It's up in your room."

"It better not be stolen."

"You're whining like a pussy. Look, it's up there. You gotta play with the ears. The reception is off."

Holman started up the stairs.

"Hey. Waitaminute. I got a couple messages for you."

Holman immediately perked up, thinking that Richie's wife had finally called. He one-eightied back to the desk where Perry was looking nervous.

"Gail called. She wants you to call her, man."

"Who else called?"

Perry was holding a note, but Holman couldn't see what was on it.

Perry said, "Now, listen, you talk to Gail, don't tell her about the goddamned car. You shouldn't have been driving and I shouldn't have rented it to you. Neither one of us needs that kind of trouble."

Holman reached for the slip.

"I'm not going to say anything. Who was the other call?"

97

Holman snagged the slip and Perry let him have it.

"Some woman from a cemetery. She said you'd know what it was about."

Holman read the note. It was an address and phone number.

> *Richard Holman*
> *42 Berke Drive #216*
> *LA, CA 90024*
> *310-555-2817*

Holman had guessed that Richie paid for his mother's burial, but this confirmed it.

"Did anyone else call? I was expecting another call."

"Just this. Unless they called while I was off paying those goddamned fines for you."

Holman put the slip of paper into his pocket.

"I'm gonna need the car again tomorrow."

"Don't say anything to Gail, for Christ's sake."

Holman didn't bother answering. He went upstairs, turned on the television, and waited for the eleven o'clock news. The television was a small American brand that was twenty years out of date. The picture wavered with hazy ghosts. Holman fought with the antennas trying to make the ghosts go away, but they didn't. They grew worse.

12

THE NEXT MORNING, Holman climbed out of bed at a quarter past five. His back hurt from the crappy mattress and a fitful night's sleep. He decided he either had to sandwich a board between the mattress and springs or pull the mattress onto the floor. The beds at Lompoc were better.

He went down for a paper and chocolate milk, then returned to his room to read the newspaper accounts of last night's developments.

The newspaper reported that three boys had discovered Juarez's body in an abandoned house in Cypress Park less than one mile from Juarez's home. The newspaper showed a picture of the three boys posing outside a dilapidated house with police officers in the background. One of the officers looked like Random, but the photo was too grainy for Holman to be sure. Police stated that a neighbor living near the abandoned house reported hearing a gunshot early during the morning following the murders. Holman wondered why the neighbor hadn't called the police when he first heard the shot, but let it go. He knew from personal experience that people heard things all the time they didn't report; silence was a thief's best friend.

Statements made by both the boys and officers at the scene described Juarez as having been seated on the floor with his back to a wall and a twelve-gauge shotgun clutched in his right hand. A representative of the coroner's office stated that death appeared instantaneous from a massive head wound fired upward through the deceased's jaw. Holman knew from Random's description that the shotgun was short, so Juarez could easily have tucked it up under his chin. Holman pictured the body and decided Juarez's finger had been caught in the trigger guard or else the shotgun would have kicked free. The buckshot would have blown out the top of his head and likely taken most of his face with it. Holman could picture the body easily enough, but something about it troubled him and he wasn't sure why. He continued reading.

The article spent a few paragraphs explaining the connection between Warren Juarez and Michael Fowler, but offered nothing Holman hadn't learned from Random and Vukovich. Holman knew men serving life sentences because they killed other men for offenses much less than the death of a sibling; veteranos who didn't regret a day of their time because their notion of pride had demanded no other response. Holman was thinking of these men when he realized what bothered him about the nature of Juarez's death. Suicide didn't jibe with the man Maria Juarez had described. Random had suggested that Juarez and his wife made the video the morning after the murders. If Random was right, Juarez had committed the murders, spent the next morning giving his daughter donkey rides and mugging for the camera, then fled to the abandoned house where he had grown so despondent that he killed himself. Mugging and donkey rides didn't add up to suicide. Juarez would have had the admiration of his homies for avenging his brother's death and his daughter would have been protected by them like a queen. Juarez had plenty to live for even if he had to spend the rest of his life behind bars.

Holman was still thinking about it when the six A.M. news opened with the same story. He put aside the paper to watch taped coverage of the press conference that had been held the night before while Holman was being interrogated. Assistant Chief Donnelly did most of the talking again, but this time Holman recognized Random in the background.

Holman was still watching when his phone rang. The sudden noise startled him and he lurched as if he had been shocked. This was the first phone call he had received since he was arrested in the bank. Holman answered tentatively.

"Hello?"

"Bro! I thought you was in jail, homes! I heard you got busted!"

Holman hesitated, then realized what Chee meant.

"You mean last night?"

"MuthuhfuckinHolman! What you think I mean? The whole neighborhood saw you get hooked up, homes! I thought they violated your ass! Whatchu do over there?"

"I just talked to the lady. No law against knocking on a door."

"Muthuhfuckin' muthuhfucker! I oughta come over

there kick your ass myself, worryin' me like this! I got your back, homes! I got your *back*!"

"I'm okay, bro. They just talked to me."

"You need a lawyer? I can set you up."

"I'm okay, man."

"You kill her old man?"

"I didn't have anything to do with that."

"I thought for sure that was you, homes."

"He killed himself."

"I didn't believe that suicide shit. I figured you took his ass out."

Holman didn't know what to say, so he changed the subject.

"Hey, Chee. I've been renting a guy's car for twenty dollars a day and it's killing me. Could you set me up with some wheels?"

"Sure, bro, whatever you want."

"I don't have a driver's license."

"I can take care of you. All we need is the picture."

"A real one from the DMV."

"I got you covered, bro. I even got the camera."

In the day, Chee had fabricated driver's licenses, green cards, and Social Security cards for his uncles. Apparently, he still had the skills.

Holman made arrangements to stop by later, then hung up. He showered and dressed, then pushed his remaining clothes into a grocery bag, intending to find a Laundromat. It was six-fifty when he left his room.

Richie's address was a four-story courtyard apartment south of Wilshire Boulevard in Westwood near UCLA. Since the address dated from Donna's burial almost two years before, Holman had spent much of the night worried that Richie had moved. He debated using the phone number, but Richie's wife had not called, so it was clear she wanted no contact. If Holman phoned now and reached her, she might refuse to see him and might even call the police. Holman figured his best chance was to catch her early and not warn her he was coming. *If* she still lived there.

The building's main entrance was a glass security door that required a key. Mailboxes were on the street side of the door, along with a security phone so guests could call to be buzzed in by the tenants. Holman went to the boxes and searched through the apartment numbers, hoping to find his son's name on 216.

He did.

HOLMAN.

Donna had given the boy Holman's name even though they weren't married, and seeing it now moved him. He touched the name—*HOLMAN*—thinking, *this was my son.* He felt an angry ache in his chest and abruptly turned away.

Holman waited by the security door for almost ten minutes until a young Asian man with a book bag pushed open the door on his way out to class. Holman caught the door before it closed and let himself in.

The interior courtyard was small and filled with lush bird-of-paradise plants. The inside of the building was ringed with exposed walkways which could be reached by a common elevator that opened into the courtyard or by an adjoining staircase. Holman used the stairs. He climbed to the second floor, then followed the numbers until he found 216. He knocked lightly, then knocked again, harder, wrapping himself in a numbness that was designed to protect him from his own feelings.

A young woman opened the door, and his numbness was gone.

Her face was focused and contained, as if she was concentrating on something more important than answering the door. She was slight, with dark eyes, a thin face, and prominent ears. She was wearing denim shorts, a light green blouse, and sandals. Her hair was damp, as if she wasn't long from the shower. Holman thought she looked like a child.

She stared at him with curious indifference.

"Yes?"

"I'm Max Holman. Richie's father."

Holman waited for her to unload. He expected her to tell him what a rotten bastard and lousy father he was, but the indifference vanished and she canted her head as if seeing him for the first time.

"Ohmigod. Well. This is awkward."

"It's awkward for me, too. I don't know your name."

"Elizabeth. Liz."

"I'd like to talk with you a little bit if you don't mind. It would mean a lot to me."

She suddenly opened the door.

"I have to apologize. I was going to call, but I just— I didn't know what to say. Please. Come in. I'm getting ready for class, but I have a few minutes. There's some coffee—"

Holman stepped past her and waited in the living room as she closed the door. He told her not to go to any trouble, but she went to her kitchen anyway and took two mugs from the cupboard, leaving him in her living room.

"This is just so weird. I'm sorry. I don't use sugar. We might have Sweeta—"

"Black is fine."

"I have nonfat milk."

"Just black."

It was a large apartment, with the living room, a dining area, and the kitchen all sharing space. Holman was suddenly overcome by being in Richie's home. He had told himself to be all business, just ask his questions and get out, but now his son's life was all around him and he wanted to fill himself with it: A mismatched couch and chair faced a TV on a pedestal stand in the corner; racks cluttered with CDs and DVDs tipped against the wall—Green Day, Beck, *Jay and Silent Bob Strike Back*; a gas fireplace was built into the wall, its mantel filled with rows of overlapping pictures. Holman let himself drift closer.

"This is a nice place," he said.

"It's more than we can afford, but it's close to campus. I'm getting my master's in child psychology."

"That sounds real good."

Holman felt like a dummy and wished he could think of something better to say.

"I just got out of prison."

"I know."

Stupid.

The pictures showed Richie and Liz together, alone, and with other couples. One shot showed them on a boat; another wearing flare-bright parkas in the snow; in another, they were at a picnic where everyone wore LAPD T-shirts. Holman found himself smiling, but then he saw a picture of Richie with Donna and his smile collapsed. Donna had been younger than Holman, but in the picture she looked older. Her hair was badly colored and her face was cut by deep lines and shadows. Holman turned away, hiding from the memories and the sudden flush of shame, and found Liz beside him with the coffee. She offered a cup, and Holman accepted it. He shrugged to encompass the apartment.

"You have a nice place. I like the pictures. It's like getting to know him a little bit."

Her eyes never left him and now Holman felt watched. Her being a psych major, he wondered if she was analyzing him.

She suddenly lowered the cup.

"You look like him. He was a little taller but not much. You're heavier."

"I got fat."

"I didn't mean fat. Richard was a runner. That's all I meant."

Her eyes filled then, and Holman didn't know what to do. He raised a hand, thinking to touch her shoulder, but he was afraid he might scare her. Then she pulled herself together and rubbed her eyes clear with the flat of her free hand.

"I'm sorry. This really sucks. This *so* really sucks. Listen—"

She rubbed her eye again, then held out her hand.

"It's good to finally meet you."

"You really think I look like him?"

She made a thin smile.

"Clones. Donna always said the same thing."

Holman changed the subject. If they got into talking about Donna he would start crying, too.

He said, "Listen, I know you have to get to class and all, but can I ask you a couple of questions about what happened? It won't take long."

"They found that man who killed them."

"I know. I'm just trying to . . . I talked to Detective Random. Have you met him?"

"Yes, I've spoken with him and Captain Levy. Levy was Richard's commander."

"Right. I've spoken with him, too, but I still have some questions about how this could happen."

"Juarez blamed Mike for what happened to his brother. Do you know that whole story?"

"Yeah, it's in the paper. You knew Sergeant Fowler?"

"Mike was Richard's training officer. They were still really good friends."

"Random told me that Juarez had been making threats ever since his brother was killed. Was Mike worried about it?"

She frowned as she thought about it, trying to remember, then shook her head.

"Mike never seemed worried about anything. It wasn't like I saw him that often, just every couple of months or so, but he didn't seem worried about anything like this."

"Did Richie maybe mention that Mike was worried?"

"The first I heard about this gang business was when they issued the warrant. Richard never said anything, but he wouldn't have. He never brought that kind of thing home."

Holman figured if some guy was shooting off his mouth and making threats, he would pay the guy a visit. He would let the guy have his shot straight up or put the guy in his place, but either way he would deal with it. He wondered if that's what the four officers were doing that night, making a plan to deal with Juarez, only Juarez got the jump on them. It seemed possible, but Holman didn't want to suggest it to Elizabeth.

Instead, Holman said, "Fowler probably didn't want to worry anyone. Guys like Juarez are always threatening policemen. Cops get that all the time."

Elizabeth nodded, but her eyes began to redden again and Holman knew he had made a mistake. She was thinking that this time it wasn't just threats—this time the guy like Juarez had gone through with it and now her husband was dead. Holman quickly changed the subject.

"Another thing I'm wondering about—Random told me Richie wasn't on duty that night?"

"No. He was here working. I was studying. He went out to meet the guys sometimes, but never that late. He told me he had to go meet them. That's all he said."

"Did he say he was going to the river?"

"No. I just assumed they would meet at a bar."

Holman took that in, but it still didn't help him.

"I guess what's bothering me is how Juarez found them. The police haven't been able to explain that yet. It'd be tough to follow someone into that riverbed and not be seen. So I'm thinking maybe if they went down there all the time—you know, a regular thing—maybe Juarez heard about it and knew where to find them."

"I just don't know. I can't believe they went down there all the time and he didn't tell me about it—it's so far out of the way."

Holman agreed. They could have sat around getting drunk anywhere, but they had gone down into a deserted, off-limits place like the riverbed. This implied they didn't want to be seen, but Holman also knew that cops were like anyone else—they might have gone down there just for the thrill of being someplace no one else could go, like kids breaking into an empty house or climbing up to the Hollywood Sign.

Holman was still thinking it through when he recalled something she mentioned earlier and he asked her about it.

"You said he almost never went out late like that, but on that night he did. What was different about that night?"

She seemed surprised, but then her face darkened and a single vertical line cut her forehead. She glanced away, then looked back and seemed to be studying him. Her face was still, but Holman felt the furious motion of wheels and cogs and levers behind her eyes as she struggled with her answer.

She said, "You."

"I don't understand."

"You were being released the next day. That's what was different that night, and we both knew it. We knew you were being released the next day. Richard never spoke about you with me. Do you mind me telling you these things? This is just so awful, what we're going through right now. I don't want to make it worse for you."

"I asked you. I want to know."

She went on.

"I tried talking to him about you—I was curious. You're his father. You were my father-in-law. When Donna was still alive we *both* tried—but he just wouldn't. I knew your release date was coming up.

Richard knew, but he still wouldn't talk about it, and I knew it was bothering him."

Holman was feeling sick and cold.

"Did he say something, how it was bothering him?"

She cocked her head again, then put down her cup and turned away.

"Come see."

He followed her back to a bedroom that was arranged as an office. Two desks were set up, one for him and one for her. The first desk, hers, was stacked with textbooks and binders and paperwork. Richie's desk was backed into a corner where corkboards were fixed to the adjoining walls. The corkboards were covered with so many clippings and Post-it notes and little slips of paper they overlapped each other like scales on a fish. Liz brought him to Richie's desk and pointed out the clippings.

"Take a look."

Shootout Ends Crime Spree, Takeover Bandits Stopped, Bystander Killed in Robbery. The articles Holman skimmed were about a pair of takeover lunatics named Marchenko and Parsons. Holman had heard about them in Lompoc. Marchenko and Parsons dressed like commandos and shot up the banks before escaping with their loot.

She said, "He became fascinated with bank robberies. He clipped stories and pulled articles off the Internet and spent all of his time in here with this stuff. It doesn't take a doctorate to figure out why."

"Because of me?"

"Wanting to know you. A way of being close to you without being close to you was my guess. We knew you were approaching your release date. We didn't know if you would try to contact us or if we should contact you or what to do about you. It was pretty clear he was working out his anxiety about you."

Holman felt a flush of guilt and hoped she was wrong.

"Did he say that?"

Elizabeth didn't look at him. Her face had closed, and now she stared at the clippings and crossed her arms.

"He wouldn't. He never talked about you with me or his mother, but when he told me he was going to see the guys, he had been in here all evening. I think he needed to talk to them. He couldn't talk to me about it, and now look—now look."

Her face tightened even more with the hardness that anger brings. Holman watched her eyes fill, but was too scared to touch her.

He said, "Hey—"

She shook her head and Holman took it as a warning—like maybe she sensed he wanted to comfort her—and Holman felt even worse. Her neck and arms were bowstrings pulled taut by her anger.

"Goddamnit, he just had to go out. He had to go. Goddamnit—"

"Maybe we should go back in the living room."

She closed her eyes, then shook her head again, but this time she was telling him she was all right—she was fighting the terrible pain and determined to kill it. She finally opened her eyes and finished her original thought.

"Sometimes it's easier for a man to show what he feels is a weakness to another male rather than to a female. It's easier to pretend it's work than to deal honestly with the emotions. I think that's what he did that night. I think that's why he died."

"Talking about me?"

"No, not you, not specifically—these bank robberies. That was his way of talking about you. The work was like an extra duty assignment. He wanted to be a detective and move up the ladder."

Holman glanced at Richie's desk, but he didn't feel comforted. Copies of what looked like official police reports and case files were spread over the desk. Holman skimmed the top pages and realized that everything was about Marchenko and Parsons. A small map of the city was push-pinned to the board with lines connecting small X's numbered from 1 to 13 to make a rough pattern. Richie had gone so far as to map their robberies.

Holman suddenly wondered if Richie and Liz believed he had been like them.

He said, "I robbed banks, but I never did anything like this. I never hurt anyone. I wasn't anything like these guys."

Her expression softened.

"I didn't mean it like that. Donna told us how you got caught. Richard knew you weren't like them."

Holman appreciated her effort, but the wall was filled with clippings about two degenerates who got off by pistol-whipping their victims. It didn't take a doctorate.

Liz said, "I don't want to be rude, but I have to finish getting ready or I'll end up blowing off class."

Holman reluctantly turned away, then hesitated.

"He was working on this before he went out?"

"Yeah. He had been here all evening."

"Were those other guys on the Marchenko thing, too?"

"Mike, maybe. He talked with Mike about it a lot. I don't know about the others."

Holman nodded, taking a last look at his dead son's workplace. He wanted to read everything on Richie's desk. He wanted to know why a uniformed officer with only a couple of years on the job was involved in a major investigation and why his son had left home in the middle of the night. He had come here for answers, but now had more questions.

Holman turned away for the final time.

"They haven't told me about the arrangements yet. For his funeral."

He hated to ask and hated it even more when the hardness again flashed across her face. But then she fought it back and shook her head.

"They're having a memorial for the four of them this Saturday at the Police Academy. The police haven't released them for burial. I guess they're still . . ."

Her voice faded, but Holman understood why. These officers had been murdered. The medical examiner was probably still gathering evidence and they couldn't be buried until all of the tests and fact-finding were complete.

Elizabeth suddenly touched his arm.

"You'll come, won't you? I would like you to be there."

Holman felt relieved. He had been worried she might try to keep him away from the services. It also wasn't lost on him that neither Levy nor Random had told him about the memorial.

"I would like that, Liz. Thank you."

She stared up at him for a moment, then lifted on her toes to kiss Holman's cheek.

"I wish it had been different."

Holman had spent the past ten years wishing everything had been different.

He thanked her again when she let him out, then returned to his car. He wondered if Random would attend the memorial. Holman had questions. He expected Random to have answers.

THE MEMORIAL SERVICE was held in the auditorium at the Los Angeles Police Department's Police Academy in Chavez Ravine, which was set between two hills outside the Stadium Way entrance to Dodger Stadium. Years earlier, the Dodgers erected their own version of the Hollywood Sign on the hill separating the academy from the stadium. It read THINK BLUE, the Dodgers color being blue. When Holman saw the sign that morning it struck him as a fitting reminder of the four dead officers. Blue was also the LAPD color.

Liz had invited Holman to accompany her and her family to the service, but Holman had declined. Her parents and sister had flown down from the Bay area, but Holman felt uncomfortable with them. Liz's father was a physician and her mother was a social worker; they were educated, affluent, and normal in a way Holman admired, but they reminded him of everything he was not. When Holman passed the gate to Dodger Stadium, he recalled how he and Chee had often cruised the parking lot for cars to steal during the middle innings. Liz's father probably had memories of all-night study sessions, frat parties, and proms, but the best Holman could manage were memories of stealing and getting high.

Holman parked well off the academy grounds and walked up Academy Road, following directions Liz had provided. The academy's parking lot was already full. Cars lined both sides of the street and people were streaming uphill into the academy. Holman glanced over their faces, hoping to spot Random or Vukovich. He had phoned Random three times to discuss what he learned from Liz, but Random had not returned his calls. Holman figured Random had dismissed him, but Holman wasn't content with being dismissed. He still had questions and he still wanted answers.

Liz had told him to meet them in the rock garden outside the auditorium. The flow of foot traffic led him up through the center of the academy to the garden, where a large crowd of people stood in small groups. Camera crews taped the crowd while reporters interviewed local politicians and the LAPD's top brass. Holman felt self-conscious. Liz had lent him one of Richie's dark suits but the pants were too tight, so Holman wore them unfastened beneath his belt. He had sweat through the suit even before he reached the garden and now he felt like a wino in hand-me-down threads.

Holman found Liz and her family with Richie's commander, Captain Levy. Levy shook Holman's hand, then took them to meet the other families. Liz seemed to sense Holman's discomfort and hung back as Levy led them through the crowd.

"You look good, Max. I'm glad you're here."

Holman managed a smile.

Levy introduced them to Mike Fowler's widow and four sons, Mellon's wife, and Ash's parents. All of them seemed drained, and Holman thought Fowler's wife was probably sedated. Everyone treated him politely and with respect, but Holman still felt conspicuous and out of place. He caught the others staring at him several times and—each time—he flushed, certain they were thinking, *That's Holman's father, the criminal*. He felt more embarrassed for Richie than for himself. He had managed to shame his son even in death.

Levy returned a few minutes later, touched Liz on the arm, then led them inside through open double doors. The floor of the auditorium was filled with chairs. A dais and podium had been erected on the stage. Large photographs of the four officers were draped with American flags. Holman hesitated at the doors, glanced back at the crowd, and saw Random with three other men at the edge of the crowd. Holman immediately reversed course. He was halfway to Random when Vukovich suddenly blocked his way. Vukovich was wearing a somber navy suit and sunglasses. It was impossible to see his eyes.

Vukovich said, "It's a sad day, Mr. Holman. You're not still driving without a license, are you?"

"I've called Random three times, but he hasn't seen fit to return my calls. I have more questions about what happened that night."

"We know what happened that night. We told you."

Holman glanced past Vukovich at Random. Random was staring back, but then resumed his conversation. Holman looked back at Vukovich.

"What you told me doesn't add up. Was Richie

working on the Marchenko and Parsons investigation?"

Vukovich studied him for a moment, then turned away.

"Wait here, Mr. Holman. I'll see if the boss has time to talk to you."

Word was spreading that it was time to be seated. The people in the rock garden were making their way to the auditorium but Holman stayed where he was. Vukovich went over to Random and the three men. Holman guessed they were high-level brass, but didn't know and didn't care. When Vukovich reached them, Random and two of the men glanced back at Holman, then turned their backs and continued talking. After a moment, Random and Vukovich came over. Random didn't look happy, but he offered his hand.

"Let's step to the side, Mr. Holman. It'll be easier to talk when we're out of the way."

Holman followed them to the edge of the garden, Random on one side of him and Vukovich on the other. Holman felt like they were shaking him down.

When they were away from the other people, Random crossed his arms.

"All right, I understand you have some questions?"

Holman described his conversation with Elizabeth and the enormous collection of material pertaining to Marchenko and Parsons he had found on Richie's desk. He still didn't buy the explanation the police put forth about Juarez. The bank robberies seemed a more likely connection if Richie was involved in the investigation. Holman floated his theory, but Random shook his head even before Holman finished.

"They weren't investigating Marchenko and Parsons. Marchenko and Parsons are dead. That case was closed three months ago."

"Richie told his wife he had an extra duty assignment. She thought Mike Fowler might have been involved in it, too."

Random looked impatient. The auditorium was filling.

"If your son was looking into Marchenko and Parsons he was doing so as a hobby or maybe as an assignment for a class he was taking, but that's all. He was a uniformed patrol officer. Patrol officers aren't detectives."

Vukovich nodded.

"What difference would it make one way or the other? That case was closed."

"Richie was home that night. He was home all evening until he got a call and went to meet his friends at one in the morning. If I was him and my buddies called that time of night just to go drinking I would have blown them off—but if we're doing police work, then maybe I would go. If they were under the bridge because of Marchenko and Parsons, it might be connected with their murder."

Random shook his head.

"Now isn't the time for this, Mr. Holman."

"I've been calling, but you haven't returned my calls. Now seems like a pretty damn good time to me."

Random seemed to be studying him. Holman thought the man was trying to gauge his strength and weaknesses the same way he would gauge a suspect he was interrogating. He finally nodded, as if he had come to a decision he didn't enjoy.

"Okay, look, you know what the bad news is? They

went down there to drink. I'm going to tell you something now, but if you repeat it and it gets back to me I'll deny I said it. Vuke?"

Vukovich nodded, agreeing that he would deny it, too.

Random pursed his lips like whatever he was about to say was going to taste bad and lowered his voice.

"Mike Fowler was a drunk. He'd been a drunk for years and he was a disgraceful police officer."

Vukovich glanced around to make sure no one was listening and looked uncomfortable.

"Take it easy, boss."

"Mr. Holman needs to understand. Fowler radioed he was going to take a break, but he wasn't supposed to be drinking and he had no business telling those younger officers to meet him in an off-limits location. I want you to keep this in mind, Holman—Fowler was a supervisor. He was supposed to be available to the patrol officers in his area when they needed his assistance, but he decided to go drinking instead. Mellon was on duty, too, and knew better, but he was a mediocre officer, also—he wasn't even in his assigned service division. Ash was off duty, but he wasn't in the running for Officer of the Year, either."

Holman sensed that Random was sweating him, but he didn't know why and he didn't like it.

"What are you telling me, Random? What does any of this have to do with Marchenko and Parsons?"

"You're looking for a reason to understand why those officers were under the bridge, so I'm telling you. I blame Mike Fowler for what happened, him being a supervisor, but no one was down there solving the crime of the century. They were problem officers with shit records and a crappy attitude."

Holman felt himself flush. Levy had told him Richie was an outstanding officer . . . one of the *best*.

"Are you telling me that Richie was a rotten cop? Is that what you're saying?"

Vukovich held up a finger.

"Take it easy, bud. You're the one who asked."

Random said, "Sir, I didn't want to tell you any of this. I had hoped I wouldn't have to."

The throbbing in Holman's head spread to his shoulders and arms, and he wanted to knuckle up. All the deep parts of him wanted to throw fists and beat down Random and Vukovich for saying that Richie was rotten, but Holman wasn't like that anymore. He told himself he wasn't like that. He forced down his anger and spoke slowly.

"Richie was working on something about Marchenko and Parsons. I want to know why he had to talk to Fowler about it at one in the morning."

"What you need to do is concentrate on making good your release and let us do our jobs. This conversation is over, Mr. Holman. I suggest you settle down and pay your respects."

Random turned away without another word and moved with the crowd into the auditorium. Vukovich stayed with Holman a moment longer before following.

Holman didn't move. He felt as if he would shatter from the horrendous rage that had suddenly made him brittle. He wanted to scream. He wanted to jack a Porsche and burn through the city as fast as it would go. He wanted to get high and suck down a bottle of the finest tequila and scream at the night.

Holman went to the double doors but could not enter. He watched people taking their seats without really seeing them. He saw the four dead men staring at him from their giant pictures. He felt Richie's dead two-dimensional eyes.

Holman turned away and walked fast back to his car, sweating hard in the heat. He stripped off Richie's jacket and tie and unbuttoned his shirt, tears filling his eyes with great hot drops that came as if they were being crushed from his heart.

Richie wasn't bad.

He wasn't like his father.

Holman wiped the snot from his face and walked faster. He didn't believe it. He wouldn't let himself believe it.

My son is not like me.

Holman swore to himself he would prove it. He had already asked the last and only person he trusted for help and had been waiting to hear back from her. He needed her help. He needed her and he prayed she would answer.

Part Two

14

FBI SPECIAL AGENT Katherine Pollard (retired) stood in the kitchen of her small tract home watching the clock above her sink. When she held her breath, a perfect silence filled the house. She watched the second hand sweep silently toward the twelve. The minute hand was poised at eleven thirty-two. The second hand touched the twelve. The minute hand released like a firing pin, jumping to eleven thirty-three—

TOCK!

The snap of passing time broke the silence.

Pollard wiped a ribbon of sweat from her face as she considered the debris that had accumulated in her kitchen: cups, grape juice cartons, open boxes of Cap'n Crunch and Sugar Smacks, and bowls showing the first stages of whole milk curdled by the heat. Pollard lived in the Simi Valley, where the temperature that day—twenty-seven minutes before noon—had already notched 104 degrees. Her air conditioner had been out for six days and wasn't likely to be fixed any time soon—Katherine Pollard was broke. She was using the heat-stroked squalor to prepare herself for the inevitable and humiliating call to beg her mother for money.

Pollard had left the FBI eight years ago after she married a fellow agent named Marty Baum and became pregnant with their first child. She had left the job for all the right reasons: She had loved Marty, they both wanted her to be a full-time mom for their son (Pollard feeling the importance of full-time mom status maybe even more than Marty), and—with Marty's salary—they had had enough money. But that was *then*. Two children, one legal separation, and— five years after the fact—Marty had dropped dead of a heart attack while scuba diving in Aruba with his then-girlfriend, a twenty-year-old waitress from Huntington Beach.

TOCK!

Pollard had been able to scrape by on Marty's death benefits, but more and more she required help from her mother, which was humiliating and defeating, and now the AC had been out for almost a week. One hour and twenty-six minutes until her children, David and Lyle, seven and six, would arrive home from camp, dirty and filled with complaints about the heat. Pollard wiped more sweat from her face, scooped up her cordless phone, then brought it out to her car.

The nuclear crystal-sky heat pounded down on her like a blowtorch. Katherine opened her Subaru, started the engine, and immediately rolled down the windows. It had to be 150 degrees inside the car. She maxed out the AC until it blew cold, then rolled up the windows. She let the icy air blow hard on her face, then lifted her T-shirt to let it blow on her skin.

When she felt she was on the safe side of heatstroke,

she turned on the phone and punched in her mother's number. Her mother's answering machine picked up, as Pollard expected. Her mother screened her calls while she played online poker.

"Mom, it's me, pick up. Are you there?"

Her mother came on the line.

"Is everything all right?"

Which was the way her mother always came on the line, immediately putting Pollard on the defensive with the implication that her life was an endless series of emergencies and dramas. Pollard knew better than to make small talk. She steeled herself and immediately got to the point.

"Our air conditioner went out. They want twelve hundred dollars to fix it. I don't have it, Mom."

"Katherine, when are you going to find another man?"

"I need twelve hundred dollars, Mom, not another man."

"Have I ever said no?"

"No."

"Then you know I live to help you and those beautiful boys, but you have to help yourself, too, Katherine. Those boys are older now and you're not getting any younger."

Pollard lowered the phone. Her mother was still talking, but Pollard couldn't understand what she was saying. Pollard saw the mail van approaching, then watched the postman shove the day's ration of bills into her mailbox. The postman wore a pith helmet, dark glasses, and shorts, and looked as if he was on a safari. When he drove away, Pollard raised the phone again.

She said, "Mom, let me ask you something. If I went back to work, would you be willing to watch the boys?"

Her mother hesitated. Pollard didn't like the silence. Her mother was *never* silent.

"Work doing what? Not with the FBI again."

Pollard had been thinking about it. If she returned to the FBI a position in the Los Angeles field office was unlikely. L.A. was a hot posting that drew far more applicants than available duty assignments. Pollard would more likely find herself posted in the middle of nowhere, but she didn't want to be just anywhere; Katherine Pollard had spent three years working on the FBI's elite Bank Squad in the bank robbery capital of the world—Los Angeles. She missed the action. She missed the paycheck. She missed what felt like the best days of her life.

"I might be able to get on as a security consultant with one of the banking chains or a private firm like Kroll. I was good on the Feeb, Mom. I still have friends who remember."

Her mother hesitated again and this time her voice was suspicious.

"How many hours are we talking about, me being with the boys?"

Pollard lowered the phone again, thinking wasn't this just perfect? She watched the postman drive to the next house, then the next. When she lifted the phone again her mother was calling her.

"Katherine? Katherine, are you there? Did I lose you?"

"We need the money."

"Of course I'll fix your air conditioner. I can't have

my grandsons living in—"

"I'm talking about me going back to work. The only way I can go back to work is if you help me with the boys—"

"We can talk about it, Katherine. I like the idea of you going back to work. You might meet someone—"

"I have to call the repairman. I'll talk to you later."

Pollard hung up. She watched the postman work his way up the street, then went to retrieve her mail. She shuffled through the letters as she returned to her car, finding the predictable Visa and MasterCard bills along with something that surprised her—a brown manila envelope showing the FBI's return address in Westwood, her old office. Katherine hadn't received anything from the Westwood Feebs in years.

When she was safely back in her car, she tore open the envelope and found a white envelope inside. It had been opened and resealed, as was all mail that was forwarded to current or former agents by the FBI. A printed yellow slip accompanied the letter: THIS PARCEL HAS BEEN TESTED FOR TOXINS AND BIOHAZARDS, AND WAS DETERMINED SUITABLE FOR RE-MAILING. THANK YOU.

The second envelope was addressed to her care of the Westwood office. It bore a Culver City return address she did not recognize. She tore the end of the envelope, shook out a one-page handwritten letter folded around a newspaper clipping, and read:

Max Holman
Pacific Garden Motels Apartments
Culver City, CA 90232

She stopped when she saw the name and broke into a crooked smile, swept up in Bank Squad memories.

"Ohmigod! Max Holman!"

She read on—

Dear Special Agent Pollard,

I hope this letter finds you in good health. I hope you have not stopped reading after seeing my name. This is Max Holman. You arrested me for bank robbery. Please know I bear no grudge and still appreshiate that you spoke on my behalf to the federal prosecutor. I have sucsessfully completed my incarceration and am now on supervised release and am employed. Again, I thank you for your kind and supportive words, and hope you will remember them now.

Katherine remembered Holman and thought as well of him as a cop could think of a man who had robbed nine banks. She felt no warmth toward him for his robberies, but for how she bagged him on his ninth caper. Max Holman had been famous for the way he went down even among the jaded agents of the FBI's Bank Squad.

She continued reading—

My son was Los Angeles Police Officer Richard Holman, which you can read about in the enclosed article. My son and three other officers were murdered. I am writing you now to ask your help and I hope you will hear me out.

Pollard unfolded the article. She immediately recognized it was a piece about the four officers who had been murdered in the downtown river basin while drinking. Pollard had seen coverage on the evening news.

She didn't bother to read the clipping, but she looked at the pictures of the four deceased officers. The last photograph was identified as Officer Richard Holman. A circle had been drawn around his picture. Two words were written outside the circle: *MY SON*.

Pollard didn't remember that Holman had a son, but she also couldn't remember what Holman looked like. As she studied the picture her memories returned. Yeah, she could see it—the thin mouth and strong neck. Holman's son looked like his father.

Pollard shook her head, thinking, *jesus, the poor bastard gets out of prison and his son gets killed, couldn't the man catch a break?*

She read on with interest—

The police believe they have identified the murderer but I still have questions and cannot get answers. I believe the police hold my status as a convicted criminal against me and that is why they will not listen. As you are an FBI Special Agent I am hoping you will get these answers for me. That is all I want.

My son was a good man. Not like me. Please call me if you will help. You can also talk to my BOP release supervisor, who will vouch for me.
Sincerely yours,
Max Holman

Beneath his name, Holman had written his home

phone, the phone number of the Pacific Gardens office, and his work number. Below his phone numbers he had written Gail Manelli's name and number. Pollard glanced at the clipping again and flashed on her own boys, older, and hoped she would never get the news Max Holman had now gotten. It had been bad enough when she was informed about Marty, even though their marriage was over and they were well on their way to a divorce. In that singular moment, their bad times had vanished and she felt as if she had lost a piece of herself. For Holman, losing his son, it must have been worse.

Pollard suddenly felt a rush of irritation and pushed the letter and the clipping aside, her nostalgic feelings for Holman and the day she bagged him gone. Pollard believed what all cops eventually learned—criminals were degenerate assholes. You could bag them, house them, dope them, and counsel them, but criminals never changed, so it was almost certain that Holman was running some kind of scam and just as certain that Pollard had almost fallen for it.

Thoroughly pissed, she scooped up the phone and the bills, then shut down her car and stormed through the heat to her house. She had humiliated herself by asking her mother for the money, then humiliated herself a second time by falling for Holman's sob story. Now she had to beg the snotty repairman to drag his ass out here to make her nightmare house livable. Pollard was all the way inside and dialing the repairman when she put down the phone, returned to her car, and retrieved Max Holman's miserable, stupid-ass letter.

She called the repairman, but then she called Gail Manelli, Holman's release supervisor.

15

HOLMAN FOUND Chee behind the counter in his East L.A. shop along with a pretty young girl who smiled shyly when Holman entered. Chee's face split into a craggy smile, his teeth brown with the morning's coffee.

Chee said, "Yo, homes. This is my youngest baby, Marisol. Sweetie, say hi to Mr. Holman."

Marisol told Holman it was a pleasure to meet him.

Chee said, "Baby, have Raul come up here, would you? In my office. Here, bro, c'mon inside."

Marisol used an intercom to summon Raul as Holman followed Chee into his office. Chee closed the door behind them, shutting her out.

Holman said, "Pretty girl, Chee. Congratulations."

"What you smilin' at, bro? You better not be thinking bad thoughts."

"I'm smiling at the notorious Lil' Chee calling his daughter 'sweetie.' "

Chee went to a file drawer and pulled out a camera.

"Girl is my heart, bro, that one and the others. I thank God every day for the air she breathes and the ground beneath her feet. Here—stand right there and look at me."

"You get me lined up with a ride?"

"Am I the Chee? Let's get you squared up with this license."

Chee positioned Holman before a dark blue wall, then lined up the camera.

"Digital, baby—state of the art. Goddamnit, Holman, this ain't a mug shot—try not to look like you want to kill me."

Holman smiled.

"Shit. You look like you're passing a stone."

The flash went off as someone knocked at the door. A short, hard-eyed young man stepped inside. His arms and face were streaked with grease from working in the body shop. Chee studied the digital image in the camera, then grudgingly decided it would do. He tossed the camera to the new guy.

"California DL, date of issue is today, no restrictions. You don't wear glasses, do you, Holman, now you got some age?"

"No."

"No restrictions."

Raul glanced at Holman.

"Gonna need an address, his date of birth, the stats, and a signature."

Chee took a pad and pen from his desk and handed them to Holman.

"Here. Put down your height and weight, too. Sign your name on a separate page."

Holman did what he was told.

"How long before I get the license? I have an appointment."

"Time you leave with the car, bro. It won't take long."

Chee had a brief conversation with Raul in Spanish, then Holman followed him out through the shop into a parking area where a row of cars was waiting. Chee eyeballed the beater.

"Man, no wonder you got pinched. That thing got 'work release' written all over it."

"Can you have someone bring it back to the motel for me?"

"Yeah, no problem. Here's what I got for you over here—a nice Ford Taurus or this brand-new Highlander, either one carry you in boring middle-class style. Both these vehicles are registered to a rental company I own without wants, warrants, or—unlike that piece of shit you driving now—traffic citations. You get stopped, I rented you the car. That's it."

Holman had never seen a Highlander before. It was black and shiny, and sat high on its big tires. He liked the idea of being able to see what was coming.

"The Highlander, I guess."

"Sweet choice, bro—black, leather trim, a sunroof— you gonna look like a yuppie on your way to the Whole Foods. C'mon, get in. I got something else for you, too, make your life a little easier now you back in the world. Look in the console."

Holman didn't know what a Whole Foods was, but he was tired of looking like he had just spent ten years in the can and he was growing worried all of this was going to take too much time. He climbed into his new car and opened the console. Inside was a cell phone.

Chee beamed proudly.

"Got you a cell phone, bro. This ain't ten years ago,

stoppin' at pay phones and digging for quarters—you got to stay on the grid twenty-four seven. Instruction book's in there with your number in it. You plug that cord into the cigarette lighter to keep it charged up."

Holman looked back at Chee.

He said, "Remember when you offered to front me some cash? I hate to do it, man, you being so nice with the car and this phone, but I gotta go back on what I said. I need a pack."

A pack was a thousand dollars. When banks wrapped used twenties, they bundled fifty bills to a pack. A thousand dollars.

Chee didn't bat an eye. He studied Holman, then touched his own nose.

"Whatever you want, homes, but I gotta ask—you back on the crank? I don't want to help you fuck yourself up."

"It's nothing like that. I got someone to help me with this thing about Richie; a professional, bro—she really knows what she's doing. I want to be ready in case there's expenses."

Holman had been both relieved and worried when Special Agent Pollard contacted him through Gail Manelli. He hadn't held much hope he would hear from her, but he had. In typical paranoid FBI fashion, she had checked him out with both Manelli and Wally Figg at the CCC before calling him, and had refused to give him her phone number, but Holman wasn't complaining—she had finally agreed to meet him at a Starbucks in Westwood to listen to his case. It wasn't lost on Holman that she gave him a location near the FBI office.

Chee squinted at him.

"What do you mean, she? What kind of professional?"

"The Fed who arrested me."

Chee's eyes tightened even more and he waved his hands.

"Bro! Holman, you lost your fuckin' mind, homes?"

"She treated me right, Chee. She went to bat for me with the AUSA, man. She helped me get a reduced charge."

"That's because you damn near gave yourself up, you dumb muthuhfuckuh! I remember that bitch runnin' into the bank, Holman! She's gonna set you up, homes! You even fart crooked this bitch gonna send you up!"

Holman decided not to mention that Pollard was no longer an agent. He had been disappointed when she told him, but he believed she would still have the connections and still be able to help him get answers.

He said, "Chee, listen, I gotta go. I have to meet her. You going to be able to help me with that money?"

Chee waved his hand again, axing away his disgust.

"Yeah, I'll get you the money. Don't mention my name to her, Holman. Do not let my name pass your lips in her presence, man. I don't want her to know I'm alive."

"I didn't mention you ten years ago when they were sweating me, homes. Why would I mention you now?"

Chee looked embarrassed and waved his hand again as he left.

Holman familiarized himself with the Highlander and tried to figure out how to use the cell phone while he waited. When Chee returned, he handed Holman a plain white envelope and the driver's license. Holman didn't look in the envelope. He tucked it into the console, then looked at the license. It was a perfect California driver's license, showing a seven-year expiration date and the state seal over Holman's picture. A miniature version of his signature had been inserted beneath his address and description.

Holman said, "Damn, this looks real."

"*Is* real, bro. That's a legitimate Cal state driver's license number straight up in the system. You get stopped, they run that license through DMV, it's gonna show you at your address with a brand-new driving record as of today. The magnetic strip on back? It shows just what it's supposed to show."

"Thanks, man."

"Give me the keys to that piece of shit you been driving. I'll have a couple of boys bring it back."

"Thanks, Chee. I really appreciate this."

"Don't mention my name to that cop, Holman. You keep me out of this."

"You're out of it, Chee. You were never in it."

Chee put his hands on the Highlander's door and leaned into the window, his eyes fierce.

"I'm just sayin', is all. Don't trust this woman, Holman. She put you in the joint once, bro. Don't trust her."

"I gotta go."

Chee stepped back, watching Holman with disgusted eyes, and Holman heard him mutter.

"Hero Bandit, my goddamned ass."

Holman pulled out into traffic, thinking he hadn't been called the Hero Bandit in years.

16

HOLMAN ARRIVED fifteen minutes early and seated himself at a table with a clear view of the door. He wasn't sure he would recognize Agent Pollard, but more importantly he wanted her to have an unobstructed view of him when she entered. He wanted her to feel safe.

The Starbucks was predictably crowded, but Holman knew this was one of her reasons for choosing it as their meeting place. She would feel safer with other people around and probably believed he would be intimidated by their proximity to the Federal Building.

Holman settled in, expecting her to be late. She would arrive late to establish her authority and to make sure he understood the power in this situation was hers. Holman didn't mind. He had trimmed his hair that morning, shaved twice to get a close shave, and polished his shoes. He had handwashed his clothes the night before and rented Perry's iron and ironing board for two dollars so he would appear as unthreatening as possible.

Holman was watching the entrance at twelve

minutes after the hour when Agent Pollard finally entered. He wasn't sure it was Pollard at first. The agent who arrested him had been bony and angular, with a thin face and light, short-cropped hair. This woman was heavier than he remembered, with dark hair to her shoulders. The longer hair was nice. She wore a straw-colored jacket over slacks and a dark shirt and sunglasses. Her expression gave her away. The serious game-face expression screamed FED. Holman wondered if she practiced it on the way over.

Holman placed his hands palms down on the table and waited for her to notice him. When she finally saw him Holman offered a smile, but she did not return it. She stepped between the people waiting for their lattes and approached the empty chair opposite him.

She said, "Mr. Holman."

"Hi, Agent Pollard. Okay if I stand? It'd be polite, but I don't want you to think I'm attacking you or anything. Could I get you a cup of coffee?"

Holman kept his hands on the table, letting her see them, and smiled again. She still didn't return the smile or offer her hand. She took her seat, brusque and all business.

"You don't have to stand and I don't have time for the coffee. I want to make sure you understand the ground rules here—I'm happy you completed your term and you're set up with a job and all that—congratulations. I mean that, Holman—congratulations. But I want you to understand—even though Ms. Manelli and Mr. Figg vouched for you, I'm here out of respect for your son. If you abuse that respect in any way, I'm gone."

"Yes, ma'am. If you want to pat me down or anything, it's okay."

"If I thought you would try something like that I wouldn't have come. Again, I'm sorry about your son. That's a terrible loss."

Holman knew he wouldn't have long to make his case. Pollard was already antsy, and probably not happy she had agreed to see him. Cops never had contact with the criminals they arrested. It just wasn't done. Most criminals—even true mental defectives—knew better than to seek out the officers who had arrested them, and those few who did usually found themselves rearrested or dead. During their one and only phone conversation, Pollard had tried to reassure him that the murder scenario the police described and their conclusions regarding Warren Juarez were reasonable, but she had had only a passing familiarity with the case and hadn't been able to answer his torrent of questions or see the evidence he had amassed. Reluctantly, she had finally agreed to familiarize herself with the news reports and let him present his case in person. Holman knew she hadn't agreed to see him because she believed the police might be wrong; she was doing it to help a grieving father with the loss of his son. She probably felt he had earned the face time for the way he went down, but the face time would be the end of her consideration. Holman knew he only had one shot, so he had saved his best hook for last, the hook he hoped she could not resist.

He opened the envelope in which he kept his growing collection of clippings and documents, and shook out the thick sheaf of papers.

He said, "Did you have a chance to review what happened?"

"Yes, I did. I read everything that appeared in the

Times. Can I speak bluntly?"

"That's what I want—to get your opinion."

She settled back and laced her fingers in her lap, her body language telling him she wanted to get through this as quickly as possible. Holman wished she would take off the sunglasses.

"All right. Let's start with Juarez. You described your conversation with Maria Juarez and expressed your doubt that Juarez would have killed himself after the murders, correct?"

"That's right. Here's a guy with a wife and kid, why would he kill himself like that?"

"If I had to guess, which is all I'm doing here, I'd say Juarez was huffing, living on crank, probably smoking the rock. Guys like this always get loaded before they pull the trigger. The drugs would contribute to paranoia and possibly even a psychotic break, which would explain the suicide."

Holman had already considered this.

"Would the autopsy report show all that?"

"Yes—"

"Could you get the autopsy report?"

Holman saw her mouth tighten. He warned himself not to interrupt her again.

"No, I can't get the autopsy report. I'm just offering you a plausible explanation based on my experience. You were troubled by the suicide, so I'm explaining how it was possible."

"Just so you know, I asked the police to let me talk to the coroner or somebody, but they said no."

Her mouth remained firm, but now her laced fingers tightened.

"The police have legal issues, like the right to privacy.

If they opened their files, they could be sued."

Holman decided to move on and fingered through his papers until he found what he wanted. He turned it so she could see.

"The newspaper ran this diagram of the crime scene. See how they drew in the cars and the bodies? I went down there to see for myself—"

"You went down into the riverbed?"

"When I was stealing cars—that was before I got into banks—I spent time down in those flats. That's what it is—flat. The bed on either side of the channel is an empty expanse of concrete like a parking lot. Only way you can get down there is by the service drive the maintenance people use."

Pollard leaned forward to follow what he was saying on the map.

"All right. What's your point?"

"The drive comes down the embankment right here in full view of where the officers were parked. See? The shooter had to come down this drive, but if he came down the drive, they would have been able to see him."

"It was one in the morning. It was dark. Besides, that thing probably isn't drawn to scale."

Holman took out a second map, one he had made himself.

"No, it's not, so I made this one myself. The service drive was way more visible from under the bridge than the newspaper drawing made it seem. And something else—there's a gate here at the top of the drive, see? You have to either climb the fence or cut the lock. Either way would make a helluva lot of noise."

Holman watched Pollard compare the two drawings.

She appeared to be thinking about it, and thinking was a good thing. Thinking meant she was becoming involved. But finally she sat back again and shrugged.

"The officers left the gate open when they drove down."

"I asked the cops how the gate was found, but they wouldn't tell me. I don't think Richie and those other officers would have left it open. If you leave the gate open, you take the chance a security patrol might see it and then you're screwed. We always closed the gate and ran the chain back through, and I'll bet that's what Richie and those other guys did, too."

Pollard sat back.

"When you were stealing cars."

Holman was setting her up for the hook and he thought he was doing pretty well. She was following his logic train even though she didn't know where he was going. He felt encouraged.

"If the gate was closed, the shooter had to open it or go over it, and that makes noise. I know those guys were drinking but they only had a six-pack. That's four grown men and a six-pack—how drunk could they be? If Juarez was stoned like you suggested, how quiet could *he* be? Those officers would have heard something."

"What are you saying, Holman? You think Juarez didn't do it?"

"I'm saying it didn't matter what the officers heard. I think they knew the shooter."

Now Pollard crossed her arms, the ultimate signal she was walling him off. Holman knew he was losing her, but he was ready with his hook and she would either go for it or pass.

He said, "Have you heard of two bank hitters named Marchenko and Parsons?"

Holman watched her stiffen and knew she was finally interested. Now she wasn't just being nice or killing time until she could jump up and run. She took off her sunglasses. He saw that the skin around her eyes had grown papery. She had changed a lot since he had last seen her, but something beyond her appearance was different that he couldn't quite place.

She said, "I've heard of them. And?"

Holman placed the map Richie made showing Marchenko's and Parsons' robberies in front of her.

"My son did this. His wife, Liz, let me make a copy."

"It's a map of their robberies."

"The night he died, Richie got a call from Fowler, and that's when he left. He was going to meet Fowler to talk about Marchenko and Parsons."

"Marchenko and Parsons are dead. That case would have closed three months ago."

Holman peeled off copies of the articles and reports he found on Richie's desk and put them in front of her.

"Richie told his wife they were working on the case. His desk at home, it was covered with stuff like this. I asked the police what Richie was doing. I tried to see the detectives who worked on Marchenko and Parsons, but no one would talk to me. They told me what you just told me, that the case was closed, but Richie told his wife he was going to see Fowler about it, and now he's dead."

Holman watched Pollard skim through the pages. He watched her mouth work, like maybe she was chewing the inside of her lip. She finally looked up, and he thought her eyes were webbed with way too many lines for such a young woman.

She said, "I'm not sure what you want from me."

"I want to know why Richie was working on a dead case. I want to know how Juarez was connected to a couple of bank hitters. I want to know why my son and his friends let someone get close enough to kill them. I want to know who killed them."

Pollard stared at him and Holman stared back. He did not let his eyes show hostility or rage. He kept that part hidden. She wet her lips.

"I guess I could make a couple of calls. I'd be willing to do that."

Holman returned all his papers to the envelope, then wrote his new cell number on the cover.

"This is everything I found in the library on Marchenko and Parsons, and what was in the *Times* about Richie's death and some of the stuff from his house. I made copies. That's my new cell number, too. You should have it."

She looked at the envelope without touching it. Holman sensed she was still struggling with the decision she had already made.

He said, "I don't expect you to do this for free, Agent Pollard. I'll pay you. I don't have much, but we could work out a payment plan or something."

She wet her lips again. Holman wondered at her hesitation, but then she shook her head.

"That won't be necessary. It might take a few days, but I just have to make a few calls."

Holman nodded. His heart was hammering, but he kept his excitement hidden along with the fear and the rage.

"Thanks, Agent Pollard. I really appreciate this."

"You probably shouldn't call me Agent Pollard. I'm not a Special Agent anymore."

"What should I call you?"

"Katherine."

"Okay, Katherine. I'm Max."

Holman held out his hand, but Pollard did not accept it. She picked up the envelope instead.

"This doesn't mean I'm your friend, Max. All it means is I think you deserve answers."

Holman lowered his hand. He was hurt, but wouldn't show it. He wondered why she had agreed to waste her time if she felt that way about him, but he kept these feelings hidden, also.

"Sure. I understand."

"It'll probably be a few days before you hear from me."

"I understand."

Holman watched her walk out of the Starbucks. She picked up speed as she passed through the crowd, then hurried away down the sidewalk. He was still watching her when he remembered the feeling that something was different about her and now he realized what—

Pollard seemed afraid. The young agent who arrested him ten years ago had been fearless, but now she had changed. Thinking these things made him wonder how much he had changed, too, and whether or not he still had what it took to see this thing through.

Holman got up and stepped out into the bright Westwood sun, thinking it felt good to no longer be alone. He liked Pollard even if she seemed hesitant. He hoped she wouldn't get hurt.

17

POLLARD WASN'T sure why she agreed to help Holman, but she was in no hurry to drive back to Simi Valley. Westwood was twenty degrees cooler and her mother would take care of the boys when they got home from camp, so it was like having a day off from the rest of her life. Pollard felt as if she had been paroled.

She walked to Stan's Donuts and ordered one plain all-American round-with-a-hole glazed donut—no sprinkles, jelly, candy, or chocolate; nothing that would cut into the silky taste of melted sugar and warm grease. Pollard's ass needed a donut like a goldfish needed a bowling ball, but she hadn't been to Stan's since she left the Bureau. When Pollard was working out of the Westwood office, she and another agent named April Sanders had snuck away to Stan's at least twice a week. Taking their donut break, they called it.

The woman behind the counter offered a donut off the rack, but a fresh batch was coming out of the fryer, so Pollard opted to wait. She brought Holman's file to one of the outside tables to read while she waited, but found herself thinking about Holman. Holman had always been a big guy, but the Holman she arrested had been thirty pounds thinner with shaggy hair, a deep tan, and the bad skin of a serious tweaker. He didn't look like a criminal anymore. Now, he looked like a forty-something man who was down on his luck.

Pollard suspected the police had answered Holman's questions as best they could, but he was reluctant to accept the facts. She had worked with grieving families during her time with the Feeb, and all of them had seen only questions in that terrible place of loss where no good answers exist. The working truth of every criminal investigation was that not all the questions could be answered; the most any cop hoped for was just enough answers to build a case.

Pollard finally turned to Holman's envelope and read through the articles. Anton Marchenko and Jonathan Parsons, both thirty-two years old, were unemployed loners who met at a fitness center in West Hollywood. Neither was married nor had a significant other. Parsons was a Texan who had drifted to Los Angeles as a teenage runaway. Marchenko was survived by his widowed mother, a Ukrainian immigrant who, according to the paper, was both cooperating with the police and threatening to sue the city. At the time of their deaths, Marchenko and Parsons shared a small bungalow apartment in Hollywood's Beachwood Canyon where police discovered twelve pistols, a cache of ammunition in excess of six thousand rounds, an extensive collection of martial arts videos, and nine hundred ten thousand dollars in cash.

Pollard had no longer been on the job when

Marchenko and Parsons blazed their way through thirteen banks, but she had followed the news about them and grew jazzed reading about them now. Reading about their bank hits filled Pollard with the same edgy juice she had known on the job. Pollard felt real for the first time in years, and found herself thinking about Marty. Her life since his death had been a non-stop struggle between mounting bills and her desire to single-handedly raise her boys. Having lost their father, Pollard had promised herself they would not also lose their mother to day care and nannies. It was a commitment that had left her feeling powerless and vague, especially as the boys grew older and their expenses mounted, but just reading about Marchenko and Parsons revived her.

Marchenko and Parsons had committed thirteen robberies over a nine-month period, all with the same method of operation: They stormed into banks like an invading army, forced everyone onto the floor, then dumped the cash drawers from the teller stations. While one of them worked the tellers, the other forced the branch manager to open the vault.

The articles Holman had copied included blurry security stills of black-clad figures waving rifles, but witness descriptions of the two men had been sketchy and neither was identified until their deaths. It wasn't until the eighth robbery that a witness described their getaway vehicle, a light blue foreign compact car. The car wasn't described again until the tenth robbery, when it was confirmed as being a light blue Toyota Corolla. Pollard smiled when she saw this, knowing the Bank Squad would have been high-fiving each other in celebration. Professionals would have used a different car for each robbery; use of the same car indicated that these guys were lucky amateurs. Once you knew they were riding on luck, you knew their luck would run out.

"Donuts ready. Miss? Your donuts are ready."

Pollard glanced up.

"What?"

"The hot donuts are ready."

Pollard had been so involved in the articles she lost track of time. She went inside, collected her donut with a cup of black coffee, then went back to her table to resume reading.

Marchenko and Parsons ran out of luck on their thirteenth robbery.

When they entered the California Central Bank in Culver City to commit their thirteenth armed robbery, they did not know that LAPD Robbery Special detectives, Special Investigations officers, and patrol officers were surveilling a three-mile corridor stretching from downtown L.A. to the eastern edge of Santa Monica. When Marchenko and Parsons entered the bank, all five tellers tripped silent alarms. Though the news story did not contain the specifics, Pollard knew what happened from that point: The bank's security contractor notified the LAPD, who in turn alerted the surveillance team. The team converged on the bank to take positions in the parking lot. Marchenko exited the bank first. In most such cases, the robber had three typical moves: He surrendered, he tried to escape, or he retreated into the bank, whereupon a negotiation ensued. Marchenko chose none of the above. He opened fire. The surveillance teams—armed with 5.56mm rifles—returned fire, killing Marchenko and Parsons at the scene.

Pollard finished the last article and realized her donut had grown cold. She took a bite. It was delicious even cold, but she paid little attention.

Pollard skimmed through the articles covering the murders of the four officers, then found what appeared to be several cover sheets from LAPD reports about Marchenko and Parsons. Pollard found this curious. Such reports were from the Detective Bureau, but Richard Holman had been a uniformed patrol officer. LAPD detectives used patrol officers to assist in searches and one-on-one street interviews after a robbery, but those jobs didn't require access to reports or witness statements, and patrol officers rarely stayed involved after the first day or two following a robbery. Marchenko and Parsons had been dead for three months and their loot had been recovered. She wondered why LAPD was maintaining an investigation three months after the fact and why it included patrol officers, but she felt she could learn the answer easily enough. Pollard had gotten to know several LAPD Robbery detectives during her time on the squad. She decided to ask them.

Pollard spent a few minutes recalling their names, then phoned the LAPD's information office for their current duty assignments. The first two detectives she asked for had retired, but the third, Bill Fitch, was currently assigned to Robbery Special, the elite robbery unit operating out of Parker Center.

When she got Fitch on the phone, he said, "Who is this?"

Fitch didn't remember her.

"Katherine Pollard. I was on the Bank Squad with the FBI. We worked together a few years ago."

She rattled off the names of several of the serial

bandits they had worked: the Major League Bandit, the Dolly Parton Bandit, the Munchkin Bandits. Serial bandits were given names when they were unknown subjects because the names made them easier to talk about. The Major League Bandit had always worn a Dodgers cap; the Dolly Parton Bandit, one of only two female bank bandits Pollard had worked, had been an ex-stripper with huge breasts; and the Munchkin Bandits had been a takeover team of little people.

Fitch said, "Oh, sure, I remember you. I heard you quit the job."

"That's right. Listen, I have a question for you about Marchenko and Parsons. You got a minute?"

"They're dead."

"I know. Are you guys still running an open case?"

Fitch hesitated, and Pollard knew this to be a bad sign. Though the FBI and the LAPD bank teams enjoyed a great working relationship, the rules stated you didn't share information with private citizens.

He said, "Are you back with the Feeb?"

"No. I'm making a personal inquiry."

"What does that mean, personal inquiry? Who are you working for?"

"I'm not working for anyone—I'm making an inquiry for a friend. I want to find out if the four officers killed last week were working on Marchenko and Parsons."

Pollard could almost see his eyes roll by the tone that came to his voice.

"Oh, now I get it. Holman's father. That guy is being a real pain in the ass."

"He lost his son."

"Listen, how in hell did he get you involved in this?"

"I put him in prison."

Fitch laughed, but then his laughter stopped as if he had flipped a switch.

"I don't know what Holman is talking about and I can't answer your questions. You're a civilian."

"Holman's son told his wife he was working on something."

"Marchenko and Parsons are dead. Don't call me again, ex-Agent Pollard."

The phone went dead in her ear.

Pollard sat with her dead phone and cold donut, reviewing their conversation. Fitch had repeatedly told her Marchenko and Parsons were dead, but he hadn't denied that an investigation was ongoing. She wondered why and thought she might know how to find out. She opened her cell phone again and called April Sanders.

"Special Agent Sanders."

"Guess where I am."

Sanders lowered her voice. This had always been Sanders' habit when taking a personal call. They hadn't spoken since Marty's death and Pollard was pleased to see that Sanders hadn't changed.

"Oh my God—is that really you?"

"Are you in the office?"

"Yeah, but not much longer. Are you here?"

"I'm at Stan's with your name on a dozen donuts. Send down a badge."

• • •

The Federal Building in Westwood was headquarters for the eleven hundred FBI agents serving Los Angeles and the surrounding counties. It was a single steel-and-glass tower set amid acres of parking lots on some of the most expensive real estate in America. The agents often joked that the United States could retire its national debt by converting their offices to condos.

Pollard parked in the civilian lot, then cleared the lobby security station to wait for her escort. It was no longer enough for someone to call down a pass. Pollard couldn't just board an elevator and punch the button for any of the eight floors occupied by the FBI; visitors and agents had to swipe their security cards and enter a valid badge number before the elevator would move.

A few moments later an elevator opened and a civilian employee stepped out. He recognized Pollard by the box from Stan's and held the door.

"Miss Pollard?"

"That's me."

"You going to Banks, right?"

"That's right."

Officially, it was known as the Federal Bureau of Investigation, Los Angeles Field Office, Bank Squad, but the agents who worked there called it Banks. Pollard's escort showed her to the thirteenth floor, then let her through a code-locked door. Pollard hadn't been through the door in eight years. She felt as if she had never left.

The Bank Squad occupied a large modern office space cut into spacious cubicles by sea-green partitions. The offices were neat, clean, and corporate, and might have belonged to an insurance firm or a FORTUNE 500 company except for the mug shots of L.A.'s ten most wanted bank robbers hanging on the wall. Pollard smiled when she saw the mug shots. Someone had stuck Post-it notes on the top three suspects, naming them Larry, Moe, and Curly.

Los Angeles and the surrounding seven counties were hit by an average of more than six hundred bank robberies every year—which meant three bank robberies each and every business day, five days per week, fifty-two weeks per year (bank robbers kicked back on Saturday and Sunday when most banks were closed). So many banks were being robbed that most of the ten elite Special Agents who worked Banks were always out in the field at any given time and today was no different. Pollard saw only three people when she entered. A bald, light-skinned African-American agent named Bill Cecil was locked in conversation with a young agent Pollard didn't recognize. Cecil smiled when he saw her as April Sanders rushed forward.

Sanders, looking panicked, covered her mouth in case lip-readers were watching. Sanders was a profound paranoid. She believed her calls were monitored, her e-mails were read, and the women's bathroom was bugged. She believed the men's bathroom was bugged, too, but that didn't concern her.

She whispered, "I should have warned you. Leeds is here."

Christopher Leeds was the Bank Squad supervisor. He had run the squad with a brilliant hand for almost twenty years.

Pollard said, "You don't have to whisper. I'm okay with Leeds."

"*Shh!*"

"No one's listening, April."

They both glanced around to find Cecil and his partner cupping their ears, listening. Pollard laughed.

"Stop it, Big Bill."

Big Bill Cecil slowly rose to his feet. Cecil was not a tall man; he was called Big Bill because he was wide. He had been on the Bank Squad longer than anyone except Leeds.

"Good to see you, lady. How are those babies?"

Cecil had always called her lady. When Pollard first joined the squad, Leeds—then as now—was as much a nightmare tyrant as he was brilliant. Cecil had taken her under his wing, counseled and consoled her, and taught her how to survive Leeds' exacting demands. Cecil was one of the kindest men she had ever known.

"They're good, Bill, thanks. You're getting fat."

Cecil eyed the donut box.

"I'm about to get fatter. One of those has my name on it, I hope."

Pollard held the box for Cecil and his partner, who introduced himself as Kevin Delaney.

They were still chatting when Leeds came around the corner. Delaney immediately returned to his desk and Sanders went back to her cubicle. Cecil, who was ripe for his pension, turned his letterbox smile on his boss.

"Hey, Chris. Look who came to visit."

Leeds was a tall humorless man known for immaculate suits and his brilliance in patterning serial bandits. Serial robbers were hunted in much the same way as serial killers. They were profiled to establish their patterns, and once their patterns were recognized, predictions were made as to when and where they would strike again. Leeds was a legendary profiler. Banks were his passion, and the agents who worked on the squad were his handpicked children. Everyone arrived before him; no one left until Leeds left. And Leeds rarely left. The workload was horrendous, but the FBI's L.A. Bank Squad was the top of the game, and Leeds knew it. Working with the squad was an honor. When Pollard resigned, Leeds had taken it as a personal rejection. The day she cleared her desk, he refused to speak to her.

Now he studied her as if he couldn't place her, but then he nodded.

"Hello, Katherine."

"Hey, Chris. I stopped by to say hello. How've you been?"

"Busy."

He glanced across the room at Sanders.

"I want you with Dugan in Montclair. He needs help with the one-on-ones. You should have left ten minutes ago."

One-on-ones were the face-to-face interviews of possible witnesses. Local shopkeepers, workmen, and pedestrians were questioned in hopes they could provide a description of the suspects or their vehicle.

Sanders peeked over the top of her cubicle.

"On it, boss."

He turned to Cecil and tapped his watch.

"Meeting. Let's go."

Cecil and Delaney hurried toward the door, but Leeds turned back to Pollard.

He said, "I appreciated the card. Thank you."

"I was sorry when I heard."

Leeds' wife had died three years ago, almost two months exactly after Marty. When Pollard heard, she had written a short note. Leeds had never responded.

"It was good to see you, Katherine. I hope you still feel you made the right decision."

158

Leeds didn't wait for her to respond. He followed Cecil and Delaney out the door like a grave digger on his way to church.

Pollard brought the donuts to Sanders' cubicle.

"Man, some things never change."

Sanders reached for the box.

"I wish I could say the same about my ass."

They laughed and enjoyed the moment, but then Sanders frowned.

"Shit, you heard what he said. I'm sorry, Kat, I gotta roll."

"Listen, I didn't stop by just to bring donuts. I need some information."

Sanders looked suspicious, then lowered her voice again.

"We should eat. Eating will distort our voices."

"Yeah, let's eat."

They fished out a couple of donuts.

Pollard said, "Did you guys close the Marchenko and Parsons case?"

Sanders spoke with her mouth full.

"They're dead, man. Those guys were iced. Why you want to know about Marchenko and Parsons?"

Pollard knew Sanders would ask, and had worried over how she should answer. Sanders had been on the squad when they tracked and busted Holman. Even though Holman had earned their respect with how he went down, many of the agents had grown resentful because of the publicity he got when the *Times* dubbed him the Hero Bandit. Within the squad, Holman's name had been the Beach Bum Bandit because of his dark tan, Tommy Bahama shirts, and shades. Bank robbers were not heroes.

She said, "I took a job. Raising two kids is expensive."

Pollard didn't want to lie, but she didn't see any other way around it. And it wasn't like it was totally a lie. It was *almost* the truth.

Sanders finished her first donut and started a second.

"So where are you working?"

"It's a private job, banking security, that kind of thing."

Sanders nodded. Retired agents often took jobs with security firms or the smaller banking chains.

Pollard said, "Anyway, I was told that LAPD was still running a case. You know anything about that?"

"No. Why would they?"

"That's what I was hoping you could tell me."

"We're not. They're not. It's a done deal."

"You sure?"

"Run a case for what? We bagged'm. Marchenko and Parsons had no accomplices inside or outside the banks. We ran this thing, man—I mean we *ran* it—so we know. We found no evidence of any other party being involved either before or after the fact, so there was no reason to continue the investigation. LAPD knows that."

Pollard thought back over her conversation with Holman.

"Were Marchenko and Parsons plugged in with the Frogtown gang?"

"Nope. Never came up."

"Any gangs other than Frogtown?"

Sanders pinched her donut between her thumb and forefinger, and ticked off the points she wanted to make on her remaining fingers.

"We questioned Marchenko's mother, their land-lord, their mailman, some dork at a video store they frequented, and the neighbors at their apartment house. These guys had no friends or associates. They didn't tell anyone—not *anyone*—what they were doing, so they sure as hell had no accomplices. And, except for a somewhat cheesy collection of gold neck-laces and a two-thousand-dollar Rolex, they sat on the money. No flashy cars, no diamond rings—they lived in a dump."

"They must have spent something. You only re-covered nine hundred K."

Nine hundred thousand was a lot of cash, but Marchenko and Parsons had hit twelve vaults. Pollard had done the math when she read the articles at Stan's. Teller drawers could yield a couple of thousand at most, but a vault could net two or three hundred thou-sand and sometimes more. If Marchenko and Parsons scored three hundred K from each of the twelve vaults, that was 3.6 million, which left two and half million missing. Pollard hadn't found this unusual because she had once bagged a thief who spent twenty thousand a night on strippers and lap dances, and a South Central gang who had flown to Vegas after their scores for two-hundred-thousand-dollar orgies of chartered jets, crack, and Texas Hold'em. Pollard assumed that Marchenko and Parsons had blown the missing money.

Sanders finished her donut.

"No, they didn't blow it. They hid it. That nine we got was a freak scene. Parsons made up a little bed with it. He liked to sleep on it and jerk off."

"How much was their take?"

"Sixteen-point-two million, less the nine."

Pollard whistled.

"Jesus Christ, that's a lot. What did they do with it?"

Sanders eyed the remaining donuts, but finally closed the box.

"We found no evidence of purchases, deposits, fund transfers, gifts—nothing; no receipts, no conspicuous consumption. We ran their phone calls for the entire year, investigating everyone they called—nothing. We worked that old lady—Marchenko's mother, man, what a nasty bitch she is, a Ukrainian? Leeds thought for sure she knew what was up, but you know what? At the end of the day we cleared her. She couldn't even afford to buy medicine. We don't know what they did with the money. It's probably sitting in a storage shed somewhere."

"So you let it drop?"

"Sure. We did what we could."

The squad's job was to bust bank robbers. Once the perpetrators of a particular crime were caught, the squad would attempt to recover any missing funds but ultimately its attention was turned to the other fifty or sixty crooks still robbing banks. Unless new evidence surfaced to indicate an at-large accomplice, Pollard knew the recovery of missing funds would be left to banking insurers.

Pollard said, "Maybe LAPD is still running the case."

"Nah, we were in with Robbery Special every step of the way so we both hit the wall at the same time. That case is closed. The banks might have pooled to run a contract investigation, but I don't know. I could find out if you want."

"Yeah. That would be great."

Pollard considered her options. If Sanders said the case was closed, then it was closed, but Holman's son told his wife he was working it. Pollard wondered if LAPD had developed a lead to the missing money.

"Listen, could you get a copy of the LAPD file on this?"

"I don't know. Maybe."

"I'd like to see their witness lists. I'd like to see yours, too. I might have to talk to those people."

Sanders hesitated, then suddenly stood to make sure the office was empty. She glanced at her watch.

"Leeds is going to kill me. I have to get going."

"How about the list?"

"You'd better not let it get back to Leeds. He'll have my ass."

"You know better than that."

"I'll have to fax it to you."

Pollard left the building with Sanders, then went to her car. It was one forty-five. Her mother would be hammering the boys to clean their room and the day was still young. Pollard had an idea how she could find out what she wanted to know, but she would need Holman's help. She found his cell number on the envelope and placed the call.

18

AFTER HOLMAN left Agent Pollard he returned to his Highlander and called Perry to let him know what was happening with the Mercury.

"A couple of guys are bringing back your car. They'll put it in the alley."

"Waitaminute. You let some other asshole drive my car? Where you get off doing something like that?"

"I got a new set of wheels, Perry. How else could I get your car back?"

"That bastard better not pick up a ticket or I'm making you pay."

"I got a cell phone, too. Let me give you the number."

"Why? In case I gotta call to say your fuckin' friends have stolen my car?"

Holman gave him the number, then got off the line. Perry was wearing him out.

Holman walked around Westwood looking for a place to have lunch. Most of the restaurants he passed looked too dressy. Holman was feeling self-conscious about his appearance since meeting with Agent Pollard.

Even though he had ironed his clothes, he knew they looked cheap. They were prison clothes, bought from secondhand shops with prison money, ten years behind the style. Holman stopped outside a Gap and watched the kids going in and out with big Gap bags. He could probably set himself up with a new pair of jeans and a couple of shirts, but spending Chee's money on clothes bothered him, so he talked himself out of it. A block later he bought a pair of Ray-Ban Wayfarers from a street vendor for nine dollars. He liked the way he looked in them, but didn't realize until he was two blocks away that they were the same style glasses he wore when he was robbing banks.

Holman found a Burger King across the street from the UCLA main gate, settled in with a Whopper and fries and the instruction manual for his new cell phone. He set up his voice mail and was programming the list of numbers he'd been keeping in his wallet into the phone's memory when the phone made a chiming sound. Holman thought he had caused the chime by pressing the wrong button, then realized he was getting a call. It took him a moment to remember to answer by pressing the Send key.

He said, "Hello?"

"Holman, it's Katherine Pollard. I have a question for you."

Holman wondered if anything was wrong. She had left him only an hour ago.

"Okay. Sure."

"Have you met or spoken with Fowler's widow?"

"Yeah. I met her at the memorial."

"Good. We're going to go see her."

"Right now?"

"Yeah. I have the free time now, so now would be good. I want you to meet me back in Westwood. There's a mystery bookstore on Broxton just south of Weyburn with a parking structure next door. Park in the structure and meet me outside the bookstore. I'll do the driving."

"Okay, sure, but why are we going to see her? Did you find out something?"

"I've asked two people if LAPD was running an investigation and they both denied it, but I think it's possible something was going on. She might be able to tell us."

"Why do you think Fowler's wife knows?"

"Your son told his wife, didn't he?"

The simplicity of that notion impressed Holman.

"Should we call her or something? What if she isn't home?"

"You never call them, Holman. When you call, they always say no. We'll take our chances. How long before you can get back to Westwood?"

"I'm already there."

"Then I'll see you in five."

Holman hung up, regretting that he hadn't bought new clothes at the Gap.

When Holman stepped out of the parking structure, Pollard was waiting in front of the bookstore in a blue Subaru with the windows raised and the engine running. It was several years old and needed a wash. He climbed into the passenger side and pulled the door closed.

He said, "Man, you got back to me really fast."

She tore away from the curb.

"Yeah, thanks, now listen—we have three things to cover with this woman: Was her husband participating in some kind of investigation involving Marchenko and Parsons? Did he tell her why he left the house to meet your son and the others that night, and what they were going to do? And, in either of the above conversations or at any other time, did he mention Marchenko and Parsons being connected with Frogtown or any other gang? Got it? That should tell us what you need to know."

Holman stared at her.

"Is this what it was like when you were on the Feeb?"

"Don't call it the Feeb, Holman. I can call it the Feeb, but I don't want to hear that kind of disrespect from you."

Holman turned to stare out the window. He felt like a child whose hand had been slapped for chewing with his mouth open.

She said, "No sulking. Please don't sulk, Holman. I'm hitting this fast because we have a lot of ground to cover and I don't have much time. You came to me, remember?"

"Yeah. I'm sorry."

"Okay. She lives up in Canoga Park. Take us about twenty minutes if we stay ahead of the traffic."

Holman was irritated, but he liked that she had taken the lead and was pushing forward. He took it as a sign of her experience and professionalism.

"So why do you think something is going on even though your friends said the case was closed?"

Pollard swiveled her head like a fighter pilot on patrol, then gunned the Subaru onto the 405, heading north. Holman held on, wondering if she always drove like this.

She said, "They never recovered the money."

"The papers said they got nine hundred thousand in Marchenko's apartment."

"Chump change. Those guys netted over sixteen mil in their heists. It's missing."

Holman stared at her.

"That's a lot of money."

"Yeah."

"Wow."

"Yeah."

"What happened to it?"

"No one knows."

They climbed the 405 out of Westwood toward the Sepulveda Pass. Holman turned in his seat to look out at the city. The city stretched away from him as far as he could see.

He said, "All that money is just . . . out there?"

"Don't mention the money to this woman, okay, Holman? If she mentions it, fine, then we've learned something, but the idea here is that we want to find out what she knows. We don't want to put ideas in her head. That's called witness contamination."

Holman was still thinking about the sixteen million dollars. His biggest single take had been three thousand, one hundred, and twenty-seven dollars. The combined take from all nine of his robberies had been eighteen thousand, nine hundred, and forty-two dollars.

"You think they were trying to find the money?"

"Finding money isn't the LAPD's job. But if they had a lead to someone who had knowingly received stolen money or was holding it for Marchenko and Parsons or was in possession of the stolen cash, then, yeah, it would be their job to conduct an investigation."

They were steaming north out of the mountains and across the Ventura Interchange. The San Fernando Valley spread out before them to the east and west, and north to the Santa Susana Mountains, a great flat valley filled with buildings and people. Holman kept thinking about the money. He couldn't get the sixteen million out of his head. It might be anywhere.

Holman said, "They were trying to find the money. You can't let that much money just go."

Pollard laughed.

"Holman, you wouldn't believe how much dough we lose. Not with guys like you who we bag alive— you bag a guy, he'll give it up if he has any left, trying to cut a deal—but the takeover guys like Marchenko and Parsons who get killed? One-point-two here, five hundred thousand there, just gone, and no one ever finds it. No one who reports it, anyway."

Holman glanced over at her. She was smiling.

"That's wild. I never thought about it."

"The banks don't want losses like that in the papers. It would only encourage more assholes to rob banks. Anyway, listen—a friend of mine is pulling the LAPD file on this thing. As soon as we have it, we'll know what's what or we'll know who to ask, so don't worry about it. In the meantime, we'll see what we get from this woman. For all we know, Fowler told her everything."

Holman nodded but did not answer. He watched the valley roll past: a pelt of houses and buildings covering the earth that reached to the mountains, cut by remote canyons and shadows. Some men would do anything for sixteen million dollars. Murdering four cops was nothing.

The Fowlers had a small tract home in a development of similar homes, all with the stucco sides, composite roofs, and tiny yards typical of the post–World War II construction boom. Ancient orange trees decorated most of the yards, so old that their trunks were black and gnarled. Holman guessed the development had once been an orange grove. The trees were older than the houses.

The woman who answered the door was Jacki Fowler, but she seemed like a coarse version of the woman Holman met at the memorial. Without make-up, her wide face was loose and blotchy, and her eyes were hard. She stared at him without recognition in a way that made Holman uncomfortable. He wished they had called.

"I'm Max Holman, Mrs. Fowler, Richard Holman's father. We met at the memorial."

Pollard held out a small bouquet of daisies. She had swung into a Vons Market to pick up the flowers when they reached Canoga Park.

"My name is Katherine Pollard, Mrs. Fowler. I'm terribly sorry for your loss."

Jacki Fowler took the flowers without comprehension, then looked at Holman.

"Oh, that's right. You lost your son."

Pollard said, "Would you mind if we come in for a few minutes, Mrs. Fowler? We'd like to pay our respects, and Max would like to talk about his son if you have the time."

Holman admired Pollard. In the time it took them to walk from the car to the door, the fast-talking frenetic driver had been replaced by a reassuring woman with a gentle voice and kind eyes. Holman was glad she was with him. He wouldn't have known what to say.

Mrs. Fowler showed them into a clean, well-kept living room. Holman saw an open bottle of red wine on a little table at the end of the couch, but no glass. He glanced at Pollard for some direction, but Pollard was still with Mrs. Fowler.

Pollard said, "This must be really hard for you right now. Are you doing all right? Do you need anything?"

"I have four sons, you know. The oldest, now he's talking the big talk about going on the police. I told him, are you out of your mind?"

"Tell him to be a lawyer. Lawyers make all the money."

"Do you have children?"

"Two boys."

"Then you know. This is going to sound terrible, but you know what I used to say? If he's going to get killed, then please God let him get T-boned by some drunk-driving movie star with millions of dollars. At least I could sue the sonofabitch. But no—he has to get killed by some piece of shit *cholo* without a pot to piss in."

She glanced at Holman.

"We should still look into that—me, you, and the other families. They say you can't get blood from a stone, but who's to know? Would you like a glass of wine? I was just about to have one, first of the day."

"No, thanks, but you help yourself."

171

Pollard said, "I'll have one."

Mrs. Fowler told them to take a seat, then continued out to her dining room. A second bottle of wine was open on the table. She poured two glasses, then returned, offering one of the glasses to Pollard. Holman realized it was a long way from being the first of her day.

As Jacki Fowler took a seat, she asked, "Did you know Mike? Is that why you're here?"

"No, ma'am. I didn't know my son very well, either. That's more why I'm here, about my son. My daughter-in-law—Richie's wife—she told me that your husband was my son's training officer. I guess they were good friends."

"I wouldn't know. It's like we lived two lives in this house. Are you a policeman, too?"

"No, ma'am."

"Are you the one was in prison? Someone at the funeral said there was a convict."

Holman felt himself flush and glanced at Pollard, but Pollard wasn't looking at him.

"Yes, ma'am. That's me. Officer Holman's father."

"Jesus, that must have been something. What did you do?"

"I robbed a bank."

Pollard said, "I used to be a police officer, Mrs. Fowler. I don't know about you, but these murders have left Max with a lot of questions, like why his son went out in the middle of the night. Did Mike tell you anything about that?"

Mrs. Fowler sipped her wine, then made a dismissive wave with the glass.

"Mike went out in the middle of the night all the damned time. He was hardly ever home."

Pollard glanced at Holman, nodding that it was his turn to say something.

"Max, why don't you tell Jacki what your daughter-in-law said? About the call he got that night."

"My daughter-in-law told me your husband called. Richie was at home, but he got a call from your husband and went out to meet him and the other guys."

She snorted.

"Well, Mike sure as hell didn't call me. He was working that night. He had the dog shift. The way it was around here, he came home when he came home. He never showed me the courtesy to call."

"I got the idea they were working on something."

She grunted again and had more of the wine.

"They were drinking. Mike was a drunkard. You know the other two—Mellon and Ash? Mike had been their T.O., also."

Now Pollard stared at Holman, and Holman shrugged.

"I didn't know that."

Pollard said, "Why don't you show her the phone bills?"

Holman unfolded his copy of Richie's phone bill.

Mrs. Fowler said, "What's this?"

"My son's phone bills for the past couple of months. You see the little red dots?"

"That's Mike's phone."

"Yes, ma'am. Ash is the yellow dots and Mellon the green. Richie was calling your husband two or three times a day almost every day. He hardly ever called Ash or Mellon, but he talked to Mike a lot."

She studied the bill as if reading the fine print in a lifetime contract, then pushed to her feet.

"I want to show you something. Just wait here. You sure you don't want any wine?"

"Thanks, Mrs. Fowler, but I've been sober for ten years. I was a drunkard along with being a bank robber."

She grunted again and walked away as if that had made no more impression on her than knowing he had been in prison.

Pollard said, "You're doing fine."

"I didn't know about the training officer business."

"Don't worry about it. You're doing fine."

Mrs. Fowler came back shuffling through several papers and returned to her spot on the couch.

"Isn't it strange you checked your son's phone records? So did I. Not your son's, I mean, but Mike's."

Pollard put down her wine. Holman saw that it was untouched.

Pollard said, "Had Mike said anything to make you suspicious?"

"It was the not saying anything that made me suspicious. He'd get these calls, not on the house line, but on his cell. He carried those damned cell phones all the time. The damn thing would ring and he'd leave—"

"What would he say?"

"He was going out. That's all he would say, I'm going out. What was I to think? What would anyone think?"

Pollard leaned forward quietly.

"He was having an affair."

"Fucking some whore is what I thought, pardon my French, so I decided to see who he was calling and who was calling him. See, here—on his cell phone bill—"

She finally found what she wanted and bent forward to show Holman the pages. Pollard came over and sat beside Holman to see. Holman recognized Richie's home and cell phone numbers.

Mrs. Fowler said, "I didn't recognize any of the numbers, so you know what I did?"

Pollard said, "You called the numbers?"

"That's right. I thought he was calling women, but it was your son and Ash and Mellon. I wish I had thought of the little dots. I asked him what are you doing with these guys, fruiting off? I didn't mean anything by that, Mr. Holman, I was just trying to be mean. You know what he said? He told me to mind my own business."

Holman ignored her comment. Richie had been calling Fowler every day, but Fowler had also been calling Richie, Ash, and Mellon. It was clear they were doing more than lining up beer parties.

Mrs. Fowler was back in the anger of that moment and rolling on.

"I didn't know what in hell they were doing. It made me angry, but I didn't say much until I had to clean up after him, then I had had enough. He came home in the middle of the night tracking dirt all over the house. I didn't find it until the next day and I was so mad. He didn't even care enough to clean up after himself. That's how little consideration he showed."

Holman had no idea what she was talking about, so he asked her, wondering if it had anything to do with Richie.

Mrs. Fowler pushed to her feet again, but this time it took more of an effort.

"Come here. I'll show you."

They followed her out through the kitchen onto a small covered patio in the backyard. A dusty Weber grill was parked at the edge of the patio with a pair of Wolverine work boots on the ground beside it, caked with dirt and weeds. She pointed at them.

"Here—he clopped through the house in the middle of the night with these things. When I saw the mess I said, Have you lost your mind? I threw them out here and told him he could clean them himself. You should have seen the mess."

Pollard stooped to look at the boots more closely.

"What night was that?"

She hesitated, frowning.

"I guess it was Thursday—two Thursdays ago."

Five days before they were murdered. Holman wondered if Richie, Mellon, and Ash had also gone out that night. He told himself to ask Liz.

Pollard, reading his mind, stood.

"Was that a night when he went out with the others?"

"I didn't ask and I don't know. I told him if he hated being here so much he should get the hell out. I was fed up with the rudeness. I had had enough with the discourtesy, coming into my house like this and not even cleaning up after himself. We had a terrible fight and I don't regret one word of it, not even now with him being dead."

Then Pollard surprised him.

She said, "Did Mike ever mention the names Marchenko and Parsons?"

"No. Are they on the police?"

Pollard seemed to study her for a moment, then made the gentle smile.

"Just people Mike used to know. I thought he might have mentioned them."

"Michael never told me a goddamned thing. It was like I didn't exist."

Pollard glanced back at Holman, then nodded toward the house, the gentle smile deadened by sadness.

"We should be going, Max."

When they reached the front door, Jacki Fowler took Holman's hand and held it an uncomfortably long time.

She said, "There's more than one kind of prison, you know."

Holman said, "Yes, ma'am. I've been there, too."

19

HOLMAN WAS ANGRY and unsettled when they left. He had wanted to find a grieving widow with straightforward answers to explain his son's death, but now he pictured Mike Fowler having secretive phone calls with his hand cupped over his mouth. He saw Fowler slipping from his home too early for the neighbors to see, then returning under cover of darkness. *What were you doing, honey? Nothing. Where did you go? Nowhere.* Holman had spent most of his life doing crime. Whatever had happened in the Fowler house felt like a crime in progress.

Pollard gunned her Subaru up the freeway on-ramp into the thickening traffic. The drive back would be ugly, but when Holman glanced at her, she was glowing as if a light had been turned on inside her.

Holman said, "What do you think?"

"Talk to your daughter-in-law. Ask if Richard went out the Thursday before they were shot and if she knows anything about where they went or what they did. Ask about the Frogtown connection, too. Don't forget that."

Holman was thinking he wanted to drop the whole thing.

"I wasn't asking about that. You said it wasn't up to the police to look for missing money."

She jacked the Subaru between two tractor-trailers, diving for the diamond lane.

"It's up to them, but recovering loot isn't a front-burner priority. No one has time for that, Holman—we're too busy trying to stop new crimes from happening."

"If someone found it, though—would they get a reward? A legal reward?"

"The banks award a recovery fee, yes, but policemen aren't eligible."

"Well, if they were doing it on their own time—"

She interrupted him.

"Don't get ahead of yourself. Deal with what you know, and right now all we know is Fowler tracked dirt in the house on Thursday night and didn't give a shit what his wife thought about it. That's all we know."

"But I checked the call dates when she showed us her phone bills. All of the calling started on the eighth day after Marchenko and Parsons died, just like on Richie's bill. Fowler called Richie and Mellon and Ash, one right after another. Like he was saying, hey, let's go find some money."

She straightened behind the wheel, crisp and sharp.

"Holman, listen—we've had exactly one interview with a woman who had a bad marriage. We don't know what they were doing or why."

"It feels like they were up to something. This isn't what I wanted in my head."

"Oh, for Christ's sake."

Holman glanced at her and saw her frowning. She swerved out of the diamond lane to zoom around two women in a sedan, then cut them off when she dived back into the diamond lane ahead of them. Holman had never driven this fast unless he was high.

She said, "We don't know enough for you to think any differently about your son, so stop it. You heard this depressed woman with her husband sneaking around and you know the money's missing, so you've jumped to this conclusion. Maybe they just liked to hang out. Maybe this fascination with Marchenko and Parsons was just a hobby."

Holman didn't believe it and felt irritated that she was trying to cheer him up.

"That's bullshit."

"You've heard of the Black Dahlia? The unsolved homicide case?"

"What does that have to do with anything?"

"That case has become a hobby for a lot of detectives. So many LAPD dicks are into that case they got together and formed a club to talk over their theories."

"I still think it's bullshit."

"Okay, forget it. But just because they were sneaking around doesn't mean they were doing anything illegal. I can think of plenty of ways we might be able to tie what they were doing with Marchenko and Parsons and Juarez."

Holman glanced at her, doubtful.

"How?"

"Did you read the obituaries for Fowler, Ash, and Mellon?"

"Just Richie's."

"If you had read Fowler's, you'd know he spent two years on the CRASH unit—that's Community Reaction Against Street Hoodlums, what the LAPD named their anti-gang unit. I'm going to call a friend of mine who used to run CRASH. I'll ask him what kind of exposure Fowler had with Frogtown."

"Fowler killed Juarez's brother. Juarez and his brother were both in Frogtown."

"Right, but maybe there's a deeper connection. Remember when we talked about a possible insider connection to Marchenko and Parsons?"

"Yeah."

"The real money is in the vault, but the amount of money in the vault varies during the week. People come in, cash their paychecks, and take the money away, right?"

"I know that. I used to rob banks, remember?"

"So once or twice a week, banks receive a shipment of new cash so they'll have enough to meet the customer draw. You said you didn't see how a couple of takeover hitters like Marchenko and Parsons could have an inside accomplice, but all it takes is someone who knows when the area branches are scheduled to receive their shipments—a secretary, somebody's assistant, a Frogtown homegirl, say, and her boyfriend passes it along to Marchenko and Parsons to get cut in on the split."

"But they hit different banks."

"It only takes one inside job to have an insider, and then the Feeb and the cops are all over it. I'm just theorizing here, Holman, not jumping at conclusions. LAPD learns of a Frogtown connection, so they turn to the cops with Frogtown experience to develop or follow up leads—i.e., Fowler. That could explain how your son leaving his house to discuss Marchenko and Parsons with Fowler led to Warren Juarez."

Holman felt a flicker of hope.

"You think?"

"No, I don't think, but I want you to understand how little we know. When you're asking your daughter-in-law about Thursday night, pick up the case reports your son had—the stuff he got from the Detective Bureau. You gave me the cover sheets, but I want to see what was in the reports. That should tell us what he was interested in."

"Okay."

"We'll know more tomorrow when I start talking to people and read those reports. I could wrap this thing up with a couple more calls."

Holman was surprised.

"You think that's all it'll take?"

"No, but it seemed like a good thing to say."

Holman stared at her, then burst out laughing.

They came down through the Sepulveda Pass and into the darkening city. Holman watched Pollard maneuvering her car through the traffic.

He said, "Why do you drive so fast?"

"I have two little boys waiting for me at home. They're with my mother, the poor kids."

"What about your husband?"

"Let's keep the personal stuff out of this, Max."

Holman went back to watching the passing cars.

"One more thing—I know you said you didn't want me to pay you, but my offer is still there. I never expected you to go to all this trouble."

"If I asked you to pay, I'd be scared you would have

to rob another bank."

"I'd find another way. I'll never rob another bank."

Pollard glanced at him and Holman shrugged.

She said, "Can I ask you a question?"

"So long as it isn't personal."

Now Pollard laughed, but then her laugh faded.

"I put you away for ten years. How come you're not pissed off at me?"

Holman thought about it.

"You gave me a chance to change."

They rode in silence after that. The lights in the shadows were just beginning to twinkle.

20

PERRY WAS STILL at his desk when Holman let himself into the lobby. The old man's leathery face twitched and trembled, so Holman read that something was wrong.

Perry said, "Hey, I want to talk to you."

"You get your car back okay?"

Perry leaned forward, lacing and unlacing his fingers. His eyes were watery and nervous.

"Here's the money I charged you, the sixty bucks, those three days for the car. Here it is right here."

As Holman reached his desk, he saw the three twenties laid out face up, waiting for him. Perry unlaced his fingers and pushed the three bills toward him.

Holman said, "What's this?"

"The sixty you paid for my car. You can have it back."

Holman wondered what in hell Perry was doing with the money laid out like that, the three Jacksons staring up at him.

"You're giving back the money?"

"Yeah. Here it is. Take the goddamned money back."

Holman still didn't move for the money. He looked at Perry. The old man looked worried, but angry, too.

Holman said, "Why are you giving this back?"

"Those wetbacks said to give it back, so you tell'm I did."

"The guys who brought back your car?"

"When they come in here to give me the keys, those gangbanging motherfuckers. I was doing you a favor, man, renting out that car, I wasn't trying to rip you off. Those bastards said I should give back your cash else they'd fuck me up good, so here, you take it."

Holman stared at the money but didn't touch it.

"We had a deal, fair and square. You keep it."

"No, uh-uh, you gotta take it back. I don't want that kind of trouble in my house."

"That's your money, Perry. I'll straighten it out with those guys."

He would have to talk to Chee in the morning.

"I don't appreciate two hoodlums comin' in here like that."

"I didn't have anything to do with it. We had a deal, fair and square. I wouldn't send two goons to shake you down for sixty bucks."

"Well, I don't appreciate it, is all. I'm just telling you. If you thought I was ripping you off, you should've said so."

Holman knew the harm had been done. Perry didn't believe him and probably would always be afraid of him.

"Keep the money, Perry. I'm sorry this happened."

Holman left the sixty dollars on Perry's desk and went up to his room. The clunky old window unit had the place like a deep freeze. He looked at Richie's picture on the bureau, eight years old and smiling. He still had a bad feeling in his stomach that Pollard's pep talk hadn't been able to shake.

He turned off the air conditioner, then went downstairs again, hoping to catch Perry still at his desk.

Perry was locking the front door, but stopped when he saw Holman.

Perry said, "That sixty is still on the desk."

"Then put it in your goddamned pocket. I wouldn't have you shaken down. My son was a police officer. What would he think if I did something like that?"

"I guess he'd think it was pretty damned low."

"I guess he would. You keep that sixty. It's yours."

Holman went back upstairs and climbed into bed, telling himself that Richie sure as hell would think it was low, shaking an old man for sixty damned dollars.

But saying it didn't make it so, and sleep did not come.

Part Three

21

POLLARD HAD NEVER been good in the morning. Every morning for as long as she could remember—months, maybe years—she woke feeling depleted, and dreading the pain of beginning her day. She drank two cups of black coffee just to give herself a pulse.

But when Pollard woke that morning, she jumped her alarm by more than an hour and immediately went to the little desk she had shared with Marty. She had stayed up the night before until almost two, comparing numbers and call times between Fowler's and Richard Holman's phone bills, and searching the Internet for information about Marchenko and Parsons. She had reread and organized the material Holman had given her, but was frustrated by not having the complete LAPD reports. She hoped Holman would get them from his daughter-in-law soon. Pollard admired Holman's commitment to his son. She felt a sudden sense of satisfaction that she had spoken on his behalf to the Assistant U.S. Attorney all those years ago. Leeds had been pissed for a month and a couple of the more cynical agents had told her she was an asshole, but Pollard thought the guy had earned a break, and she felt even more strongly about it now. Holman had been a career criminal, but the evidence suggested he was basically a decent guy.

Pollard reviewed her notes from the night before, then set about drawing up a work plan for the day. She was still working on it when her oldest son, David, pushed at her arm. David was seven and looked like a miniature version of Marty.

"Mom! We're gonna be late for camp!"

Pollard glanced at her watch. It was ten before eight. The camp bus arrived at eight. She hadn't even made coffee or felt the time pass, and she had been working for more than an hour.

"Is your brother dressed?"

"He won't come out of the bathroom."

"*Lyle!* Get him dressed, David."

She pulled on a pair of jeans and a T-shirt, then slammed together two bologna sandwiches.

"David, is Lyle ready?"

"He won't get dressed!"

Lyle, who was six, shouted over his brother.

"I hate camp! They stick us with pins!"

Pollard heard the fax phone ring as she was packing the sandwiches into lunch-size paper bags. She ran back to the office bedroom to see the first page emerging. She smiled when she saw the FBI emblem cover page—April was delivering the goods.

Pollard ran back to the kitchen, topped off the sandwiches with two containers of fruit cocktail, two bags of Cheetos, and a couple of boxes of juice.

David pounded breathlessly in from the living room.

"Mom! I can hear the bus! They're gonna leave us!"

Everything had to be a drama.

Pollard sent David out to stop the bus, then forced a T-shirt over Lyle's head. She had Lyle and the lunches through the front door just as the bus rumbled to a stop.

Lyle said, "I miss Daddy."

Pollard looked down at him, all hurt eyes and knotted frown, then squatted so they would be the same height. She touched his cheek, and thought it was as soft as when he was newborn. Where David looked like his father, Lyle looked like her.

"I know you do, baby."

"I dreamed he got eaten by a monster."

"That must have been very scary. You should have come into bed with me."

"You kick and toss."

The bus driver beeped his horn. He had a schedule to keep.

Pollard said, "I miss him, too, little man. What are we going to do about that?"

It was a script they had played before.

"Keep him in our hearts?"

Pollard smiled and touched her youngest son's chest.

"Yeah. He's right here in your heart. Now let's get you on the bus."

The pebbles and grit on the driveway hurt Pollard's bare feet as she walked Lyle to the bus. She kissed her boys, saw them away, then hurried back to the house. She went directly back to work and skimmed through the fax. April had sent sixteen pages, including a witness list, interview summaries, and a case summation. The witness list contained names, addresses, and phone numbers, which was what Pollard wanted. Pollard was going to compare the numbers against the calls that appeared on Richard Holman's and Mike Fowler's phone bills. If Holman or Fowler were running their own investigation into Marchenko and Parsons, they would have called the witnesses. If so, Pollard would ask the witness what they talked about, and then Pollard would know.

She called her mother and arranged for her to stay with the boys when they got home from camp.

Her mother said, "Why are you spending so much time in the city all of a sudden? Did you take a job?"

She had always resented her mother's questions. Thirty-six years old, and her mother still questioned her.

"I have things to do. I'm busy."

"Doing what? Are you seeing a man?"

"You'll be here at one, right? You'll stay with the boys?"

"I hope you're seeing a man. You have to think of those boys."

"Goodbye, Mom."

"Go easy on the desserts, Katherine. Your bottom isn't as small as it used to be."

Pollard hung up and went back to her desk. She still hadn't made coffee, but she didn't take the time to make it now. She didn't need the coffee.

She sat down with her case plan, then paged through all the documents she had read and reread the night before. She studied the map of the crime scene that Holman had sketched, then compared it with the drawing that had appeared in the *Times*. The Feeb had taught her that all investigations begin at the crime scene, so she knew she would have to make the drive. She would have to see for herself. Alone there in her little house in the Simi Valley, Pollard broke into a smile.

She felt as if she was in the game again.

She was back in the hunt.

22

PERRY WASN'T at his desk when Holman came downstairs that morning. Holman was relieved. He wanted to pick up the reports from Liz before she left for class and didn't want to get bogged down in another argument with Perry.

But when Holman stepped outside to go to his car, Perry was hosing off the sidewalk.

Perry said, "You got a call yesterday I forgot to tell you about. Guess it slipped my mind, having to fight off your thugs."

"What is it, Perry?"

"Tony Gilbert over at that sign company. Said he's your boss and wants you to call."

"Okay, thanks. When did he call?"

"During the day, I guess. Good thing it wasn't while those gangbanging fucks were putting the arm on me else I would've missed the message."

"Perry, look—I didn't tell those guys to do that. All they were supposed to do was bring back the car and give you the keys. That's it. I already apologized."

"Gilbert sounded pissed off, you ask me. I'd call

him. And since you have a job, you might consider fronting the cash for an answering machine. My memory isn't what it used to be."

Holman started to say something, then thought better of it and went around the side of the motel to his car. He didn't want to start his day with Gilbert, either, but he hadn't been to work in a week and didn't want to lose the job. Holman climbed into his Highlander to make the call and was pleased he could bring up Gilbert's number on his phone's memory without having to refer to the owner's manual. It felt like a step into real life.

As soon as Gilbert came on the line, Holman knew his patience was wearing thin.

He said, "Are you coming back to work or not? I need to know."

"I'm coming back. I've just had a lot to deal with."

"Max, I'm trying to be a good guy here, what with your son and all, but what in hell are you doing? The police were here."

Holman was so surprised he didn't respond.

"Max?"

"I'm here. What did the police want?"

"You just got out, man. Are you going to wash ten years down the drain?"

"I'm not washing anything down the drain. Why were the police there?"

"They wanted to know if you'd been coming to work and what kind of people you've been associating with, like that. They asked whether or not you've been using."

"I haven't been using. What are you talking about?"

"Well, they asked, and they asked if I knew how you

were supporting yourself without working. What am I supposed to think? Hey, listen, my friend, I'm trying to run a business here and you disappeared. I told'm I gave you some time off for your son, but now I gotta wonder. It's been a week."

"Who was it asking about me?"

"Some detectives."

"Did Gail send them?"

"They weren't from the Bureau of Prisons. These were cops. Now listen, are you coming back to work or not?"

"I just need a few more days—"

"Ah, hell."

Gilbert hung up.

Holman closed his phone, feeling a dull ache in his stomach. He had expected Gilbert to bitch him out for missing so much work, but he hadn't expected the police. He decided the cops were following up his visit to Maria Juarez, but he also worried that someone had put him together with Chee. He didn't want to bring any heat down on Chee, mostly because he wasn't sure Chee was completely straight.

Holman considered calling Gail Manelli about the police, but he was worried about missing Liz, so he put away his phone and headed for Westwood. As he turned out of the parking lot, he saw Perry still on the sidewalk, watching him. Perry waited until Holman had driven past, then flipped him off. Holman saw it in the mirror.

When Holman drew closer to Westwood, he called Liz to let her know he was coming.

When she answered, he said, "Hey, Liz, it's Max. I need to stop by to see you for a few minutes. Can I bring you a coffee?"

"I'm on my way out."

"This is kind of important. It's about Richie."

She hesitated, and when she spoke again her voice was cold.

"Why are you doing this?"

"Doing what? I just need to—"

"I don't want to see you anymore. Please stop bothering me."

She hung up.

Holman was left sitting in traffic with his dead phone. He called back, but this time her message machine picked up.

"Liz? Maybe I should've called earlier, okay? I didn't mean to be rude. Liz? Can you hear me?"

If she was listening she didn't pick up, so Max ended the call. He was only five blocks from Veteran Avenue by then, so he continued on to Liz's apartment. He didn't take the time to find a parking spot, but left his car in a red zone by a fire hydrant. If he got a ticket he'd just pay Chee back with his own money.

The usual morning rush of students on their way to class meant Holman didn't have long to wait before he could get inside the building. He took the stairs two at a time, but slowed when he reached her apartment, catching his breath before he knocked.

"Liz? Please tell me what's wrong."

He knocked softly again.

"Liz? This is important. Please, it's for Richie."

Holman waited.

"Liz? Can I come in, please?"

She finally opened the door. Her face was tight and pinched, and she was already dressed for the day. Her eyes were hard with a brittle tension.

Holman didn't move. He stood with his hands at his sides, confused by her hostility.

He said, "Did I do something?"

"Whatever you're doing, I want no part of it."

Holman kept his voice calm.

"What do you think I'm doing? I'm not doing anything, Liz. I just want to know what happened to my son."

"The police were here. They cleaned out Richard's desk. They took all his things and they questioned me about *you*. They wanted to know what you were doing."

"Who did? Levy?"

"No, not Levy—Detective Random. He wanted to know what you were asking about and said I should be careful around you. They warned me not to let you in."

Holman wasn't sure how to respond. He took a step away from her and spoke carefully.

"I've been inside with you, Liz. Do you think I would hurt you? You're my son's wife."

Her eyes softened and she shook her head.

She said, "Why did they come here?"

"There was someone with Random?"

"I don't remember his name. Red hair."

Vukovich.

She said, "Why did they come?"

"I don't know. What did they tell you?"

"They didn't tell me anything. They said they were investigating you. They wanted to know—"

The apartment next door opened and two men came out. They were young, both wearing glasses and book bags over their shoulders. Holman and Liz stood quietly as they passed.

When the two men were gone, Liz said, "I guess you can come in. This is silly."

Holman stepped inside and waited as she closed the door.

Holman said, "Are you all right?"

"They asked if you said anything to indicate you were involved in criminal activity. I didn't know what in hell they were talking about. What would you say to me: Hey, you know any good banks to rob?"

Holman thought about describing his conversation with Tony Gilbert, but decided against it.

"You said they took things from his desk? Can I see?"

She brought him to their shared office, and Holman looked at Richie's desk. The newspaper clippings still hung from the corkboard, but Holman could tell the items on Richie's desk had been moved. Holman had been through everything himself and remembered how he had left it. The LAPD reports and documents were gone.

She said, "I don't know what they took."

"Some reports, it looks like. Did they say why?"

"They just said it was important. They wanted to know if you had been in here. I told them the truth."

Holman wished she hadn't, but nodded.

"That's okay. It doesn't matter."

"Why would they go through his things?"

Holman wanted to change the subject. The reports were gone now, and he wished he had read them when he had the chance.

He said, "Did Richie go out with Fowler the Thursday

before they were killed? It would have been at night, late."

Her brow furrowed as she tried to remember.

"I'm not sure . . . Thursday? I think Rich worked that night."

"Did he come home dirty? Fowler went out that night and came home with his boots caked with dirt and weeds. It would have been late."

She thought more, then slowly shook her head.

"No, I—wait, yes, it was Friday morning I took the car. There was grass and dirt on the driver's-side floor. Richie had the shift Thursday night. He said he had chased somebody."

Her eyes suddenly took on the hardness again.

"What were they doing?"

"I don't know. Didn't Richie tell you?"

"He was on duty."

"Did Richie ever say that Marchenko and Parsons were connected with any Latin gangs?"

"I don't think so. I don't remember."

"Frogtown? Juarez was a member of the Frogtown gang."

"What did Juarez have to do with Marchenko and Parsons?"

"I don't know, but I'm trying to find out."

"Waitaminute. I thought Juarez killed them because of Mike—because Mike killed his brother."

"That's what the police are saying."

She crossed her arms, and Holman thought she looked worried.

She said, "You don't believe it?"

"I gotta ask you something else. In all this time when he was telling you about Marchenko and Parsons, did he ever tell you exactly what he was doing?"

"Just . . . that he was working on the case."

"What case? They were dead."

A lost and hopeless cast came to her eyes, and Holman could see she didn't remember. She finally shook her head, holding her arms even tighter.

"An investigation. I don't know."

"Trying to find an accomplice, maybe?"

"I don't know."

"Did he mention missing money?"

"What money?"

Holman studied her, and part of him wanted to explain, thinking that maybe it would trigger some memory in her that would help him, but he knew he was done. He didn't want to bring this part of it to her. He didn't want to leave her thinking about the money and wondering whether her husband was working as a cop in an investigation or was trying to find the missing cash for himself.

"It's nothing. Listen, I don't know what Random was talking about, all that stuff about investigating me. I haven't done anything illegal and I'm not going to do anything, you understand? I wouldn't do that to you and to Richie. I couldn't."

She stared up at him for a moment, and then she nodded.

"I know. I know what you're doing."

"Then you know a helluva lot more than me."

She raised on her toes to kiss his cheek.

"You're trying to take care of your little boy."

Richie's wife hugged him long and tight, and Holman was glad for it, but he cursed himself for being too late.

23

HOLMAN WAS FURIOUS as he crossed the street, heading back to his car. He was pissed that Random had questioned Liz about him and implied he was involved in some kind of criminal activity. Holman now assumed Random was the cop who got him in trouble with Tony Gilbert, but he was even more furious that Random warned Liz not to trust him. Random had jeopardized his only remaining connection to Richie, and Holman didn't know why. He didn't believe Random was harassing him, which meant that Random suspected him of something. He wanted to drive to Parker Center to confront the sonofabitch, but by the time he reached the Highlander he knew this would be a bad idea. He needed a better idea of what Random was thinking before he called him on it.

After the lousy start to his morning, Holman expected to find a ticket waiting under the Highlander's windshield wiper, but the windshield was clean. He hoped he hadn't used up his good luck for the day by ducking a lousy parking ticket.

Holman got into his car, started the engine, and

spent a few minutes thinking through the rest of his day. He had a lot to do and couldn't allow an asshole like Random to move him off track. He wanted to call Pollard, but it was still on the early side and he didn't know what time she woke. She said something about having kids, so the mornings were probably rough—getting the kids up and fed, getting them dressed and ready for their day. All the stuff Holman had missed out on with Richie. It was an inevitable thread of regret that left Holman in a funk whenever he made the mistake of following it. He decided to call Chee about Perry. Chee probably thought he was doing Holman a favor, but Holman didn't need that kind of help. Now he would have to deal with Perry's resentment on top of everything else.

Holman found Chee's number in the memory, and was listening to Chee's line ring when a grey car slid up fast beside him, blocking him against the curb. Holman saw the doors open as Chee answered—

"Hello?"

"Hang on—"

"Homes?"

Random and his driver stepped out of the gray car as Holman caught a flash of movement from the curb. Vukovich and another man were stepping off the sidewalk, one from the front and one from the back. They were holding pistols down along their legs. Chee's tinny voice squawked from the phone—

"Holman, is that you?"

"Don't hang up. The cops are coming—"

Holman let the phone slip to the seat and put both hands on the steering wheel, motionless and in plain sight. Chee's voice was an electronic squeak.

"Homes?"

Random pulled open the door, then stepped aside. His driver was shorter than Holman but as wide as a bed. He jerked Holman out from behind the wheel and shoved him face-first against the Highlander.

"Don't fucking move."

Holman didn't resist. The short guy patted him down while Random leaned into the car. Random turned off the ignition, then backed out of the car with Holman's phone. He held it to his ear, listened, then closed the phone and tossed it back into the car.

Random said, "Nice phone."

"What are you doing? Why are you doing this?"

"Nice car, too. Where'd you get a car like this? You steal it?"

"I rented it."

The short guy shoved Holman harder against the car.

"Keep your face planted."

"It's hot."

"Too fucking bad."

Random said, "Vuke, run the car. You can't rent a car without a driver's license and a credit card. I think he stole it."

Holman said, "I got a driver's license, goddamnit. It came yesterday. The rental papers are in the glove box."

Vukovich opened the far passenger door to check the glove box as the short guy pulled Holman's wallet.

Holman said, "This is bullshit. Why are you doing this?"

Random pulled Holman around so they were facing each other while the short guy brought the wallet to his car and went to work on their computer. Three students stopped on the sidewalk, but Random didn't seem concerned. His eyes were dark knots focused on Holman.

"You don't think Jacki Fowler is suffering enough?"

"What are you talking about? So I went to see her? So what?"

"Here's a widow with four boys and a dead husband, but you had to invade her privacy. Why would you want to upset a woman like that, Holman? What do you expect to gain?"

"I'm trying to find out what happened to my son."

"I told you what happened when I told you to let me do my job."

"I don't think you're doing your job. I don't know what in fuck you're doing. Why did you go to my boss? What the fuck is that, asking if he thinks I'm on drugs?"

"You're a drug addict."

"Was. *Was.*"

"Drug addicts always want more, and I'm thinking that's why you're leaning on the families. You're looking to score. Even from your own daughter-in-law."

"*Was!* Fuck you, motherfucker."

Holman fought hard for his self-control.

"That's my son's wife, you sonofabitch. Now it's me telling you to stay away from her. You goddamn leave her alone."

Random stepped closer and Holman knew he was being provoked. Random wanted him to swing. Random wanted to take him inside.

"You don't have a right to tell me anything. You were nothing to your son, so don't give yourself airs. You didn't even meet the girl until last week, so don't pretend she's your family."

Holman felt a deep throbbing in his temples. His vision grayed at the edges as the throbbing grew. Random floated in front of him like a target, but Holman told himself no. Why did Random want him inside? Why did Random want him out of the way?

Holman said, "What was in those reports you took?"

Random's jaw flexed, but he didn't answer, and Holman knew the reports were important.

"My daughter-in-law claims you took something that belonged to my son from her house. Did you have a warrant, Random? Did it list what you went there to find or were you grabbing whatever you wanted? That sounds like theft, if you had no warrant."

Random was still staring when Vukovich backed out of the car with the rental papers. He held them out to show Random.

"He's got a rental agreement here in his name. Looks legit."

Holman said, "It is legit, Detective, just like your warrant. Call'm and see."

Random studied the papers.

"Quality Motors of Los Angeles. You ever heard of Quality Motors?"

Vukovich shrugged as Random called over his shoulder.

"Teddy? You get the plate?"

The short guy was Teddy. Teddy returned and handed Holman's license and wallet to Random.

"Vehicle registered to Quality Motors, no wants, warrants, or citations. His DL shows good, too."

Random glanced at the driver's license, then Holman.

"Where'd you get this?"

"The Department of Motor Vehicles. Where did you get your warrant?"

Random put the license back in Holman's wallet but held on to it along with the rental papers. Random had backed off, and now Holman knew the reports were important. Random wasn't pressing because he didn't want Holman to make a stink about the reports.

Random said, "I want to make sure you understand the situation, Holman. I asked you one time nice. This is me telling you a second time. I'm not going to let you make it more difficult for these families. Stay away from them."

"I'm one of those families."

Something like a smile played at Random's lips. He stepped closer and whispered.

"Which family? Frogtown?"

"Juarez was Frogtown. I don't know what you're talking about."

"You like White Fence any better?"

Holman kept his face empty.

"How's your friend Gary Moreno—L'Chee?"

"I haven't seen him in years. Maybe I'll look him up."

Random tossed Holman's wallet and rental papers into the Highlander.

"You're fucking me up, Holman, and I cannot tolerate that and will not allow it. I will not allow it for the four men who died. And I will not allow it for their families in which, as we all know, you are not included."

"Can I go now?"

"You claim you want answers, but you have made it harder for me to find those answers, and I take that personally."

"I thought you knew the answers."

"Most of the answers, Holman. Most. But now because of you an important door just closed in my face and I don't know if I'll be able to open it again."

"What are you talking about?"

"Maria Juarez disappeared. She split, man. She could have told us how Warren put it together, but now she's gone and that one is on you. So if you feel like undercutting me with your daughter-in-law again, you get the urge to make these families doubt what we're doing and keep their grief fresh, you explain to them how you delayed the case by being an asshole. Are we clear?"

Holman did not respond.

"Don't try my patience, boy. This isn't a fucking game."

Random went back to his car. Vukovich and the other guy vanished. The grey car pulled away. The three kids on the sidewalk were gone. Holman climbed back into the Highlander and picked up his phone. He listened, but the line was dead. He got out again, went around to the passenger side, and felt under the seat. He checked the floorboards and glove box and panel pocket in the door, then checked the rear floors and back seats, too, worried that they had planted something in his car.

Holman didn't believe Random's false concern for the families or even that Random believed he was looking to score. Holman had been fronted and leaned on by a hundred cops, and he sensed something deeper was at play. Random wanted him out of the way, but Holman didn't know why.

24

POLLARD WAS ON her way downtown to check out the crime scene. She had picked up the Hollywood Freeway and dropped down into the belly of the city when April Sanders called.

Sanders said, "Hey. You get the faxes okay?"

"I was going to call you to say thanks, girl. You really came through."

"Hope you still think so after I tell you the rest. LAPD froze me out. I can't get their file."

"You're kidding! They must have something in play."

Pollard was surprised. The Feeb's Bank Squad and the LAPD's Bank Robbery team worked together so often on the same cases they shared information freely.

April said, "I don't know why they wouldn't come across. I asked the putz—you remember George Hines?"

"No."

"Probably came on after you left. Anyway, I said, what gives with that, I thought we were butt buddies, what happened to agency cooperation?"

"What did he say?"

"He said they didn't have the case anymore."

"How could they not have the case anymore? They're the Robbery bank team."

"What I said. After they closed the file someone upstairs pulled the whole damned thing. I'm like, *who* upstairs, the chief, God? He said it wasn't their case anymore and that's all he could tell me."

"How could it not be Robbery's case? It was a *robbery*."

"If those guys knew what they were doing they would be *us*, not them. I don't know what to tell you."

Pollard drove for a few seconds, thinking.

"But he said the case was closed?"

"Those were his words. Shit—gotta run. Leeds—"

The line went dead in Pollard's ear. If LAPD had closed the book on Marchenko and Parsons, it increased the odds that Richard Holman had been involved with Fowler and the others in something off the books. It was bad news for Holman, but Pollard already had bad news to share—April's witness list had included the names and numbers of thirty-two people who had been interviewed by the FBI in the matter of Marchenko and Parsons. Marchenko's mother, Leyla, had been among them. Pollard had checked the thirty-two telephone numbers against the outgoing numbers appearing on both Richard Holman's and Mike Fowler's phone records and come up with a hit. Fowler had phoned Marchenko's mother twice. It was highly unlikely that a uniformed field supervisor would have a legitimate reason to contact a witness, so Pollard now felt sure Fowler had been conducting some kind of rogue investigation. Fowler's contact indicated

Holman's son was almost certainly involved in something inappropriate or illegal. Pollard didn't look forward to telling Holman. She found his need to believe in his son moving.

Pollard dropped off the Hollywood Freeway at Alameda, then cruised south down Alameda parallel with the river. When she reached Fourth Street, she used the Fourth Street Bridge to cross over to the eastern side of the river. The east side was thick with warehouses and train yards and congested with eighteen-wheel cargo trucks. Pollard had been to the river only twice before, once as part of a task force targeting the importation of Iranian drugs and the other as part of a task force tracking a pedophile who brought children from Mexico and Thailand. Pollard had arrived on the scene in the drug case after the body had already been found, but she hadn't been so lucky in the pedophile case. Pollard had discovered the bodies of three small children in a container car, one boy and two girls, and she had not slept after that for weeks. It wasn't lost on Pollard that here she was again, drawn back to the river by death. The Los Angeles River left her feeling creeped out and queasy. Maybe more now because she knew she might break the law.

Pollard was a cop; even though she had left the Feeb eight years ago, she still felt like part of the law enforcement community. She had married a cop, most of her friends were cops, and, like almost every cop she knew, she didn't want to get in trouble with other cops. The L.A. River was a restricted area. Jumping the fence to check out the crime scene would be a misdemeanor offense, but Pollard knew she had to see if Holman's description held up. She had to see for herself.

Pollard drove along Mission Road, following the fence past trucks and workmen until she found the service gate. She parked beside the fence, locked her car, then went to the gate. A dry breeze came out of the east that smelled of kerosene. Pollard was wearing jeans and Nikes and had a pair of Marty's work gloves in case she had to climb. The gate was locked and had been secured with a secondary chain, which she had expected. She also expected that security patrols along the gates had been increased, but so far she hadn't seen anyone. Pollard had hoped she could see the scene well enough from above, but as soon as she reached the gate she knew she would have to climb.

The riverbed was a wide concrete plain cut by a trough and bordered by paved banks that were crowned with fences and barbed wire. She could see the Fourth Street Bridge from the gate, but not well enough to envision the crime scene in her head. Cars crossed the bridge in both directions and pedestrians moved on the sidewalks. The bright morning sun painted a sharp shadow beneath the bridge, cutting across the river. Pollard thought everything about the scene was ugly and industrial—the nasty concrete channel with its lack of life; the muddy trickle of water that looked like a sewer; the weeds sprouting hopelessly from cracks in the concrete. It looked like a bad place to die, and an even worse place for an ex-FBI agent to be arrested for unauthorized entry.

Pollard was pulling on her gloves when a white pickup truck drove out from one of the loading docks and beeped its horn. Pollard thought it was a security patrol, but when the truck drew close she saw it belonged to one of the shipping companies. The driver braked to a stop by the gate. He was a middle-aged man with short grey hair and a fleshy neck.

"Just letting you know. You're not supposed to be here."

"I know. I'm with the FBI."

"I'm just telling you. We had some murders down here."

"That's why I'm here. Thanks."

"They have security patrols."

"Thanks."

Pollard wished he would get the hell on with his business and leave her alone, but he didn't move.

"You have some identification or something?"

Pollard put her gloves away and walked over to the truck, staring at him the way she had stared at criminals she was about to handcuff.

"You have some authority to ask?"

"Well, I work over there and they asked us to keep an eye out. I don't mean anything by it."

Pollard pulled out her wallet, but didn't open it. She had turned in her badge and FBI commission card—which agents called their creds—when she left the Feeb, but her wallet had been a gift from Marty. He had purchased it at the FBI gift shop in Quantico because it was emblazoned with the FBI seal. Pollard kept her hard stare on the driver as she tapped her wallet, making no move to open it but letting him see the red, white, and blue seal.

"We got a report someone down here was taking tourists on tours of the crime scene. Tourists, for Christ's sake. You know anything about that?"

"I never heard anything like that."

Pollard studied him as if she suspected him of the crime.

"We heard it was someone in a white truck."

The fleshy neck quivered and the man shook his head.

"Well, we got a million white trucks down here. I don't know anything about it."

Pollard studied him as if she was making a life-or-death decision, then slipped her wallet back into her jeans.

"If you want to keep your eye out for something, watch for the white truck."

"Yes, ma'am."

"One more thing. Are you down here at night or just during the day?"

"The day."

"Okay then, forget it. You're doing a good job keeping an eye on things. Now move on and let me do my job."

Pollard waited as he drove away, then turned back to the gate. She climbed the gate without much difficulty, then walked down the service drive. Entering the riverbed was like lowering herself into a trench. Concrete walls rose around her, cutting off the city from view, and soon all she could see were the tops of a few downtown skyscrapers.

The smooth flat channel stretched in both directions and the air was still. The kerosene breeze couldn't reach her down here. Pollard could see the Sixth Street and Seventh Street bridges to the south, and the First Street Bridge beyond the Fourth Street Bridge to the north. The channel walls in this part of the river were twenty-foot verticals topped by the fence. They reminded Pollard of a maximum security prison and their purpose was the same. The walls were designed to contain the river during the rainy season. During the rains, the normally pathetic trickle would quickly overflow its trough and climb the higher walls like a raging beast, devouring everything in its path. Pollard knew that once she left the safety of the service ramp, the walls would become her prison, too. If a rush of water surged through the channel, she would have no way out. If a police car rolled up to the fence, she would have no place to hide.

Pollard made her way to the bridge and stepped out of the sun into the shade. It was cooler. Pollard had brought the *Times*'s drawing of the crime scene and Holman's sketch, but she didn't need them to see where the bodies had lain. Four shining irregular shapes were visible on the concrete beneath the bridge, each shape brighter and cleaner than the surrounding pavement. It was always this way. After the bodies had been removed and the crime scene cleared by the police, a hazmat crew had disinfected the area. Pollard had once seen them work. Blood was soaked up with absorbent granules, then vacuumed into special containers to remove all human tissue. Contaminated areas were sprayed with disinfectant, then scoured with high-pressure steam. Now, more than a week later, the ground where each man died glowed like a shimmering ghost. Pollard wondered if Holman had known what they were. She did not step on the clean places; she carefully stepped around them.

Pollard stood between the body shapes and considered the service ramp. It was about eighty yards away and sloped directly toward her. Pollard had an uninterrupted view of the ramp, but she knew this was in broad daylight with no cars parked in the area. Perspectives often changed in the darkness.

No marks remained to locate the positions of the cars, so Pollard opened the map that appeared in the *Times*. The three cars were pictured under the bridge in a loose triangle between the east columns and the river, with the car at the top of the triangle extending past the north side of the bridge. The car at the left base of the triangle was completely under the bridge, with the last car angled across its rear and a little bit to the east to form the right base. The bodies in the drawing were located relative to the cars and columns and were labeled by name.

Mellon and Ash had been together at the back of Ash's radio car, which was the car at the top of the triangle. A six-pack carton of Tecate had been found on their trunk with four of the bottles missing. Fowler's car was the left base of the triangle; completely under the bridge and nearest the river. His body was shown near the right front fender. Richard Holman's car formed the right base of the triangle, with his body midway between his car and Fowler. Pollard decided that Mellon and Ash had arrived first, which was why they had parked at the north side of the bridge, leaving room for the others. Fowler had probably arrived second and Holman last.

Pollard folded the map and put it away. She studied the four steam-blasted spots on the concrete, no longer drawings on a page but the fading residue of four lives—Mellon and Ash together and Richard Holman nearest the column. Pollard was standing next to Fowler. She moved away and tried to picture their cars and how they were standing at the moment they were shot. If the four men were talking, both Fowler and Holman would have had their backs turned to the ramp. Fowler had probably been perched on his right front fender. Holman might have been leaning against his car, but Pollard couldn't know. Either way, they were facing away from the ramp and wouldn't have seen someone approaching. The shooter had come from behind.

Pollard moved to stand with Mellon and Ash. She positioned herself where their car had been parked. They had been facing south toward Fowler. Pollard imagined herself leaning against their car, having a beer. Mellon and Ash had a clear view of the ramp.

Pollard moved away to circle the columns. She wanted to see if there was another way down to the north, but the walls were hard verticals all the way to the Fourth Street Bridge and beyond. She was still searching to the north when she heard the gate clatter like the rattle of chains. She walked back under the bridge and saw Holman coming down the ramp. Pollard was surprised. She hadn't told him she was coming to the bridge and hadn't expected him to appear. She was wondering what he was doing here when she realized she had heard the gate. Then she heard the scruffing his shoes were making on the gritty concrete surface. He was half a football field away, but she heard him walking, and then she knew why. The towering walls trapped sound just like they trapped water and channeled it like the river.

Pollard watched him approach, but didn't say anything until he arrived, and then she gave him her expert opinion.

"You were right, Holman. They would have heard him coming just like I heard you. They knew the person who killed them."

Holman glanced back at the ramp.

"Once you're down here there's no other way to see it. And at night it's even more quiet than this."

Pollard crossed her arms and felt sick. That was the problem—there was no other way to see it, but the police claimed they saw it another way.

25

POLLARD WAS still trying to decide what this meant when Holman interrupted her. He seemed nervous.

"Listen, we shouldn't spend too much time down here. Those guys at the loading docks might call the police."

"How'd you know I would be here?"

"Didn't. I was up on the bridge when you came down the ramp. I saw you jump the fence."

"You just happened to be up there?"

"I've come here a dozen times since it happened. C'mon, let's go back up. I was going to call you—"

Pollard didn't want to go back to the gate; she wanted to figure out why the police had overlooked such an obvious flaw in their case, and was thinking about something Holman had said.

"Waitaminute, Holman. Have you been here at night?"

Holman stopped in the edge of the bridge's shadow, split in two by the light.

"Yeah. Two or three times."

"How's the light at that time of night?"

"They had a three-quarter moon with scattered clouds on the night they were killed. I checked the weather report. You could've read a newspaper down here."

He turned back toward the gate again.

"We better leave. You could get arrested, being down here."

"So could you."

"I've been arrested before. You won't like it."

"Holman, if you want to wait up at the gate, go on. I'm trying to figure out what happened down here."

Holman didn't leave, but it was obvious he wasn't happy about staying. Pollard circled the murder scene, trying to picture the cars and the officers on the night they were killed. She changed their positions like mannequins in a store window, turning each time to stare at the ramp. She rearranged the cars in her mind's eye, thinking maybe she had missed some obvious explanation.

Holman said, "What are you trying to figure out?"

"I'm trying to see if there was some way they wouldn't have seen him."

"They saw him. You just told me they saw him."

Pollard went to the edge of the channel and peered at the water. The channel was a rectangular trough about two feet deep with a sickly trickle along its bottom. The shooter could have hidden down here or maybe behind one of the columns, but only if he had known when and where to expect the four officers, and both possibilities were absurd. Pollard knew she was reaching. The primary rule of an investigation was that the simplest explanation was the most likely. It was no more likely the shooter had lain in wait than he had jumped down from the bridge like a ninja.

Holman said, "Did you hear me?"

"I'm thinking."

"You need to listen. I went to see Liz this morning to get the reports, but the police got to her first. They cleaned out Richie's desk. They took the reports."

Pollard turned away from the channel, surprised.

"How did they know she had the reports?"

"I don't know if they went for the reports, but they knew she's been helping me. They made it sound like they had to search his things because I had been there—like they wanted to see what I was up to. Maybe that's when they saw the reports."

"Who?"

"That detective I told you about, Random."

"Random's the homicide detective running the task force?"

"That's right. When I was leaving, Random and three other guys jumped me. They told me Maria Juarez split and they're blaming me for it, but I don't think that's why they jumped me. They knew we went to see Mike Fowler's wife and they didn't like it. They didn't mention you, but they knew about me."

Pollard didn't give a damn if they knew about her or not, but she wondered why a homicide detective had taken robbery reports about Marchenko and Parsons. The same reports April told her were no longer available from Robbery Special because they had been pulled upstairs.

Pollard figured she knew the answer but asked anyway.

"Did you have a chance to speak with Mellon's and Ash's families?"

"I called after I left Liz, but they wouldn't speak to me. Random had already seen them. He told me not to bother Liz anymore. Richie's wife, and he warned me to stay away from her."

Pollard then circled the crime scene again, shaking her head, careful not to step on the clean places where the bodies had dropped. She was glad Holman hadn't asked her about them.

She said, "I want to see what's in those reports."

"They took them."

"That's why I want to see what's in them. What did she say about Thursday night?"

Pollard circled back to her starting point, and realized Holman hadn't answered.

"Did you remember to ask her about Thursday?"

"The floorboard of his car was messy with dirt and grass, she said."

"So Richard was out with Fowler."

"I guess. You think they were down here?"

Pollard had already considered the river and discounted it.

"There's no grass and damned little mud, Holman. Even if they jumped down in the water and waded around, they wouldn't pick up mud and weeds like we saw on Fowler's boots."

Pollard stared at the ramp again, then Holman. Where he was standing, he was perfectly split by the bridge's shadow, half in light, half in darkness.

"Holman, you and I aren't Sherlock-fucking-Holmes. Here we are in the kill zone, and it's obvious the shooter could not have approached without being seen. He wasn't hiding down here and he did not lay in wait—he walked down that ramp, came over here, and

222

shot them. This is freshman detective work. Fowler, your son, Mellon, and Ash—they let him get close."

"I know."

"That's the point. You and I aren't the only two people who would see this. The cops who came down here would have seen it, too. They would know Juarez could not have ambushed these guys, but all their statements in the press claimed that's how it happened. So either they're ignoring the obvious or they're lying about it or there is some mitigating factor that explains it, but I don't see what that might be."

Holman stepped back into the shade and was no longer split by the light.

"I understand."

Pollard wasn't sure he did. If a mitigating factor didn't exist, then the police had been lying about what happened down here. Pollard didn't want to let herself believe it until she had seen the reports. She still held out hope that something in the papers would make it all right.

She said, "Okay, here's where we are. I went through the witness list from the Marchenko case and checked the witnesses against the calls your son and Fowler made. Here's the bad news—Fowler called Marchenko's mother two times."

"That means they were investigating the robberies."

"It means they were investigating the robberies. It doesn't tell us whether or not they were doing it in an official capacity or doing it for themselves. We should talk to this woman and find out what Fowler wanted."

Holman seemed to think about it, then looked away.

"Maybe tomorrow. I can't do it today."

Pollard checked her watch and felt a tick of irritation. Here she was, humiliating herself with her mother to help out Holman, and he couldn't put himself out.

She said, "You know, I don't have all the time in the world for this, Holman. I'm set up to help you today, so today would be a good day to do this."

Holman's mouth tightened and he turned red. He started to say something, then glanced at the ramp before turning back to her again. She thought he looked embarrassed.

He said, "You're really going above and beyond. I appreciate this—"

"Then let's go see her."

"I gotta go see my boss. I haven't been to work in a week, and the guy reamed me out today. He's been really good to me, too, but Random went to see him. I can't lose this job, Agent Pollard. I lose the job, and I'm fucked with my release."

Pollard watched Holman squirming, and felt terrible she had pressed him. She also wondered again why Random was coming down so hard on a poor bastard who had just lost his son. She checked her watch again, then felt like an idiot for being such a slave to the clock.

"Okay, we can go see Marchenko's mother tomorrow. I know a man who might be able to help get the reports. I guess I could do that today."

Holman looked back at the ramp.

"We should go. I don't want you to get in trouble."

Neither spoke as they walked back, but their footsteps were loud in the silence. With every step, Pollard grew more convinced that the investigation into the murder of the four officers was bad, and she wanted to find out the truth.

Pollard thought about Detective Random. He was pulling the shades on Holman's sources of information, which was never a smart move for an officer to make. Pollard had dealt with dozens of journalists and overanxious family members during her own investigations, and shutting them out had always been the worst thing to do—they always dug harder. Pollard felt Random would know this, too, but wanted to protect something so badly he was willing to take the risk.

It was a dangerous risk to take. Pollard wanted to know what he was protecting and she would keep digging to find it.

26

POLLARD LEFT Holman at the river, but didn't drive far. She crossed back over the bridge, then followed Alameda north into Chinatown to a tall glass building where Pacific West Bank kept their corporate headquarters. Pollard believed she had only one possible way to see the reports Random had confiscated from Richard Holman's apartment, and that was through Pacific West Bank—if she could pull it off.

Pollard no longer had their phone number, so she called information and was connected with a Pacific West receptionist.

Pollard said, "Is Peter Williams still with the company?"

It had been nine years, and she hoped he would remember her.

"Yes, ma'am. Would you like his office?"

"Yes, please."

A second voice came on the line.

"Mr. Williams' office."

"Is he available for Katherine Pollard? Special Agent Pollard of the FBI."

"Hold, please, and I'll see."

Pollard's most dramatic bust during her time with the Bank Squad was taking down the Front Line Bandits, a team of four Ukranians who were later identified as Craig and Jamison Bepko, their cousin Vartan Bepko, and an associate named Vlad Stepankutza. Leeds tagged the Front Line with their name because of their size; Varton Bepko, the lightest, weighed in at two hundred sixty-four pounds; Stepankutza tipped the scales at an even two-eighty; and brothers Craig and Jamison clocked in at three hundred sixteen and three hundred eighteen pounds respectively. The Front Line hit sixteen branches of Pacific West Bank over a two-week period, and almost put Pacific West out of business.

The Front Line foursome were one-on-one bandits who operated as a team. They entered a bank together, joined the teller line, then intimidated other customers into dropping out of the line. They approached the available tellers en masse to fill the bank counter with a wall of flesh, then made their demands. The Front Line didn't whisper or pass notes like most one-on-one bandits; they shouted, cursed, and often grabbed tellers by the arm or punched them, apparently not caring that everyone now knew the bank was being robbed. Each man stole only the money of his particular teller, and they never attempted to rob the vault. Once they had the money, they fled as a group, punching and kicking customers and bank employees out of their way. The Front Line Bandits robbed four Pacific West branches on their first day in business. Three days later, they robbed three more branches. It went on like that for two weeks, a reign of nightly-news terror that became a public-relations nightmare for Pacific West Bank, a small regional chain with only forty-two branches.

Leeds assigned the case to Pollard after the first group of robberies. By the end of the second group of robberies, Pollard had a good fix on how she would identify the bandits and solve the case. First, they were only hitting branches of Pacific West Bank. This indicated a connection to Pacific West, and most likely some kind of grudge—they weren't just stealing money; they were trying to hurt Pacific West. Second, Pacific West tellers were trained to slip explosive dye packs disguised as cash in with the regular money. The Front Line Bandits successfully recognized and discarded these dye packs before leaving the teller windows. Third, once the Front Line Bandits reached the tellers and demanded the money, they never stayed in a bank longer than two minutes. Pollard was convinced a knowledgeable employee of Pacific West had taught these guys about the dye packs and the Two Minute Rule. Because of the grudge factor, Pollard began screening the bank for disgruntled employees. On the morning of the day the Front Line Bandits committed robberies fifteen and sixteen, Pollard and April Sanders questioned one Kanka Dubrov, a middle-aged woman who had recently been fired as an assistant manager from a Glendale branch of Pacific West. Pollard and Sanders didn't have to resort to torture or truth serum; the moment they flashed their creds and told Ms. Dubrov they wanted to ask her about the recent robberies, she burst into tears. Vlad Stepankutza was her son.

Later that day when Stepankutza and his associates arrived home, they were met by Pollard, Sanders, three LAPD detectives, and a SWAT Tactical Team that had been deployed to assist in the arrest. The general manager and chief operations officer of Pacific West, a man named Peter Williams, presented Pollard with their Pacific West Bank Meritorious Service Award of the Year.

"This is Peter. Katherine, is that you?"

He sounded pleased to hear from her.

"The very one. I wasn't sure if you'd remember."

"I remember those hulking monsters who almost put me out of business. You know what we nicknamed you after you brought those men down? Kat the Giant Killer."

Pollard thought, perfect.

"Peter, I need five minutes with you. I'm in Chinatown now. Can you make time for me?"

"Right now?"

"Yes."

"May I ask what this is regarding?"

"Marchenko and Parsons. I need to discuss them with you, but I'd rather do it face-to-face. It won't take long."

Williams grew distracted for a moment, and Pollard hoped he was making room on his calendar.

"Sure, Katherine. I can do that. When can you be here?"

"Five minutes."

Pollard left her car in a parking lot next to the building, then took an elevator to the top floor. She felt anxious and irritated at having left Williams with the impression she was still with the FBI. Pollard didn't like lying, but she didn't trust telling the truth. If Williams turned her down, she had no other hope of seeing the reports Random was trying to hide.

When Pollard got off the elevator she saw that Peter had been promoted. A burnished sign identified him as the president and CEO. Pollard considered this a lucky break—if she was going to lie she might as well lie to the boss.

Peter Williams was a fit man in his late fifties, short and balding with a tennis player's tan. He seemed genuinely pleased to see her and brought her into his office to show off the sweeping views that let him look out over the entire Los Angeles Basin. Peter didn't retreat to his desk. He brought her to a wall covered with framed photographs and plaques. He pointed at one of the pictures, high in the right corner.

"You see? Here you are."

It was a picture of Peter presenting her with the Pac West Meritorious Service Award nine years earlier. Pollard thought she looked a lot younger in the picture. And thinner.

Peter offered her a seat on the couch, then sat in a leather club chair.

"All right, Agent. What can I do for Kat the Giant Killer after all this time?"

"I'm not with the FBI anymore. That's why I need your help."

Peter seemed to stiffen, so Pollard gave him her most charming smile.

"I'm not talking about a loan. It's nothing like that."

Peter laughed.

"Loans are easy. What can I do?"

"I'm interviewing with private contractors as a security specialist. Marchenko and Parsons have the highest profile of the recent takeover teams, so I need to know those guys inside and out."

Peter was nodding, going along.

"They hit us twice."

"Right. They hit you on their fourth and seventh robberies, two of the thirteen."

"Fucking animals."

"I need the backstory in detail, but LAPD won't share their files with a civilian."

"But you were an FBI agent."

"From their side I can see it. They have to dot the i's and cross the t's, and the Feeb is even worse. Leeds hates it when an agent goes into the private sector. He considers us traitors. But traitor or not, I have two kids to support and I want this job, so if you can help me I'd appreciate it."

Pollard thought she had done a pretty good job with the subtle hint that the welfare of her children depended upon his cooperation. Most major banks and banking chains had their own security office that worked hand in hand with authorities to identify, locate, and apprehend bank robbers, as well as prevent or deter future robberies. To that end, banks and authorities openly shared information in an ongoing evolution that began with the initial robbery. What was learned during robbery number two or six or nine might very well help the police capture the bandits during robbery number sixteen. Pollard knew this because she had been part of the process herself. The Pacific West security office had likely been copied on all or part of the LAPD's detail reports as they were developed. They might not have all of it, but they might have some, even if in redacted form.

Peter frowned, and she could tell he was working it through.

"You know, we have security agreements with these agencies."

"I know. You signed some of those forms for me when I was profiling the Front Line gang and I shared our interview summaries."

"They're supposed to be for our internal use and ours alone."

"If you want me to read them at your security office, that would be fine. They don't have to leave the premises."

Pollard held his eyes for a moment, then looked at the Kat the Giant Killer picture. She stared at it for several seconds before looking back at him.

"And if you'd like me to sign a confidentiality agreement, of course I'd be happy to sign it."

She stared at him, waiting.

"I don't know, Katherine."

Pollard sensed the whole effort going south, and suddenly grew worried he might ask LAPD for their permission. His security office had almost daily contact with robbery detectives and FBI agents. If the Robbery Special dicks found out she was running an end-around after they already turned her down, she would be screwed.

She studied the picture again, then took her final shot.

"Those bastards are getting out in two years."

Peter made a noncommittal shrug that was not encouraging.

"Tell you what. Leave your contact information with my assistant. Let me think about it and I'll be in touch."

Peter stood, and Pollard stood with him. She couldn't think of anything else to say. He walked her out. She left her information, then rode down in the elevator alone, feeling like a brush salesman who had struck out for the day.

Pollard missed her credentials—the badge and commission card that identified her as an agent of the FBI. The creds gave her the weight and moral authority to ask questions and demand answers, and she had never hesitated to knock on any door or ask any question and she had almost always gotten the answers. She felt worse than a brush salesman. She felt like a chiseler stealing sugar packs from a diner. She felt like nothing.

Pollard drove back to the Simi Valley to make dinner for her kids.

27

HOLMAN WATCHED Pollard drive away from the river with a numb feeling in his chest. He hadn't told her the real reason he had seen her under the bridge. He had been on his way to Chee's shop. And he had also lied when he told her he had been to the bridge a dozen times. Holman had returned to this place twenty or thirty times. He found himself at the bridge several times every day and two or three times each night. Sometimes he would find himself at the bridge as if he had fallen asleep at the wheel and the car had driven itself. He didn't always jump the fence. Most times he cruised the bridge without stopping, but other times he parked, leaning far over the rail to see those terrible scrubbed patches from every possible angle. Holman hadn't told her the truth about those visits, and knew he could never tell anyone, not about his terrible moments with those bright patches of light.

Holman thought through everything he and Pollard talked about, then decided not to go to Chee's. He still needed to talk to Chee, but he wanted to keep Chee out of the rest of it.

He turned back toward Culver City and called Chee on his cell.

"Homes! 'Sup, bro? How you like those wheels?"

"I wish you hadn't sent your boys after the old man. It made me look bad."

"Homes, please! Muthuhfuckuh billin' you twenty a day for a cop magnet like that, a man in your position! He knew what he was doing, bro—I couldn't let him get away with that."

"He's an old man, Chee. We had a deal. I knew what I was getting into."

"You knew he had warrants on that piece of shit?"

"No, but that's not the point—"

"What you want me to do, send him some flowers? Maybe a little note sayin' I'm sorry?"

"No, but—"

Holman knew he wasn't going to get anywhere and was already sorry he brought it up. He had more important things to discuss.

"Look, I'm not asking you to do anything, I guess I just wanted to mention it. I know you meant well."

"I got your back, bro, don't ever forget that."

"This other thing, I heard Maria Juarez disappeared."

"She left her cousins?"

"Yeah. The cops issued a warrant, and now they're blaming me for making her run. Think you can ask around?"

"Whatever, bro. I'll see what I can see. You need anything else?"

Holman needed something, but not from Chee.

He said, "Something else. I got fronted by the cops today about this Juarez thing. Have the cops been talking to you?"

"Why would the cops be talkin' to me?"

Holman told him that Random had mentioned Chee by name. Chee was silent for a moment, and then his voice was quiet.

"I don't like that, bro."

"I didn't like it, either. I don't know if they've been following me or they're into my phone at the room, but don't call me on that phone anymore. Just on the cell."

Holman put down the phone and drove in silence across the city. He spent almost an hour driving from the Fourth Street Bridge to the City of Industry. Traffic always got heavy at the end of the day when people were getting off work. Holman grew worried he would get there too late, but he reached the sign company a few minutes before quitting time.

Holman didn't turn into the parking lot and he didn't intend to see Tony Gilbert. He parked in a red zone across the street and stayed in the car, waiting for five o'clock. The workday ended at five.

Holman glanced at his father's watch with its frozen hands. Maybe that was why he wore it—time had no meaning. He checked the dashboard clock and watched the minutes tick past.

At exactly five o'clock, men and women came out of the printing plant and filed through the parking lot to their cars. Holman watched Tony Gilbert go to a Cadillac and the two front-office girls get into a Jetta. Three minutes later he watched Pitchess exit the building and get into a Dodge Charger that was almost as bad as Perry's beater.

Holman waited until Pitchess pulled out, then

slipped into traffic a few cars behind him. He followed the Charger for almost a mile until he was sure no one else from the printing plant was around. He accelerated around the cars ahead, and swerved back into the lane so he was directly behind Pitchess.

Holman tapped his horn and saw Pitchess's eyes go to the rearview mirror, but Pitchess kept driving.

Holman tapped his horn again, and when Pitchess looked, Holman gestured for him to pull over.

Pitchess got the message and turned into a Safeway parking lot. He stopped near the entrance, but didn't get out of his car. Holman thought the sonofabitch was probably scared.

Holman parked behind him, got out, and walked forward. Pitchess's window rolled down as Holman approached.

Holman said, "Can you get me a gun?"

"I knew I'd see you again."

"Can you get me a gun or not?"

"You got the money?"

"Yeah."

"Then I can get whatever you need. Get in."

Holman went around to the passenger side and climbed in.

28

WHEN HOLMAN got home that night Perry's usual parking spot was empty. The beater was gone.

Holman avoided the water raining from the window units and let himself in through the front door like always. It was almost ten, but Perry was still at his desk, reading a magazine with his feet up.

Holman decided to move quickly to the stairs without speaking, but Perry put down his magazine with a big smile.

"Hey, those boys came back today. You must've straightened'm out real good, Holman. Thanks."

"Good. I'm glad it worked out."

Holman didn't want to hear about it now. He wanted to get upstairs, so he kept going, but Perry swung his feet from the desk.

"Hey, wait—hang on there. What's that in the bag, your dinner?"

Holman stopped, but held the paper Safeway bag down along his leg like it was nothing.

"Yeah. Listen, Perry, it's getting cold."

Perry pushed the magazine aside and smiled so wide

his lips peeled off his gums.

"If you want a beer to go with it I got a couple in my place. We could have dinner together or something."

Holman hesitated, not wanting to be rude but also not wanting to get involved with Perry. He wanted to bring the bag upstairs.

"It's just a little bit of chow mein. I already ate most of it."

"Well, we could still have that beer."

"I'm sober, remember?"

"Yeah. Listen, I'm just trying to thank you for whatever you did. When those boys walked in, I thought, holy shit, they're gonna bust my guts."

Now Holman was curious. He also figured the sooner Perry got it out, the sooner he'd be able to go upstairs.

"I didn't know they were coming back."

"Well, shit, you must've told'm somethin'. Did you notice that ol' Mercury is gone?"

"Yeah."

"They're gonna fix it up for me, kind of like an apology. Pound out those dents and hit the rust that's eating up my headlights and paint the sonofabitch. Have it back good as new, they said."

"That's real good, Perry."

"Hell, Holman, I appreciate this. Thanks, man."

"No problem. Listen, I want to get this upstairs."

"Okay, partner, I just wanted to let you know. You change your mind about that beer, you come knock."

"Sure, Perry. Thanks."

Holman went up to his room, but left his door open. He turned off his AC unit to cut the noise of its blower, then returned to his door. He heard Perry lock the front door, then move through the lobby turning off lights before heading back along the hall to his room. When Holman heard Perry's door close, he slipped off his shoes. He crept down to the utility closet at the end of the hall where Perry kept mops, soaps, and cleaning supplies. Holman had raided the closet a couple of times, looking for Pine-Sol and a plunger.

In addition to the cleaning supplies, Holman had noticed a water shutoff valve in a rectangular hole cut into the wall between two studs. He pushed the bag into the hole beneath the valve. He didn't want to keep the gun in his room or car. The way things had been going, the cops would search his room. If they had found something when they searched his car that morning, he would be back in federal custody right now.

Holman shut the closet and returned to his room. He was too tired for a shower. He washed up as best he could in the sink, then put the air conditioner back on and climbed into bed.

When Holman first saw problems with how the police were explaining Richie's death, he believed the police were incompetent; now he believed he was dealing with conspiracy and murder. If Richie and his friends had been trying to find the sixteen million in missing money, Holman was pretty sure they weren't the only people trying to find it. And since the missing money was a secret, the only other people who knew about it were policemen.

Holman tried to imagine what sixteen million dollars in cash looked like, but couldn't. The most he had ever had in his possession at one time was forty-two hundred bucks. He wondered if he could lift it. He wondered if he could put it into his car. A man might do anything for that much cash. He wondered if Richie was such a man, but thinking about it made his chest ache so he forced the thoughts away.

Holman turned to Katherine Pollard and what they discussed under the bridge. He liked her and found himself feeling bad he had gotten her involved. He thought he might like to know her a little bit better, but he held no real hope of that. Now here he was with the gun. He hoped he wouldn't have to use it, but he would even though it meant going back to prison. He would use it as soon as he found his son's killer.

29

THE NEXT MORNING, Pollard called to tell Holman they were on with Leyla Marchenko. Mrs. Marchenko lived in Lincoln Heights not far from Chinatown, so Pollard would pick him up at Union Station and they would drive over together.

Pollard said, "Here's the deal, Holman—this woman hates the police, so I told her we were reporters."

"I don't know anything about reporters."

"What's to know? The point is she hates cops and that's our in. I told her we were doing a story about how the cops mistreated her when they were investigating her son. That's why she's willing to talk to us."

"Well, okay."

"Why don't I do this without you? No reason you have to tag along."

"No, no—I want to go."

Holman felt bad enough she was working for free; he didn't want her to think he was leaving it all to her.

Holman took a fast shower, then waited until he heard Perry hosing the sidewalk before he returned to the closet. He had tossed and turned throughout the night, regretting that he had gotten the gun. Now Pitchess knew he had a gun and if Pitchess got pinched for something he wouldn't hesitate to cut a deal for himself by ratting Holman out. Holman knew with a certainty Pitchess would get pinched because guys like Pitchess always got pinched. It was only a matter of time.

Holman wanted to check his hiding place in the better light of day. The water valve and exposed pipes were thick with dust and cobwebs, so it was unlikely Perry or anyone else would reach down between the studs. Holman was satisfied. If Pitchess ratted him out, he would deny everything and the cops would have to find the gun. Holman positioned the mop and broom in front of the valve, then went to meet Pollard.

Holman had always liked Union Station, even though it was a block away from the jail. He liked the deco Spanish look of the place with its stucco and tile and arches, which reminded him of the city's roots in the Old West. Holman had loved watching westerns on TV when he was a child, which was the only thing he remembered ever doing with his father. The old man brought him down to Olvera Street a few times, mostly because Mexican guys walked around dressed like Old West vaqueros. They had bought churros, then walked across the street to see the trains at Union Station. It had all seemed to fit together— Olvera Street, the vaqueros, and Union Station looking like an old Spanish mission—there at the birthplace of Los Angeles. His mother had brought him the one time, but only the one. She brought him into the passenger terminal with its enormously high ceiling and they sat on one of the long wooden benches where people wait. She bought him a Coke and a Tootsie

Pop. Holman had been five or six, something like that, and after a few minutes she told him to wait while she used the bathroom. Five hours later his father claimed him from the station attendants because she hadn't come back. Two years later she died and the old man finally told him his mother had tried to abandon him. She had boarded a train, but only got as far as Oxnard before she ran out of guts. That's the way his father had put it—she ran out of guts. Holman still liked Union Station anyway. It reminded him of the Old West that had always looked pretty good when he was watching it on TV with his dad.

Holman parked in the lot alongside the passenger terminal, then walked over to wait at the main entrance. Pollard picked him up a few minutes later and they drove to Lincoln Heights. It was only a few minutes away.

Anton Marchenko's mother lived in a low-income neighborhood between Main and Broadway, not far from Chinatown. The tiny houses were poorly kept because the people here had no money. The houses would be overcrowded with two or three generations and sometimes more than one family, and it took everything they had just to hang on. Holman had grown up in a similar house in another part of town and found the street depressing. Back in the day when Holman was stealing, he didn't bother with a neighborhood like this because he knew firsthand they had nothing worth stealing.

Pollard said, "Okay, now listen—she's going to rant about how the cops murdered her son, so we'll just have to listen to it. Let me direct the conversation to Fowler."

"You're the boss."

Pollard reached around to the backseat and brought out a folder. She put it in Holman's lap.

"Carry this. Here we come, up here on the right. Try to act like a reporter."

Leyla Marchenko was short and squat, with a wide Slavic face showing small eyes and thin lips. When she answered the door, she was wearing a heavy black dress and fluffy house slippers. Holman thought she seemed suspicious.

"You are the newspaper people?"

Pollard said, "Yes, that's right. You spoke with me on the phone."

Holman said, "We're reporters."

Pollard cleared her throat to shut him up, but Mrs. Marchenko pushed open the door and told them to come in.

Mrs. Marchenko's living room was small, with spotty furnishings pieced together from lawn sales and secondhand stores. Her house wasn't air-conditioned. Three electric table fans were set up around the room, swinging from side to side to churn the hot air. A fourth fan sat motionless in the corner, its safety cage broken and hanging on the blades. Except for the fans, it reminded Holman of his old house and he didn't feel comfortable. The small closed space felt like a cell. He already wanted to leave.

Mrs. Marchenko dropped into a chair like a dead weight. Pollard took a seat on the couch and Holman sat beside her.

Pollard said, "All right, Mrs. Marchenko, like I told you on the phone, we're going to do a story exploring how the police mistreated—"

Pollard didn't have to say more than that. Mrs. Marchenko turned bright red and launched into her complaints.

"They were nasty and rude. They come in here and make such a mess, me alone, an old woman. They break a lamp in my bedroom. They break my fan—"

She waved at the motionless fan.

"They come in here stomping around the house and here I was alone, thinking I might be raped. I don't believe any of those things they say and I still don't. Anton did not commit all those robberies like they say, maybe that last one, but not those others. They blame him so they can say they solved all those cases. They murdered him. This man on TV, he say Anton was trying to give up when they kill him. He say, they use too much force. They tell those terrible lies to cover up themselves. I am going to sue the city. I am going to make them pay."

The old woman's eyes reddened along with her face, and Holman found himself staring at the broken fan. It was easier than seeing her pain.

"Max?"

"What?"

"The folder? Could I have the folder, please?"

Pollard had her hand out, waiting for the folder. Holman handed it to her. Pollard took out a sheet and passed it to Mrs. Marchenko.

"I'd like to show you some pictures. Do you recognize any of these men?"

"Who are they?"

"Police officers. Did any of these officers come to see you?"

Pollard had clipped the pictures of Richie and

Fowler and the others from the newspaper and taped them to the sheet. Holman thought this was a good idea and knew he probably wouldn't have thought of it.

Mrs. Marchenko peered at the pictures, then tapped the one of Fowler.

"Maybe him. No uniform. A suit."

Holman glanced at Pollard, but Pollard showed no reaction. Holman knew it was a telling moment. Fowler had worn civilian clothes because he had been pretending he was a detective. He had hidden the fact that he was a uniformed officer and was pretending to be something else.

Pollard said, "How about the others? Were any of them here either with the first man or at another time?"

"No. Another man came with him, but not these."

Now Pollard glanced over at Holman and Holman shrugged. He was wondering who in hell this fifth man was and whether or not the old woman was making a mistake.

Holman said, "You sure the other man isn't one of the guys in the pictures? Why don't you take another look to be sure?"

Mrs. Marchenko's eyes narrowed into angry slits.

"I don't need to see again. It was some other man, not one of these."

Pollard cleared her throat and jumped in. Holman was glad.

"Do you remember his name?"

"I don't give those bastards the time of day. I don't know."

"About when were they here, you think? How long ago?"

"Not long. Two weeks, I think. Why do you ask

247

about them? They did not break my lamp. That was another one."

Pollard put away the pictures.

"Let's just say they might be nastier than most, but we'll focus on everyone in the story."

Holman was impressed with how well Pollard lied. It was a skill he had noticed before in cops. They often lied better than criminals.

Pollard said, "What did they want?"

"They wanted to know about Allie."

"And who is Allie?"

"Anton's lady friend."

Holman was surprised and he could tell Pollard was surprised, too. The papers had described Marchenko and Parsons as a couple of friendless loners and had hinted at a homosexual relationship. Pollard stared down at the folder for a moment before continuing.

"Anton had a girlfriend?"

The old woman's face grew rigid and she tipped forward.

"I am not making this up! My Anton was not a sissy boy like those horrible people said. Many young men have roommates to share in the cost. Many!"

"I'm sure of it, Mrs. Marchenko, a handsome young man like him. What did the officers want to know about her?"

"Just questions, they ask—did Anton see her a lot, where she lives, like that, but I am not going to help these people who murdered my son. I made like I don't know her."

"So you didn't tell them about her?"

"I say I don't know any girl named Allie. I am not going to help these murderers."

248

"We'd like to speak with her for the article, Mrs. Marchenko. Could you give me her phone number?"

"I don't know the number."

"That's okay. We can look it up. How about her last name?"

"I am not making this up. He would call her when he was here watching the television. She was so nice, a nice girl, she was laughing when he gave me the phone."

Mrs. Marchenko had once more flushed, and Holman saw how desperately she needed them to believe her. She had been trapped in her tiny house by the death of her son, and no one was listening and no one had listened for three months and she was alone. Holman felt so bad he wanted to jump up and run, but instead he smiled and made his voice gentle.

"We believe you. We just want to talk to the girl. When was this you spoke to her?"

"Since before they murdered my Anton. It was a long time. Anton would come and we would watch the TV. Sometimes he would call her and put me on the phone, here, Mama, talk to my girl."

Pollard pouched out her lips, thinking, then glanced at the phone at the end of Mrs. Marchenko's couch.

"Maybe if you showed us your old phone bills we could figure out which number belongs to Allie. Then we could see if Detective Fowler treated her as badly as he treated you."

Mrs. Marchenko brightened.

"Would that help me sue them?"

"Yes, ma'am, I think it might."

Mrs. Marchenko pushed up from her chair and waddled out of the room.

Holman leaned toward Pollard and lowered his voice.

"Who's this fifth guy?"

"I don't know."

"The papers didn't say anything about a girlfriend."

"I don't know. She wasn't on the FBI witness list, either."

Mrs. Marchenko interrupted them by returning with a cardboard box.

"The bills I put in here after I pay them. It's all mixed up."

Holman settled back and watched them go through the bills. Mrs. Marchenko didn't make many calls and didn't phone many different numbers—her landlord, her doctors, a couple of other older women who were friends, her younger brother in Cleveland, and her son. Whenever Pollard found a number Mrs. Marchenko couldn't identify, Pollard called the number on her cell phone, but the first three she dialed were two repairmen and a Domino's. Mrs. Marchenko remembered the repairmen, but frowned when Pollard reached the Domino's.

"I never have the pizza. That must have been Anton."

The Domino's call had been placed five months ago. The following number on the list was also a number Mrs. Marchenko couldn't identify, but then she nodded.

"That must be Allie. I remember the pizza now. I tell Anton it has a nasty taste. When the man brought it, Anton gave me the phone when he went to the door."

Pollard smiled at Holman.

"Well, there we go. Let's see who answers."

Pollard dialed the number, and Holman watched as her smile faded. She closed her phone.

"It's no longer in service."

Mrs. Marchenko said, "Is this bad?"

"Maybe not. I'm pretty sure we can use this number to find her."

Pollard copied the number into her notebook along with the time, date, and duration of the call, then searched through the remaining bills, but found the number only one other time on a call placed three weeks before the first.

Pollard glanced at Holman, then smiled at Mrs. Marchenko.

"I think we've taken enough of your time. Thank you very much."

Mrs. Marchenko's face folded in disappointment.

"Don't you want to talk about the fan and how they lied?"

Pollard stood and Holman stood with her.

"I think we have enough. We'll see what Allie has to say and we'll get back to you. Come on, Holman."

Mrs. Marchenko waddled after them to the door.

"They did not have to kill my boy. I don't believe any of those things they said. Will you put that in your story?"

"Goodbye and thank you again."

Pollard walked out to the car, but Holman hesitated. He felt awkward just leaving.

Mrs. Marchenko said, "Anton was trying to give up. Put in your story how they murdered my son."

Pollard was waving for him to join her, but here was this old woman with her pleading eyes, thinking they were going to help her and they were going to leave her with nothing. Holman felt ashamed of himself. He looked at the broken fan.

"You couldn't fix it?"

"How could I get it fixed? My Anton is dead. How could I get it fixed until I sue and get the money?"

Pollard beeped the horn. Holman glanced at her, then turned back to Mrs. Marchenko.

"Let me take a look."

Holman went back into the house and examined the fan. The safety cage was supposed to be attached at the back of the motor by a little screw, but the screw was broken. It had probably snapped when the cops knocked over the fan. The head of the screw had popped off and the body of the screw was still in the hole. It would have to be drilled and rethreaded. It would be cheaper to buy a new fan.

"I can't fix it, Mrs. Marchenko. I'm sorry."

"This is outrageous, what they did to my son. I am going to sue them."

The horn beeped.

Holman went back to the door and saw Pollard waving, but he still didn't leave. Here was this woman with her son who had robbed thirteen banks, murdered three people, and wounded four others; her little boy who had modified semiautomatic rifles to fire like machine guns, dressed up like a lunatic, and shot it out with the police, but here she was, defending her son to the last.

Holman said, "Was he a good son?"

"He came and we watched the TV."

"Then that's all you need to know. You hang on to that."

Holman left her then and went to join Pollard.

30

WHEN HOLMAN pulled the door closed, Pollard roared back toward Union Station.

"What were you doing? Why'd you go back inside?"

"To see if I could fix her fan."

"We have something important here and you're wasting time with that?"

"The woman thinks we're helping her. I didn't feel right just leaving."

Holman felt so bad he didn't notice that Pollard had gone silent. When he finally glanced over, her mouth was a hard line and her brow was cut by a vertical line.

He said, "What?"

"It might not have dawned on you, but I did not enjoy that. I don't like lying to some poor woman who lost her son and I don't like sneaking around pretending to be something I'm not. This kind of thing was easier and simpler when I was on the Feeb, but I'm not, so this is what we have. I don't need you making me feel even worse."

Holman stared at her. He had spent much of the night regretting he had gotten her involved, and now he felt like a moron.

"I'm sorry. I didn't mean it like that."

"Forget it. I know you didn't."

She was clearly in a bad mood now, but Holman didn't know what to say. The more he thought about everything she was doing for him, the more he felt like an idiot.

"I'm sorry."

Her mouth tightened, so he decided not to apologize again. He decided to change the subject.

"Hey, I know this Allie thing is important. Can you find her with a disconnected number?"

"I'll have a friend of mine at the Feeb do it. They can run the number through a database that will show prior subscribers even though it's no longer in use."

"How long will it take?"

"It's computers. Milliseconds."

"Why wasn't she on the witness list?"

"Because they didn't know about her, Holman. Duh."

"Sorry."

"That's why this is important. They didn't know about her, but Fowler did. That means he learned about her from some other source."

"Fowler and the new guy."

Pollard glanced over at him.

"Yeah, and the new guy. I'm looking forward to talking with this girl, Holman. I want to find out what she told them."

Holman grew thoughtful. They were driving west on Main Street toward the river. He was thinking about what she might have told them, too.

"Maybe she told them to meet her under the bridge to cut up the money."

Pollard didn't look at him. She was silent for a moment and then she shrugged.

"We'll see. I'll go back through his phone bills to see if and when they made contact, and I'll see if we can find her. I'll call you later with whatever I find."

Holman watched her drive, feeling even more guilty that she would be spending her afternoon with this.

"Listen, I want to thank you again for going to all this trouble. I didn't mean to put my foot in it back there."

"You're welcome. Forget it."

"I know you already said no, but I'd like to pay you something. At least gas money since you won't let me drive."

"If we have to get gas I'll let you pay. Will that make you feel better?"

"I'm not trying to be a pain. I just feel bad with you putting in so much time."

Pollard didn't respond.

"Your husband doesn't mind you spending all this time?"

"Let's not talk about my husband."

Holman sensed he had stepped over a line with her, so he backed off and fell silent. He had noticed she didn't wear a ring the first time he saw her at Starbucks, but she had mentioned her kids so he didn't know what to make of it. Now he regretted bringing it up.

They drove on without speaking. As they crossed the river, Holman tried to see the Fourth Street Bridge, but it was too far away. He was surprised when Pollard suddenly spoke.

"I don't have a husband. He's dead."

"Sorry. It was none of my business."

"It sounds worse than it was. We were separated. We were on our way to a divorce we both wanted."

Pollard shrugged, but still didn't look at him.

"How about you? How'd it go between you and your wife?"

"Richie's mom?"

"Yeah."

"We never got married."

"Typical."

"If I could go back and do it all over again I would have married her, but that was me. I didn't learn my lesson until I was in prison."

"Some people never learn, Holman. At least you figured it out. Maybe you're ahead of the curve."

Holman had been spiraling down into the inevitable funk, but when he glanced over he saw Pollard smiling.

She said, "I can't believe you went back to fix her fan."

Holman shrugged.

"That was cool, Holman. That was very, very cool."

Holman watched Union Station swing into view and realized he was smiling, too.

31

HOLMAN DIDN'T immediately leave Union Station when Pollard dropped him off. He waited until she had gone, then walked across to Olvera Street. A Mexican dance troop garbed in brilliant feathers was performing Toltec dances to the rhythms of a beating drum. The drumbeats were fast and primitive, and the dancers soared around each other so quickly they appeared to be flying.

Holman watched for a while, then bought a churro and moved through the crowd. Tourists from all over the world crowded the alleys and shops, buying sombreros and Mexican handicrafts. Holman drifted among them. He breathed the air and felt the sun and enjoyed the churro. He wandered along a row of shops, stopping in some when the notion struck him and bypassing others. Holman felt a lightness he hadn't known in a while. When long-term convicts were first released they often experienced a form of agoraphobia—a fear of open spaces. The prison counselors had a special name for this type of agoraphobia when they attributed it to convicts—the fear of life. Freedom gave a man choices and choices could be terrifying. Every choice was a potential failure. Every choice could be another step back toward prison. Choices as simple as leaving a room or asking for directions could leave a man humiliated and unable to act. But now Holman felt the lightness and knew he was putting the fear behind him. He was becoming free again and it felt good.

It occurred to him he could have asked Pollard to join him for lunch. Since she wasn't letting him pay for her time he should have offered to buy her a sandwich. He imagined the two of them having a French Dip at Philippe's or a taco plate at one of the Mexican restaurants, but then he realized he was being stupid. She would have taken it wrong and probably wouldn't have seen him again. Holman told himself to be careful with stuff like that. Maybe he wasn't as free as he thought.

Holman no longer felt hungry, so he picked up his car and was heading for home when his phone rang. He hoped it was Pollard, but the caller ID window showed it was Chee. Holman opened the phone.

"Hey, bro."

"Where are you, Holman?"

Chee's voice was quiet.

"On my way home. I just left Union Station."

"Come see me, bro. Drop around the shop."

Holman wasn't liking how Chee sounded.

"What's wrong?"

"Nothing's wrong. Just come see me, okay?"

Holman was certain that something was wrong and he wondered if it had to do with Random.

"Are you all right?"

"I'll be waiting."

Chee hung up without waiting for an answer.

Holman picked up the freeway and headed south. He wanted to call Chee back, but he knew Chee would have already told him if he wanted to say it over the phone, and that worried him even more.

When he reached Chee's shop he pulled into the lot and was parking his car when Chee came out. As soon as Holman saw him he knew it was bad. Chee's face was grim, and he didn't wait for Holman to park. He motioned Holman to stop, then climbed into the passenger seat.

"Let's take a little drive, bro. Swing on around the block."

"What's wrong?"

"Just drive, bro. Get away from this place."

As they pulled into traffic, Chee swiveled his head left and right as if searching the surrounding cars. He adjusted the outside passenger mirror so he could see behind them.

He said, "It was the cops told you Maria Juarez went on the run?"

"Yeah. They put out a warrant."

"That's bullshit, man. They fed you bullshit."

"What are you talking about?"

"She didn't go on the run, bro. The fuckin' cops took her."

"They said she split. They put out a warrant."

"Night before last?"

"Yeah, it would've been—yeah, the night before last."

"Their warrant can kiss my ass. They bagged her in the middle of the night. Some people over there, they saw it happen, *ese*. They heard the noise and saw these two muthuhfuckuhs shove her in a car."

"A police car?"

"A car car."

"How do they know it was the police?"

"It was that red-haired guy, homes—that same fuckin' guy who jumped you. That's how they know. These are the people who told me that you got bagged, homes! They said it was the same fuckin' guy who grabbed you."

Holman drove in silence for a while. The red-haired man was Vukovich, and Vukovich worked for Random.

"They get the plate?"

"No, man, that time of night?"

"What kind of car?"

"Dark blue or brown Crown Victoria. You tell me anyone who drives a Crown Vic but the cops?"

Holman fell silent, and Chee shook his head.

"What the fuck are those cops doin', homes? What you got into?"

Holman kept driving. He was thinking. He had to tell Pollard.

32

POLLARD CALLED IT the blood tingle. She blasted up the Hollywood Freeway, high-fiving the dashboard and pumping her fist, feeling the electric buzz in her fingers and legs that had always come with making a breakthrough in a case—the blood tingle. Now she wasn't just covering someone else's old case notes—the girlfriend was new. Pollard had turned up a new lead and now the investigation felt totally hers.

She called April Sanders as she hit Hollywood and climbed the Cahuenga Pass.

"Hey, girl, can you talk?"

April came back whispering so softly Pollard could barely understand.

"Office. You got more donuts?"

"I have an out-of-service phone number and I'm in my car. Can you pull the subscriber for me?"

"Yeah, I think—hang on."

Pollard smiled. She knew Sanders would be peeking out of her cubicle to make sure she wasn't being watched.

"Yeah, sure. What is it?"

Pollard read off the number.

"Three-ten area code."

"Stand by. I show a Verizon account for one Alison Whitt, W-H-I-T-T, billed to what looks like a Hollywood POB. You want it?"

"Yeah. Go."

The address appeared to be a private mailbox service on Sunset Boulevard.

"What was the date of termination?"

"Last week . . . six days ago."

Pollard thought about it. If Fowler had discovered her number at about the time he visited Leyla Marchenko he would have been able to contact her. Maybe Fowler's contact is why she dropped the number.

"April, see if she has a new listing."

"Ah . . . hang on. No, negative. No Alison Whitt in the listings."

Pollard found the absence of a new listing notable but not unusual. Unlisted numbers didn't show on the regular database, so Whitt's new number might be unlisted. Also, it was possible Whitt had taken a number under a different name or was sharing a phone billed to another party. The bad news was that none of this would help Pollard find her.

"Listen, one more thing. I hate to ask, but could you check this girl in the system?"

"The NCIC?"

"Whatever. The DMV should be fine. I'm trying to find her."

"Is this something I should know about?"

"If it turns out to be I'll let you know."

Sanders hesitated, and Pollard thought she might be

peeking at the office again. Running a government database check couldn't be handled at her desk. Sanders returned to the line.

"I can't right now. Leeds is here but I can't see him. I don't want him to ask what I'm doing."

"So call me later."

"Out."

Pollard felt good about the progress she was making. The disconnection of Alison's phone number so close in time to Fowler's questioning of Mrs. Marchenko was too coincidental. Coincidences occurred, but, like all cops, Pollard had learned to be suspicious of them. She put down her phone, anxious to go through Fowler's phone records and hear back from Sanders. If Sanders struck out, Pollard knew she could try for contact information through the mailbox service. Learning anything from the mail service would be difficult without her creds, but it left her an avenue for investigation and she found herself smiling again.

Pollard knew she might not hear back from Sanders until the end of the day, so she had her car washed, then went to Ralphs. She stocked up on food and toilet paper and bought extra treats for the boys. They ate like starving wolves and seemed to eat more every day. She found herself wondering if Holman had once bought boxes of Jujubes for his little boy, and suspected that no, he hadn't. This left her feeling sad. Holman seemed like a pretty good guy now that she had gotten to know him, but she also knew he had been a criminal for much of his life. Every thug she ever arrested had a story—debt, drug addiction, abusive parents, no parents, learning disabilities, poverty, whatever. None of that mattered. All that mattered was whether or not you broke the law. If you did the crime, you did the time, and Holman had done the time. Pollard thought it was a shame he hadn't had a second chance with his son.

Once she had the groceries away, she straightened the house, then sat on her living room couch with Fowler's phone bills. She read through the outgoing numbers beginning with the date Fowler visited Mrs. Marchenko and found Alison Whitt's phone number only a few days later. Fowler had called her on the same Thursday he and Holman's son went out late and came home muddy. Fowler had called her, but Mrs. Marchenko claimed she did not give Fowler any information about Allie, which meant Fowler had gotten her number from another source. Pollard read through the rest of Fowler's bills, but the Thursday call was the only time he called her. Pollard searched through Richard Holman's bills next, but found nothing.

Pollard wondered how Fowler had learned about Alison Whitt. She reviewed the FBI's witness list. The summaries referenced Marchenko's landlord and neighbors, but did not include anyone named Alison Whitt. If one of the neighbors reported that Marchenko or Parsons had a girlfriend, the investigators would have followed the trail and named her in the witness list, but just the opposite had occurred—the neighbors uniformly stated that neither man had friends, girlfriends, or other visitors to their apartment. Yet somehow Fowler had learned of Whitt before he visited Mrs. Marchenko. Maybe the fifth man had known. Maybe the fifth man's phone number was somewhere in Fowler's bills.

Pollard was still thinking about it when her doorbell rang. She pushed the papers together, went to the door, and squinted through the peephole. It was still too early for her mother to bring the boys home.

Leeds and Bill Cecil were at the door, Leeds scowling at something down the street. He didn't look happy. He frowned at his watch, rubbed his chin, then rang her bell again.

Though Cecil had been to her home on several occasions when she and Marty entertained, Leeds had never been to her house. She had not seen him outside the office since she left the Feeb.

He was reaching to ring the bell again when Pollard opened the door.

"Chris, Bill, this is—what a surprise."

Leeds didn't look particularly happy to see her. His blue suit hung loose off his hunched frame and he towered over her like a spindly scarecrow who no longer liked his job. Cecil stood a halfstep behind him, expressionless.

Leeds said, "I would think so. May we come in?"

"Of course. Absolutely."

She stepped out of the way to let them in, but she didn't know what to do or say. Leeds entered first. As Cecil passed, he raised his eyebrows, warning her Leeds was in a mood. Pollard moved to join Leeds in the living room.

"I'm stunned. Were you in the area?"

"No, I came up here to see you. This is very nice, Katherine. You have a lovely home. Are your boys here?"

"No. They're at camp."

"Too bad. I would have liked to meet them."

Pollard felt the creepy sensation of being a child again in the presence of her father. Leeds looked around as if he was inspecting her house, while Cecil stood just inside the door. Leeds finished his slow tour of the living room and settled on her like a sinking ship finding rest on the bottom.

He said, "Have you lost your mind?"

"Excuse me?"

"Why on earth would you get involved with a convicted criminal?"

Pollard felt the blood rush to her face as her stomach knotted. She started to open her mouth, but he shook his head, stopping her.

"I know you're helping Max Holman."

She had been about to deny it, but she lied.

"I wasn't going to deny it. Chris, he lost his son. He asked me to talk to the police about it—"

"I know about his son. Katherine, the man is a criminal. You should know better than this."

"Than what? I don't know why you're here, Chris."

"Because you were on my team for three years. I picked you and I was goddamned pissed off to lose you. I could never forgive myself if I let you do this to yourself without speaking up."

"Do what? Chris, I'm just trying to help the man get answers about his son."

Leeds shook his head as if she was the dumbest rookie alive and he could see right through her into the creases and folds of her innermost secrets.

He said, "Have you gone Indian?"

Pollard felt a fresh surge of blood brighten her face. It was an old expression. A cop went Indian when he turned crooked . . . or fell in love with a crook.

"No!"

"I hope to hell not."

"This is really none of your business—"

"Your personal life is *absolutely* none of my business, yes, you're right—but I still give a damn so here I am. Have you let him into your home? Have you exposed your children to him or given him money?"

"Chris? You know what? You should go—"

Cecil said, "Maybe we should leave now, Chris."

"When I'm finished."

Leeds didn't move. He stared at Pollard, and Pollard suddenly remembered the papers on her couch. She edged toward the door to draw his eye away.

"I'm not doing anything wrong. I haven't broken any laws or done anything my children would be ashamed of."

Leeds placed his palms together as if he was praying and tipped his fingers at her.

"Do you really know what this man wants?"

"He wants to know who killed his son."

"But is that *really* what he wants? I've spoken with the police—I know what he's told them and I'm sure he's told you the same thing, but can you be sure? You put him in prison for ten years. Why would he turn to you for help?"

"Maybe because I got his sentence reduced."

"And maybe he sought you out because he knew you were soft. Maybe he thought he could use you again."

Pollard felt a growing tickle of anger. Leeds had been furious when the *Times* dubbed Holman the Hero Bandit, and he had been livid at her for speaking in Holman's favor with the U.S. Attorney.

"He didn't use me. We didn't discuss it and he didn't ask me to intervene. He earned that reduction."

"He isn't telling you the truth, Katherine. You can't trust him."

"What isn't he telling me the truth about?"

"The police believe he's consorting with a convicted felon and active gang member named Gary Moreno, also known as Little Chee or L'Chee. Ring a bell?"

"No."

Pollard was growing scared. She sensed Leeds was directing the conversation. He was judging her reactions and trying to read her as if he suspected she was lying.

"Ask him. Moreno and Holman were known associates throughout Holman's career. The police believe Moreno has funded Holman with cash, a vehicle, and other items for use in a criminal enterprise."

Pollard tried to keep her breath even. Here was Holman fresh out of prison with a brand-new car and cell phone. Holman had told her a friend loaned him the car.

"Why?"

"You know why. You can feel it. Here—"

Leeds touched his stomach, then gave her the answer.

"To recover the sixteen million dollars stolen by Marchenko and Parsons."

Pollard worked to show nothing. She didn't want to admit anything until she had time to think. If Leeds was right, she might need to talk with a lawyer.

"I don't believe it. He didn't even know about the money until—"

Pollard realized she was already saying too much when Leeds gave her a sad but knowing smile.

"You told him?"

She forced herself to take a slow breath, but Leeds seemed able to see her fears.

"It's difficult to think when your emotions are

involved, but you need to rethink this, Katherine."

"My emotions aren't involved."

"You felt something for the man ten years ago and now you've let him back into your life. Don't lose yourself to this man, Katherine. You know better than that."

"I know I would like you to leave."

Pollard kept her face even, staring at him when the phone rang. Not her house phone, but the cell. The loud chirp broke the silence like a stranger entering the room.

Leeds said, "Answer it."

Pollard didn't move toward the phone. It sat on the couch near the file with Holman's papers, ringing.

"Please go. You've given me a lot to think about."

Cecil looked embarrassed and went to the door. He opened it, trying to get Leeds out of her house.

"Come on, Chris. You've said what you wanted to say."

The phone rang. Leeds studied it as if he was thinking of answering it himself, but then he joined Cecil at the door. He looked back at her.

"Agent Sanders will no longer be helping you."

Leeds walked out, but Cecil hesitated, looking sad.

"I'm sorry about this, lady. The man—I don't know, he hasn't been himself. He meant well."

"Goodbye, Bill."

Pollard watched Cecil leave, then went to the door and locked it.

She walked back to the phone.

It was Holman.

33

HOLMAN DROPPED Chee a block from his shop, then turned toward Culver City. He played and replayed the news about Maria Juarez, trying to cast it in a light that made sense. He wanted to drive to her house to speak with her cousins, but now he was afraid the same cops would be watching. Why would they bag her, then claim she had split? Why would they issue a warrant for her arrest if they had already arrested her? News of her flight and the warrant had even been in the newspaper.

Holman didn't like any of it. The police who thought she fled had been lied to by the cops who knew different. The police who obtained the warrant didn't know that other cops already knew her whereabouts. Cops were keeping secrets from other cops, and that could only mean one thing: bad cops.

Holman drove a mile from Chee's shop, then turned into a parking lot. He speed-dialed Pollard's number and listened as it rang. The ringing seemed to go on forever, but finally she answered.

"Now isn't a good time."

Pollard didn't sound like Pollard. Her voice was remote and failing, and Holman thought he might have gotten the wrong number.

"Katherine? Is this Agent Pollard?"

"What?"

"What's wrong?"

"Now isn't a good time."

She sounded terrible, but Holman believed this was important.

"Maria Juarez didn't run. The cops took her. That same cop with the red hair who bounced me—Vukovich. It isn't like the police have been saying. Vukovich and another cop took her in the middle of the night."

Holman waited, but heard only silence.

"Are you there?"

"How do you know this?"

"A friend knows some people who live on her street. They saw it. Just like they saw those guys get me."

"What friend?"

Holman hesitated.

"Who?"

Holman still didn't know what to say.

"Just . . . a friend."

"Gary Moreno?"

Holman knew better than to ask how she knew. Asking would be defensive. Being defensive would imply guilt.

"Yeah, Gary Moreno. He's a friend. Katherine, we were kids together—"

"So tight he gave you a car?"

"He runs a body shop. He has lots of cars—"

"And so much money you don't have to work?"

"He knew my little boy—"

"A multiple felon and gang member and you didn't think it worth mentioning?"

"Katherine—?"

"What are you doing, Holman?"

"Nothing—"

"Don't call me again."

The line was dead.

Holman hit the speed-dial, but her voice mail picked up. She had turned off the phone. He spoke as fast as he could.

"Katherine, listen, what should I have said? Chee's my friend—that's Gary's nickname, Chee—and yes he's a convicted felon, but so am I. I was a criminal all my life; the only people I know are criminals."

Her voice mail beeped, cutting him off. Holman cursed and hit the speed-dial again.

"Now he's straight just like I'm trying to be straight and he's my friend so I went to him for help. I don't know anyone else. I don't have anyone else. Katherine, please call back. I need you. I need your help to get through this. Agent Pollard, please—"

Her voice mail beeped again, but this time Holman lowered his phone. He sat in the parking lot, waiting. He didn't know what else to do. He didn't know where she lived or how to reach her except through her phone. She had kept it that way to protect herself. Holman sat in his car, feeling alone the way he had been alone on his first night in jail. He wanted to reach out to her, but Agent Pollard had turned off her phone.

34

POLLARD'S MOTHER called at dinnertime. That's the way they had been working it. Her mother would meet the boys when they were brought home from camp, then bring them to her condo in Canyon Country where the boys could play by the pool while her mother played online poker. Texas Hold'em.

Pollard, knowing it would be awful and steeling herself for the pain, said, "Could they camp out with you tonight?"

"Katie, do you have a man there?"

"I'm really tired, Mom. I'm just beat, that's all. I need the break."

"Why are you tired? You're not sick, are you?"

"Could they stay?"

"You didn't catch anything, did you? Did you catch something from some man? You need a husband but there's no reason to become a slut."

Pollard lowered the phone and stared at it. She could hear her mother still talking, but couldn't understand the words.

"Mom?"

"What?"

"Could they stay?"

"I guess it would be all right, but what about camp? They'll be heartbroken if they miss their camp."

"Missing one day won't kill them. They hate camp."

"I don't understand a mother who needs a break from her children. I never needed a break from you or wanted one."

"Thanks, Mom."

Pollard put down the phone and stared at the clock over her sink. She was in the kitchen. The house was quiet again. She watched the second hand sweep and waited for the tock.

TOCK.

Like a gunshot.

Pollard got up and went back into the living room, wondering if Leeds was right. She had felt a kind of admiration for Holman both back in the day and now, for how he went down and how he had brought himself back. And she had felt a kind of attraction, too. Pollard didn't like admitting to the attraction. It made her feel stupid. Maybe she had gone Indian without even knowing it. Maybe that's the way going Indian happened. Maybe it snuck up on you when you weren't looking and took over before you knew.

Pollard stared at the papers on the couch and felt disgusted with herself. Her Holman file.

She said, "Jesus Christ."

Sixteen million dollars was a fortune. It was buried treasure, a winning lotto ticket, the pot of gold at the end of the rainbow. It was the Lost Dutchman Mine and the Treasure of the Sierra Madre. Holman had robbed nine banks for a total score of less than forty thousand. He had pulled ten years and come out with nothing, so why wouldn't he want the money? Pollard wanted the money. She had dreamed about it, seeing herself in the dream, opening a shitty garage door in a shitty neighborhood, everything covered in grime; pushing up the door and finding the money, a great huge vacuum-packed block of it, sixteen million dollars. She would be set up for life. The boys would be set. Their kids would be set. Her problems would be solved.

Pollard, of course, would not steal it. Keeping the money was just a fantasy. Like finding Prince Charming.

But Holman was a lifelong degenerate criminal who had stolen cars, ripped off warehouses, and robbed nine banks—he probably wouldn't think twice about stealing the money.

The phone rang. Her house phone, not the cell.

Pollard's gut clenched because she was sure it was her mother. The boys had probably bitched about staying over, and now her mother was calling to lay on both barrels of guilt.

Pollard returned to the kitchen. She didn't want to answer, but she did. She was already guilty enough.

April Sanders said, "Are you really helping out the Hero?"

Pollard closed her eyes and shouldered a fresh load of guilt.

"I am so sorry, April. Are you in trouble?"

"Oh, fuck Leeds. Is it true about the Hero?"

Pollard sighed.

"Yes."

"Are you fucking him?"

"No! How could you even ask a question like that?"

275

"I'd fuck him."

"April, shut up!"

"I wouldn't marry him, but I'd fuck him."

"April—"

"I found Alison Whitt."

"Are you still going to help me?"

"Of course I'm going to help you, Pollard. Give a sista some credit."

Pollard reached for a pen.

"Okay, April. I owe you, girl. Where is she?"

"The morgue."

Pollard froze with her pen in the air as April's voice turned somber and professional.

"What have you gotten yourself into, Pollard? Why are you looking for a dead girl?"

"She was Marchenko's girlfriend."

"Marchenko didn't have a girlfriend."

"He saw her on multiple occasions. Marchenko's mother spoke with her at least twice."

"Bill and I ran his phone logs, Kat. If we had ID'd a potential girlfriend on the callbacks we would have followed up on her."

"I don't know what to tell you. Maybe he never phoned her at home or maybe he only called her from his mother's."

Sanders hesitated and Pollard knew she was thinking about it.

Sanders said, "Whatever. The sheet shows a couple of busts for prostitution, shoplifting, drugs—the usual. She was just a kid—twenty-two years old—and now she's been killed."

Pollard felt the blood tingle again.

"She was murdered?"

"The body was found in a Dumpster off Yucca in Hollywood. Ligature marks on the neck indicate strangulation, but the cause of death was cardiac arrest brought on by blood loss. She was stabbed twelve times in the chest and abdomen. Yeah, I'd call that murder."

"Was there an arrest?"

"Nope."

"When was she killed?"

"The same night Holman's son was killed."

Neither of them spoke for a moment. Pollard was thinking of Maria Juarez. She wondered if Maria Juarez would turn up dead, too. Finally, Sanders asked the question.

"Kat? Do you know what happened to this girl?"

"No."

"Would you tell me if you did?"

"Yes, I would tell you. Of course I would."

"Okay."

"What was the time of death?"

"Between eleven and eleven-thirty that night."

Pollard hesitated, unsure what this might mean or how much she should say, but she owed April the truth.

"Mike Fowler knew her or knew of her. Do you recognize Fowler's name?"

"No, who's that?"

"One of the officers killed with Richard Holman that night. He was the senior officer."

Pollard knew Sanders was taking notes. Everything she now said would be part of Sanders' records.

"Fowler approached Marchenko's mother about a girl named Allie. He knew Allie and Anton Marchenko were linked, and asked Mrs. Marchenko about her."

"What did Mrs. Marchenko tell him?"

"She denied knowing the girl."

"What did she tell you?"

"She gave us the first name and allowed us to look through her phone bills to find the number."

"You mean you and the Hero?"

Pollard closed her eyes again.

"Yeah, me and Holman."

"Huh."

"Stop."

"When were the four officers killed that night?"

Pollard knew where Sanders was going and had already considered it.

"One thirty-two. A shotgun pellet broke Mellon's watch at one thirty-two, so they know the exact time."

"So it was possible Fowler and these guys killed the girl earlier. They had time to kill her, then get to the river."

"It's also possible someone else killed the girl, then went to the river to kill the four officers."

"Where was the Hero that night?"

Pollard had already thought of that, too.

"He has a name, April. Holman was still in custody. He wasn't released until the next day."

"Lucky him."

"Listen, April, can you get the police report on Alison Whitt?"

"Already have it. I'll fax you a copy when I get home. I don't want to do it from here."

"Thanks, babe."

"You and the Hero. Man, that's a shiver."

Pollard put down the phone and returned to her living room. Her home didn't seem quiet anymore, but she knew the sounds now came from her heart. She con-

278

sidered the papers on her couch, thinking more papers would soon be added. The Holman file was growing. A girl had been murdered before his release and now Holman believed the police were lying about Maria Juarez. She wondered again if Maria Juarez was going to turn up dead and whether the fifth man would have something to do with it.

Pollard thought about the timing and found herself hoping that Holman's son had nothing to do with murdering Alison Whitt. She had seen him struggle with the guilt he felt about his son's death and agonize over the growing evidence that his son had been involved in an illegal scheme to recover the stolen money. Holman would be crushed if his son was a murderer.

Pollard knew she had to tell him about Alison Whitt and find out more about Maria Juarez. Pollard picked up the phone, but hesitated. Leeds' appearance had taken a toll. His comments about her going Indian had left her feeling foolish and ashamed of herself. She hadn't gone Indian, but she had been thinking about Holman in ways that disturbed her. Even Sanders had laughed. *You and the Hero. Man, that's a shiver.*

Pollard had to call him, but not just yet. She tossed the phone back onto the couch and went back through the kitchen into the garage. It was hotter than hell even though the sun was down and night had fallen. She waded around bicycles, skateboards, and the vacuum cleaner to a battered grey file cabinet layered with dust. She hadn't opened the damned thing in years.

She pulled the top drawer and found the folder containing her old case clippings. Pollard had saved press clippings from her cases and arrests. She had almost tossed the stuff a hundred times, but now was glad she

hadn't. She wanted to read about him again. She needed to remember why the *Times* had called him the
Hero Bandit, and why he deserved a second chance.

She found the clip and smiled at the headline. Leeds
had thrown the paper across the room and cursed the
Times for a week, but Pollard had smiled even then.
The headline read: *Beach Bum a Hero.*

Pollard read the clippings at her kitchen table and
remembered how they had met...

The Beach Bum Bandit

*The woman ahead of him shifted irritably, making
a disgusted grunt as she glanced at him for the fourth
time. Holman knew she was working herself up to say
something, so he ignored her. It didn't do any good.
She finally pulled the trigger.*

*"I hate this bank. Only three tellers, and they move
like sleepwalkers. Why three tellers when they have
ten windows? Shouldn't they hire more people, they
see a line like this? Every time I come here it sucks."*

*Holman kept his eyes down so the bill of his cap
blocked his face from the surveillance cameras.*

*The woman spoke louder, wanting the other people
in line to hear.*

*"I have things to do. I can't spend all day in this
bank."*

*Her manner was drawing attention. Everything
about her drew attention. She was a large woman
wearing a brilliant purple muumuu, orange nails, and
an enormous shock of frizzy hair. Holman crossed his
arms without responding and tried to become invisible. He was wearing a faded Tommy Bahama beach-
comber's shirt, cream-colored Armani slacks, sandals,*

and a Santa Monica Pier cap pulled low over his eyes. He was also wearing sunglasses, but so were half the people in line. This was L.A.

The woman harrumphed again.

"Well, finally. It's about time."

An older man with pickled skin in a pink shirt moved to a teller. The large woman went next, and then it was Holman's turn. He tried to even his breathing, and hoped the tellers couldn't see the way he was sweating.

"Sir, I can help you over here."

The teller at the end of the row was a brisk woman with tight features, too much makeup, and rings on her thumbs. Holman shuffled to the window and stood as close as he could. He was carrying a sheet of paper folded in half around a small brown paper bag. He put the note and the bag on the counter in front of her. The note was composed of words he had clipped from a magazine. He waited for her to read it.

THIS IS A ROBBERY

PUT YOUR CASH IN

THE BAG

Holman spoke softly so his voice wouldn't carry.

"No dye packs. Just give me the money and everything's cool."

Her tight features hardened even more. She stared at him and Holman stared back; then she wet her lips and opened her cash drawer. Holman glanced at the clock behind her. He figured she had already pressed a silent alarm with her foot and the bank's security company had been alerted. An ex-con Holman knew cautioned him you only had two minutes to get the cash and get out of the bank. Two minutes wasn't *long, but it had been long enough eight times before.*

●●●

FBI Special Agent Katherine Pollard stood in the parking lot of the Ralphs Market in Studio City sweating in the afternoon sun. Bill Cecil, in the passenger seat of their anonymous beige g-ride, called out to her.

"You're gonna get heatstroke."

"All this sitting is killing me."

They had been in the parking lot since eight-thirty that morning, a half hour before the banks in the area opened for business. Pollard's butt was killing her, so she got out of the car every twenty minutes or so to stretch her muscles. When she got out, she left the driver's-side window down to monitor the two radios on her front seat even though Cecil remained in the car. Cecil was the senior agent, but he was only on hand to assist. The Beach Bum Bandit was Pollard's case.

Pollard bent deep at the hips, touching her toes. Pollard hated stretching in public with her big ass, but they had been hovering in the Ralphs lot for three days, praying the Beach Bum would strike again. Leeds had dubbed this one the Beach Bum Bandit because he wore sandals and a Hawaiian shirt, and had shaggy hair pulled back into a ponytail.

A voice crackled from one of the radios.

"Pollard?"

Cecil said, "Hey, lady, that's the boss."

It was Leeds on the FBI channel.

Pollard dropped into her car and scooped up the radio.

"Hey, boss, I'm up."

"LAPD wants their people on something else. I agree. I'm pulling the plug on this."

Pollard glanced at Cecil, but he only shrugged and shook his head. Pollard had been dreading this moment. Forty-two known serial bank robbers were operating in the city. Many of them used violence and guns, and most of them had robbed way more banks than the Beach Bum.

"Boss, he's going to hit one of my banks. Every day he hasn't drives up the odds that he will. We just need a little more time."

Pollard had patterned most of the serial bandits operating in Los Angeles. She believed the Beach Bum's pattern was more obvious than most. The banks he hit all were located at major surface inter-sections and had easy access to two freeways; none employed security guards, Plexiglas barriers, or ban-dit-trap entry doors; and all of his robberies had fol-lowed a progressive counterclockwise route along the L.A. freeway system. Pollard believed his next target would be near the Ventura/Hollywood split, and had identified six banks as likely targets. The rolling stakeout she now oversaw covered those six banks.

Leeds said, "He isn't important enough. LAPD wants their people on gunslingers and I can't afford to have you and Cecil tied up any longer, either. The Rock Stars hit in Torrance today."

Pollard felt her heart sink. The Rock Stars were a takeover crew who got their name because one of them sang during their robberies. It sounded silly until you knew the singer was stoned out of his mind and strumming a MAC-10 machine pistol. The Rock Stars had killed two people during sixteen robberies.

Cecil took the radio.

"Give the girl one more day, boss. She's earned it."

"I'm sorry, but it's done, Katherine. The plug has been pulled."

Pollard was trying to decide what else to say when the second radio popped to life. The second radio was linked with Jay Dugan, the LAPD surveillance team leader assigned to the stakeout.

"Two-eleven in progress at First United. It's going down."

Pollard dropped the FBI radio into Cecil's lap and snatched up her stopwatch. She hit the timer button, started her car, then radioed back to Dugan.

"Time on the lead?"

"Minute thirty plus ten. We're rolling."

Cecil was already filling in Leeds.

"It's happening, Chris. We're rolling out now. Go, lady—drive this thing."

The First United California Bank was only four blocks away, but the traffic was heavy. The Beach Bum had at least a ninety-second jump on them and might already be exiting the bank.

Pollard dropped her car into gear and jerked into the traffic.

"Time out, Jay?"

"We're six blocks out. Gonna be close."

Pollard steered through traffic with one hand, blowing her horn. She drove hard toward the bank, praying they would get there in time.

•••

Holman watched the teller empty her drawers one by one into the bag. She was stalling.

"Faster."

She picked up the pace.

Holman glanced at the time and smiled. The second hand swept through seventy seconds. He would be out in less than two minutes.

The teller pushed the last of the cash into the bag. She was being careful not to make eye contact with the other tellers. When the last of the cash was in the bag, she waited for his instructions.

Holman said, "Cool. Just slide it across to me. Don't shout and don't tell anyone until I'm out the door."

She slid the bag toward him exactly as Holman wanted, but that's when the bank manager brought over a credit slip. The manager saw the paper bag and the teller's expression, and that was all she needed to know. She froze. She didn't scream or try to stop him, but Holman could tell she was scared.

He said, "Don't worry. Everything's going to be okay."

"Take it and go. Please don't hurt anyone."

The old man in the pink shirt had finished his transaction. He was passing behind Holman when the manager asked Holman not to hurt anyone. The old man turned to see what was happening and, like the manager, realized that the bank was being robbed. Unlike the manager, he shouted—

"We're being robbed!"

His face turned bright red, then he clutched his chest and made an agonized gurgle.

Holman said, "Hey."

The old man stumbled backwards and fell. When he hit the floor his eyes rolled and the gurgle turned into a fading sigh.

The loud woman in the muumuu screamed, "Oh my God!"

Holman snatched up the money and started toward the door, but no one was moving to help the old man.

The large woman said, "I think he's dead! Someone call nine-one-one! I think he's dead!"

Holman ran to the door, but then he looked back again. The old man's red face was now dark purple and he was motionless. Holman knew the old man had suffered a heart attack.

Holman said, "Goddamnit, don't any of you people know CPR? Someone help him!"

No one moved.

Holman knew the time was slipping away. He was already over the two-minute mark and falling farther behind. He turned back toward the door, but he just couldn't do it. No one was trying to help.

Holman ran back to the old man, dropped to the ground, and went to work saving his life. Holman was still blowing into the old man's mouth when a woman with a gun ran into the bank, followed by this inhumanly wide bald guy. The woman identified herself as an FBI agent and told Holman he was under arrest.

Between breaths, Holman said, "You want me to stop?"

The woman then lowered her gun.

"No," she said. "You're doing fine."

Holman kept up the CPR until the ambulance arrived. He had violated the two-minute rule by three minutes and forty-six seconds.

The old man survived.

Part Four

35

HOLMAN WAS doing push-ups when someone knocked at his door. He was mechanically grinding them out, one after another, and had been for most of the morning. He had left two more messages on Pollard's phone the previous evening and was working up his nut to call again. When he heard the knock he figured it was Perry. No one else ever came to his door.

"Hang on."

Holman pulled on his pants, opened the door, but instead of Perry he found Pollard. He didn't know what to make of Pollard showing up like this, so he stared at her, surprised.

She said, "We need to talk."

She wasn't smiling. She seemed irritated, and she was holding the folder with all the papers he had given her. Holman suddenly realized he was shirtless with his flabby, sweaty white skin, and wished he had pulled on a shirt.

"I thought you were someone else."

"Let me in, Holman. We have to talk about this."

Holman backed out of the door to let her pass, then

glanced into the hall. Perry's head disappeared behind the far corner. Holman turned back into his room, but left the door open. He felt embarrassed by his appearance and the shitty room and thought for sure she wouldn't feel comfortable being inside alone with him. He pulled on a T-shirt to hide himself.

"You get my messages?"

She went back to the door and closed it, but stood with her hand on the knob.

"I did, and I want to ask you something. What are you going to do with the money?"

"I don't know what you're talking about."

"If we find the sixteen million. What do you want to do?"

Holman stared at her. She looked serious. Her face was intent, with her mouth pooched into a tight little knot. She looked like she had come to cut up the pie.

Holman said, "Are you kidding me?"

"I'm not kidding."

Holman studied her a moment longer, then sat on the edge of his bed. He pulled on his shoes just to give himself something to do even though he needed a shower.

"I just want to find out what happened to my boy. We find that money, you can have it. I don't care what you do with it."

Holman couldn't tell if she was disappointed or relieved. Either way, he didn't give a damn except he still wanted her help.

"Listen, you want to keep it, I won't rat you out. But just one thing—I won't let the money keep me from finding Richie's killer. If it gets down to a choice—keeping that money or finding out what happened—

then that money is going back."

"What about your friend, Moreno?"

"Did you listen to my messages? Yes, he loaned me the car. What's the big deal with that?"

"Maybe he expects a cut."

Holman was growing irritated.

"What's up with you and Moreno? How'd you hear about him?"

"Just answer my question."

"You haven't asked a goddamned question. I never mentioned the money to him, but I don't give a rat's ass if he keeps it, either. What do you think we're doing, planning a capital crime?"

"What I think is the police have put you and Moreno together. How would they come to do that?"

"I've been over to see him three or four times. Maybe they have him under surveillance."

"Why would they be watching him if he's gone straight?"

"Maybe they figured out he helped me find Maria Juarez."

"Are he and Juarez connected?"

"*I asked him to help.* Listen, I'm sorry I didn't tell you Chee loaned me the fucking car. I'm not looking for the money—I'm looking for the sonofabitch who killed my son."

Holman finished with his shoes and looked at her. She was still staring at him, so he stared back. He knew she was trying to read him, but he wasn't sure why. She finally seemed to make up her mind and let go of the knob.

"Nobody's keeping that money. If we find it, we're turning it in."

"Fine."

"You good with that?"

"I said it was fine."

"Your friend Chee good?"

"He loaned me the goddamned car. So far as I know he doesn't even know about the money. You want to go see him, we'll go. You can ask him yourself."

Pollard studied him a moment longer, then took several sheets from the folder.

"Marchenko's girlfriend was named Alison Whitt. She was a prostitute."

Pollard brought over the sheets and handed them to him. Holman scanned the top sheet as Pollard talked and saw it was a copy of an LAPD records and identification document on a white female named Alison Whitt. The black-and-white reproduction of her booking photo was crude, but she looked like a kid—midwestern-fresh with light sandy hair.

"Approximately two hours before your son and the other three officers were murdered, Whitt was murdered, too."

Pollard continued but Holman no longer heard what she was saying. Pictures were snapping through his mind that drowned her out and left him afraid: Fowler and Richie in a dark alley, faces lit by the flashes of their guns. Holman barely heard himself speak.

"Did they kill her?"

"I don't know."

Holman clenched his eyes, then opened them, trying to stop the pictures, but Richie's face only grew larger, lit by the silent flash of his pistol as Pollard went on.

"Fowler called her on the Thursday they came back

with the dirt. They spoke for twelve minutes that afternoon. That night was the night Fowler and Richard were out late and came back with dirty shoes."

Holman stood and went around his bed to the air conditioner, trying to walk away from the nightmare in his head. He focused on the picture of eight-year-old Richie on his dresser, not yet a thief and a killer.

"They killed her. She told them where the money was or maybe she lied or whatever and they killed her."

"Don't go there yet, Holman. The police are concentrating on johns and customers she might have met on her day job. The hooking was just a sometimes thing—she was a waitress at a place on Sunset called the Mayan Grille."

"That's bullshit. That's too coincidental, her getting killed on the same night like that."

"I think it's bullshit, too, but the guys running this case probably don't know about her connection with Marchenko. Don't forget the fifth man. We have five people in Fowler's group now, and only four of them are dead. The fifth man could be the shooter."

Holman had forgotten about the fifth man, but now he grabbed on to the thought like a life preserver. The fifth man had been trying to find Allie, too, and now everyone else was dead. He suddenly remembered Maria Juarez.

"Did you find out about Juarez's wife?"

"I talked to a friend this morning. LAPD still maintains she fled."

"She didn't flee; she was taken. That guy who grabbed me took her—Vukovich—he works with Random."

"My friend is following up. She's trying to get the videotape Maria made of her husband. I know you told me Random said it was faked, but our people can examine it, too, and we have the best people in the world."

Our. Like she was still with the Fed.

Holman said, "You're still going to help me?"

She hesitated, then turned back to the door with her file.

"You'd better not be lying to me."

"I'm not lying."

"You'd better not be. Get yourself cleaned up. I'll be downstairs in the car."

Holman watched Pollard let herself out, then hurried into the shower.

36

THE MAYAN GRILLE was a small diner on Sunset near Fairfax that served only breakfast and lunch. Business was good. People were waiting on the sidewalk and the outside tables were packed with young, good-looking people eating pancakes and omelets. Holman hated the place as soon as he saw it and he hated the people outside. He didn't think about it much at the time, but just looking at them filled him with disgust.

Holman hadn't spoken as they drove toward the Mayan Grille. He had pretended to listen as Pollard filled him in about Alison Whitt, but mostly he thought about Richie. He wondered if criminal tendencies were inherited as Donna once feared or if a lousy home life could drive someone to crime. Either way, Holman figured the responsibility came back to him. Thinking these things left him feeling sullen as he followed Pollard through the crowd into the restaurant.

Inside was crowded, too. Holman and Pollard were faced with a wall of people, all waiting to be seated. Pollard had trouble seeing past the crowd, but Holman, taller than most everyone else, could see just fine. Most of the guys were dressed in baggy jeans and T-shirts, and most of the girls were wearing belly shirts that showed tattoos across the top of their butts. Everyone seemed more interested in schmoozing than eating, as most of the bused plates were full. Holman decided either none of these people had jobs or they worked in show business or both. Holman and Chee used to cruise the parking lots of places like this, looking for cars to steal.

Pollard said, "The police identified one of the waitresses, a girl named Marki Collen, as having been close to Whitt. She's the one we want to see."

"What if she's not here?"

"I called to make sure. We just have to get her to talk to us. That's not going to be easy with them being this busy."

Pollard told him to wait, then worked her way forward to a hostess who was overseeing a sign-up sheet for the waiting customers. Holman watched them speak and saw someone who looked like a manager join them. The manager pointed toward a waitress who was helping a busboy clear a table in the rear, then shook his head. Pollard didn't look happy when she returned.

"They got twenty people waiting to be seated, they're shorthanded, and he won't let her take a break. It's going to be a while before she can talk to us. You want to go get a coffee and come back when she gets off?"

Holman didn't want to wait or go anywhere else. Now he was supposed to dick around while a bunch of Hollywood wannabes with nothing better to do than

talk about their latest audition ordered food they did-
n't eat. Holman's already bad mood darkened.

"That was her, the one in the back he pointed out?"

"Yeah, Marki Collen."

"Come on."

Holman shouldered through the crowd past the
hostess and went to the table. The busboy had just
wiped it clean and was putting out new setups. Holman
pulled a chair and sat, but Pollard hesitated. The hostess had already called two men to be seated, but now
she saw Holman had taken the table and was glaring.

Pollard said, "We can't do this. You're going to get
us thrown out."

Holman thought, no fucking way.

"It's going to be fine."

"We need their cooperation."

"Trust me. They're actors."

Marki Collen was delivering an order to the table
behind Holman. She looked harried and pressed, as did
every other waitress and busboy in the place. Holman
dug out Chee's money, keeping his wad hidden under
the table. He leaned back and tapped Marki's hip.

"I'll be with you in a minute, sir."

"Look at this, Marki."

She glanced around at her name and Holman
showed her a folded hundred-dollar bill. He watched
her eyes to make sure it registered, then slipped it into
her apron.

"Tell the hostess I'm a friend and you told us to take
this table."

The hostess had flagged the manager, and now they
were steaming back toward the table with the two
men behind them. Holman watched Marki intercept

them, but part of him was hoping the two guys who wanted the table would get in his face. Holman wanted to kick their asses all the way out onto Sunset Boulevard.

Pollard touched his arm.

"Stop it. Stop looking at them like that. Jesus, what's with this hostility?"

"I don't know what you're talking about."

"You want to fight them over the goddamned table? You're not on the yard anymore, Holman. We need to talk to this girl."

Holman realized she was right. He was giving them jailhouse eyes. Holman forced himself to stop staring. He glanced at the surrounding tables. Most every guy in the diner was about Richie's age. Holman told himself this was why he was so angry. These people were sopping up pancakes, but Richie was bagged in the morgue.

"You're right. Sorry."

"Just take it easy."

Marki squared things with the manager, then returned to the table with a big smile and two menus.

"That was cool, sir. Have I waited on you before?"

"No, it's not that. We need to ask you about Alison Whitt. We understand you were friends."

Marki didn't look moved one way or the other when Holman mentioned Alison's name. She just shrugged and held her pad as if she was waiting for them to order.

"Well, yeah, kinda. We were buds here at the grill. Listen, this isn't the greatest time. I have all these tables."

"A hundred covers a lot of tips, honey."

298

Marki shrugged again and shifted her weight.

"The police already talked to me. They talked to everyone here. I don't know what else I can say."

Pollard said, "We don't want to know about her murder so much as a former boyfriend. Did you know she worked as a prostitute?"

Marki giggled nervously, then glanced at the nearest tables to make sure no one was listening before lowering her voice.

"Well, yeah, sure. The police told everyone about it. That's what they asked us about."

"Her record shows two arrests about a year ago, but none since. Was she still working?"

"Oh, yeah. That girl was wild—she grooved on the life. She had all these great stories."

Holman was keeping an eye on the manager, who was pissed off and watching them. Holman was pretty sure he was going to come over because Marki was having a conversation instead of working.

Holman said, "Tell you what, Marki. Put in a couple of orders so your boss doesn't freak out, then come back for the stories. We'll look at the menus."

When she went away, Pollard leaned toward him.

"Did you give that girl a hundred dollars?"

"What of it?"

"I'm not trying to fight with you, Holman."

"Yes. A hundred."

"Jesus Christ. Maybe I should have let you pay me."

"Chee's money. You wouldn't want to get contaminated."

Pollard stared at him. Holman felt a flush of embarrassment and glanced away. He was in a terrible mood and had to get a grip on himself. He looked at the menu.

"You want something to eat? As long as we're here we might as well eat."

"Fuck off."

Holman stared at the menu until Marki returned. Marki told them she could hang for a minute, and Pollard went back to the point as if Holman hadn't just made an ass of himself.

"Did she ever tell you about her johns?"

"She had funny stories about her johns. Some of them were celebrities."

"We're trying to find out about a guy she was with four or five months ago. He might have been her boyfriend, but it's more likely he was a john. He had an unusual name—Anton Marchenko. A Ukrainian dude?"

Marki smiled, recognizing the name right away.

"That was the pirate. Martin, Marko, Mar-something."

"Marchenko."

Holman said, "How was he a pirate?"

Now her smile morphed into a giggle.

"'Cause that was his thing. Allie said he couldn't get off without pretending he was this badass pirate, you know, yo-ho-ho and a bottle of rum, how he lived a life of adventure and had all this buried treasure."

Holman glanced at Pollard and saw the corner of her mouth curl. She returned his glance and nodded. They had something.

Holman looked back at Marki and turned on his friendliest smile.

"No shit? He told her he had buried treasure?"

"He said all kinds of silly stuff. He used to take her to the Hollywood Sign. That's where he had to do it. He'd never take her back to his place or do it in the car or use a motel. They had to go up to the Hollywood Sign so he could make these speeches and look out over his kingdom."

Marki giggled again, but Holman saw a problem.

He said, "Allie told you they went to the sign?"

"Yeah. Four or five times."

"You can't get to the sign. It's fenced off and covered by security cameras."

Marki seemed surprised, then shrugged as if it didn't matter to her either way.

"That's what she told me. She said it was a big pain because you have to hike up, but the guy was loaded. He paid her one thousand dollars just for, you know, oral. She said she'd hike up there all day for a thousand dollars."

A nearby table waved Marki over, leaving Holman and Pollard alone again. Holman was starting to doubt Allie's story about going up to the sign.

He said, "I've been up there. You can get close, but you can't get to the sign. They have video cameras all over up there. They even have motion detectors."

"Now waitaminute, Holman—this is making sense. Marchenko and Parsons lived in Beachwood Canyon. The sign is right at the top of their hill. Maybe they hid the money up there."

"You couldn't bury sixteen million dollars anywhere around that sign. Sixteen million dollars is big."

"We'll see when we get there. We'll go take a look."

Holman still had his doubts, but when Marki returned Pollard resumed her questions.

"We're almost finished, Marki. We'll be out of your hair in a minute."

"Like he said, a hundred covers a lot of tips."

"Did Allie know why it always had to be the sign?"

"I don't know. That's just where he liked to go."

"Okay, you mentioned something about speeches. What kind of speeches did he make?"

Marki scrunched her face, thinking.

"Not really speeches, maybe—more like pretend. Like if he was a pirate and kidnapped her, he would screw her on all his stolen treasure. She had to act like that made her really hot, you know, like it would be this big turn-on to get screwed on all these hard gold coins."

Pollard nodded, encouraging.

"Like that was his turn-on, to do it on the money?"

"I guess."

Pollard glanced at Holman again, and this time Holman shrugged. Banging on bucks might have been Marchenko's fantasy, but Holman still couldn't see planting sixteen million in cash in such a public place. Then he remembered that Richie and Fowler had come home covered in grass and dirt.

Holman said, "When the cops were here before, did you tell them about Marchenko?"

Marki looked surprised.

"Should I have? It was so long ago."

"No. I was just wondering if they asked."

Holman was ready to leave, but Pollard wasn't looking at him.

Pollard said, "Okay, just one more. Do you know how Allie hooked up with this guy?"

"No, uh-uh."

"Did she have a madam or work for an outcall service?"

Marki screwed up her face again.

"She had someone looking out for her, but he wasn't a pimp or anything."

Holman said, "What does that mean, someone looking out for her?"

"It sounds kinda silly. She told me I wasn't supposed to tell anyone."

"Allie's gone. The statute of limitations ran out on that one."

Marki glanced at the nearby tables, then lowered her voice again.

"Okay, well. Allie worked for the police. She said she didn't have to worry about getting in trouble 'cause she had this friend who could make it go away. She even got paid for telling about her clients."

This time when Holman glanced at Pollard, Pollard had turned white.

"Alison was a paid informant?"

Marki made an uneasy grin and shrugged.

"She wasn't getting rich or anything. She told me they had some kinda cap or something on the amount. Every time she wanted some money this guy hadda get it approved."

Holman said, "Did she tell you who she worked for?"

"Uh-uh."

Holman looked back at Pollard, but Pollard was still pale. Holman touched her arm.

"Anything else?"

Pollard shook her head.

Holman peeled off another hundred and slipped it into Marki's hand.

37

A DEPRESSED ACTRESS named Peg Entwistle killed herself in 1932 by jumping from the top of the letter H. The letters were fifty feet tall, then and now, and these days the sign stretched some four hundred fifty feet across the top of Mount Lee in the Hollywood Hills. After years of neglect, the Hollywood Sign was rebuilt in the late seventies, but vandals and dickweeds took their toll, so not long thereafter the city closed the area to the public. They surrounded the sign with fences, closed-circuit video cameras, infrared lights, and motion detectors. It was like they were guarding Fort Knox, which wasn't lost on Holman as he directed Pollard up to the top of Beachwood Canyon. Holman had been going up to the sign since he was a kid.

Pollard looked worried.

"You know how to get there?"

"Yeah. We're almost there."

"I thought we had to go through Griffith Park."

"This way is better. We're looking for a little street I know."

Holman still didn't think they would find anything,

but he knew they had to look. Every new discovery they made brought them back to the police, and now they knew a policeman had also been connected to Alison Whitt. If Whitt told her contact officer about Anton Marchenko, then the cops might have known about the Hollywood Sign. Putting the sign together with Marchenko's fantasy would have inspired them to search the area. Richie might have been part of the search. Holman wondered if Alison Whitt had seen Marchenko in the news. It was likely. She had probably realized her pirate was the bank robber and offered up what she knew to her cop. This had probably inspired her death.

Pollard said, "These canyons are shit. I can't get a cell signal."

"Do you want to turn around?"

"No, I don't want to turn around. I want to check out whether or not this girl was really an informant."

"They have some kind of informant hotline you can call?"

"Don't try to be funny, Holman. Please."

They wound their way up narrow residential streets higher into Beachwood Canyon. The Hollywood Sign grew above them, sometimes visible between houses and trees and sometimes hidden by the mountain. When they reached the top of the ridge, Holman told her to turn.

"Slow down. We're coming up on it. You can pull over in front of these houses."

Pollard pulled over and they got out of the car. The street ended abruptly at a large gate. The gate was locked and was hung with a large sign reading CLOSED TO THE PUBLIC.

305

Pollard looked dubious as she studied the sign.

"This is your shortcut? It's closed."

"It's a fire road. We can follow it up around the peak to the back of the sign. This way cuts a couple of miles off going up through Griffith Park. I've been coming up here since I was a kid."

Pollard tapped the sign, CLOSED.

"Have you *ever* obeyed the law?"

"No, not really."

"Jesus Christ."

Pollard squeezed around the side of the gate. Holman followed, and they started up the road. It was steeper than Holman remembered, but he was older and in lousy shape. He was breathing hard before long, but Pollard seemed to be doing fine. The fire road joined with a paved road, and the paved road grew steeper as it curved around to the back side of the peak. The Hollywood Sign disappeared from view, but the radio tower perched above it steadily grew.

Holman said, "There's no way those guys brought all that money up here. It's too far."

"Marchenko brought his girlfriend up here."

"She could walk. Would you leave sixteen million laying around in a place like this?"

"I wouldn't rob thirteen banks and shoot it out with the cops, either."

The road wrapped around the back side of the mountain as they neared the peak, but curved to the front face again, and suddenly all of Los Angeles spread out before them as far as Holman could see. Catalina Island floated in the mist almost fifty miles to the southwest. The pudgy cylinder of the Capitol Records Building marked Hollywood, and tight clusters of skyscrapers pushed up like islands dotting the cityscape sea from downtown to Century City.

Pollard said, "Wow."

Holman didn't give a damn about the view. The Hollywood Sign was about thirty feet below them, walled off by a green six-foot chain-link fence that ran along the edge of the road. The radio tower waited at the end of the road, bristling with antennas and microwave dishes and surrounded by yet more fences. Holman waved his hand at the sign.

"There it is. You still think they buried the money up here?"

Pollard hooked her fingers into the fence and gazed down at the sign. The downslope was steep. The bases of the letters were too far below them to see.

Pollard said, "Goddamn. Can you get down there?"

"Only if we climb the fence, but it isn't the fence you'd have to worry about. See the cameras?"

Closed-circuit video cameras were mounted on metal poles dotting the fence by the communications station. The cameras were trained on the sign.

Holman said, "These cameras watch the sign twenty-four hours a day. They have cameras all along the length of the sign and more cameras down below at the base so they can see it from all angles. They're also set up with infrared so they can watch it at night, and they have motion sensors."

Pollard stood on her toes, trying to see as far down the slope as possible, then squinted up the road at the communications station. A bristle of cameras sprouted at the station, too. Uphill from the road was a steep slope climbing another twenty or thirty feet to the summit. Pollard glanced uphill, then back to the cameras.

"Who's on the other end of the cameras?"

"The Park Service. Rangers are watching this thing twenty-four seven."

Pollard looked uphill again.

"What's up there?"

"Weeds. It's just the top of the hill. There's some old geologic survey gear, but that's all."

Pollard set off toward the communications station and Holman followed. She stopped from time to time to peer down at the sign.

She said, "Can we come up from below the sign?"

"That's why they have the motion detectors. The cameras at the bottom cover the approaching hillsides."

"Damn, it's steep. Does it flatten out at the base of the letters?"

"A little, but not much. It's more like a wide spot in a trail. The sign is pretty much set into the side of the mountain."

The communications station was surrounded by an even taller fence. The eight-foot fence was topped by barbed wire and concertina wire. The road they were on dead-ended directly into a gate that cut across the road like a wall. They were boxed in by the steep upslope on one side, the fence on the other, and the gate in front of them. Holman thought it felt like being in a chain-link tunnel.

Holman said, "There's supposed to be a helipad on the other side of the antenna, but I've never seen it. That's how they come up if someone triggers the alarms. They send a chopper."

Pollard stared up at the surrounding cameras, then gazed back along the road at the way they had come.

She looked disappointed.

"You were right, Holman. This place is a fucking compound."

Holman tried to picture Richie and Fowler and the other two cops coming up here in the middle of the night, but just couldn't see it. If they suspected Marchenko had hidden the money at or near the sign, where and how would they search? The Hollywood Sign covered a lot of ground and even policemen couldn't approach the sign without being seen by the Rangers. Holman thought they might have tried telling the Rangers they were conducting an official police investigation, but the chances of that were slim. It would have been a bad move, made even worse by conducting their search at night. The Rangers would have had questions, and stories of the late-night search would have spread beyond the park. If they had tried to bluff their way past the Rangers they would have made their search during the day. Coming out at night meant their search had been a secret.

Pollard said, "You know what I'm thinking about?"

"What?"

"Blow jobs."

Holman felt himself flush. He glanced away and cleared his throat.

"Yeah?"

Pollard turned in a little circle, spreading her arms at their surroundings.

"So Marchenko brings her up here to have sex, what did he do, just drop trou for his blow job right here in the road? Cameras are everywhere. Other people might come walking up the road. There isn't any privacy. This is a lousy place for a blow job."

Holman was uncomfortable with Pollard talking about sex. He glanced at her, but couldn't bring himself to make eye contact. She suddenly turned and stared up the steep slope rising above them.

"Is there a way up to the top?"

"Yeah, but nothing's up there."

"That's why I want to see it."

Holman realized her instincts were right. The summit was the only private place on the hill.

They squeezed between the hillside and the corner of the fence by the communication station, then scrambled up a narrow, steep path. It wasn't easy going like the fire road. Pollard twice fell to her knees, but pretty soon they crested the summit and reached a small clearing at the top of the hill. The only things up here were the survey equipment Holman remembered and brush. Pollard looked around at the 360-degree view that surrounded them and smiled.

"*That's* what I'm talking about! If they were doing the nasty, this is where they were doing it."

Pollard was right. From the clearing, they could see if anyone was approaching on the fire road. The cameras that dotted the fences were below them, and pointed downhill toward the sign. No one was watching the summit.

But Holman still didn't believe Marchenko and Parsons had buried their money up here. Carrying that much cash would have taken several trips, and each trip would have increased the odds they would be discovered. Even if they were stupid enough to bring the money up here, the hole needed to bury it would have been the size of five or six suitcases. It would have been difficult to dig in the rocky soil, and anyone else who visited the summit would have easily noticed the large area of disturbed soil.

Holman pointed out the heel prints and scuff marks that had been scratched into the clearing.

"Maybe he had the girl up here, but there's no way they brought the money. You see all these footprints? Hikers come up here all the time."

Pollard considered the prints, then walked around the edges of the clearing. She seemed to be studying it from different angles.

She said, "This little hill isn't so big. There's not a lot of room up here."

"That's my point."

Pollard gazed down at Hollywood.

"But why did he have to come up here to be with the girl? He could've pretended to be a pirate anywhere."

Holman shrugged.

"Why'd he rob thirteen banks dressed like a commando? Freaks happen."

Holman wasn't sure she heard him. She was still staring down into Hollywood. Then she shook her head.

"No, Holman, coming up here was important to him. It meant something. That's one of the things they taught us at Quantico. Even madness has meaning."

"You think that money was up here?"

She shook her head, but she was still staring down into the canyon.

"No. No, you're right about that. They didn't bury sixteen million dollars up here, and Fowler and your boy sure as hell didn't find it and dig it up. That hole would look like a bomb crater."

"Okay."

She pointed down toward the city.

"But he lived right down there in Beachwood Canyon. You see it? Every day when he stepped out of his apartment, he could look up and see this sign. Maybe they didn't keep the money in their apartment or hide it up here, but something about this place made him feel safe and powerful. That's why he brought the girl up here."

"You can see forever. Maybe it made him feel like he was in a crow's nest, like on one of those old sailing ships."

Pollard still wasn't looking at him. She was staring down into Beachwood Canyon like the answers to all of her questions were waiting to be found.

"I don't think so, Holman. Remember what Alison told Marki? It always had to be here. He couldn't perform without his fantasies, and the fantasies were about treasure—having sex on the money. Money equals power. Power equals sex. Being here made him feel close to his money, and the money gave him the power to have sex."

She looked at him.

"Fowler and your son could have picked up dirt and grass in any vacant lot in L.A., but if they knew what Alison knew, they would have come up here. Look around. It isn't that big. Just look."

Pollard walked off into the brush, scanning the ground as if she had lost her car keys. Holman thought they were wasting their time, but he turned in the opposite direction.

The only man-made artifact on the summit was a device Holman thought looked like a metal scarecrow.

Holman had seen it before. The scarecrow had been set into the ground years ago and bore what appeared to be U.S. Geological Survey markings. Holman guessed it was something for monitoring seismic activity, but he didn't know.

Holman was in a brushy area ten feet beyond the cage when he found the turned earth.

"Pollard! Agent Pollard!"

It was a small egg-shaped depression about a foot across. The darker, turned earth at its center stood out from the surrounding undisturbed ground.

Pollard appeared at his side, then knelt by the depression. She probed the turned soil with her fingers and tested the surrounding area. She scooped a handful of loose soil from the center, then scooped more. By clearing away the loose soil, she revealed a hard perimeter. She continued clearing loose soil until she finally sat back on her heels. It hadn't taken long.

Holman said, "What is it?"

She looked at him.

"It's a hole . . . Holman. See the hard edge where the shovel bit? Someone dug up something. You saw how it was a depression? Someone removed something, so there wasn't enough dirt to fill the empty space when they refilled the hole. Hence, the depression."

"Anyone could have dug this."

"Yes, anyone could have dug it. But how many people would be up here digging, and what could have been here that someone would want to remove?"

"They had sixteen million dollars. You couldn't fit sixteen million in a little hole like that."

Pollard stood, and then both of them stared down at the hole.

"No, but you could hide something that led to the sixteen million—GPS coordinates, an address, keys—"

Holman said, "A treasure map."

"Yep. Even a pirate's treasure map."

Holman glanced up, but Pollard was walking away. He looked down at the hole again as an emptiness grew in his heart. The hole in his heart was larger than this little hole and felt larger than the canyon beneath the Hollywood Sign. It was the emptiness of a father who had failed his only child and cost that child his life.

Richie had not been a good man.

Richie had made a play for the money.

And now Richie had paid the price.

Holman heard Donna's voice echoing across the cavernous emptiness that filled him, the same four words over and over:

Like father, like son.

38

POLLARD BRUSHED at the dirt on her hands, wishing she had a Handi Wipe. Dirt was caked under her nails and would be hell to get out, but she didn't care. Pollard had a high level of confidence the hole was connected with Marchenko and Parsons and the search for their money, but confidence wasn't proof. She opened her phone. The signal bars showed she had an excellent connection, but she didn't yet place the call. A man accompanied by a white dog was hiking up the fire road below the summit. She watched them, then considered the cameras perched on their poles, and decided that at least one of the cameras probably included a view of the fire road. The Park Service almost certainly recorded the video feed, but Pollard knew most security videos were stored digitally on a hard drive that recorded over itself as its memory filled. Most security captures in her experience weren't kept more than forty-eight hours. She doubted that images remained of Fowler and the other officers hiking up the fire road in the middle of the night—if any had ever existed. One or more of the officers had probably made an initial visit during the day. They would have seen the cameras and planned to avoid them, just as they had planned how and where to search.

Pollard studied the surroundings and decided it was possible. She and Holman had followed the fire road as it wrapped around the peak to bring them to the communications facility at the top of the Hollywood Sign. The cameras probably included views of the road as it approached the sign and the antenna, but no one was watching the road on the back side of the mountain. Pollard moved to the edge of the summit and studied the rear-facing slope. It was steep, but Pollard thought it was doable. Scrambling up the slope on a dewy night with poor footing probably even explained the mud on Fowler's boots.

Pollard opened her phone again and punched up Sanders' cell number from the memory. Pollard knew Sanders wasn't in the office because she answered in a normal voice.

"Let me ask you a question, Pollard—what in hell are you and the Hero doing?"

Pollard glanced across the summit at Holman. He was still standing by the hole. She lowered her voice.

"The same thing we were doing yesterday and the day before. Why?"

"Leeds has been getting serious heat from the police is why. Parker Center has been calling and Leeds is going to meetings he won't tell anyone about and he's coming apart at the seams."

"Has he said anything specifically about me?"

"As a matter of fact. He said if any of us were contacted by you we were to report that contact immediately.

He also said if any of us were using government time and resources to aide a civilian endeavor—he looked at me when he said it—he would bring disciplinary charges and transfer our asses to Alaska."

Pollard hesitated, debating how much she should say.

"Where are you?"

"The marina. Some homeless dude pulled a note job, then fell asleep in the park across the street."

"Are you going to report this call?"

"Are you breaking the law?"

"For God's sake, no, I am not breaking the law."

"Then fuck Leeds. I just want to know what's going on."

"I'll tell you, but let me ask first—have you been able to get a copy of the Juarez tape?"

Sanders didn't immediately answer, but when she did her tone was guarded.

"They told me the tape had been erased. An unfortunate accident, they said."

"Hang on—Juarez's alibi tape was destroyed?"

"What they said."

Pollard took a breath. First Maria Juarez had disappeared, and now her tape had been destroyed, the same tape Maria claimed as her husband's alibi. Pollard found herself smiling, though without any humor. A hot breeze had picked up, but felt good on her face. She liked being on the summit.

Pollard said, "I'm going to tell you some things. I don't know everything yet, so do not repeat this."

"Please."

"Who's calling Leeds?"

"I don't know. The calls come from Parker Center

and Leeds doesn't tell us a goddamned thing. He hasn't even been in the office for two days."

"All right. I think we're looking at a criminal conspiracy among police officers growing out of the Marchenko and Parsons robberies. That conspiracy includes the murder of Holman's son and the other three officers under the Fourth Street Bridge."

"Are you shitting me?"

Pollard's phone beeped with an incoming call.

Sanders said, "What's that?"

"Incoming call."

Pollard didn't recognize the number so she let it go to her voice mail. She resumed her conversation with Sanders.

"We believe the four dead officers plus at least one additional officer were conducting an off-the-books investigation to find the missing sixteen million."

"Did they find it?"

"I believe they did—or identified its location. My guess now is that once the money was found, at least one member of the conspiracy decided to keep everything for himself. I don't know that yet, but I'm positive about the conspiracy. I believe this fifth person was connected with Alison Whitt."

"How does Whitt fit into this?"

"Alison Whitt claimed she was a registered police informant. If that's true, she might have told what she knew about Marchenko to her contact officer. That officer is potentially a party to the conspiracy."

Sanders hesitated.

"You want me to identify her contact officer."

"If she's registered, she'll be on an informant list and so will the name of the cop who signed her up."

"This is going to be tough sledding. I told you how they're coming down on us."

"Parker Center is coming down on you. Whitt's murder is being handled on the divisional level out of Hollywood Station. You might still be able to get some cooperation."

"All right. Okay, yeah, I'll see what I can do. You really think this is cop-on-cop murder?"

"That's the way it's shaping up."

"You can't sit on this, for Christ's sake. You're a civilian. You're talking about murder."

"When I have something that stands up I'll give it to you. You can bring it forward through the FBI. Now one more thing—"

"Jesus, more?"

"I want this on record with you. Mike Fowler left a pair of dirty boots on the patio in his backyard. Soil and vegetation samples should be taken from his boots and compared with samples from the summit above the Hollywood Sign."

"*The* Hollywood Sign? Why the friggin' sign?"

"That's where I am. Marchenko and Parsons hid something related to their robberies up here. I believe Fowler and Richard Holman came here searching for it, and I believe they found something. If you end up bringing this thing forward, you'll want to see if the soil samples match."

"Okay. I'm on it. You keep me advised, okay? Stay in touch."

"Let me know when you get something on Whitt."

Pollard ended the call, then retrieved the incoming message. It was Peter Williams' assistant, calling from Pacific West Bank.

"Mr. Williams has arranged for you to access the files you requested. You'll have to read them here on our premises during normal business hours. Please contact me or our chief security officer, Alma Wantanabe, to make the arrangements."

Pollard put away her phone and felt like pumping her fist. Williams had delivered and now everything was coming together. Pollard sensed they were close to making a breakthrough and wanted to read the Pacific West files as quickly as possible.

She turned toward Holman and saw he was now squatting beside the hole. She hurried over.

She said, "What are you doing?"

"Putting the dirt back. Someone could break a leg."

Holman was slowly pushing dirt back into the hole with measured mechanical motions.

"Well, stop playing in the dirt and let's go. Pacific West has a copy of the police summaries. This is good, Holman. If we can match your cover sheets with the reports, we'll know what Random took from your son's desk."

Holman stood as if he were made of lead and started back down the trail. Pollard related what she had learned about Maria Juarez's videotape. She considered this development telling, and grew annoyed when Holman didn't react.

She said, "Did you hear me?"

"Yeah."

"We're getting close, Holman. We catch a break with these reports or with Whitt being an informant, and everything will come together. That's what you want, isn't it?"

Pollard got pissed off when he didn't answer. She

was about to say something when Holman finally spoke.

He said, "I guess they did it."

Pollard realized what was bothering him, but she wasn't sure what to say. Holman had probably been holding out hope his son wasn't a bad cop but now that hope was gone.

"We still have to find out what happened."

"I know."

"I'm sorry, Max."

Holman kept walking.

When they reached the car, Holman got in without a word, but Pollard tried to be encouraging. She turned the car around and headed back down the canyon into Hollywood, telling him what she hoped to find when they reached Pacific West Bank.

He said, "Listen, I don't want to go to Chinatown. I'd like you to bring me home."

Pollard felt another flash of irritation. She felt bad for Holman with what he was going through, but here he was with the big shoulders filling the other side of her car like a giant depressed lump, not even looking at her. He reminded her of herself when she sat in the kitchen staring at the goddamned clock.

She said, "We won't be at the bank that long."

"I have something else to do. Just drop me home first."

They were on Gower heading south to the freeway, stopped at a traffic light. Pollard planned to hop on the 101 for an easy slide into Chinatown.

"Holman, listen, we are close, okay? We are really close to making this case happen."

He didn't look at her.

"We can make it happen later."

"Goddamn it, we're halfway to Chinatown. If I have to bring you to Culver City it's really out of the way."

"Forget it. I'll ride the fuckin' bus."

Holman suddenly pushed open the door and stepped out into traffic. Pollard was caught off guard, but she jammed on the brake.

"Holman!"

Horns blew as Holman trotted across traffic.

"Holman! Would you come back here? What are you doing?"

He didn't look at her. He kept walking.

"Get back in the car!"

He walked south on Gower toward Hollywood. The cars behind her leaned on their horns and Pollard finally crept forward. She watched Holman walking, wondering what he so badly wanted to do. He no longer moved like a zombie or seemed depressed. Pollard thought he looked furious. She had seen his expression on men before, and it frightened her. Holman looked like he wanted to kill someone.

Pollard didn't turn onto the freeway. She let the traffic flow around her, then eased to the curb, letting Holman walk, but keeping him in sight.

Holman hadn't lied about taking the bus. Pollard watched him board a westbound bus on Hollywood Boulevard. Following it was a pain in the ass because it stopped at damn near every corner. Each time it stopped she had to wedge her Subaru to the curb even when there was no place to park, then crane her head to see past pedestrians and vehicles in case Holman got off.

When Holman reached Fairfax he finally stepped off,

then caught a Fairfax bus heading south. He stayed on the Fairfax bus to Pico, then changed buses again, once more heading west. Pollard believed Holman was going home like he had said, but she couldn't be sure and didn't want to lose him, so she followed him, furious at herself for wasting so much time.

Holman left the bus two blocks from his motel. Pollard was worried he might see her, but he never once looked around. Pollard found that odd, as if he had no awareness of his surroundings or maybe he no longer cared.

When he reached his motel she expected him to go inside, but he didn't. He continued around the side and got into his car, and then she was following him again.

Holman picked up Sepulveda Boulevard and dropped south through the city. Pollard stayed five or six cars back, following him steadily south until Holman surprised her. He stopped near a freeway off-ramp and bought a bouquet of flowers from one of the vendors who haunt the ramps.

Pollard thought, what in hell is he doing?

She found out a few blocks later when Holman arrived at the cemetery.

39

THE LATE-MORNING sun was breathtakingly hot as Holman turned onto the cemetery grounds. Polished head markers caught the light like coins strewn onto the grass, and the immaculate rolling lawn was so bright Holman squinted behind his sunglasses. The outside temperature gauge on his dashboard showed 98 degrees. The dashboard clock showed 11:19. Holman caught a glimpse of himself in the mirror, and froze—in that instant, he saw the dated Ray-Ban Wayfarers with his hair shaggy over the temples and was his younger self; the same Holman who ran wild with Chee, doing dope and stealing cars until his life spun out of control. Holman took off the Wayfarers. He must have been stupid, buying the same glasses.

With the midweek morning and the heat, only a few other visitors were scattered throughout the cemetery. A burial was taking place on the far side of the grounds, but only the one, with a small crowd of mourners gathered around a tent.

Holman followed the road up to Donna and parked

exactly where he had parked the last time he came. When he opened his car the heat crushed into him like a wave and the glare made him wince. He started to reach for the sunglasses, but thought, no, he didn't want to remind her of what he used to be.

Holman brought the flowers to her grave. His earlier flowers were now black and brittle. Holman collected the old flowers, then policed the headstone of dead leaves and petals. He took the dead stuff to a trash can by the drive, then brought the fresh flowers back and put them on her grave.

Holman felt badly he hadn't brought some kind of vase. In this heat, without water, the flowers would be shriveled and dead by the end of the day.

Holman grew even angrier with himself, thinking maybe he was just one of those people who fucked up everything.

He squatted and pressed his hand onto Donna's marker. The hot metal burned his palm, but Holman pressed harder. He let it burn.

He whispered, "I'm sorry."

"Holman?"

Holman glanced over his shoulder to see Pollard coming toward him. He pulled himself up.

"What did you think I was going to do, rob a bank?"

Pollard stopped beside him and gazed down at the grave.

"Richard's mother?"

"Yeah. Donna. I should've married this girl, but . . . you know."

Holman let it drop. Pollard looked up and seemed to study him.

"You okay?"

"Not so good."

Holman studied Donna's name on the marker. Donna Banik. It should have been Holman.

"She was proud of him. So was I, but I guess the kid never really had a chance, not with the way I was."

"Max, don't do this."

Pollard touched his arm, but Holman barely felt it, a gesture with no more weight than a wave from a passing car. He studied Pollard, who he knew to be a bright and educated woman.

"I tried to believe in God when I was in prison. That's part of the twelve-step thing—you have to give yourself to a higher power. They say it doesn't have to be God, but, c'mon, who are they kidding? I really wanted there to be a Heaven, man—Heaven, angels, God on a throne."

Holman shrugged, then looked back at the marker. Donna Banik. He wondered if she would mind if he had it changed. He could save up the money and buy a new marker. Donna Holman. Then his eyes suddenly filled when he thought, no, she would probably be ashamed.

Holman wiped at his eyes.

"I got this letter—Donna wrote when Richie finished the police academy. She said how proud she was he wasn't like me, here he was a policeman and nothing like me. Now, you might think she was being cruel, but she wasn't. I was grateful. Donna made our boy good and she did it alone. I didn't give them a goddamned thing. I left them with nothing. Now I hope there's no goddamned Heaven. I don't want her up there seeing all this. I don't want her knowing he turned out like me."

Holman felt ashamed of himself for saying such things. Pollard was as rigid as a statue. Her mouth was a tight line and her face was grim. When Holman glanced at her, a tear leaked down from behind her sunglasses and rolled to her chin.

Holman lost it when he saw the tear and a sob shuddered his body. He tried to fight it, but he gasped and heaved as tears flooded his eyes, and all he knew in that moment was how much pain he had caused.

He felt Pollard's arms. She murmured words, but he did not understand what she was saying. She held him hard, and he held her back, but all he knew were the sobs. He wasn't sure how long he cried. After a while Holman calmed, but he still held her. They just stood there, holding each other. Then Holman realized he was holding her. He stepped back.

"Sorry."

Pollard's hand lingered on his arm, but she didn't say anything. He thought she might, but she turned aside to wipe her eyes.

Holman cleared his throat. He still needed to talk with Donna and he didn't want Pollard to hear.

"Listen, I want to stick around here for a while. I'll be okay."

"Sure. I understand."

"Why don't we call it quits for today?"

"No. No, I want to see the reports. I can do that without you."

"You don't mind?"

"Of course not."

Pollard touched his arm again and he reached to touch her hand, but then she turned away. Holman watched her walk to her car in the brutal heat and watched as she drove away. Then he looked back at Donna's marker.

Holman's eyes filled again, and now he was glad Pollard had gone. He squatted once more and adjusted the flowers. They were already beginning to wilt.

"Bad or not, he was ours. I'll do what I have to do."

Holman smiled, knowing she wouldn't like it, but at peace with his fate. You just couldn't beat the bad blood.

"Like son, like father."

Holman heard a car door close behind him and glanced up into the sun. Two men were coming toward him.

"Max Holman."

Two more men were coming from the direction of the burial, one with bright red hair.

40

VUKOVICH AND FUENTES were coming from one side and two more men from the other. Holman could not reach his car. They spread apart as they came like they expected him to run and were ready for it. Holman stood anyway, his heart pounding. The empty plain of the cemetery left him exposed like a fly on a dinner plate with no place to hide and no way to lose them.

Vukovich said, "Easy now."

Holman started for the gate, and both Fuentes and one of the men behind him widened out.

Vukovich said, "Don't be stupid."

Holman broke into a trot and all four men suddenly ran forward. Holman shouted at the burial party.

"Help! Help me!"

Holman reversed course toward his car, knowing he couldn't make it even as he tried.

"Over here! Help!"

Mourners at the far tent turned as the first two officers converged on him. Holman lowered his shoulder at the last moment and drove into the smaller guy hard, then spun, making a sprint for his car as Vukovich shouted.

"Take him down!"

"Help! Help here!"

Someone slammed into Holman from behind, but he kept on his feet and turned as Fuentes charged from the side, Vukovich shouting, "Stop it, goddamnit— give it up."

Everything blurred into bodies and arms. Holman swung hard, catching Fuentes in the ear, then someone tackled his legs and he went down. Knees dug into his back and his arms were twisted behind him.

"Help! Help!"

"Shut up, asshole. What do you expect those people to do?"

"Witnesses! People are watching, you bastards!"

"Calm down, Holman. You're being dramatic."

Holman didn't stop struggling until he felt the plastic restraints cut into his wrists. Vukovich lifted his head by the hair and twisted him around so they could see each other.

"Relax. Nothing's going to happen to you."

"What are you doing?"

"Taking you in. Relax."

"I haven't fucking done anything!"

"You're fucking up our shit, Holman. We tried to be nice, but could you take the hint? You're fucking up our shit."

When they lifted him to his feet, Holman saw that everyone in the burial party was now watching them. The two motorcycle cops who had escorted the hearse were walking over, but Fuentes was trotting out to meet them.

Holman said, "They're witnesses, goddamnit. They're gonna remember this."

"All they're going to remember is some asshole getting arrested. Stop being stupid."

"Where are you taking me?"

"In."

"Why?"

"Just relax, man. You're going to be fine."

Holman didn't like the way Vukovich told him he was going to be fine. It sounded like something you heard before you were murdered.

They stood him up outside their car and went through his pockets. They took his wallet, keys, and cell phone, then checked his ankles, waist, and groin. Fuentes came back and the two motorcycle cops returned to their funeral. Holman watched them go as if they were life preservers drifting away on the current.

Vukovich said, "Okay, load'm up."

Holman said, "What about my car?"

"We'll get your car. You're in the limo."

"People know, damnit. People know what I'm doing."

"No, Holman, no one knows anything. Now shut the fuck up."

Fuentes drove away in Holman's Highlander as the two new guys pushed him into the backseat of their car. The larger man got into the back with Holman and his partner climbed in behind the wheel. They pulled away as soon as they had the doors locked.

Holman knew they were going to kill him. The two cops didn't speak to each other or look at him, so Holman made himself think. They were in a typical

Crown Victoria detective's car. Like all police cars, the rear seats and windows locked from the front. Holman wouldn't be able to open the doors even if he could get his hands free. He would have to wait until he was out of the car, but by then it might be too late. He tested his wrists. The plastic ties had no give and did not slide over his skin. He had heard cons say these new plastic ties were stronger than steel, but Holman had never worn them before. He wondered if they would melt.

Holman studied the two cops. They were both in their thirties with solid builds and burnished faces as if they spent time outdoors. They were fit men and young, but neither had Holman's heavy shoulders and weight. The man seated beside Holman was wearing a wedding ring.

Holman said, "Did either of you know my son?"

The driver shot a glance in the mirror, but neither answered.

"Was it one of you fuckers gunned him down?"

The driver glanced again and started to say something, but the backseat man cut him off.

"That's up to Random to tell him."

Holman figured Random was probably the fifth man, but now Vukovich, Fuentes, and these two guys were also part of the action. Add in Fowler, Richie, and the other two, and that made nine. Holman wondered if anyone else was involved. Sixteen million was a lot of money. There was still plenty to go around. Holman wondered what they knew about Pollard. They had probably followed him from his apartment and they would have seen her at the cemetery. They probably didn't like the idea of stirring up the FBI, but they wouldn't be willing to take the chance. When they got rid of him they would get rid of her.

They drove for about fifteen minutes. Holman thought they would take him out into the middle of nowhere or maybe a warehouse, but they turned off Centinela onto a cluttered middle-class street in Mar Vista. Small houses set on narrow lots lined both sides of the street, separated by hedges and shrubs. Fuentes had already arrived. Holman saw his Highlander parked ahead at the curb. Fuentes wasn't in the car and no one was standing nearby. Holman's heart started to pound and his palms grew cold. He was getting close and he would have to make his move soon. It felt like walking into a bank or circling a hot Porsche. His life was on the line.

They pulled across the drive of a small yellow house. A narrow drive ran past the side of the house under an arching carport to a garage at the rear of the property, and a blue sedan was parked beneath the arch. Holman didn't recognize the sedan. Fuentes was probably already inside, but he didn't know about Vukovich and Random. The entire house might be crawling with people.

The driver shut off their car and unlocked the back doors. The driver got out first, but the backseat man waited. The driver opened Holman's door, but stood close as if he wanted to block Holman's way.

"Okay, dude. Get out, but don't move away from the car. When you're out, stand straight up, then turn to face the car. You understand what I'm telling you?"

"I think I can handle it."

They didn't want the neighbors to see that Holman's hands were bound behind his back.

"Get out and turn."

Holman stepped out and turned. The driver immediately stepped up behind him and took a firm grip on his wrists.

"Okay, Tom."

Tom was the backseater. He got out, then moved to the front of the car, waiting for Holman and the driver.

Holman took in the surrounding houses. Bikes in the front yards and knotted ropes hanging from trees told him this was a family neighborhood. An outboard powerboat was parked in a drive two houses away. He glimpsed low chain-link fences through breaks in the shrubs. No one was outside, but people would be inside with their air conditioners, mostly women with small children this time of day. He could scream his ass off, but no one would hear. If he ran, he would have to go over fences. He hoped none of these people had pit bulls.

Holman said, "You'd better tell me what you want me to do so I don't fall."

"We're going around the front of the car."

"We going to the front door?"

"Straight down the drive to the carport."

Holman had already guessed they would use the carport. The front door was open, but the kitchen probably opened under the arch. The door would be hidden. Holman wasn't going to let them bring him into the house. He figured he would die in the house. If he was going to die he wanted to die out in the open where someone might see, but Holman didn't plan on dying that day. He glanced at the powerboat again and then at his Highlander.

Holman stepped away from the car. The driver

closed the door, then nudged him toward the front. Holman slowly shuffled forward. Tom waited for them at the drive, then walked a few paces ahead, and would reach the door first.

The driver said, "Jesus, you can walk faster than that."

"You're bumping my feet. Why don't you back off and give me some room, for Christ's sake. You're going to trip me."

"Fuck that."

The driver moved up even closer behind him, which was what Holman wanted. He wanted the driver as close behind as possible in the narrow space between the house and the blue sedan.

Tom stepped under the arch between the house and the car and went to the door. He waited for Holman and the driver, then opened the screen. When the screen door was open, Tom was on one side and Holman and the driver were on the other, sandwiched between the house and the blue sedan.

Holman didn't wait for the door to open. He swung his right foot high against the house and shoved the driver backwards against the sedan as hard and fast as he could. He jerked his left foot up to join with his right, and crushed hard with both legs, pressing so hard the sedan rocked. He slammed his head backwards and the solid bone-on-bone impact made his eyes sparkle. He hammered backwards again, driving with his thick neck and shoulders and felt the driver go limp as Tom realized what was happening.

"Motherfuck—hey!"

Tom scrambled to get the door closed, but Holman was already running. He didn't look back. He didn't run across the street or away from the yellow house. He cut hard across the front yard, then turned again, racing for the backyard. He wanted to get out of sight as quickly as possible. He plowed headfirst through bushes and shrubs and fell across a fence. He heard someone shouting inside the house, but he didn't stop. When he reached the rear of the house he rolled over another fence into the neighbor's backyard and kept going. Limbs and branches and sharp things tore at him, but he couldn't feel their claws. He sprinted across the neighbors' yard head-on into a wall of shrubs and kicked his way over another fence like an animal. He landed on a sprinkler head. He struggled to his feet and ran, falling over a tricycle as he cut across their yard. Inside, a small dog snarled and snapped at him through a window. He heard shouts and voices two houses away and knew they would be coming, but he moved up along the side of the house toward the street because that's where he had seen the boat. The boat was in the drive.

Holman crept to the corner of the house. Vukovich and Tom were in the street by their car, Vukovich holding a radio.

Holman crept forward to the boat with its big Mercury outboard motor. He twisted around to push the plastic tie onto the edge of the propeller blade and sawed as hard as he could, hoping that con was wrong about these things being stronger than steel.

He pushed with all of his weight and sawed the tie back and forth. He pushed so hard the tie cut into his skin, but the pain only drove him to push harder and then the tie popped and his hands were free.

Fuentes and Tom were now moving in the opposite

direction, but Vukovich was walking down the middle of the street in his direction.

Holman crabbed backwards away from the boat, then slipped across the backyard in the direction from which he had come. They were fanning away from the house and wouldn't expect him to double back, but this was an old trick he learned as a teenager when he first started breaking into apartments. He jumped back over the fence into the next yard and saw a stack of patio bricks. He took one, and he would need it for what he had planned. He continued across the yard, not crashing across as he had before, but moving quietly and listening. He eased over the fence and was again behind the yellow house. The backyard was empty and quiet. He slipped along the side of the house toward the street, stopping, starting, listening. He couldn't take too much time because Vukovich and the others would return when they couldn't find him.

Holman slipped along the side of the yellow house, staying beneath the windows. He could see the Highlander sitting in the street. They would probably see him when he made his move, but if he got lucky they would be too far away to stop him. He edged closer, and that's when he heard a woman's voice coming from inside the house.

The voice was familiar. He slowly raised up enough to see into the house.

Maria Juarez was inside with Random.

Holman should never have looked. He knew not to look from years of breaking into houses and apartments and stealing cars, but he made the mistake. Random caught the movement. Random's eyes widened, and he turned for the door. Holman didn't wait. He lurched to his feet and crashed through the shrubs. He only had seconds, and now those seconds might not be enough.

He ran for the Highlander as hard as he could and heard the front door open behind him. Vukovich was already on his way back and broke into a run. Holman shattered the Highlander's passenger-side window with the patio brick, then reached in and unlocked the door, Random screaming behind him.

"He's here! Vuke! Tommy!"

Holman threw himself inside. Chee had given him two keys, and Holman had left the spare in the console. He jacked it open, fished out the key, then pushed himself into the driver's seat.

Holman ripped away from the curb and didn't look back until he was gone.

338

41

HOLMAN WANTED to dump the Highlander as quickly as possible. He turned at the next intersection, punched out of the turn, and powered up the street. He resisted the urge to turn again at the next cross-street because turning and zigging were sure ways to lose a pursuit. Amateur car thieves and drunks fleeing arrest always thought they could shake the police in a maze of streets, but Holman knew they couldn't. Every turn cost speed and time and gave the police an opportunity to draw closer. Speed was life and distance was everything, so Holman powered forward.

Holman knew he had to get out of the residential neighborhoods and into an area with businesses and traffic. He hit Palms Boulevard on the fly, turned toward the freeway, and jammed into the first and largest shopping center he found, a big open-air monster anchored by an Albertsons supermarket.

The Highlander was large, black, and easy to spot, so Holman didn't want to leave it in the main parking lot. He turned into the service lane behind the shops and stores, and drove along the rear of the shopping center. He pulled over, shut the engine, and looked at himself. His face and arms were scratched and bleeding and his shirt was torn in two places. Streaks of dirt and grass stains striped his clothes. Holman slapped off the dirt as best he could, then spit on his shirt tail to wipe away the blood, but he still looked like hell. He wanted to get away from the Highlander, but the remaining plastic restraint was still attached to his left wrist. Holman had cut the right loop on the boat's propeller, and now the strands from the severed loop dangled from his left wrist like two strands of spaghetti. He studied the clasp. The restraints worked like a belt except the buckle only worked in one direction. The tongue of the belt could be slipped through the buckle, but tiny teeth prevented the tongue from being withdrawn. The plastic ties had to be cut, only now Holman didn't have a blade.

Holman started the engine again, turned the air conditioner on high, then pushed in the cigarette lighter. He tried not to think about what he was going to do because he knew it was going to hurt. When the lighter popped out, he pulled the tie as far from his skin as possible and pressed the glowing end onto the plastic. Holman clenched his jaw and held firm, but it burned like a sonofabitch. He had to heat the lighter three more times before the plastic melted through.

Vukovich had taken his keys, wallet, money, and cell phone. Holman searched the floorboards and console, and came up with seventy-two cents. That was it. That was all he had.

Holman locked the Highlander and walked away without looking back. He made his way through a pet store filled with cages of chirping birds and found a pay phone outside the Albertsons. He wanted to warn Pollard and he needed her help, but when he reached the phone he couldn't remember her number. Holman stood with the phone in his hand, drawing a total blank. He had programmed her number into his cell phone's memory, but now his phone was gone and he couldn't remember the number.

Holman started to shake. He slammed the phone into its cradle and shouted.

"Are you fucking *kidding* me?"

Three people entering the store stared at him.

Holman realized he was losing it and told himself to calm down. More people were looking. His cuts were bleeding again, so he wiped at his arms, but all that accomplished was smearing the blood. Holman scanned the parking lot. No patrol cars or anonymous Crown Victorias crept past the store. Holman began to calm down after a few minutes and decided to call Chee. He didn't remember Chee's number, either, but Chee's shop was listed.

Holman fed in his coins, then waited while the information operator made the connection.

Chee's phone rang. Holman expected someone to answer on the first couple of rings, but the ringing went on. Holman cursed his lousy luck, thinking the operator had given him the wrong connection, but then a young woman answered in a tentative voice.

"Hello?"

"I'm calling for Chee."

"I'm sorry, we're closed."

Holman hesitated. It was the middle of the day during the work week. Chee's shop should not have been closed.

"Marisol? Is this Marisol?"

Her voice came back, even more tentative.

"Yes?"

"This is Max Holman—your dad's friend. I need to talk to him."

Holman waited, but Marisol didn't respond. Then he realized she was crying.

"Marisol?"

"They took him. They came—"

She broke into full-blown sobs and Holman's fear level spiked.

"Marisol?"

Holman heard a man saying something in the background and Marisol trying to answer, and then the man came on the line, his voice also guarded.

"Who is this?"

"Max Holman. What's she talking about? What's going on over there?"

"This is Raul, man. You remember?"

Raul was the kid who put together Holman's driver's license.

"Yes. What was she talking about? Where's Chee?"

"They hooked him up, man. This morning—"

"Who?"

"Fuckin' cops. They arrested him."

Holman's heart started pounding again and he once more scanned the parking lot.

"What the fuck happened? Why did they arrest him?"

Raul lowered his voice like he didn't want Marisol to hear, but his voice became strained.

"I don't know what the fuck happened. They came in this morning with warrants, dogs, fuckin' assholes

342

with machine guns—"

"The police?"

"LAPD, FBI, SWAT, even the fuckin' ATF—if it's in the alphabet they were here. They ate this shit up and took his ass in."

Holman's mouth had grown dry, but the phone was slippery in his grip. He watched the parking lot and forced himself to breathe.

"Was he hurt? Is he okay?"

"I don't know."

Holman almost shouted.

"Why don't you know? It's a simple goddamned question."

"You think they let us stand around an' watch, muthuhfuckuh?! My ass was proned out! They brought us here in the fuckin' office!"

"Okay, okay—take it easy. Warrants for what? What were they looking for?"

"Assault rifles and explosives."

"Jesus Christ, what was Chee doing?"

"*Nothin'*, bro! Chee's not into anything over here, fuckin' explosives! His daughter works here. You think he'd keep explosives? Chee won't even let us deal stolen air bags."

"But they arrested him?"

"Hell, yes. They put him in the car right in front of his daughter."

"Then they must have found something."

"I don't know what the fuck they found. They loaded some shit into a truck. They had the fuckin' Bomb Squad here, Holman! They had those fuckin' dogs sniffin' everywhere, but we didn't have anything like that."

A computerized voice came on the line, telling Holman he had only one minute left. Holman was out of quarters. His time was running out.

Holman said, "I gotta go, but one more thing. Did they ask about me? Did they try to connect Chee with me in any way?"

Holman waited for the answer, but the line was already dead. Raul had hung up.

Holman put down the phone and studied the parking lot. He believed Chee had been set up, but he didn't understand why. Chee didn't know anything of value about Holman that couldn't be learned from Gail Manelli or Wally Figg or Tony Gilbert. Holman hadn't even told Chee about the missing sixteen million and his growing suspicions of a police conspiracy, but maybe someone thought he had; maybe someone thought Chee knew more than he did, and this was their way of trying to make him talk. Thinking about it made Holman's head hurt. Nothing made sense, so Holman stopped thinking about it. He had more immediate problems. No one was coming to give him a ride and more money and a car. Holman was on his own, and his only hope now was to reach Pollard. Reaching Pollard might be her only hope, too.

Holman went back to the Albertsons. He searched out the produce section, then headed for the rear of the store. Every produce section in every market in America had a swinging door in the back, through which produce clerks could push their carts laden with fruits and vegetables. Behind the door was always a refrigerated room into which the perishables were delivered and stored, and all such rooms had still more doors that opened onto loading docks.

Holman let himself out and was once more behind the shopping center. He returned to the Highlander, opened the rear cargo door, and pulled out the floor mats. The emergency tool kit had a screwdriver, pliers, and a jack handle. Holman hadn't stolen a car in a dozen years, but he still remembered how.

Holman went back to the parking lot.

42

WHEN POLLARD left Holman at the cemetery she climbed onto the freeway in a confused daze and headed for Chinatown, her head so busy she barely noticed the surrounding cars.

Pollard hadn't known what to expect when she followed Holman from Hollywood, but he had surprised her yet again. Here was Holman, who allowed himself to get pinched for bank robbery rather than let an old man die. Here was Holman, apologizing to his dead girlfriend for screwing up their son. Pollard hadn't wanted to leave. She had wanted to stay, just hold his hand and comfort him and lose herself to her feelings.

Pollard's heart broke when Holman started crying, not so much for him as for herself. Here was Holman, and she knew she could love him. Now, driving away, she fought the frightening suspicion she already did.

Max Holman is a degenerate career criminal ex-con and former drug abuser with no education, no skills, and absolutely no legitimate prospects short of an endless series of minimum-wage jobs. He has no respect for Black Letter law and his only friends are known felons. He will almost certainly end up back in jail within the next year. I have two little boys. What kind of example would he set? What would my mother say? What would everyone say? What if he doesn't find me attractive?

Pollard arrived at the Pacific West Building in Chinatown forty-five minutes later where Alma Wantanabe, the Pac West operations officer, showed her to a windowless conference room on the third floor. Two institutional blue boxes were waiting on a table.

Wantanabe explained that the LAPD summaries were divided into two distinct groups. One group consisted of divisional files specific to the robberies within those divisions—Newton Division Robbery detectives investigating robberies that had occurred in Newton. The second group of files was compiled by Robbery Special, who had synthesized the divisional reports into their larger, citywide investigation. Pollard knew from experience this was a function of resources. Though Robbery Special had been in charge of the citywide investigation, they employed divisional robbery detectives to pound the pavement on robberies in their local divisions. The divisional detectives then shipped their reports up the food chain to Robbery Special, who worked across divisional boundaries to coordinate and direct a Big Picture investigation.

Wantanabe cautioned her again not to remove or copy any material from the files, then left Pollard alone to work.

Pollard opened her own file for the cover-sheet copies Holman had made before Random confiscated the reports. The cover sheets told Pollard nothing except the case and witness numbers, and the witness numbers told her nothing without the identifying witness list:

Case # 11-621

Witness # 318

Marchenko/Parsons

Interview Summary

Pollard hoped to identify the witnesses through the witness lists, then see what they had to say. She didn't know the source of the cover sheets, so she started with the box of divisional reports. She emptied the box, then methodically searched for witness lists. She found three lists, but it soon became apparent that the divisional numbering system did not match with her cover sheets. She put the divisional files aside and turned to the Parker Center reports.

Her interest spiked the instant she opened the second box. The first page was a case file introduction signed by the commander of Robbery Special and the two lead detectives in charge of the case. The second lead detective was John B. Random.

Pollard stared at his name. She knew Random from his investigation into the murder of the four police officers. She had assumed he was a homicide detective, yet here he was in charge of a robbery investigation. The same robbery that now overlapped with the murders.

Pollard flipped through the following reports until she found the witness list. It was a thirty-seven-page document listing three hundred forty-six numbered names beginning with witness number one, who was identified as a teller employed at the first bank Marchenko and Parsons robbed. The lowest witness number on Pollard's cover sheets was #318, followed in consecutive order by 319, 320, 321, 327, and 334. All of her witnesses had come late in the case.

Pollard began matching the numbers on her cover sheets to names, and immediately saw a pattern.

#318 was identified as Lawrence Trehorn, who managed the four-unit apartment building in Beachwood Canyon where Marchenko and Parsons lived.

The next three witnesses were their neighbors.

#327 was an attendant at the West Hollywood health club Marchenko visited.

And #334 was Anton Marchenko's mother.

Pollard located the individual summaries, but did not immediately read them. She checked for the names of the detectives who conducted the interviews. Random had signed off on Trehorn and Mrs. Marchenko, and Vukovich had signed off on one of the neighbors. Vukovich had been one of the officers with Random who confronted Holman outside his daughter-in-law's apartment—another detective investigating the murders who had also investigated Marchenko and Parsons.

Pollard thought about Fowler and the fifth man going to see Mrs. Marchenko. She wondered if Fowler had gone to see these other five people, also.

Pollard copied the names and contact information of the five new witnesses, then read through the summaries. She half suspected that at least one of the summaries would reference Alison Whitt, the Hollywood Sign, or the Mayan Grille, but the reports provided nothing except a list of people who were personally known to Marchenko and Parsons. Pollard decided this was the key. None of these summaries were specific to

349

the actual robberies, but all were potentially relevant to establishing what Marchenko and Parsons had done with the money. This would have been why Richard Holman had them, but the questions remained: How had he gotten them and why had Random removed them from Richard's apartment? It was as if Random didn't want anyone to have proof that Fowler and his little group were trying to find the money.

When Pollard finished, she returned the summaries to the file in their proper order, then placed the files in their boxes. She kept thinking about Random taking the files. Pollard considered the possibility that Richard had gotten the files from Random, but something about this bothered her. Random knew what was in the summaries. If he was involved with Richard and Fowler, he could have told them what he knew—he didn't have to give them the files.

Pollard left the boxes on the table, then thanked Alma Wantanabe, who walked her to the elevators. As Pollard rode down, she checked her messages, but Sanders hadn't yet called. She felt a flash of frustration, then realized she had something almost as good with which to work—Mrs. Marchenko. If Random was the fifth man, Pollard did not need to see the informant list—Mrs. Marchenko would be able to identify him, which would put Random together with Fowler. Finding Alison Whitt's contact officer would then be icing on the cake.

Pollard decided to call Holman. She wanted to tell him what she had found, then go to Mrs. Marchenko. She was dialing his number when the elevator opened.

Holman was in the lobby, filthy and streaked with dried blood.

43

HOLMAN REMEMBERED she was going to the Pacific West Building, but he didn't know if she was still there or how to reach her and he had no money left to make a call. He didn't want to go to the building. If someone had followed Pollard from the cemetery Holman would be giving himself back to them, but he didn't know how else to reach her. Holman circled the building until he was scared he would miss her, then waited in the lobby like a nervous dog. He was about to leave when the elevator opened and Pollard stepped out. In that double-take moment when she saw him, her face went white.

"What happened to you? Look at you—what happened?"

Holman was still shaking. He led her away from the elevators. A lobby security guard had already questioned him twice and Holman wanted to leave.

"We gotta get out of here. Vukovich and those guys—they grabbed me again."

Pollard saw the guard, too, and lowered her voice.

"You're bleeding—"

"They might have followed you. I'll tell you outside—"

Holman desperately wanted to leave.

"Who?"

"The cops. They jumped me at the cemetery after you left—"

The shaking grew worse. Holman tried to bring her toward the door, but she pulled him the other way.

"This way. Come with me—"

"We have to go. They're looking for me."

"You're a mess, Max. You stand out. In here—"

Holman let her pull him into the women's bathroom. She led him to the lavatories, then jerked paper towels from a dispenser and wet them in the sink. Holman wanted to run, but he couldn't make himself move—the bathroom felt like a rat trap ready to spring.

"They brought me to a house. It was Vukovich and—Random was there. They didn't arrest me. It wasn't a goddamn arrest. They fuckin' *took* me—"

"Shh. You're shaking. Try to calm down."

"We have to get out of here, Katherine."

She wiped blood from his face and arms, but he couldn't stop talking any more than he could stop the trembling in his voice. Then he remembered his phone was missing and the terrible helpless feeling he had when he couldn't reach her.

"I need something to write with—a pen. You got a pen? I tried to call you, but I couldn't remember your number. I couldn't fuckin' remember—"

The trembling grew worse until Holman felt he was shaking apart. He was losing control of himself, but he didn't seem able to stop.

Pollard tossed the bloody towels, then gripped his arms.

"Max."

Her eyes seemed to draw him. She stared into his eyes and Holman stared back. Her fingers dug into his arms, but her eyes were calm and her voice was soothing.

"Max, you're here with me now—"

"I was scared. They had Maria Juarez—"

Holman couldn't stop looking into her eyes as her fingers massaged his arms.

"You're safe. You're with me now, and you're safe."

"Jesus, I was so fuckin' scared."

Holman stayed with her eyes, but the corners of her lips held a gentle curl that slowed him like an anchor would slow a drifting boat.

His shaking eased.

"You okay?"

"Yeah. Yes, I'm better."

"Good. I want you okay."

Pollard found a pen in her jacket, then took his arm. She wrote her cell number on the inside of his forearm, then looked up again with softer eyes.

"Now you have my number. You see, Max? Now you can't lose it."

Holman could feel that something was now different. She moved closer to him, then slipped her arms around him and rested her head on his chest. Holman stood stiff as a mannequin. He was uncertain and didn't want to offend her. She whispered into his chest.

"Just for a moment."

Holman hesitantly touched her back. She didn't run or jump away. He put his arms around her and laid his cheek on her head. Little by little, he let himself hold her and breathed her in and felt the badness drain away. After a bit Holman felt her stir, and they stepped apart at the same time. Pollard smiled.

"Now we can go. You can tell me what happened in my car."

Pollard was parked in the building's basement. Holman described how they had taken him at the cemetery and how he had escaped and what he had seen. She frowned as she listened, but made no comment and asked no questions until he was finished, even when he told her he had stolen a car. She didn't speak until he was finished, but even then she seemed uncertain.

"All right, it was Vukovich and three other men— one named Fuentes and one named Tom—who arrested you at the cemetery?"

"They didn't arrest me. They hooked me up, but they didn't bring me to a station—they brought me to a *house*. This wasn't any damn *arrest*."

"What did they want?"

"I don't know what they wanted. I got the hell out of there."

"Didn't they say anything?"

"*Nothing*—"

Then Holman remembered.

"At the cemetery, Vukovich said I was fucking them up, how they tried to be nice but I was fucking them up. He told me they were taking me in, but instead they took me to a goddamned house. I saw that house, there was no way I was going in, no way."

Pollard frowned harder as if she was trying to make sense of it, but couldn't.

"All right, and Random was at the house?"

354

"Yes. With Maria Juarez. Chee said the cops took her and he was right. And now they have Chee. They arrested him this morning."

Pollard didn't respond. She still seemed troubled and finally shook her head.

"I don't get what's happening here. They grabbed Maria Juarez and now they grabbed you—what were they going to do, hold you prisoner? What could they hope to gain?"

Holman thought it was obvious.

"They're getting rid of everyone who's rocking the boat about Random's case against Warren Juarez. Think about it. Random put the murders on Warren Juarez and closed the case, but Maria said Warren didn't do it—so they grabbed her. Then I didn't buy the story they floated, either. They tried to make me back off, and when that didn't work they bagged me, too. Now they have Chee."

"Random arrested him?"

"A task force raided his shop this morning looking for guns and explosives. That's bullshit. I've known Chee my whole life and I am telling you that's bullshit. These bastards must have set him up."

Pollard still didn't seem convinced.

"But why involve Chee?"

"Maybe they think I told him about the money. Maybe because he's been helping me. I don't know."

"Could you find the house again, the one where they took you?"

"Absolutely. I can take you there right now."

"We're not going there now—"

"We have to. Now that I know where they have her, they'll clear out. They'll take that woman with them."

"Max, listen to me—you're right. They left as soon as you left and if they were holding Maria Juarez against her will, then they took her with them. If we go back now we'll find an empty house. If we go to the police about this, what can we tell them? You were kidnapped by four LAPD officers who may or may not have had criminal intent?"

Holman knew she was right. He was a criminal. He had no proof, and no reason to think anyone would believe him.

"Then what can we do?"

"We have to find the fifth man. If we can prove Random is the fifth man we can tie him to Fowler and make our case—"

Pollard paged through her folder and pulled out a newspaper clipping about Richard's murder. The clipping included a picture of two cops making a statement at Parker Center, and one of the cops was Random.

"I want to show this picture to Mrs. Marchenko. If she fingers Random as the fifth man, I can take what we know to my friends at the FBI. I can make a case with this, Max."

Holman glanced at Random's grainy face, then nodded at Pollard. Once more, he knew she was right. She knew this stuff. She was a professional.

Holman reached out to touch the curve of her cheek. She didn't move away.

"Funny how things work."

"Yeah."

Holman turned to open the door.

"I'll see you over there."

Pollard grabbed his arm before he could leave.

"Hey! You're coming with me! You can't drive around in a stolen car. You want to get bagged for grand theft auto?"

Pollard was right again, but Holman knew he was right in a different way. Random and Vukovich had come for him. They would come for him again. For all he knew, every cop in the city was looking for him, and they would set him up just like they set up Chee.

Holman gently lifted her hand.

"I might have to run, Katherine. I don't want to run in your car. I don't want you caught with me."

Holman squeezed her hand.

"I'll see you at her place."

He didn't give her a chance to respond. Holman slid out of her car and trotted away.

44

HOLMAN LEFT the parking structure as if he was sneaking away from a bank he had just robbed. He still worried that someone had followed Pollard from the cemetery, so he studied the cars and pedestrians outside the building but found no one suspicious. He waited in his stolen car until Pollard pulled into traffic, then followed her to Mrs. Marchenko.

Holman felt better now that he had spoken with Pollard. He sensed they were close to finding out who murdered Richie, and why, and he suspected this was why Random had moved against him. Random had been a major player in the Marchenko case and now he controlled the investigation into the murder of the four officers. How convenient. Random would have known about the missing sixteen million and had probably put together a team to find it that included Fowler, Richie, and the others. Holman bitterly recalled how Random described them—problem officers; drunks and bums who would sell out for the pot of gold. Random wanted to pin the murders on Warren Juarez; Maria Juarez had proof her husband wasn't the shooter, so the proof disappeared and so did Maria Juarez. Richie had been in possession of reports Random had written, and Random had made the reports disappear. Holman had asked too many questions, so first they cut him off from the other families, then tried to scare him off, and finally tried to make him disappear, too. This was the only explanation Holman could see that made everything fit together. He still didn't understand how Chee was involved, but he felt sure they had enough. The noose was tightening, so Random was trying to tie off the loose ends and get rid of the hangman. When Holman realized he was the hangman, he smiled. It had to be Random—and he wanted to be Random's hangman.

When they reached Mrs. Marchenko's house, Holman parked across the street. Mrs. Marchenko opened her front door even as Holman joined Pollard on the sidewalk.

Pollard said, "I called her from the car."

Mrs. Marchenko didn't seem happy to see them. She looked even more suspicious than before.

"I been lookin' for that article. I don' see it."

Pollard smiled brightly.

"Soon. We're here to tack down a few last details. I have a picture I want to show you."

Holman followed Pollard and Mrs. Marchenko into her living room. He noticed the broken fan was still broken.

Mrs. Marchenko dropped into her usual chair.

"What picture?"

"Remember the pictures we showed you last time? You were able to identify one of two officers who came to see you?"

"Yes."

"I'm going to show you another picture. I want to know if he was the other man."

Pollard took the clipping from her folder and held it out. Mrs. Marchenko studied it, then nodded.

"Oh, him I know, but that was before—"

Pollard nodded, encouraging.

"Right. He interviewed you after Anton was killed."

"Right, yah—"

"Did he come back to see you with the other man?"

Mrs. Marchenko settled back in her chair.

"No. It wasn't him."

Holman felt a swirl of anger. They were close; they were at the very edge of breaking this thing open and now the old lady was being a roadblock.

"Why don't you look again—"

"I don't need to look again. Wasn't him with that man. Him, I know from before. He was one of that bunch came broke my lamp."

The old lady looked so smug and contrary that Holman was convinced she was jerking them around.

"For Christ's sake, lady."

Pollard held up a hand, warning him to stop.

"So think about that other man, Mrs. Marchenko. Try to remember what he looked like. He didn't look like this man?"

"No."

"Can you describe him?"

"He looked like a man. I don't know. A dark suit, I think."

Holman suddenly wondered if the fifth man might have been Vukovich.

"Did he have red hair?"

360

"He was wearing a hat. I don't know. I told you, I not pay attention."

Holman's certainty at nailing Random fell apart like a dream shattered by an alarm clock. Holman was still on the run; Chee was still in jail; Maria Juarez was still a prisoner. Holman snatched the clipping from Pollard and stalked over to Mrs. Marchenko. She jerked backwards as if she thought he might hit her, but Holman didn't care. He pointed at Random's picture.

"Are you *sure* it wasn't him?"

"Wasn't him."

"Max, stop it."

"How about if I told you he was the sonofabitch who shot your son? Would it look like him then?"

Pollard pushed up from the couch, rigid and angry.

"That's enough, Max. That's it."

Mrs. Marchenko's bulldog face hardened.

"Was him? Was he the one killed Anton?"

Pollard took the clipping and pushed Holman toward the door.

"No, Mrs. Marchenko. I'm sorry. He didn't have anything to do with Anton's death."

"Then why he say that? Why he say a thing like that?"

Holman stalked out of the house and didn't stop until he reached the street. He felt like an asshole. He was angry and confused and ashamed of himself all over again, and when Pollard came out she looked furious.

Holman said, "I'm sorry. How could it not be Random? It *had* to be Random! He's what ties this all together."

"Shut up. Just stop. All right, so the fifth man

361

wasn't Random or Vukovich. We know he wasn't your son or Mellon or Ash, but he had to be somebody."

"Random had three or four other guys with him at that house. Maybe it was one of them. Maybe Random has the whole fucking police department working for him."

"We still have Alison Whitt—"

She already had her cell phone out and was speed-dialing a number.

"If Random was her contact officer, we can still—"

She held up a hand, cutting him off as the person she called answered.

"Yeah, it's me. What did you get on Alison Whitt?"

Holman waited, watching as Pollard stiffened. Holman knew it was bad even before Pollard lowered the phone. He could read it in the way her shoulders dipped. Pollard stared at him for a moment, then shook her head.

"Alison Whitt was not a registered informant with the Los Angeles Police Department."

"So what do we do?"

Pollard didn't answer right away. He knew she was thinking. He was thinking, too. He should have expected it. He knew better than to expect anything to work out.

Pollard finally answered.

"I have her arrest record at my house. I can see who the arresting officers were. Maybe we were wrong in thinking she was a registered informant. Maybe she was just feeding some guy on the sly and I'll recognize a name."

Holman smiled, and, again, it was more for himself than her. He took in the lines of her face and the way her hair fell, and remembered again the first time he saw her, pointing a gun at him in the bank.

"I'm sorry I got you into this."

"We are *not* finished with this. We're close, Max. Random is all over both sides of this crazy thing and all we need is the one missing piece to have it make sense."

Holman nodded, but he felt only loss. He had tried to play this the right way, the way you're supposed to play it when you live within the law, but the right way hadn't worked out.

"You're a special person, Agent Pollard."

Her face tightened and she was that young agent again.

"My name is Katherine. Call me by my goddamn name."

Holman wanted to hold her again. He wanted to hold her close and kiss her, but doing so could only be wrong.

"Don't help me anymore, Katherine. You'll only get hurt."

Holman started toward his car, and now Pollard followed him.

"Waitaminute. What are you going to do?"

"Get new stuff and drop off the grid. They had me and they're going to come for me again. I can't let that happen."

He got into his car, but she stood inside the door and wouldn't let him close it. Holman tried to ignore her. He wedged his screwdriver into the busted ignition and twisted it to start the engine. Pollard still didn't get out of the way.

"What are you going to do for money?"

"Chee gave me some money. I have to go, Katherine. Please."

"Holman!"

Holman looked up at her. Pollard stepped back, then closed the door. She leaned into the window and touched his lips with hers. Holman closed his eyes. He wanted it to go on forever, but knew, like every other good thing in his life, it would not last. When he opened his eyes again, she was watching him.

She said, "I'm not going to quit."

Holman pulled away. He told himself not to look back. He had learned the hard way that looking back was when you got into trouble, so he told himself not to look, but he glanced in the mirror anyway and saw her in the street, watching him, this incredible woman who had almost been part of his life.

Holman wiped his eyes.

He stared ahead.

He drove.

They hadn't been able to put the pieces together, but that no longer seemed to matter. Holman was not going to let them get away with Richie's murder.

45

POLLARD WAS FURIOUS. Marki had used all the right terms in relating what Whitt told her about being an informant—the registration, the cap, the approval; civilians didn't know these things unless they knew them firsthand, so Pollard still believed Whitt had been telling the truth.

Pollard one-handed a call back to Sanders as she blasted up the Hollywood Freeway. She hadn't wanted to get into it in front of Holman, but now she wanted details.

"Hey, it's me. Can you still talk?"

"What's wrong?"

"This girl was an informant. I want you to check again."

"Hey. Whoa. I'm doing you a favor, remember? Leeds would have my ass if he found out."

"I'm sure this girl wasn't lying. I believe her."

"I know you believe her. I can hear your belief coming through the phone, but she wasn't on the list. Look—maybe some cop was paying her out of his own pocket. That happens all the time."

"If somebody was using her off the books she wouldn't have known about payouts being capped and having to be approved. Think about it, April—she was the real thing and she had a cop backing her."

"Listen to me: She was not on the list. I'm sorry."

"Maybe she's under an alias. Check her arrest record for—"

"Now you're being stupid. Nobody gets paid under an alias."

Pollard drove in silence for a while, embarrassed by her desperation.

"Yeah, I guess you're right."

"You know I'm right. What's going on with you, girl?"

"I was sure."

"She was a whore. Whores lie. That's what they do—you're my best lover, you made me come so good. C'mon, Kat. She made it sound good for her friend because she can make anything sound good. That's what they do."

Pollard felt ashamed of herself. Maybe it was Holman. Maybe she needed it to work out for him so badly she had lost her common sense.

"I'm sorry I freaked out on you."

"Just bring me some more donuts. I'm starting to lose weight. You know I like to keep my weight up."

Pollard couldn't even bring herself to smile. She closed her phone and brooded about it as she drove home, her thoughts swinging between her disappointment that Alison Whitt had lied about being an informant and her surprise that Mrs. Marchenko had not identified Random as the fifth man.

It was as if she and Holman had uncovered two

separate cases, with Random on both sides—Fowler's search for the missing money and Warren Juarez's alleged murder of the four officers. Random had been a principal in the Marchenko investigation and now he controlled the investigation into the murders. Random had immediately closed the murder investigation by naming Warren Juarez the assailant even though unanswered questions remained. He had denied that Fowler and the others were in any way connected to Marchenko and had actively suppressed further inquiry; *so* actively, it was clear he was hiding something.

Only Fowler and his boys *had* been searching for the money, and they hadn't been searching alone; at least one other person was involved—the fifth man. Someone had given them copies of Robbery Special reports they otherwise would not have been able to acquire, and two of those reports had been written by Random, who later confiscated those reports from Richard Holman's apartment. Someone had also accompanied Fowler to see Mrs. Marchenko, and Pollard believed it likely this was the same person who provided Fowler with information learned from Alison Whitt. Pollard believed Alison Whitt was now the telling key and would still likely connect everything to Random.

But Pollard still had a problem with Maria Juarez. When she disappeared, Random had issued a warrant for her arrest, yet Chee claimed the police had taken her from her cousins' home. Now, Holman had seen her in Random's custody. If Random was covering the true murderer of the four officers, why would he hold Maria Juarez captive and not simply kill her? Since her visit to the murder scene, Pollard believed the four officers had knowingly let their killer approach. If the killer was Juarez and if the officers were at the bridge that night on their search for the money, then Juarez must have had a connection with Marchenko. Maybe Maria Juarez knew what her husband had known, and Random needed her help to find the money. This would explain why she was still alive, but Pollard wasn't happy with the explanation. She was guessing, and guesses were a sucker's game in any investigation.

Pollard was trying to reconcile why so much of what she had didn't add up when she pulled into her drive. She hurried through the hellish heat and let herself into the house. She stepped through the front door, her irritation about Alison Whitt now being replaced by her dread at the inevitable phone call to her mother. She was lost in thought as she entered her house, thinking how absolutely nothing was going to work out, when a red-haired man waiting inside pushed the door out of her hands, slamming it shut.

"Welcome home."

Pollard startled so badly she jerked backwards as another man stepped from the hall, this man holding a credential case with a badge.

"John Random. We're the police."

46

POLLARD SPUN into Vukovich, driving her elbow hard into his ribs. Vukovich grunted and jerked to the side.

"Hey—"

Pollard spun in the opposite direction, thinking she had to get to the kitchen and then out the back door, but Random was already blocking her path.

"*Hold it!* We're not going to hurt you. *Hold it!*"

Random had stopped between Pollard and the kitchen and had come no closer. He was holding up both hands with his badge dangling over his head and Vukovich had made no further move. Pollard edged sideways to see both of them at the same time.

Random said, "Take it easy now. Just relax. If we wanted to hurt you would we be standing here like this?"

Random lowered his hands, but made no move forward. It was a good sign, but Pollard still edged to the side, eyes going between them, kicking herself for leaving her service pistol in the box in her closet, thinking, how stupid could you be? Thinking she might be able to get one of the kitchen knives, but she'd hate to fight these bastards with a knife.

"What do you want?"

Random studied her for a moment longer, then put away his badge.

"Your cooperation. You and Holman have been messing things up for us. Will you give me a chance to explain?"

"Is that why you grabbed him, to explain?"

"I wouldn't be here now and telling you what I'm about to tell you if you hadn't forced my hand."

Vukovich was leaning against the door, watching her, but his eyes were curious and his manner relaxed. Random seemed irritated, but his eyes were tired and his suit was rumpled. Nothing about their body language was threatening. Pollard felt herself begin to relax, but she was still wary.

She said, "Question."

Random opened his hands, saying go ahead, ask.

"Who murdered those men?"

"Warren Juarez."

"Bullshit, Random. I don't believe you and I don't believe they just happened to be under that bridge. They were looking for Marchenko's money."

Random opened his hands again and shrugged, the shrug saying he could take it or leave it whether she believed him.

"Yes, they were looking for the money, but Juarez was the shooter. He was hired by someone to kill them. We're trying to identify the person who hired him."

"Stop lying to me. Holman saw Maria Juarez with you at the house."

"Not lying. That house is a safe house. She was there voluntarily at our request."

"Why?"

"Juarez didn't commit suicide. The person who hired him murdered him. We believe he was hired because of his connection with Fowler and that the person who hired him planned to kill him from the beginning. We grew worried that this person might also murder his wife. We brought Holman to the house so Maria could tell him herself. I didn't expect him to believe me otherwise."

Pollard watched Random as he spoke and believed he was telling the truth. Everything he was saying made sense. She thought it through and finally nodded.

"All right. Okay, I buy that, but why did you have Chee arrested? I don't get that."

Random glanced at Vukovich before looking back at her. He shook his head.

"I don't know what you're talking about."

"Holman's friend, Chee—Gary Moreno. He was raided this morning and taken into custody. We thought that was you."

"I don't know anything about it."

"What are we talking about, Random? Am I supposed to believe it was a coincidence?"

Random looked blank, but he glanced at Vukovich again.

"Vuke, see what you can find out."

Vukovich took out a cell phone and drifted into the dining room toward the kitchen. Pollard could hear him mumbling as she continued with Random.

"If you knew another person was involved with Juarez, why did you close the case?"

"His killer set up the murder to look like a suicide. I wanted him to think we bought it. I wanted him to believe we didn't know he existed so he would feel safe."

"Why?"

"We believe this person is a high-level police officer."

Random said it matter-of-factly and without hesitation. This was exactly what Pollard and Holman had been thinking, only they had figured it was Random. Pollard suddenly realized how the disparities between the two Randoms made sense, and how all the inconsistencies about him could be consistent.

"The fifth man."

"What's the fifth man?"

"We knew someone else was involved. We called him the fifth man. We thought it was you."

"Sorry to disappoint you."

"You've been running an investigation within an investigation, one public, the other secret—a secret investigation."

"There was no other way to approach this. The only people who know what we're doing are my team, the chief, and one assistant chief. This investigation began weeks before those guys were killed. I was informed a group of officers were making a play for the money. We identified most of them, but someone with an intimate knowledge of Marchenko and Parsons was feeding information to Fowler, and Fowler was protecting the sonofabitch like a pit bull. Fowler was the only one who knew this person, the only one who spoke or met with him, and that's who we were trying to identify."

"And then the shooting started."

Random's face tightened.

"Yes. Then the shooting started, and you and Holman have been kicking so many rocks even divisional officers are beginning to notice. I need you to stop, Pollard. If this man starts feeling the heat we'll lose him."

Now Pollard understood the calls Leeds had received from Parker Center. The A-Chief had been trying to find out what she was doing and reaming Leeds to make her stop.

"How is it you know so much about what Fowler did and didn't do? How do you know Fowler was the only one?"

Random hesitated. It was the first time he had hesitated in answering her questions. Pollard felt a knot in her stomach because she suddenly knew the answer.

She said, "You had someone inside."

"Richard Holman was working for me."

The icy air-conditioning grew warm. The house filled with silence, as if it was spreading from her kitchen like spilled syrup. Everything Holman had told her about his conversations with Random flickered in her head.

"You sonofabitch. You should have told him."

"Telling him would have compromised this investigation."

"You let the man think his son was dirty. Do you have any idea how much this has been hurting him? Do you give a shit?"

The soft flesh around Random's eyes tightened. He wet his lips.

"Rich Holman contacted me when Fowler tried to recruit him. Rich had refused, but I convinced him to call Fowler back. I put him in with them, Ms. Pollard, so yes, I give a shit."

Pollard went to her couch. She paid no attention to Random. She had nothing to say. She thought about Holman. She blinked hard when her eyes began to fill because she didn't want Random to see her cry: Richie wasn't a bad guy anymore; Richie was good. Holman wouldn't have to apologize to Donna.

Random said, "Do you see why it had to be this way?"

"If you're looking for absolution, forget it. Maybe it did have to be this way, Random, but you're still an asshole. The man lost his son. All you had to do was talk to him like a human being instead of a dirtbag and none of this would be happening."

"Will you call him? I need to get you people on board with this before it's too late."

Pollard laughed.

"Well, I would, but I can't. Your guys took his cell phone at the cemetery. I have no way to reach him."

Random clenched his jaw, but didn't respond. Vukovich returned from the dining room saying someone would call him back, but Pollard paid no attention. She was wondering if everything she and Holman had done was pointless. The fifth man was probably already gone.

"Well, did they find the money or not? I'm guessing they must have or this suspect you're looking for wouldn't have killed these people."

"We're not sure. If the money was located, it was found after the murders."

"They must have found the money, Random. What did they find at the Hollywood Sign?"

Random was clearly surprised.

"How did you know about that?"

"Kicking rocks, you asshole. They found something on the Thursday night, before they were murdered. Whatever they found was buried in a hole approximately twelve inches wide and eighteen inches deep. What was it?"

"Keys. They found twenty-two keys in a blue metal thermos bottle."

"Just keys? What kind of keys?"

"Rich didn't see them. It was Fowler who opened the thermos. He told the others what they had, but kept them in his possession."

"There was nothing about how to find the locks?"

"Just the keys. The next day, Fowler told the others that his partner thought maybe he could figure out what the keys opened. We believe that's why the meeting was called on the night they were murdered. The last report I got from Rich, he said everyone thought they were going to learn about the money."

Pollard was thinking about the keys when she realized almost everything Random knew came from Rich Holman. If Fowler shared the wealth, then Rich passed it on to Random, but Fowler had protected his partner. He kept secrets. Pollard suddenly wondered if she didn't know more about this case than Random.

"Do you know why Marchenko hid those keys at the Hollywood Sign?"

Pollard could see by his expression he didn't have a clue. He shrugged, guessing at the reason.

"Remote. Close to his apartment."

"Alison Whitt."

Random was lost.

375

"Alison Whitt was a prostitute. Marchenko used to have sex with her up at the sign. You didn't know this?"

Vukovich shook his head.

"That's not possible. We interviewed everyone even remotely connected to Marchenko and Parsons. Everyone we talked to said these clowns were eunuchs. They didn't even have *male* friends."

"Holman and I learned about her from Marchenko's mother. Random, listen to this—approximately a week before the murders, Fowler and another man went to see Marchenko's mother. They went specifically to ask about Alison Whitt. The man with Fowler that day wasn't Rich or Mellon or Ash. He must have been Fowler's partner. She didn't have a name for him, but you could work her with an artist."

Random shot a glance at Vukovich.

"Call Fuentes. Have someone go with an artist."

Vukovich turned away again with his cell phone as Random turned back to Pollard.

"What's the story on Whitt?"

"Bad. She was murdered on the same night as the others. Whitt's the connection here, Random. Holman and I learned about her from Mrs. Marchenko, but Fowler and his friend knew about Whitt *before* they saw Marchenko's mother. Whitt claimed she was a registered informant, so I figured the fifth man might be her contact, but that didn't pan out."

"Waitaminute—how did you find out all this if Whitt was already dead?"

Pollard told him about Marki Collen and the Mayan Grille and Alison Whitt's stories about Marchenko. Random took out a pad and made notes. When she finished,

Random studied what he had written.

"I'll check her out."

"You won't find anything. I had a friend at the Feeb run her name through the roster at Parker. She isn't on your list."

Random made a dark smile.

"Thank your friend, but I'll check it myself."

Random took out his phone and went to the window as he made his call. While he was talking, Vukovich returned to Pollard.

"Got word on your boy, Chee. It was a righteous bust. Bomb Squad got a tip from the Feeb and rolled in with Metro. They pulled six pounds of C-4 plastic explosive and some det cord out of his shop."

Pollard stared at Vukovich, then looked at Random, but Random was still talking on his phone.

"The FBI put them onto this?"

"What the man said. Part of a conspiracy investigation, he said, so they rolled over to check it out."

"When did the call go in?"

"This morning. Early sometime. Is that important?"

Pollard shook her head, feeling a numbness settle low in her legs.

"You sure it was the Feeb?"

"What the man said."

The numbness spread up into her body.

Random finished his call, then took a business card from his wallet and brought it to Pollard.

"Holman will want to talk to me. That's okay. Once you reach him, call me, but you have to make him understand he has to back off. That's imperative here. You can't tell anyone what I've said, and Holman can't tell his daughter-in-law. You see why we're playing it like this, don't you? I hope to Christ it's not already too late."

Pollard nodded, but she wasn't thinking about how Random was playing it. She waited stiffly at the door as they walked away, then turned to face the emptiness of her home. Pollard didn't believe in coincidence. They taught it at Quantico and she had learned it over hundreds of investigations—coincidence did not occur.

A tip from the Feeb.

Pollard went to her bedroom and dragged a chair into her closet. She pulled the box from her high shelf, the highest shelf where the boys couldn't reach, and took down her gun.

Pollard knew she might have made a grave and serious mistake. Marki told them Whitt was a registered informant with a cop taking care of her, but "cop" didn't necessarily mean a policeman and LAPD wasn't the only law enforcement agency using registered informants. Sheriffs, Secret Service agents, U.S. Marshals, and ATF agents all thought of themselves as cops, and all of them employed registered informants.

Alison Whitt could have been an informant for the FBI. And if she had—

The fifth man was an FBI agent.

Pollard hurried out into the heat and drove into Westwood.

47

REGISTERED INFORMANTS could be and often were integral in solving crimes and obtaining indictments. The information they provided and their methods of obtaining it were included as part of the legal record in investigators' reports, writs, warrants, grand jury indictments, motions, briefs, and ultimately trials. The true names of informants were never used, as many of these documents were in the public record. In all such documents, the informant's name was replaced by a number. This number was the informant's code number, and the codes—along with investigators' reports regarding the informant's reliability and pay vouchers when informants were paid for their information—were held under lock and key to protect the anonymity of the informants. Where and how this list was safeguarded varied by agency, but no one was guarding nuclear launch codes; all an agent had to do was ask his boss for the key.

Pollard had used informants only four times during her three years on the Squad. On each of those four occasions she had requested the Bank Squad's informant list from Leeds and watched him open a locked file cabinet in which he stored the papers. Each time, he used a brass key taken from a small box he kept in his upper right-hand desk drawer. Pollard didn't know if the box and the key and the file would be in their same places after eight years, but Sanders would know.

The sky over Westwood was a brilliant clear blue when Pollard rolled into the parking lot. It was eight minutes after two. The black tower shimmered against the sky; an optical trick played by the sun.

Pollard studied the tower. She tried telling herself this was the one-in-a-million chance when a coincidence was just a coincidence, but she didn't believe it. Alison Whitt's name was going to be on a form in Leeds' office. The agent who recruited and used her was almost certainly responsible for murdering six people. That agent might be anyone.

Pollard finally opened her phone to call Sanders. She needed a pass into the building, but Sanders did not answer. Her voice mail picked up on the first ring, indicating Sanders was probably at a crime scene interviewing fresh victims.

Pollard cursed her bad luck, then dialed the Squad's general number and waited as it rang. On days when the Squad was spread throughout L.A., a duty agent remained in the office to field incoming calls and attend to his or her paperwork. Whenever Pollard had been the duty agent she usually ignored the calls.

"Bank Squad. Agent Delaney."

Pollard remembered the young agent she met with Bill Cecil. New guys always answered because they weren't yet jaded.

"This is Katherine Pollard. I met you up in the office

with the donuts, remember?"

"Oh, sure. Hi."

"I'm downstairs. Is April up there?"

Pollard knew Sanders wasn't in the office, but asking about Sanders was a setup for asking about Leeds. She had to find out if Leeds was in his office because Leeds controlled the list. Pollard wanted Leeds gone.

Delaney said, "I haven't seen her. I'm pretty much alone here. Everyone's out on a call."

"How about Leeds?"

"Um, he was here earlier—no, I don't see him. It's pretty busy today."

Pollard was relieved, but tried to sound disappointed.

"Damn. Kev, listen—I have some things for Leeds I wanted to drop off along with a box of donuts for the Squad. Would you send down a badge?"

"Sure. No problem."

"Great. I'll see you in a minute."

Pollard had picked up a box of donuts from Stan's to justify her visit to the office. She tucked her gun under the seat, then carried the donuts and her file into the building. She brought the file so she would have an excuse to enter Leeds' office. Pollard waited for her escort like before, then rode up to the thirteenth floor.

When she entered the squad area she scanned the room. Delaney was alone in a cubicle near the door. Pollard flashed a big smile at Delaney as she approached him.

"Man, I used to *hate* having the duty. I think you need a donut."

Delaney fished a donut from the box, but seemed uncertain where to put it and had probably taken it only to be polite. His desk was covered in paperwork.

Pollard said, "You want me to leave the box with you?"

Delaney glanced at his desk, noting there was no place to put it.

"Why don't you leave it in the coffee room?"

"You bet. I'm going to drop these things in Leeds' office, then I'll be out of your hair."

She gestured with the file so he would see it, then turned away. Pollard tried to move with an easy grace, as if her actions were expected and normal. She dropped off the donuts in the coffee room, then stole a glance at Delaney as she stepped back into the squad area. His head was down, busy with his work.

Pollard went to Leeds' office. She opened the door without hesitation and entered the dragon's lair. Pollard had not been in Leeds' office since the day she resigned, but it was as intimidating now as she remembered. Pictures of Leeds with every president since Nixon adorned the walls, along with an inscribed portrait of J. Edgar Hoover, who Leeds revered as an American hero. An actual Wanted poster of John Dillinger hung among the presidents, presented to Leeds by President Reagan.

Pollard took in the office to get her bearings and was relieved to see the file cabinet was still in the corner and Leeds' desk was unchanged. She hurried to the desk and opened the upper right-hand drawer. Several keys were now in the box, but Pollard recognized the brass key. Now she hurried to the cabinet, worried Delaney would start wondering why she was taking so long. She unlocked the cabinet, opened the drawer, and scanned through the file folders, which were divided alphabetically. She found the W's, pulled out the folder, then searched through the files. Each file was labeled by the informant's name and code number.

She was still hoping this would be the one-in-a-million coincidence when she saw the name: Alison Carrie Whitt.

Pollard opened the file to the cover sheet, which contained Alison Whitt's identifying information. She scanned down the page, searching for the fifth man's name—

"What in the hell are you doing?"

Pollard jerked at the sound of his voice. Leeds filled the door, his face furious.

"Pollard, *stand up*! Get away from those files. Delaney! Get in here!"

Pollard slowly stood, but she didn't put down the file. Delaney appeared in the door behind Leeds. She studied them. Either of their names might be on the sheet, but she didn't believe it would be Delaney. He was too new.

Pollard pulled herself together. She stood tall and looked Leeds in the eye.

"An agent in this office was involved in the murder of the four officers under the Fourth Street Bridge."

Even as she said it she thought: Leeds. It could be Leeds.

He advanced toward her across the office, moving carefully.

"Put down the file, Katherine. What you're doing now is a federal crime."

"Murdering four police officers is a crime. So is murdering a registered federal informant named Alison Whitt—"

Pollard held out the file.

"Is she your informant, Chris?"

Leeds glanced at Delaney, then hesitated. Delaney was her witness. Pollard went on.

"She's in your file—Alison Whitt. She was a friend of Marchenko's. An agent in this office knew that because he knew her. That same agent was involved with Mike Fowler and the other officers in trying to find the sixteen million dollars."

Leeds glanced at Delaney again, but now Pollard read his hesitancy in a different light. He didn't seem threatening; now, he was curious.

"What kind of proof do you have?"

She nodded toward the file with all of Holman's notes and articles and documents.

"It's all in there. You can call an LAPD detective named Random. He'll back me up. Alison Whitt was murdered on the same night as the four officers. She was murdered by the person named in her file."

Leeds stared at her.

"You think it's me, Katherine?"

"I think it could be."

Leeds nodded, then slowly smiled.

"Look."

Pollard skimmed the last few entries on the cover sheet until she found the name.

The name she found was Special Agent William J. Cecil.

Bill Cecil.

One of the kindest men she had ever known.

48

HOLMAN CRUISED three mall parking lots before he found a red Jeep Cherokee similar to the one he had stolen. Swapping plates with the same make, model, and color vehicle was a trick Holman learned when he stole cars for a living—now if an officer checked Holman's plate, the vehicle report wouldn't show that his Jeep had been stolen.

Holman switched the plates, then headed for Culver City. He did not like the idea of returning to his apartment, but he needed the money and the gun. He didn't even have change to call Perry to see if anyone had come around. Holman kicked himself for not asking Pollard to loan him a few bucks, but it hadn't occurred to him until later. And this stolen Jeep was clean. He searched the floorboards, seats, console, and cushions, and found nothing—not even trash.

The lunch-hour crush was beginning to ease when Holman reached the Pacific Gardens. He circled the block, looking for loiterers and people waiting in parked cars. Pollard had made good points about the confusing nature of Random's actions, but whatever their intentions Holman was certain they would come for him again. He circled the block twice more, then parked up the street, watching the motel for almost twenty minutes before he decided to make his move.

Holman left the Jeep on the street alongside the motel and entered through the rear by Perry's room. He stopped at the bottom of the stairs, but heard and saw nothing unusual. Perry wasn't at his desk.

Holman moved back to Perry's room and rapped lightly at the door. Inside the room, Perry answered.

"What is it?"

Holman kept his voice low.

"It's me. Open up."

Holman heard Perry cursing, but soon the door opened enough for Perry to see out. His pants were bunched around his thighs. Only Perry would answer a door this way.

"I was on the goddamned crapper. What is it?"

"Has anyone been here looking for me?"

"Like who?"

"Like anyone. I thought some people might come around."

"That woman?"

"No, not her."

"I've been out there all mornin' til my bowels started to move. I didn't see anyone."

"Okay, Perry. Thanks."

Holman returned to the lobby, then crept up the stairs. When he reached the second floor, he checked the hall in both directions but the hall was empty. Holman didn't stop at his room; he went directly to the utility closet and eased open the door. Holman pushed the mops out of the way and reached into the wall beneath the water valve. The wad of cash and the gun were still behind the pipe. Holman was fishing them out when the muzzle of a gun dug hard behind his left ear.

"Leave go whatever you've got, boy. Nothing better come out of there but your hand."

Holman didn't move. He didn't even turn to look, but went rigid with his hand in the wall.

"Pull that hand out slow and empty."

Holman showed his hand, opening his fingers wide so the man could see.

"That's good. Now stand there while I cop a feel."

The man felt Holman's waist and his crotch and the seat of his pants, then checked down along the inside of his legs to his ankles.

"All right then. You and I have a little problem, but we're gonna work it out. Turn around slow."

Holman turned as the man stepped back, giving himself room to react if Holman tried something. Holman saw a bald light-skinned black man wearing a blue suit. The man slipped his pistol into his coat pocket, but held on to it, showing Holman it was ready to go. It took a minute before Holman recognized him.

"I know you."

"That's right. I helped put your ass away."

Holman remembered—FBI Special Agent Cecil had been with Pollard that day in the bank. Holman wondered if Pollard had sent him, but the way Cecil was holding the gun told him Cecil was not here as his friend.

"Am I under arrest?"

"Here's what we're going to do—we're going down those stairs like we're the best buddies in the world. That old man down there says anything or tries to stop us, you tell him you'll see him later and keep walking. We get outside, you'll see a dark green Ford parked out front. You get in. You do anything but what I'm telling you, I'll kill you in the street."

Cecil stepped out of the way and Holman went down the stairs and got into the Ford, wondering what was happening. He watched Cecil cross in front of the car, then get in behind the wheel. Cecil took the pistol from his pocket and held it in his lap with his left hand as he pulled away from the curb. Holman studied him. Cecil's breath was fast and shallow and his face sheened with sweat. His eyes were large, darting between traffic and Holman like a man watching for snakes. He looked like a man who had stolen a car and was trying to get away.

Holman said, "What the fuck are you doing?"

"Going to get us sixteen million dollars."

Holman tried to show nothing, but his right eye watered as the skin surrounding it flickered. Cecil was the fifth man. Cecil had killed Richie. Holman glanced at the gun. When he looked up Cecil was watching him.

"Oh, yeah. Yeah, yeah, I was in with them, but I didn't have anything to do with those killings. Me and your boy were partners until Juarez lost his mind. Sonofabitch went nuts killing everybody, figuring he could keep the money, I guess. That's why I took him out. I took him out for killing those people."

Holman knew Cecil was lying. He saw it in how Cecil made eye contact, arching his eyebrows and nodding his head to fake sincerity. Fences and dope dealers had lied to Holman the same way a hundred times. Cecil was trying to play him, but Holman didn't understand why. Something had driven Cecil into revealing himself and now the man clearly had a plan that included Holman.

Images of Cecil under the bridge flashed in Holman's head like a shotgun in the darkness: Cecil cutting loose at point-blank range, the white-gold plume, Richie falling . . .

Holman glanced at the gun again, wondering if he could get it or push it aside. Holman wanted the sonofabitch—everything he had done since that morning in the CCC when Wally Figg told him Richie was dead had led to finding this man. If Holman could keep from being shot he might be able to punch Cecil out, but then where would he be? He would have to shoot Cecil right there or the cops would come and Cecil would flash his creds—who would they believe? Cecil would split while Holman was trying to talk himself out of a squad car.

Holman thought he might be able to jump out of the car before Cecil shot him. They had just turned onto Wilshire Boulevard, where traffic slowed.

"You don't have to jump. We get where we're going, I'm gonna let you out."

"I'm not going anywhere."

Cecil laughed.

"Holman, I've been hooking up guys like you for almost thirty years. I know what you're going to think even before you think it."

"You know what I'm thinking right now?"

"Yeah, but I won't hold it against you."

"I'm thinking why the fuck are you still here if you have sixteen million dollars."

"Know where it is, just couldn't get it. That's where you come in."

Cecil took a cell phone from the console and dropped it in Holman's lap.

"Here. Call your boy Chee, see what's shaking."

Holman caught the phone but did nothing. He stared at Cecil and now he felt a different kind of dread, one that had nothing to do with Richie.

"Chee was arrested."

"You already know? Well, good, save us a call. Chee was in possession of six pounds of C-4. Among the evidence confiscated from that shithole he calls a body shop are the telephone numbers of two people suspected of being Al Qaeda sympathizers and the plans for building an improvised explosive device. You see where I'm going with this?"

"You set him up."

"Ironclad, baby, ironclad. And only I know who planted that shit in his shop, so if you don't help me get this goddamned money your boy is fucked."

Without warning, Cecil slammed on the brakes. The car screeched to a stop, throwing Holman into the dash. Horns blew and tires screamed behind them, but Cecil didn't react. His eyes were hard black chips that stayed on Holman.

"Do you get the picture?"

More horns blew and people cursed, but Cecil's eyes never wavered. Holman wondered if he was crazy.

"Just take the money and go. What in hell do I have to do with this?"

"Told you—couldn't get it by myself."

"Why the hell not? Where is it?"

"Right there."

Holman followed Cecil's nod. He was looking at the Beverly Hills branch of Grand California Bank.

49

CECIL PULLED his car to the curb out of the flow of traffic, and stared at the bank as if it were the eighth wonder of the world.

"Marchenko and Parsons hid all that money in a goddamned bank."

"You want me to rob a bank?"

"They didn't *deposit* the goddamned money, dumb-ass. It's in twenty-two safe-deposit boxes, the big kind, not those little ones."

Cecil reached under his seat and took out a soft pouch that tinkled. He dropped it into Holman's lap and took back the phone.

"Got the keys here, all twenty-two."

Holman poured the keys into his hand. The name MOSLER was cut into one side along with a seven-digit number. A four-digit number was on the opposite side.

"This is what they hid at the sign."

"Guess he figured if he got pinched for something, those keys would be safe up there. Wasn't anything saying which bank, either, but the manufacturer keeps a record. One phone call, I had it."

Holman stared down at the keys filling his hand. He shifted them like coins. Sixteen million dollars.

Cecil said, "So now you're thinking, if he had the keys and knew where it was, why didn't he just go get the money."

Holman already knew. Every bank manager in L.A. would recognize Cecil and the other Bank Squad agents on sight. A bank employee would have to accompany him into the vault with the master key because safe-deposit boxes always required two keys—the customer's and the bank's—and Cecil would have to sign their ledger. Sixteen million spread among twenty-two boxes was a lot of trips in and out of a bank where you were recognized by the employees and everyone knew you were not a customer and had rented no boxes. Cecil would have been questioned. His comings and goings would have been recorded by security cameras. He would have been made.

"I know why you didn't get the money. I was wondering how much sixteen million dollars weighs."

"I can tell you exactly. Bank gets hit, they tell us how many of each denomination was lost. Tally that up, you know how many bills; you have four hundred fifty-four bills in a pound, doesn't matter what denominations—just do the math. This particular sixteen million weighs eleven hundred forty-two pounds."

Holman considered the bank again, then glanced back at Cecil. The man was still staring at the bank. Holman would have sworn his eyes glittered green.

"Did you go look at it?"

"Went in one time. Opened box thirty-seven-oh-one. Took thirteen thousand dollars and never went back. Too scared."

Cecil frowned at himself, disgusted.

"Even wore a goddamn pissant disguise."

Cecil had gold fever. Men in the joint used to talk about it, trying to make their bad decisions sound romantic by comparing themselves to Old West prospectors; men who got high by dreaming about the pot-of-gold score that would set them up. They thought about it until they thought about nothing else; they obsessed on it until it consumed them and they had nothing else in their lives; they became desperate for it until their desperation made them stupid. This idiot was looking at six first-degree murder hits and all he could see was the money. Holman saw his way in. He smiled.

Cecil said, "What are you smiling at?"

"I thought you knew what I was thinking before I thought it."

"I do. You're thinking, why on earth did this pathetic motherfucker pick me?"

"That would be right."

Cecil's wet eyes hardened with anger.

"Who would you expect me to get, my *wife*? You think this is my *preferred* plan of action? Motherfucker, believe me, I was going to work this out—that money is just *sitting* there! I had all the time I needed, but you and that bitch got me jammed in a corner. A week ago I had forever; now, I got fifteen minutes, so who in hell *should* I ask? Call my brother in Denver, maybe the kid who caddies when I play golf? And say *what*, come help me steal some money? This shit is on *you*! I will *not* walk away from sixteen million dollars.

I refuse! So here we are. It's you because I don't have anyone else. Except for your friend Chee. I own that boy. You fuck me over, I swear to God Almighty that boy will pay the price."

Cecil settled back like he had run out of gas, but the gun in his lap never wavered.

Holman considered the gun.

"You'll be gone. What could you do for Chee?"

"You bring out this money, I'll give you the man who planted those things—tell you when he got the stuff, where, how—everything you need to clear the boy."

Holman nodded like he was thinking about it, then stared at the bank. He didn't want Cecil to read his face. Cecil could shoot him right now or wait until Holman brought out the money, but Cecil was going to shoot him either way—this stuff about dealing for Chee was bullshit. Holman knew it and Cecil probably knew he knew it, but Cecil was so crazy needful of the money he had talked himself into believing it like he talked himself into killing four police officers. Holman thought about pretending to go along so he could get away, but then Cecil might escape. Holman wanted the sonofabitch to answer for killing his son. He was beginning to get an idea how he could do it.

"How do you see this playing out?"

"Go to the customer service manager. Tell'm right up front you're going to be making a lot of trips—you're picking up tax records and court documents you put here for safekeeping. Make a joke about it, like how you hope they weren't going on a coffee break. You know how to lie."

"Sure."

"The money in those boxes is still bagged up. You're

394

going to open four boxes at a time. I figure the bag in each box weighs about fifty pounds, two on each shoulder, two hundred pounds, a big guy like you oughta be able to handle that."

Holman wasn't listening. He was thinking about something Pollard told him when they believed Random was the fifth man—if they could put Random with Fowler they would own him. Holman decided if he could put Cecil together with the money, Cecil would never be able to explain it away or beat the conviction.

Holman said, "Twenty-two boxes at four boxes a trip. That's six trips carrying two hundred pounds of money each time. You think they're not going to stop me?"

"I'm thinking something is better than nothing. Anything goes wrong, just walk away. You're not robbing the goddamned place, Holman. Just walk away."

"What if they want to see in the bags?"

"Keep walking. We get what we get."

Holman had a plan. He thought he could pull it off if he had enough time. Everything depended on having enough time.

"It's going to take a long time, man. I hate being in a bank that long. I have bad memories."

"Fuck your memories. You just think about Chee."

Holman stared at Cecil like he was the stupidest asshole on earth. He wanted Cecil drunk with knowing the money was so close. He wanted Cecil stoned on gold.

"Fuck Chee. I'm the guy risking his ass. What's in it for me?"

Cecil stared at him, and Holman pressed forward.

395

"I want half."

Cecil blinked at him. He glanced at the bank, wet his lips, then looked back at Holman.

"You fuckin' kidding me?"

"I am not. I figure you owe me, motherfucker, and you know why. You don't like it, get that fuckin' money yourself."

Cecil wet his lips again and Holman knew he was in.

Cecil said, "The first four bags are mine. After that, every four bags you bring out, you get one."

"Two."

"One, then two."

"I can live with that. You be here when I get back with the money or I'm selling your ass to the cops."

Holman got out of the car and walked toward the bank. His stomach was cramping as if he was going to throw up, but Holman told himself he could make this thing happen if Cecil gave him enough time. Everything depended on Cecil giving him the time.

Holman held the door for a young woman leaving the bank. He smiled at her pleasantly, then stepped inside and took in his surroundings. Banks were usually busy during the lunch hour, but now it was almost four. Five customers were waiting in line for two tellers. Two manager types were at desks behind the teller cages and a young man who was probably a customer service rep manned a desk on the lobby floor. Holman knew right away this bank was a target for robberies. It had no man-trap doors at the entrance, no Plexiglas bandit barriers shielding the tellers, and no security guards. It was a robbery waiting to happen.

Holman went to the head of the customer line, glanced at the customers, then turned to the tellers and raised his voice.

"This is a motherfucking robbery. Empty the drawers. Give me the money."

Holman checked the time. It was 3:56.

The clock was running.

50

LARA MYER, age twenty-six, was in the final hour of her shift as a security dispatcher at New Guardian Technologies when her computer flashed, indicating a 2-11 alarm was being received from the Grand California Bank on Wilshire Boulevard in Beverly Hills. This was no big deal. The time log on her screen showed the time at 3:56:27.

New Guardian provided electronic security services for eleven area banking chains, two hundred sixty-one convenience stores, four supermarket chains, and several hundred warehouses and businesses. On any given day, half of the incoming alarms were false, triggered by power surges, computer glitches, electronic or electrical failure, or human error. Twice a week—every week—a bank teller somewhere in the greater L.A. area accidentally tripped an alarm. People are people. It happens.

Lara followed procedure.

She brought up the Grand Cal (Wilshire-BH branch) page on her screen. This page listed the managers and physical particulars of the bank (number of employees, number of teller windows, security enhancements if any, points of egress, etc). More important, the page allowed her to run a system diagnostic particular to the bank. The diagnostic would check for system problems that could trigger a false alarm.

Lara opened the diagnostic window, then clicked the button labeled CONFIRM. The diagnostic automatically reset the alarm as it searched for power anomalies, hardware malfunctions, or software glitches. If a teller had accidentally triggered the alarm, they sometimes reset at the bank, which automatically canceled and cleared the alarm.

The diagnostic took about ten seconds.

Lara watched as the confirmation appeared.

Two tellers at the Grand Cal Beverly Hills branch had triggered their silent alarms.

Lara swiveled in her chair to call over her shift supervisor.

"We got one."

Her shift supervisor came over and read the confirmation.

"Call it in."

Lara pressed a button on her console to dial the Beverly Hills Police Department's emergency services operator. After she notified Beverly Hills, Lara would call the FBI. She patiently waited as the phone rang four times.

"Beverly Hills emergency services."

"This is New Guardian operator four-four-one. We show a two-eleven in progress at Grand California Bank on Wilshire Boulevard in your area."

"Stand by, one."

Lara knew the emergency services operator would

now have to confirm that Lara was for real and not making a crank call. No cars would be dispatched until this was done and Lara had provided all necessary information about the bank.

She glanced at the clock.

3:58:05.

51

HOLMAN THOUGHT it was going pretty well. No one made a break for the door or fell out with a heart attack like last time. The tellers quietly emptied their drawers. The customers stayed together in their line, watching him as if they were waiting for him to tell them what to do. All in all, they were excellent victims.

Holman said, "Everything's going to be okay. I'll be out of here in a few minutes."

Holman pulled the pouch of keys from his pocket and went to the young man standing at the customer service desk. Holman tossed him the pouch.

"What's your name?"

"Please don't hurt me."

"I'm not going to hurt you. What's your name?"

"David Furillo. I'm married. We have a two-year-old."

"Congratulations. David, these are safe-deposit box keys, box number on each key just like always. Take your master and open four of these boxes, any four, doesn't matter. Go do that right now."

David glanced at the women standing by the desks behind the counter. One of them was probably his boss. Holman touched David's chin away from the woman so he was looking at Holman.

"Don't look at her, David. Do what I say."

David opened his desk for the master box key, then hurried toward the box room.

Holman trotted back across the lobby to the front door. He edged to the door, careful not to expose himself, and peered out. Cecil was still in the car. Holman turned back to the customers.

"Who's got a cell phone? C'mon, I need a phone. It's important."

They milled around uncertainly until a young woman tentatively drew a phone from her purse.

"You can use mine, I guess."

"Thanks, honey. Everybody stay calm. Everybody relax."

Holman checked the time as he opened the phone. He had been in the bank two and a half minutes. He was past the window of safety.

Holman trotted back to the door to check Cecil, then held out his arm to read the number on the inside of his forearm.

He called Pollard.

52

LEEDS HAD cautioned Pollard that Cecil's connection to Alison Whitt did not ensure a conviction, so they were making arrangements to see if Mrs. Marchenko could pick Cecil's picture from a six-pack. In the moments when Leeds was placing his call to Random, Pollard had tried to reach Holman by phoning his apartment. When she got no answer, she phoned Perry Wilkes, who told her Holman had been there but had since departed. Wilkes was able to offer no other information.

Alison Whitt's informant registration form indicated Cecil had first recruited and used her as an informant three years earlier. Cecil had learned of Whitt while investigating the involvement of a onetime singer turned B-level movie star who was suspected of bankrolling a gang of South Central dealers in their dope importation business. In lieu of being arrested for prostitution and possession, Whitt agreed to provide ongoing information about the singer's contacts with certain gang members. Cecil stated in her registration document that Whitt provided regular and accurate information that aided the prosecution.

Now Pollard was sitting in a cubicle outside Leeds' office when her phone rang. Hoping it was Holman or Sanders, she checked the caller ID, but did not recognize the number. She decided to let it go to her voice mail, then grudgingly changed her mind.

Holman said, "It's me."

"Thank God! Where are you?"

"I'm robbing a bank."

"Hang on—"

Pollard called out to Leeds.

"I've got Holman! Holman's on the phone—"

Leeds left his desk as Pollard returned to the call. He stood in the door, murmuring into his phone as he watched her.

Pollard said, "The fifth man is an FBI agent named Bill Cecil. He was—"

Holman interrupted her.

"I know. He's in a green Ford Taurus outside the bank right now. He's waiting for me—"

Now Pollard interrupted him.

"Whoa, waitaminute. I thought you were kidding."

"I'm in the Grand California on Wilshire Boulevard in Beverly Hills. Marchenko stashed the money here in safe-deposit boxes. Cecil had the keys—that's what they found at the Sign—"

"*Why are you robbing the bank?*"

Leeds frowned.

"What is he doing?"

Pollard waved him quiet as Delaney came over to watch.

Holman was saying, "You know a faster way to get the cops here? We flushed him, Katherine—Cecil had the keys, but he was scared to get the money. I've been inside three and a half minutes. The police will be here soon."

Pollard cupped the phone, glancing at Leeds and Delaney.

"Grand California on Wilshire in B.H. See if they're reporting a two-eleven."

She returned to Holman as Delaney ran to call the FBI dispatcher.

"Has anyone been hurt?"

"It's nothing like that. I want you to tell the cops what's happening. I figure they won't listen to me."

"Max, this is a *bad* idea."

"I want the cops to catch him with the money in his possession. He was scared to come in, so I'm gonna bring the money to him—"

"Where's Cecil now?"

"Parked outside. He's waiting for the money."

"Green Taurus?"

"Yeah."

Pollard cupped the phone and spoke again to Leeds.

"Cecil's in a green Ford Taurus in front of the bank."

Leeds relayed the information to Random as Delaney returned, excited.

"Beverly Hills confirms a two-eleven alarm at the location. Units en route."

Pollard went back to Holman.

"Holman, listen, Cecil is dangerous. He's already killed six people—"

"He made the mistake of killing my son."

"Stay in the bank, okay? Do *not* go outside. This is dangerous and I'm not just talking about Cecil— the responding officers don't know you're a good guy.

They will not know—"

"*You* know."

Holman hung up.

In that instant the line died. A pressure swelled in Pollard as if she was being crushed from the inside out, but she pushed through it and struggled to her feet.

"I'm going to the bank."

"Let Beverly Hills handle it. You don't have enough time."

Pollard ran as fast as she could.

53

BILL CECIL watched the bank, nervously tapping his foot. The car was in Park, the engine was running, the air conditioner was blowing cold. Cecil sweated as he imagined what was happening inside the bank.

First, Holman would have to make bullshit conversation with the customer service rep. If the dude already had a customer, Holman would have to wait. Cecil thought Holman should be smart enough to come wave or something, let him know if that was the case, but so far he hadn't. Cecil took this as a good sign, but that didn't make the waiting any easier.

Next up, the customer rep would bring Holman into the box vault, and he might be one of those lazy laid-back bastards who walked in slow motion.

Once they were inside, Holman would have to sign the ledger while the rep unlocked the master locks on each of the four boxes. The small ones always had an inner steel contents box you could slide in and out, keep your insurance and wills and stuff together, but not the big boxes. The big boxes were just big empty boxes. Holman would use his keys to make sure everything unlocked okay, but he wouldn't open the boxes until the rep had stepped out.

So then he would pull the money bags, close and relock the boxes, and amble on out of the bank. He'd probably have to say something cute to the rep, but after that it was only ten seconds to the door.

Cecil figured—start to finish without having to wait for another customer—that the entire process should take six minutes. Holman had been in the bank for four minutes, maybe four and a half. No reason to worry.

Cecil tapped his pistol on the lower edge of the steering wheel, thinking he would go peek through the door in another ten seconds.

54

HOLMAN CLOSED the phone, then glanced out the front door again, worried the police would arrive too soon. It was almost impossible for police to respond in two minutes, but every second after that gave them more time to reach the scene. Holman had now been in the bank two minutes longer than any of his robberies except the one in which he was arrested. He thought back. It had taken Pollard almost six minutes to arrive and they had been on a rolling stakeout, waiting and ready to go. Holman still had a few seconds.

He went back to the customers and returned the girl's phone.

"Everyone okay? Everybody still cool?"

A man in his forties with wire-rimmed glasses said, "Are we hostages?"

"No one is a hostage. Just stay cool. I'll be outta your hair in a minute."

Holman called toward the vault.

"Hey, David! How we doin' in there?"

David's voice came from the vault.

"They're open."

"You people just stay where you are. The police are on the way."

Holman trotted across the lobby to the vault. David had four large safe-deposit boxes open and had dragged four nylon gym bags into the center of the floor. Three were blue and one was black.

David said, "What's in the bags?"

"Somebody's bad dream. You stay in here, bud. You'll be safe in here."

Holman lifted the bags one by one, hooking the straps over his shoulders. Felt heavier than fifty pounds.

David said, "What about these other keys?"

"You keep'm."

Holman staggered out of the vault and immediately noticed that two of the customers were missing.

The girl who had loaned him her phone pointed at the door.

"They ran away."

Holman thought, oh shit.

55

CECIL TOLD himself to give Holman another ten seconds. He wanted the goddamned money, but he didn't want to die for it or get caught, and the odds of both increased the longer Holman remained in the bank. Cecil finally decided to see what was taking so long. If they had Holman proned out he was going to get the hell out of here as fast as his tired fat ass could carry him.

Cecil shut off the engine as a man and woman ran out of the bank. The woman stumbled as she came through the door and the man almost tripped over her. He pulled her to her feet, then took off running.

Cecil immediately started the engine, ready to drive away, but no one else emerged.

The bank was quiet.

Cecil shut the engine again, slipped his pistol into his holster, then got out of the car, wondering why those people had run. No one else was running, so what could be happening? Cecil started toward the bank, then hesitated, thinking he should get back in the goddamned car and get the hell away.

He glanced up and down Wilshire, but saw no lights or police cars. Everything seemed fine. He looked back at the bank, but now Holman was in the glass door with all these big-ass nylon bags hanging from his shoulders—just standing there. Cecil waved him over, thinking hurry up, what are you waiting for?

Holman didn't leave the bank. He dropped two of the bags, then gestured for Cecil to come get them.

Cecil didn't like it. He kept thinking about the two people running away. He flipped out his cell phone and hit a speed-dial button he had already programmed. Holman waved again, so Cecil held up a finger, telling him to wait.

"Beverly Hills Police Department."

"FBI Special Agent William Cecil, ID number six-six-seven-four. Suspicious activity at the Grand California on Wilshire. Please advise."

"Copy. We have a two-eleven alarm at that address. Units en route."

Cecil felt a burning knot in his chest. His eyes flickered. Everything he wanted was sixty feet away, but now it was gone. Sixteen million dollars—gone.

"Ah, confirm the two-eleven. Suspect is a white male, six-two, two-thirty. He is armed. I say again, he is armed. Customers in the bank appear down and disabled."

"Understand you are FBI six-six-seven-four. Do not approach. Units en route. Thanks for the advisory."

Cecil stared at Holman, then saw lights in the corner of his eye. Red and blue flashers were turning onto Wilshire three blocks away.

Cecil ran back to his car.

56

HOLMAN WATCHED Cecil with a bad feeling, confused why the man would be wasting time on his phone when he was so close to the sixteen million. He waved again for Cecil to come get the money, but Cecil kept talking. Holman had the skin-prickling sense something was wrong, then Cecil turned back toward his car. A heartbeat later, red and blue flashes reflected off the glass buildings across the street, and Holman knew his time had run out.

He shoved through the door, the heavy bags of cash swinging like lead pendulums. Two blocks away, cars were pulling to the curbs to let the police cars pass. The cops would be here in seconds.

Holman ran at Cecil as hard as he could, pinballing off two pedestrians. Cecil reached the Taurus, threw open the door, and was climbing inside when Holman caught him from behind. Holman pulled Cecil backwards and both of them fell.

Cecil, trying to climb back into the car, said, "What the fuck are you doing, man? Get out of here."

Holman dragged himself up Cecil's leg, hammering

at the man with his fist.

Cecil said, "Get off me, goddamnit. Let go!"

Holman should have been more afraid. He should have thought through what he was doing to realize Cecil was a blooded FBI agent with thirty years' training and experience. But all Holman saw in those moments was Richie running alongside his car, red-faced and crying, calling him a loser; all he knew was the eight-year-old gap-toothed boy in a picture that would continue to fade; all he felt was the blind-furious need to make this man pay.

Holman didn't see the gun. Cecil must have pulled it while Holman pounded on Cecil's back as Cecil was crawling toward the car. Holman was still punching, still blindly trying to anchor Cecil to the street, when Cecil rolled over. An exploding white light flashed three times and the sound of thunder echoed on Wilshire Boulevard.

Holman's world stopped. He heard only the sound of his beating heart.

He stared at Cecil, waiting for the pain. Cecil stared back, his mouth working like a fish. Behind them, the patrol cars slid to a stop as an officer's amplified voice shouted words Holman did not hear.

Cecil said, "Sonofafuckinbitch."

Holman looked down. The bags of money were wedged in front of his chest, scorched where the cash had trapped the three bullets.

Cecil shoved the gun across the money into Holman's chest, but this time he didn't fire. He dropped the gun into Holman's arms, then rolled away, coming to his knees with his FBI credentials high over his head, shouting—

414

"FBI! FBI agent!"

Cecil rolled away, hands up, shouting and pointing at Holman.

"Gun! He's got a gun! I've been shot!"

Holman glanced at the gun, then at the patrol cars. Four uniformed officers were crouched behind their vehicles. Young men about Richie's age. Aiming.

The amplified voice boomed again in the Wilshire canyon, now behind the sound of approaching sirens.

"Put down the weapon! Drop the weapon but make no sudden moves!"

Holman wasn't holding the weapon. It was on the money bag directly under his nose. He didn't move. He was too scared to move.

People had spilled out of the bank. They pointed at Holman as they shouted to the officers.

"That's him! It was him!"

Cecil staggered to his feet, crabbing away as he waved his credentials.

"I see his hand! I see it, goddamnit! *He's reaching for the gun!*"

Holman saw the young men shift behind their weapons. He closed his eyes, held himself perfectly still, and—

—nothing happened.

Holman looked up, but now the four young officers had their guns in the air, surrounded by milling officers. BHPD tactical officers with rifles and shotguns ran toward Cecil, shouting for him to get down on the ground. They tackled him hard, proned him out, then two of them peeled toward Holman.

Holman still didn't move.

One of the tactical officers stayed back with his

shotgun up and ready, but the other approached.

Holman said, "I'm the good guy."

"Don't fuckin' move."

The near officer lifted away Cecil's pistol, but he didn't slam down on Holman or prone him out. Once he had the gun he seemed to relax.

The cop said, "You Holman?"

"He killed my son."

"That's what they tell me, buddy. You got him."

The second cop joined the first.

"Wits said there was shooting. Were you shot?"

"I don't think so."

"Stay down. We're getting a medic."

Pollard and Leeds shoved through the growing crowd of officers. When Holman saw Pollard he started to rise, but she motioned him to stay down so he did. Holman figured he had come too far to take any chances.

Leeds went to Bill Cecil, but Pollard came directly to Holman, breaking into a trot as she came. She was wearing a blue FBI windbreaker like the first time he saw her. When Pollard arrived, she gazed down at him, breathing hard, but smiling, then held out her hand.

"I'm here now. You're safe."

Holman slipped out of the money bags, took her hand, and let her help him up. He stared at Cecil, still spread-eagled on the street. He watched the officers fold Cecil's hands behind his back to bind his wrists. He saw Leeds, his face livid and twisted, kick Cecil in the leg, whereupon the Beverly Hills cops shoved Leeds away. Holman turned back to Pollard. He wanted to tell her why everything that happened here and everything that led up to it had been his fault, but his mouth was dry and he was blinking too hard.

She held tight to his hand.

"It's okay."

Holman shook his head and toed the bags. It wasn't okay and never could be.

He said, "Marchenko's money. This is what Richie wanted."

She touched his face, turning him.

"No. Oh, no, Max, it wasn't that way."

She cupped his face in both her hands.

"Richie wasn't doing what we thought. Listen—"

Pollard told him how his son died and, more important to Holman, how Richie had lived. Holman broke down, crying there on Wilshire Boulevard, but Pollard held on tight, letting him cry and keeping him safe.

Part Five
32 DAYS LATER

57

WHEN HOLMAN came downstairs Perry was at his desk. Perry usually called it quits by seven o'clock to hole up in his room to watch *Jeopardy!*, but here he was. Holman figured Perry was waiting for him.

Perry wrinkled his nose.

"Jesus Christ, you smell like a whorehouse. What in hell are you wearing, perfume?"

"I'm not wearing anything."

"My dick may not work as well as it used to, but there's nothing wrong with my nose. You smell like a goddamn woman."

Holman knew Perry would keep hammering at him, so he decided to fess up.

"I bought this new shampoo. It's supposed to smell like a tropical garden."

Perry leaned back and cackled.

"I guess it does. And what flower would that be— pansies?"

Perry was killing himself, laughing.

Holman glanced out the front door, hoping to see Pollard's car, but the curb was empty.

Perry, still enjoying himself, said, "Look at how slicked up you are. My, my—I guess we have a date."

"It's not a date. We're just friends."

"That woman?"

"Stop calling her 'that woman.' I'll knock you on your ass."

"Well, she looked pretty fine to me. I was you, I'd tell people this was a date."

"Well, you're not me, so shut up. I'll have Chee send those boys back, bust up your fancy car."

Perry stopped laughing and scowled. Once everything about Chee had been straightened out, his boys rebuilt Perry's old beater like they promised. Perry took great pride in tooling around in the pristine classic. A man driving a Range Rover had offered him five thousand dollars for it.

Perry leaned forward again and hunched over his desk.

"I want to ask you a question. I'm being serious now."

"Aren't you missing *Jeopardy!*?"

"Now just wait—you think you got a future with this woman?"

Holman went back to the door but Pollard still had not arrived. He glanced at his father's watch. He had finally had it repaired and now it kept time pretty well. Pollard was running late.

"Perry, look, I have enough trouble dealing with the present. Katherine is an FBI agent. She has two little boys. She doesn't want anything to do with a guy like me."

After the fallout from Cecil, Leeds was left with an opening on the Bank Squad and had offered it to Pollard. Allowing an ex-agent to return to such a sought-after post was highly unusual, but Leeds had the clout to make it happen. Pollard would be able to apply her prior service toward her seniority and eventual retirement. Holman thought it was a good deal and encouraged her to take it.

Perry said, "Well, Jesus Christ, that new pansy shampoo must have made you stupid. The woman wouldn't be coming here if she didn't want anything to do with you."

Holman decided to wait on the sidewalk. He went outside, but thirty seconds later Perry appeared in the door. Holman raised both palms.

"Please, I'm begging you—let it rest."

"I just want to tell you something. All you know about me is I'm a cranky old man in this shitbag motel. Well, I wasn't always this way. I was young once and I had chances and opportunities in my life. I made choices that put me here. I sure as hell would make different choices if I had it to do over. You think about that."

Perry stomped off into the empty motel.

Holman stared after him, then heard a horn. He looked up the street. Pollard was a block away, but she had seen him. Holman raised his hand and saw Pollard smile.

Holman thought about what Perry said, but Perry didn't understand—Holman was afraid. Katherine Pollard deserved a good man. Holman was trying hard to be better than he had ever been in his life, but he still had a long way to go. He wanted to earn Katherine Pollard. He wanted to deserve her. And he believed—one day he would.